On My Way To You

R. BAGLIERE

Table of Contents

Acknowledgments

Like any work of literature, writing is not done in a void. While the author may be the master of his work, there are many others who become involved in its creation. These men and women provide literary and professional critiques, research, artwork, copy and creative editing, and formatting for final publication. I would like to acknowledge a few of those who have given their precious time in providing insightful critiques and encouragement. They have been an invaluable resource to me in the development of this novel.

First and foremost, a huge thank you to my monthly critique group—Mary, Millisa, Julie, Debbie, and Martin—who provided a sounding board for me in the writing of this novel. I trust them completely because we have known each other a long time. To Paul, who gave of his time to proof this novel, I am most grateful for his detailed eye in catching all the little things that make for better reading. All of you always know what I want to say, and you help me say it better.

For my friends in Nepal—Binod, Gokul and Dan— I give my gratitude for your help in filling in some of the little holes that escaped me. While I have been in their world, there is so much to know that can't be contained in my notebooks.

To P.A. David Hammack, who was kind enough to look over my shoulder and guide me through all the medical issues that came up, I offer a huge thank you! It is so comforting to know I got things right. For my editor, Jenna, who did a fabulous job of catching all my little typos, my sincerest thanks. For all my beta readers who brought up things I hadn't thought about, I am forever grateful.

And to my publisher, Creativia; as always you are right there to take care of all the little things and bumps in the road. Thank you all!

Glossary

There are a few terms/foreign words used throughout this text the reader may or may not be familiar with. To assist in enjoying the reading experience, the author has included an abridged glossary.

ABC: Annapurna Base Camp

AMS: Acute Mountain Sickness, also referred to as HAPE (High Altitude Pulmonary Edema) or HACE (High Altitude Cerebral Edema), Hypothermia.

Buff: An elastic band of head clothing that is used to ward off cold wind and dust to the face and head.

Butter Tea: Traditionally made from tea leaves, yak butter, water, and salt.

CamelBak: a portable water bladder with an attached drinking tube that fits in the pouch of a daypack or backpack.

Chhaang: A traditional Nepalese beverage similar to beer. It is usually drunk at room temperature in summer, but is often served hot in brass bowls or wooden mugs when the weather is colder.

Chomolungma: Also known as Mount Everest or the Snow Goddess. The name means: Goddess Mother of Mountains.

Dal Bhat: A staple dish of the Nepalese and Tibetans consisting of rice and lentil soup.

Diamox: A diuretic medication that has additional qualities effective in combatting the affects of high altitude exposure for extended times.

EBC: Everest Base Camp

Kaju Katli: Also known as kaju Katari or kaju barfi, is an Indian dessert similar to a barfi. *Kaju* means cashew nut in Hindi. Barfi is often but not always, made by thickening milk with sugar and other ingredients (dry fruits and mild spices).

Kat: Slang for Katmandu

Khata: Tibetan ceremonial traditional scarf symbolizing purity and compassion.
Also used in Nepalese culture.

Lassi: A popular traditional yogurt-based drink from the Indian Subcontinent. Lassi is a blend of yogurt, water, spices and sometimes fruit.

Mani walls: Stone plates, rocks and/or pebbles, inscribed with the six-syllabled mantra as a form of prayer in Tibetan Buddhism. Mani stones are intentionally placed along the roadsides and rivers or placed together to form mounds or cairns or sometimes long walls, as an offering to spirits of place.

MFD: Nepalese National Weather Division (Meteorological Forecasting Department)

Serac: a pinnacle or ridge of ice on the surface of a glacier.

Stuppa: A mound-like or hemispherical structure containing relics (typically the remains of Buddhist monks or nuns) used as a place of meditation.

The Annapurna Circuit

(The Apple Trail)

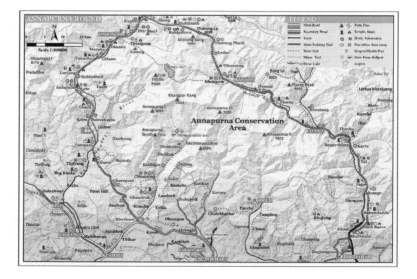

Chapter 1

John

Pokhara – April 22^h

John Patterson woke up in a fog. Putting his hands to his temples, he pushed away shoulder length hair as his stomach churned. He'd managed to crawl in off the porch last night and find his way to the couch. After the banging between his ears eased, he opened his eyes. Yellow sunlight bathed the tiny Spartan living room. Take-out containers, empty soda cans, and crumpled-up food wrappers were scattered on the threadbare carpet. An open pizza box sat on a wooden crate that filled in for a coffee table. A lingering odor of cold fried chicken, garlic potatoes and curry permeated the room.

He blinked and pushed himself upright and bent forward, causing his bladder to bear down on him. He sighed, went to stand and almost fell. He sat back looking for his prosthetic limb, which he kept nearby when he went to sleep, but it wasn't there. He frowned.

"Shit! God damn it," he muttered. He slid down the couch away from the crate, rocked forward and got up. The journey down the hall to the bathroom would be like hopping through a minefield. The last thing he needed was to trip and plant his face on the floor. He palmed the wall as he went. Behind him, his cell phone rang out. Whoever it was would have to wait. With a grunt, he shut the bathroom door behind him and navigated to the toilet. He needed something for his headache and the gnawing pain in his leg. Without looking up, he reached beside him and pawed through the collection of razors, tangled hair ties, and wadded tissues on the vanity. After knocking most of them

16

in the sink or on the floor, he found his bottle of goodies. He tipped it, expecting to see a little, white, hand-pressed pill drop into his palm, but nothing rolled out. He stared down into the empty blue tube as his brain spun.

Suddenly, the ache in his leg exploded into a rage. He flung the bottle at the wall in front of him and groped for the Tylenol, which, of course, tipped over, spilling its contents on the floor.

"Shit!"

He swept the remaining toiletries away, scattering them around the room.

Get it together.

He reached down beside him and picked up the scattered pills and hair ties within arm's length. An hour later he had his leg on, bed made and things picked up – maybe not shining clean, but presentable enough for his own tastes. He brushed the mud off the boots that were living in the kitchen sink, put them on and opened the tiny refrigerator. There wasn't much in it: a few forgotten leftovers, a carton of milk and a carton of eggs. He frowned.

"Okay, eggs it is," he muttered, and took them out along with the milk. As he scrambled up his breakfast in a cereal bowl, his phone went off again. He dug it out of his pocket and stared at the number flashing on the screen. Putting it on speakerphone, he forced a smile.

"Frank!"

"Hi John."

"What's up?" John said, crossing his arms and leaning back against the stove. The last time they'd spoken had been in October right after Andersen had assigned him to run the Annapurna Circuit. Frank had shown up on his doorstep out of the blue, proposing that he run Khum Jung Mountaineering. Told him he could get back in the game. Run things as he saw fit.

It had all sounded good until Frank said it was the least he could do to show his thanks for saving his life, as if he was trying to even the score. As if!

"So, how you doing, John?"

"I'm doing. You?"

Frank paused. "Been better."

"I bet. I heard what happened up on the Fall. God-awful thing. I assume you were there?" John said, grabbing the carton of milk beside him. He popped it open and caught an unpleasant whiff.

Damn it!

"Unfortunately, yes." There was a long pause as John dumped the spoiled milk down the drain. Finally, Frank lowered his voice. "John, Da-wa was roping the course at the time."

John blinked as the words rammed into him. He and Da-wa went back a ways, and although they'd parted on less than friendly terms, he still had high regard for the sherpa. He leaned back against the stove and cleared his throat.

"Damn. That sucks."

"Yeah, it does," Frank said and paused before going on. "You probably heard about the meeting of the minds up on the mountain?"

"A little. I guess things got a bit hot up there," John said. He pulled out a battered frying pan and greased it up.

"To say the least. You know as well as I the Sherpa are getting screwed. A death bennie of a million and a half rupees and a measly comp of forty thousand – are you kidding me? It's next to nothing."

"Right," John said, having a distinct feeling Frank was going to hit him up for something. He turned the knob on the stove, struck a match and put it to the burner. When a flame popped up, he set the pan over it and sucked a lip.

Wait for it.

"Anyway, I'm trying to put together a fundraiser in Kat, so I'm hitting up all the outfits on the mountain. I called Terry, but I was directed to a Brandon Carson. Is Terry still at Andersen?"

"Yeah, he's there, but he's not as involved as he used to be," John said.

"Really?"

"Family issues, or so I've heard," John said.

"I guess that explains the run-around I got. So this Carson guy...he's running things in Nepal, I take it?"

"Something like that. Terry brought him on to evaluate our expeditions." *And screw with my life.* "Another bean counter who only looks at the bottom line."

"Hence the lukewarm response I got," Frank said. He paused then went on, "I know we haven't always gotten along, but could you get me connected with Terry?"

John rolled his eyes. "I'm not exactly on his speed-dial list, Frank. I've only seen him a few times over the last three years."

"Whatever you can do, I would really appreciate," Frank said and paused again. "I've missed you on the mountain the last two years. Things aren't the same without you stalking around up there."

"I bet," John said, grabbing a spatula and folding the eggs in the skillet. "I'll be back there soon enough."

"I'm sure you will. So, they're keeping ya busy?"

"Yep. They got me straightening things out on the Circuit now."

"That's a two-hundred K hike."

"From what I hear," John said, understanding the gist of Frank's comment. But his leg could handle it. He turned off the stove and took a bowl out of the dish drainer. After he set it on the counter, he dumped his breakfast into it. "Hey, look, gotta get at the paperwork here. You know how it is – everyone wants to get paid. Anyway, I'll do my best with Terry."

"Okay, and thanks. In any case, whether Andersen ponies up or not, I'll save you a table at the event."

"You do that," John said. "Later."

John pulled his beaten, gray 2002 Santo sedan into the torrent of weaving motorbikes, cars, buses, and trucks heading east along the crumbling macadam road. As he drove past the shores of Phewa Tal, he was mindful of the surging crowds gathered around the end of the lake that reflected the white-capped mountains to the north. He rolled his window down and turned his radio on as he negotiated the madness of weaving traffic that obeyed only one law: keep moving.

Fifteen minutes later, he parked outside a rundown, whitewashed stucco building with a ragged blue canvas canopy over the front entry. Overlooking the Seti Gandaki River, Sanjay's Internet café was a regular haunt for local guides, offering up decent Nepalese food and wireless internet connections, all at reasonable prices. When he opened the front door, he was met with a ubiquitous balsamic fragrance. He waved to one of the regulars and walked past a bank of desktop computers to the back of the room. There, he took a table near the sit-down dining bar.

Unlike the touristy restaurants of Pokhara that were flush with hanging swag lamps, mandala tapestries and Brahma and Vishnu golden statuettes, Sanjay's was understated - a few pictures of the mountains and Phewa Tal on the walls, solid hardwood tables and chairs, hardwood floors and a few large planters bearing leafy jade and philodendron in the corners.

This was his office, so to speak. He spread out a map of the Annapurna region and opened his laptop while he waited for his sherpa assistant guides, Orson and Kembe, to arrive. As he went over the Circuit Trail map, Nabin came rushing up to take his order. The rail-thin, coffee-skinned kid really didn't need to ask what he wanted. John had been coming there almost daily for the better part of a year. But that was how the Nepalese were: never leaving anything to chance.

Nabin pulled out his pad and pencil. "Namaste, Mr. Patterson! Same as always?"

John nodded. "Same as always. Is the man around?"

"Hō, he in kitchen. You want me to get him for you?"

"Yes, please." John dug two one-thousand-rupee notes out of his wallet and tucked them into Nabin's shirt pocket. "For your piggy bank," he said, knowing the boy was saving every penny he could to attend the Nepalese Mountain Guide School.

Nabin's dark eyes lit and a broad smile flashed across his face. "Thank you, Mr. Patterson, thank you, thank you!"

John put his hand up. "Nabin, how many times I got to tell you? There's no need to thank me. And for God's sake, you need to stop with the 'Mr. Patterson' bullshit. John works just fine, okay?"

The boy nodded. "Okay, whatever you say, Mr. Patterson."

Whatever.

John rolled his eyes and turned back to his computer, scrolling through his email. As usual, his mother had sent him her weekly note about the goings-on at home in Oak Creek, Colorado, land of the snow bunnies. He made a mental note to email her before he went to bed tonight then sorted through the rest of the unsolicited spam. As he deleted the last of it, Sanjay showed up with his order.

Besides owning the café, Sanjay had a side business in pharmaceuticals – homemade pharmaceuticals – some of which were herbals he sold openly and others that were sold more discretely. The latter consisted of opiates, which was John's primary interest at that moment. He eyed the short, dark man who had a warm, friendly smile. Over the last year, the two of them had struck up more than a passing business relationship. They were friends, and John never saw Sanjay as anything less than an herbalist trying to provide for his family as well as for the locals who couldn't afford the government-approved drugs.

"Namaste, John. What can I do for you?" Sanjay said as he put a basket of roti with a bowl of lassi on the table.

"Hey, Sanjay," John said. Nabin hustled over with his Masala tea. The boy set it on the table and dashed away. John waited until Nabin was out of earshot then leaned forward. "My leg is killing me."

Sanjay wiped his hands on his apron. "John, you must be careful…"

John put his hand up. "I know, I know, and I am. It's just bothering me more than usual. Help me out, okay?"

"I sorry, I have none to give just now. You come back later, maybe?

John gritted his teeth. "Yeah, sure," he said, feeling his body tighten up. He sat back, tore off a piece of roti and dunked it in the yogurt and apricot-blended parfait.

When John looked up from his notes a couple hours later, Mick Hanson stood in front of him with a thick Pendaflex folder stuffed with paperwork pinned under his arm. John grinned at the man who worked for High Trails Adventures and motioned to Orson and Kembe, who had joined him an hour ago to hold off on filling him in on the logistics of the Circuit. He'd known Mick since he'd come to Nepal, and counted him as the closest thing he had to a friend.

Mick pulled a chair back, set his laptop and Pendaflex on the table. "Hey Nabin," Mick called out sitting down, "a Thermos of butter tea and a plate of Kaju Katli."

John shook his head. How Mick could stomach the combination of the gagging bitter brew and coma-inducing sweet-cakes was beyond him. Then again, not too many things were out of the burly man's diet.

"I see you're doing your homework on the Circuit," Mick said, nodding toward the maps.

"Yeah. My punishment for being a Good Samaritan," John said, and called Nabin over for a refill on his tea. "What happened to you last night?"

"What do you mean?" Mick said.

"You wimped out on me."

"Had a fire to put out," Mick said as Nabin brought his order over. "You want a piece?" He pointed to one of the small diamond shaped cakes on the plate.

"Umm…no," John said, clearing away a stack of papers in front of him. "This here is Sherpa Orson and Sherpa Kembe."

Mick put his hand out to the two men. "Hey."

They shook his hand but said nothing.

"So what'cha think?" Mick said, nodding toward the Circuit map.

"I think I'm being screwed up the a-hole, is what I think," John said.

"Don't worry, you'll get back to Everest," Mick said. "Just have to give it time."

"My leg works just fine," John said.

"They just want to make sure you're ready."

John scowled. "They? You mean Carson. He's just looking for a way to shove me out the door. Sending me on this yellow brick road is his way of letting me know about it, too." He paused. "No matter. So, High Trails is still planning on running all their treks?"

Mick drilled a finger into his ear. "Yep...all except Everest." He eyed the two sherpas critically then went on, "It's all a tizzy up there."

Orson nodded and finally said, "Government act like nothing happen. 'Go climbing' they say at EBC. No one care about sherpa side of story."

"I know," Mick said, nodding in agreement, "and to my way of thinking you have a right to be raising a stink."

"We tired of Ministry dictating how things go," Kembe put in. "All we want is what's ours. No offense, but we fed up from being used by big companies and government."

Mick nodded. "Well, I can't speak for anyone else, but High Trails treats our sherpas fair. The sad thing is, there's a lot of folks up there who can't see their hands in front of their faces which puts everyone at risk."

"Yeah, I know. I heard the ministry offered to raise the death benny to fifteen K," John said, remembering what Frank had told him. He sipped his tea, and waited to hear what Mick would say.

"Yeah, big joke," Orson said.

"I agree, Orson," Mick said. "Personally, some of these outfits shouldn't be on the mountain. They have no interest in safety or who should climb or not; only the green that comes flowing in." He took a drink of his butter tea. "And get this—I heard some idiot has contracted choppers to haul their sorry asses up over the Ice Fall to Camp 2 so they can continue a summit attempt. What the hell?"

"You wouldn't be talking about Andersen, now would you, good buddy?" John said.

Mick cranked his brow up and eyed him with one of his did-you-really-just-say-that looks. He helped himself to another piece of cake. "Sure you don't want a piece?"

John shook his head. "I'll pass."

Mick washed his cake down with a sip of tea and sat back with a speculative gaze. "You know, you could look elsewhere."

"What do you mean?"

"What about Eckert? They're a good outfit?"

"They are, 'cept they're all filled out at the moment," John said.

Mick nodded. "Well, there's always Frank's offer."

"Out of the question, and let's not go there again, okay?" John said, narrowing his gaze on the man. At length, he paused, sucked a sip of tea. "So, High Trails gonna go for an Annapurna summit?"

"Yeah, in the fall. I'll be running Base Camp," Mick said and bit into a piece of his Kaju Katli. "In the meantime, they got me training a couple new guys for the Circuit."

"Better you than me," John said and chuckled.

Mick flipped him the bird. "Well, at least one of them is experienced. Came from the States. California, I think. The other one's from Nevada," he said, and helped himself to the last piece of dessert. He bit into it and said, "The California kid even has an Everest summit under his belt."

"No shit," John said, sitting back. A queer feeling ran through him. "When'd he summit?"

Mick wiped his mouth with a napkin. "2011, I think. Hey, that was the year you-"

"Yeah. Don't remind me," John said. The uneasy feeling intensified and for a moment he didn't know why, only that his breath quickened with dread. And then it hit him.

No f'ing way.

"You know which company he climbed with?"

Mick sat back looking off for some time as John's heart thumped. Finally, the man rubbed his chin and shook his head. "Geeze, you know I can't remember."

John closed his eyes, trying to shoo the bad feeling away. He waved his hand. "No matter. So, want to hit the Golden Monkey tonight for a few?"

"Yeah, why not?" Mick said.

John turned toward Orson and Kembe. "I believe we're done here."

The sherpas pushed back in their chairs and stood. Orson said, "So, we meet you next week for first Circuit run?"

"Wouldn't miss it," John said as the men headed for the front door.

When they were alone, Mick glanced toward the door the sherpas left through and said, "Good men there, Shanks. They'll do you good."

"Yeah, I think so," John said. "Well, I got to be heading out. Till tonight then, and don't be late."

"Not if you're buying, I won't be" Mick said. He grabbed his Pendaflex and got up, then wrinkled his brow. "Hold on, wait a minute. It just came to me."

John gathered his paperwork and shut his laptop. "What?"

"The guy you just asked me about." Mick opened his Pendaflex and slid a handful of documents out as John looked on. Rifling through them, he came to a sheet that caught his attention and pulled it out. "Here it is...says he was with Khum Jung Mountaineering. Name's Greg Madden."

John felt hot blood rush into his face.

Son of a bitch!

Chapter 2

Michelle

Cornwall, Canada – May 3ʳᵈ

Michelle dragged her daypack off the kitchen table and slung it over her shoulder. "Come, Merlin," she called to her girlfriend's chocolate Lab who was watching her from the kitchen archway. She opened the door to the attached garage of her one-story ranch and waited for him to scoot through. Outside, Cam was loading the last of their hiking gear into an idling 2013 Highlander. Michelle took one last look around the kitchen, making sure she wasn't forgetting anything, then grabbed her hiking poles. After locking up, she joined the woman she'd known for over twenty-five years.

"So, grab coffee at Ernie's?" Cam said as Merlin jumped into the back seat.

Michelle threw her pack in the back of the car and shut the tailgate. Looking up at the cloudless blue sky, she breathed deep and wondered if she'd break down once she was out on the trail. Hiking in the wilderness of Algonquin Provincial Park had been her special time with her husband Adam, but with him gone now, she wondered how she'd react. She shut the tailgate and put on a smile. "Perfect!"

Cam hopped in the driver's seat, and as Michelle got in, put her long blond hair up. Slipping her Expos cap on, she entered their destination into her GPS. "Got your passport, right?"

"Right here," Michelle said, patting the breast pocket of her trail jacket. "Looks like we have a good day for it."

Cam buckled up, put the car in gear, and they were off for the hour and half jaunt over the border to Saranac Lake in the States. There, they'd hike the Ampersand Trail. Training for the real stuff Cam, called it—the real stuff being the Himalayas. When Cam suggested they travel to Nepal to fulfill Adam's bucket list wish, she was all in, even though the idea of traveling halfway around the world scared her.

Michelle could still see the intense gaze coming back from her sister-in-law's bright hazel eyes. Cam was right! *He would've wanted this!*

Despite losing her brother and going through her own grief, Cam had never wavered in her support for her. She was the one who forced her out of the house on weekends: took her on field trips, to dinner or just anywhere to hang out and talk. And what was more, Cam never tried to fix her, but instead just listened when she blamed herself for what happened on the day Adam was taken away from her. Cam was the one who kept her from sliding off into the abyss when the world turned into a shit storm.

"So," Cam said, "you'll never believe who messaged me this morning."

Michelle assumed it was a guy and shrugged. Cam had so many of them chasing her, she needed a scorecard. "I haven't a clue, who?"

Cam shot her a sideways glance. "Matt. Remember him?" she said.

Michelle cocked her brow, remembering Cam telling her about the date from Hell whose idea of an outing was a jaw-jarring ride on the back of his all-terrain four-wheeler through the forest. "You mean Lumberjack Boy?"

"One and the same. The caveman wanted to know what I was up to."

"Did you answer him?"

"No," Cam said, drawing out the word. She was quiet a moment, then in a brittle tone, added, "I think I need to give up dating for a while. There's just nothing out there."

Now it was Michelle's turn to be quiet. Cam was venting, but she knew she wasn't serious. Not that Cam dated anything that walked upright, but still!

Cam tightened her jaw. "You think I'm kidding."

"No," Michelle said and smiled.

"What?"

"Nothing," Michelle said.

Cam eyed her and sighed. "You're probably right."

"About what?"

"What you're thinking. That I like *it* a little too much."

Michelle shrugged. "You could be a little more selective. I mean, mind-blowing sex alone does not make for a meaningful relationship."

"I know...I know. And hey, I'm picky!" Cam protested."

"Right."

They were quiet a moment. Finally, Cam said, "There's Ernie's."

Cam pulled in and they ordered a couple of coffees along with a sausage biscuit for Merlin from the drive-thru. Once they were off again, Cam said, "So, I'm all set. What about you?"

Michelle tossed the biscuit wrapper in a trash bag. "All set with what?"

Cam shook her head. "Duh, the paperwork for the trip. Insurance, paying off Andersen?"

"Oh, yeah. All set," Michelle said. She sipped her coffee as a recurring vision of them searching for their Andersen connection at a strange airport where no one spoke a lick of English flashed before her. She'd never traveled abroad, and the thought of being swept away in a sea of humanity to God knows where unsettled her. It was a dark thought she'd been keeping to herself for some time, but as the date of the trip loomed ahead, it began to assert itself more and more.

She took a deep breath, trying to squash her anxiety. "So, do we know how many guys are in our tour group yet?"

Cam fidgeted in her seat as they fell in line with traffic that was slowing down at the border crossing. "I think all of them are guys except us, but I can't be sure. Grab my passport from my purse, would you? It's right on top."

Michelle sighed as she dug Cam's passport out and added her own with it.

"What?"

"Oh…nothing. Just thinking."

"About what?" Cam said, taking a sip of her coffee.

Michelle looked off at the other cars crowding around the border patrol booths, wondering if she should say anything. They'd had similar conversations about her concerns in the past, and always Cam had made light of her worries. But the reality was, since Adam had died, she hadn't laced her hiking boots up once. Finally, she said, "I'm nervous about slowing everyone down."

"Oh, please. No one's in a race to get around the Circuit, 'Chelle."

"Maybe, but I'm sure I'll bog everyone down," she said.

Cam huffed. "You need to let go of that before you drive both of us crazy. You'll be just fine," she said as the car at the border patrol booth was waved through. Putting the car in drive, she pulled ahead.

The interrogation with the tall Border Control officer, whose cholate brown eyes glanced up and down Cam's body, was brief. Even so, Michelle was fairly sure Cam was aware of his looking her over by the way her voice softened in answering him. After they were waved through and on their way to Saranac, Michelle said, "You sure know how to manage the border boys. I get the full deal coming through customs and they just wave you on through."

Cam shrugged. "Most of them just want their egos stroked." She broke into a wicked smile and added, "Among other things."

"Oh my God, did you just say that?"

"I think I did," Cam said and smirked.

"You are so bad," Michelle said, then burst out laughing. But deep inside, she envisioned Cam on the trail surrounded by guys while she brought up the rear alone.

They drove into the depths of the Adirondack Park on a winding road that snaked through the towering spruce and pine. As they drove, veering east through the isolated villages of Gabriels and Harrietstown, Michelle tried to ease her anxious mind. She knew she was catastrophizing (Cam's word for it) and that all of her worst fears had never come to pass.

Five miles later, they were driving through the dense wood, and by the time they came to the village of Saranac Lake, the sun was high in a cloudless blue sky. Cam pulled off the main road that bordered the sparkling blue lake and parked next to a country store/gas station. While Cam went inside, Michelle waited with Merlin, watching people going in and out of the quaint roadside shops bellying up to the lake.

When Cam came back out and joined her, they looked over the water where jet skis were darting back and forth. Michelle tilted her head back and took a breath of the pine-scented air.

Cam tapped Michelle on the arm. "I believe that's our destination," she said, pointing to the rising treed landscape overlooking the lake.

Michelle followed the leading edge of the ridge that rose above the lesser peaks and nibbled her lip.

"What?" Cam said as Merlin sat beside them, sniffing the air.

"Nothing."

"Don't you worry. You'll do just fine," Cam said, turning toward her. She put her hand on Michelle's shoulder and stared her in the eye. "This is for Adam, never forget that."

"I know," Michelle said and steeled herself.

Cam gave Michelle's shoulder a squeeze. "You've worked hard in the gym. You're in good shape. Come on, let's go. Daylight's wasting."

While Michelle couldn't argue about her being in better shape, she still worried. It had been two years since she'd been on a real trail, before.... Her breath caught as the thought passed through her like a knife.

I'm not going to go down this dark well – not now!

Michelle closed her eyes and swallowed the heartbreaking image of her husband, forcing it back to the private place in her heart where she held him safe.

Ampersand's beaten trail beat a level path under the canopy of the forest for the first kilometer before taking to a moderate uphill slope. As she followed it with Merlin dashing back and forth on the trail, Michelle gazed at the sea of green ferns and trillium that dominated the understory. Here and there, fallen trees and decaying stumps poked up through the sun-dappled verdant blanket. Above, squirrels raced along the clacking branches and birds flitted about from limb to limb. The whine of insects permeated the spring air that was warming up. Cam, who was walking ahead, stopped and waited for her to catch up.

"The trail's busy this morning," she said, nodding at the group of teens who'd just tromped past them.

Michelle watched the bare legged girls marching ahead with tank-topped boys leading the way. The majority of them were wearing sneaks and ankle socks. A couple of them carried backpacks. Michelle shook her head, and waved a couple of black flies away from her face.

"They're gonna get torn up pretty good."

"Oh, yeah," Cam said, bending over and retying her boot. She looked up at Michelle. "Say nothing of ending up with a blister or two. City kids, probably."

Michelle was quiet a minute. All of a sudden, she was noticing things that were bringing back memories of Adam. Images of Adam in his dress blues, of him stepping off the military transport plane into her arms, of them hiking the Seaway Trail, camping in the provincial park and canoeing; things they'd still be doing if she hadn't forgotten to get gas that fateful morning.

They started off, walking at a steady pace as Merlin bounced ahead. Sometimes they passed people who were admiring the forest until at last the ground ramped up to a steep rocky incline. As it did, they met strewn boulders. Poling along, Cam led the way. Her long legs able to bridge the substantial stepped heights of the helter-skelter stone riprap. Michelle tacked her way up behind her and after a solid hour of uphill going, they took a moment to relax and slake their thirst.

Michelle sat on one of many boulders marching up the ragged mount and mopped a river of sweat off her face. Looking up, she hoped to find the top. They'd been climbing for what felt like forever, and she was ready to get off this winding, steep trail cutting into the mountain.

Cam dropped her daypack beside her and leaned against a thick maple. "You okay?" she said, digging a bag of trail mix out of her pack.

"Yeah, I'm good. How much farther, you think?" Michelle said as Merlin bounded back from above where he'd been exploring. The dog nestled beside Cam, his tongue lolling and tail wagging.

Cam looked upward. "Don't know," she said. "Can't be too much farther."

"I'll be glad to get into open air."

"I hear that," Cam said, stepping up to Michelle. She offered the bag of trail mix to Michelle. "Want some?"

Michelle dug in and grabbed a handful. She glanced at Adam's sister from the corner of her eye, put her hand over Cam's and smiled.

"What?"

"Nothing. I was just thinking how good it is to be out here. I've missed the woods."

Cam studied her a moment with a crooked smile. Finally, she said, "Yes it is, and we better get moving before the bugs find us."

An hour later, Michelle sat on the undulating granite slabs of Ampersand's summit overlooking the rolling land of spiked pine and spruce. Beside her, Cam sat cross-legged near the edge of the down-sloping rock that dove into the forest.

The last hundred meters up the side of the mountain had tested Michelle, but she was proud of herself, despite being scared a couple of times when the trail turned into a wreck of fallen trees and slick-faced boulders. Her reward was an angry red scrape above her ankle, which she was presently dealing with.

Cam nodded at Michelle's leg and then at her woolen sock lying beside her. "You're not wearing liners?"

"Couldn't find any," Michelle said, digging a bandage out of her pack. She peeled the tabs off and fixed it over the sore, hoping the field dressing would get her down the mountain. "Don't worry, I'll be fine." She stretched her injured leg out, buttoned her canvas med kit up and put it away.

"Okay. Keep an eye on it, though," Cam said as Merlin came loping back from another exploration. She looked off toward Mount Marcy and was quiet for some time. Finally, she said, "It's beautiful up here, don't you think? I can only imagine what it'll be like in Nepal."

Michelle pulled a ham sandwich out, ignoring the dog's hopeful gaze, and took a bite. "The people where I work think I'm nuts going there, except my boss, Don.

Which is a good thing because we're gone for a month. Speaking of which, how did the partners take your news?"

Cam smiled. "Like a baby takes a bottle."

"I should have you break the news to my brother and dad," Michelle said, and smiled.

"Well, my family isn't high on me going either. But hey, I'm not a kid anymore. I'm 43," Cam said and grabbed a sandwich from her pack and unwrapped it. "Hey, wait, you haven't told them yet?"

Michelle shrugged. "Umm…nope, not until I'm ready," she said.

"Oh my God! Really?"

"Yep. You know CJ. He'll go off like a Roman candle, and I'm not interested in dealing with it until I'm ready. Don't worry, we're good," Michelle said, and petted Merlin. Then, sensing the time was right to bring up the phone call, she added, "By the way, he phoned me last night."

"Oh? And?"

"He mentioned there's a house near his neighborhood for sale. Told me he'd buy it and give it to me if I moved up north."

Cam's eyes widened. "Why?"

Michelle looked off. "He wants his family around him, says he's worried about Dad, especially after his heart attack. I know what you're thinking. Don't worry. I'm not going."

"Still, your father would love having you nearby." Cam was quiet a moment, then added, "What's Monica have to say about it?"

"Don't know," Michelle said, trying to hide her reservations toward her brother's wife. "She probably likes the idea of me being there so she can have CJ back to herself."

"Don't sugarcoat it," Cam said. "We both know Monnie wants you to daddysit."

Michelle couldn't argue with that. "You think?"

Cam rolled her eyes. "Daddy's little princess."

There was that. Monica was spoiled growing up and had a sense of entitlement. For the life of her, Michelle couldn't understand what CJ saw in her. Then again, CJ had been driven to make something of his life after putting his family through hell, and marrying into the Mannington family had gone a long way in doing that. Michelle supposed she couldn't blame him.

That Monica had given CJ two beautiful children, even though they were a tad spoiled (okay, a lot spoiled) sealed the deal. But he was a good father and he grounded his children from a world of glitter that spun around them like so many sugarplums on Christmas morning.

Cam took a bite of her lunch, looked toward the valley below and said, "What did you tell him?"

"Nothing...yet." Michelle said, and cleared her throat. "Hey, wanna get a room in town and drive back tomorrow?"

Cam turned back with a start. "That sounds great except what do we do with Merlin?" She tilted her head toward the dog.

"Oh...yeah, right," Michelle said, and pulled Merlin tight to her. "I'm sorry buddy. Your auntie wasn't thinking, was she?" The dog bent his head back, trying to lick her face.

"Hey, I have an idea," Cam said.

"What's that?"

"What about my place? The wine's free there, too."

"Hmm...I like that idea," Michelle said. "And we can stop at Bernie's on the way back and pick up takeout. I'll buy."

"Sounds like a plan," Cam said.

They ran into torrential rain on the way home and by the time they pulled into Cam's driveway, the scrape on Michelle's leg was a raging fire. She opened the car door and stepped out into the cool, damp evening with Merlin piling out behind her. As she did, she sucked a breath and gritted her teeth.

Cam grabbed the takeout and headed for her side door. Unlocking it, she pushed it open and glanced back, catching Michelle limping after her. "You gonna make it, Hop-Along?"

"Very funny," Michelle grumbled as she ducked in behind her. "I think I screwed up royally."

"Ya think. You could have told me you needed liners this morning when we left and I would have stopped at TrailTown, you know."

"I know. I just didn't want to hold us up," Michelle said as she plopped down with a grimace onto one of Cam's kitchen chairs. Bending over, she untied the laces and tugged her boots off. As she did so, Cam glanced at the bloodstained sock that covered the bandage on the side of her leg.

"Ouch! Sit right there and I'll go grab my med kit and get you cleaned up," Cam said setting their takeout on the kitchen table. A minute later, she was back with a small plastic case and a large towel tucked under her arm.

"Merlin, stop sniffing around that table," she said to the dog as she slid her hands into a pair of latex gloves. The dog darted glances between their takeout and them, then reluctantly retreated to the corner of the room. Cam kneeled before Michelle, placed the towel under her foot and peeled the sock off revealing the bloody bandage. Sitting back, she sighed and looked up guardedly.

"What?" Michelle said.

Cam turned the leg into the light. The area around the blister was swollen and red. "I'll do what I can, but tomorrow we'll need to get you to the clinic and have this looked at," she said, dousing a cotton ball with peroxide. She pulled the bandage away and exposed the wound. "This is going to sting a bit."

Michelle looked down as Cam lifted her foot. As she dabbed the Q-tip on the wound, Michelle jerked her foot back and winced. "Easy there, Nurse Ratched!"

"Hold still," Cam said.

"Sorry, but easy, okay?" Michelle said.

Cam took hold of her leg and went about cleaning the wound. "You're going to need to stay off this for the rest of the night."

"So, no shower?" Michelle said. She gritted her teeth while she watched Cam cut away a shriveled flap of skin.

"'Fraid not," Cam said looking over her work. She reached into her case and pulled out a surgical sponge and tamped the area around the wound lightly, then slathered ointment on it. "We'll let it drain for a bit then I'll bandage it up."

"What about a bath...if I keep my foot out of the water," Michelle said.

Cam sat back on her heels. "I suppose that'd be okay. Just be careful." She put her medical stuff away and got up. "You need help getting to the bathroom?"

"No, I think I can make it," Michelle said and got up.

"Okay, I'm gonna grab a fresh towel for you and get you a robe," Cam said, and headed down the hallway. Over her shoulder, she added, "Remember what I said, keep that hoof out of the water."

Michelle shed her clothes and was about to toss them in a wicker hamper when Cam knocked on the door. Thinking nothing of it, Michelle told her to come in.

"Here, let me take those from you," Cam said hanging a robe on the back of the door and reaching out for Michelle's pants and shirt. Michelle handed them off and turned to draw a bath. As she did, she heard Cam come in.

Flashing her a smile, Cam handed her a handful of bath beads then left.

Michelle dashed them in the water and watched it bubble up as she tied her hair back. Before long, the bathroom was saturated with lavender scents. She straddled the rim of the oval garden tub, careful not to get her wounded ankle wet, and sank down into bliss. For a minute, she lay there submerged with eyes closed breathing in the floral scented water.

The door opened again and Cam came in with a couple glasses of wine. "Takeout's in the oven keeping warm. Thought I'd bring some wine in and get our party started."

"Oh, this is perfect. Thanks," Michelle said, taking the glass. She took a sip, savoring a hint of peach.

"You want the lights dimmed?" Cam said. "It's a bit bright, don't you think?"

Michelle shrugged. "Sure, why not."

A moment later, the room was in a soft yellow glow. "So, how's the water?" she said taking a seat on the toilet next to the tub.

"Heavenly."

Cam sipped her wine and ran her finger through the water. "It is nice. Think I'll be taking one later myself." She was quiet a moment, as if debating something. Finally, she said, "You making out okay financially?"

"Yeah," Michelle said. "I'm okay." She looked at her best friend who was sipping her wine. Cam had been on her own since forever. "Ask you a question?"

"Shoot."

"You ever get lonely?"

Cam shrugged. "On occasion."

They were both silent a moment as Nora Jones' voice floated out from the other room. Finally, Cam said, "It gets easier with time."

But Michelle wasn't so sure it would ever get easier for her. Yet, she couldn't see herself with anyone else but Adam. "I guess."

Cam tilted her head and peered down at her. "It's not easy for you, I know." She looked away a moment. "I miss him, too."

"I know."

Cam turned back. "You need to get out there again. It's been two years 'Chelle. I know how much you loved my brother, but he's gone."

"I know, I know." Michelle sighed. "But I wouldn't know where to start, and to be honest, I'm not ready."

Cam pursed her lips. "You keep telling yourself that and you'll end up alone." She paused. "You might not believe this, but it's possible to fall in love again. All you have to do is make yourself available. They can't find you if you're hiding in your house all the time."

Michelle frowned. "I get out."

"Yeah, when I drag you."

Michelle looked away. She couldn't argue with that. But a parade of men running through her life? She didn't think so. It wasn't who she was, or ever had been. She turned back. "I'm not a bar hopper like you."

"Who says I'm a bar hopper?" Cam said. "I go out with friends. Have a good time. Sometimes, I meet someone. See where it goes."

"Sometimes?" Michelle said and smiled.

"Okay, a lot of times. Point is, I put myself out there."

Michelle thought about putting herself out there. She was no Cam, didn't have the long legs and curves, the attributes that summoned men effortlessly. She forced a smile. "I'll think about it."

.

Chapter 3

John

Pokhara – May 12th

In the depths of sleep, John heard a soft ringing, growing steadily until his eyes opened. He lay a second in the dark, coming to himself, then groped for the phone on the nightstand beside his bed. Something hit the floor in the process, click-clacking as it rolled away. Blinking at the blurred number flashing on the screen, he answered.

"John, it's Peg," his sister said. Her voice was jittery and rushed.

"Yeah, I see that." He pulled the phone away from his ear and looked at the time. 2:00 a.m. "You know I'm twelve hours ahead of you, right?"

"John, listen to me. It's Mom. She's had a stroke."

It took a moment for the words to register. He'd just spoken with his mother not two days ago, enduring fifty minutes of the latest gossip of Oak Creek's mucky-mucks. He sat up. "Stroke? What the hell you talking about? When?"

"This morning. I found her on the floor when I came to take her grocery shopping. I've been in the hospital ever since." She paused and he heard her take a shaky breath. "John, she's in the ICU and she's not good. Can you come home?"

"Umm…yeah, yeah. I'll…I'll book a flight as soon as I can," he said, trying to wrap his head around this whirlwind that had just blown into his life. All at once, his world narrowed into one focused point. His mother. He tried to think, but it was like swimming in molasses.

"John, John you there?" she said.

"Yeah…I was just trying to sort things out," he said, scrambling to get control of the situation. He raked his fingers through his hair, adding the flight hours and subtracting a day. But his math depended on a perfect world where everything ran smoothly. In Nepal, things ran on their own time and sometimes, no time at all. At last, he said, "If I can make the flight out of Pokhara to Kat, I can make the Hong Kong to Denver leg this afternoon and get to you by six tomorrow morning your time."

"Okay. When you get flight numbers and times, let me know and I'll have Mom's girlfriend, Helen, pick you up at the airport."

John leaned over and reached to the foot of the bed for his prosthetic. As he dragged it next to him, he said, "I'll call you when I hit Hong Kong. I should know my ETA then."

"Sounds good. And John…"

"Yeah?"

"Hurry."

Frazzled, John ended the call, threw a change of clothing and a few incidentals into his day-pack and got dressed. First thing was to check his credit card balance and find a flight. He booted his laptop up and logged onto his account. Thirty-two hundred and change, more than enough to get home. Next, he searched for a flight to Kat. He groaned. Even if he got to Kat with three hours to spare, the circuslike atmosphere at Tribhuvan's International airport guaranteed he'd need a minor miracle to make the trans-Pacific connection to San Francisco.

He scrolled down the list of departure times on Buddha Airline's website and found a flight leaving at 7:37 a.m., arriving in Kathmandu at 8:05a.m. Dragon Airlines - a partner with Cathay-Pacific - had a flight leaving for Hong Kong out of Kathmandu at 11:15 p.m. It was a super tight connection, considering he was going to have to switch terminals – if you could call Tribhuvan's antiquated masonry building a terminal.

At 6:30 a.m., John's taxi pulled up to the front entry of Pokhara's regional airport. He paid the driver, grabbed his daypack and got out, marching briskly into the crowded terminal that was humming with tourists and trekkers heading to Kathmandu, Jomsom and Manang. As he waited in a long queue to get his boarding pass, he pulled his phone out and dialed his sister. Although he'd said he'd call her in Hong Kong, he had to know if anything had changed with their mother. After giving her his flight itinerary, he pressed her for news and found out Mom had stabilized – at least for the time being - but the doctors cautioned against hope for a recovery. A CT scan revealed another embolism deep within the temporal lobe that was inoperable.

John's shoulders sagged after he hung up. His mother was going to die. This was impossible! The thought of her not being in the world was incomprehensible. He felt untethered and suddenly adrift in his own life, and it frightened him. Until now, he'd always considered himself independent and in control. But now, life had jumped the tracks. Esther May Patterson, retired school bus driver, librarian for Oak Creek Elementary, church deacon, and everyone's favorite mother was going to die. It was as if someone had ripped his guts out, and he found it hard to breathe as he stepped ahead in line.

The runway of Denver's International Airport raced up beneath John's passenger window. Remarkably, the travel gods had smiled on him and he'd been able to make his connection in Kathmandu to Hong Kong with five minutes to spare. Now, twenty-one hours later, he was back in the states, feeling as if he'd been dragged through a knothole. When the plane made the gate, he collected his daypack from the overhead compartment and waited with his phone glued to his ear as the passengers deplaned onto the jetway.

"I'm down," he said to his sister. "How's Mom?"

"Hanging in there. How was the flight?"

"Long. At least I didn't get hung up at customs. Is my ride here?" Having never met Helen, or for that matter, any of his mother's girlfriends since he'd taken the job with Andersen so many years ago in pursuit of his dreams, he asked what the woman looked like.

"Helen should be waiting at baggage. She has shoulder-length brown hair, oversized glasses, and is wearing a bright red sweater. I gave her a sign with your name on it so you should be able to find her pretty easy."

"Okay, I'll be there as quick as I can," he said following the moving passengers off the plane. "See you in forty-five."

He ended the call and marched past the deplaning passengers into the bustling, carpeted concourse. The escalators leading to the baggage claim on the ground floor were several gates down the long sprawling terminal. Slinging his daypack over his shoulder, he made a bee-line toward them, weaving in and out of the sea of humanity. Suddenly, he was rushing forward, faster than he should on his prosthetic and he would have taken a tumble had he not caught himself at the last minute on one of the large round columns stretching to the terminal's vaulted ceiling. Clinging to its smooth metal surface, he huffed as people darted glances his way.

Sucking a breath, he forced himself onward to the escalator leading to the baggage claim. Stepping onto it, he peered down over the rail, searching for a woman with a red sweater and a sign among the scattered crowds heading for their destinations. He found Helen standing on the fringe of the baggage carousels. When she saw him coming down the escalator, she raised her sign.

"You'd be John, I assume," she said after he made his way to her.

"Yep, Helen?" John said, catching a faint hint of a British accent.

She held her hand out. "Pleased to meet you. Tell you what: I'll go fetch my car while you collect your luggage."

John shook his head. "No need to. Got it right here," he said, patting the daypack on his shoulder. "Let's go."

Helen steered her lime-green Ford Focus past the line of waiting taxis and security vehicles in front of the entry terminal. As she went, John stared out his passenger-side window, barely noticing the idling cars dropping off or picking up friends and family from their flights. Five minutes later, they were motoring down Pena Boulevard to the 470 expressway with her giving him a rundown of her friendship with his mother, telling him how they'd met and what a good friend she'd been to her after losing her husband to colon cancer.

John nodded, trying to be polite, but his mind was focused on getting to his mother. He wished she'd pick up her speed and glanced at the speedometer. She was doing sixty in a seventy-five, and cars were flying past them like they were standing still. He pulled his phone out and dialed his sister. When she answered, he said, "Hey, we're on our way."

"Oh, good, you found Helen. Mom's hanging in there, so take your time."

John glanced over at Helen, whose dark blue eyes were focused on the road. He made his tone urgent. "Yeah, we're coming as quick as we can." But if Helen heard him, she wasn't letting on. The needle remained pinned on sixty. So much for that idea, he thought.

Peg said, "John, didn't you hear me? Everything's okay. She's not in any danger right now."

He looked up and saw their exit for Route 2 coming up in one mile. "Yeah, I know. Coming up on the 2 in a minute. See you in fifteen." He ended the call, slipped his phone back in his pocket and drummed his fingers on the armrest as the sprawling factory parks and low-rise office buildings slid past his window.

Helen looked over at him as they came to the interchange. "Don't fret. We'll get there just fine, I promise." She paused as they followed the line of cars exiting the highway then said, "So, your mum told me you work in Nepal. How did you ever end up there?"

"I'm an expedition leader," John said. "I went there because that's where the real mountains are."

She turned onto the southbound lane of Route 2 and, picking up speed, went on, "But don't we have mountains here? Some pretty big ones, I might say."

John almost smiled. "The ones around here are nothing but hills compared to what's over there."

"So, what's an expedition leader do?" she said.

"Depends on what the expedition is for," he said, and remembered he was supposed to meet Orson and Kembe in four days. He pulled his phone out and typed a quick note to himself to let them know he wouldn't be there to meet them at the bus.

She was quiet a moment, then said, "I see. And what kinds of expeditions do you lead?"

"Summit attempts," John said, putting his phone away.

"So, you're a climber. My goodness! Your mum never told me that. What mountains have you climbed? Everest?" She said the mountain's name almost as if she was afraid to hear the answer.

John eyed her, dismissing the awestruck expression on her round face. "As a matter of fact, yes."

She turned to him, and her eyes were large behind her oversized round-rimmed glasses. "Good Lord, young man. If I was your mum, I'd be worried sick."

"She doesn't know," John said as she turned onto East Hale Parkway and headed to the hospital down around a sweeping tree-lined bend. "And I aim to keep it that way."

"Well, not to worry. She won't hear anything from me," she said pulling into the hospital entrance. She drove up to the front door and stopped. "Her room's on the fourth floor. 4132. Off you go. I'll park and be up in a bit."

He grabbed his pack, got out and found his way up to the fourth floor. His sister was at the nursing station talking with a nurse. When she saw him, she broke off the conversation and hurried into his arms, clutching him tight to her feather-light body. For a minute he thought the worst had happened, that their mother had suddenly passed, but when she pulled back studying him with her soft blue eyes, he relaxed and drank in the long Patterson family face. She'd lost weight she didn't need to lose since the last time he saw her three years ago.

At last, she patted his shoulder. "Come."

She led him down the hallway under the hum and glare of fluorescent lights, past idle x-ray machines, portable medical documentation stations and janitorial carts to the wide sliding glass doors of their mother's ICU room.

When he peered through them, he shuddered. His mother's ageless, ever-present upright posture had melted into a limp wraith-like form on the bed. He glanced at his sister as the full weight of the impending future settled on his shoulders. She pressed her pencil thin lips together, and the look of pity, acceptance, and sorrow in her eyes struck him like a fist barreling into his chest. Suddenly, his legs wouldn't move and his throat tightened.

His sister drew a breath then straightened her shoulders. Though he'd never admit it to anyone, she was the strong one – the one he looked to for answers when he was young and life was shitting on him – like it was doing right now, and had been for the last three years. She turned to him with an unspoken invitation to step into the room ahead of her.

At his mother's bedside, sat Bob Murphy, a longtime friend of the family. The man got up with a forlorn expression on his long face. He'd been there a while, as far as John could tell. His dark eyes were a little red around the edges, as if he hadn't slept. Bob put his mottled hand on John's shoulder, pressing his spindled fingers into him to convey his sympathy, and stepped aside. Clearing his throat, he said, "I'll...um...go grab a cup of coffee."

John nodded at the gesture, and turned his eyes to his mother. When he came to her bedside, Peg said, "She's in a coma and probably won't come out of it."

He reached over the bed rail. "She feels cold," he muttered, laying his hand over his mother's.

"I know," Peg whispered.

His gaze narrowed in on the withered woman lying on the bed. He traced the lines of her lop-sided, wrinkled face under the oxygen mask and saw the drooped cheek and the purple bruise over her brow. This was his mother, a simple woman who could exhaust and embarrass him to no end, but in his heart, he knew she was the one person in this world he could trust without question – who'd stand by him even when he went off half-cocked and still be there waiting for him when he came back home.

I should've been here, God damn it!

He felt Peg's hand on his shoulder. "I know you don't want to hear this, John, and I don't want to talk about it, but it has to be said. The doctors...they, umm...they think it'd be best if we sign a DNR so when it happens, they don't have to put her through unnecessary pain and discomfort, and I agree. But I told them I needed to hold off until you got here."

John looked up at her, searching the unwavering, defeated gaze coming back along with the set jaw that betrayed a quivering tremor. He knew she was right, but he couldn't bring himself to say the words, as if, in doing so, he'd be condemning their mother to die. At last, he looked away, fighting with all his might to keep the river of tears dammed inside him, and said, "Do what you need to do."

He bolted from the room then and marched down the hall, his eyes downcast, not wanting to meet anyone's face. He knew it was wrong, that he shouldn't have shot out of his mother's room, but he had to get out of there, had to breathe, get a handle on himself. And the irony of walking out on the one person who really mattered - like his father had done to his mother so many years ago - wasn't lost on him, and he hated himself for it.

John opened the door to his mother's bungalow as Peg pulled away from the curb to go home and check on her husband, Stu, and the kids. It had been a long day for both of them, too long, and he was totally spent. He bent over and rubbed his leg where the prosthetic connected, remembering Nabin's little painkillers falling to the floor and rolling away this morning, or was it yesterday? Christ, he didn't know. All he did know was that he'd give just about anything he had right now for one of those little white pills.

He gritted his teeth.

Suck it up, Buttercup.

Finally, he stepped inside the house he'd grown up in. As always, coming back home was like walking into the past - as if he'd never left it. He surveyed the room as a faint citrus odor surrounded him along with the ticking of the clock on the mantel. Again, the wave of feeling out of control swept over him. He gazed into the gloom of the early evening shadows casting geometric shapes on the walls. In the far corner, an old marble-topped, cherry pedestal table sat with a large Tiffany lamp on top. The stained glass lamp was an heirloom, which had been in the family since before he was born. Two oil paintings of a streetscape of some tiny village in New York were placed prominently over the fireplace. They were the work of his great grandmother, or so his mother had told him once.

He dropped his pack beside him and flipped the light switch, chasing the shadows out of the broad rectangular room. Soft, golden light from a pair of floor lamps bathed the space that was pretty much the way it had been when he'd left home. The only exceptions were a new flat screen TV, wall-to-wall brown carpeting and a two-tone tan upholstered couch.

Wandering in, he ran his fingers over the back of a wingback chair and down its polished cherry trim. Peg had told him she'd found their mother on the floor beside it. This was his mother's chair, where she worked her crossword puzzles or read from her exhaustive collection of classic novels by Michener, Nabokov, Salinger, Caldwell, and Brontë. Forcing away the unbidden image of his mother lying helpless on the floor, he sat in her chair. The chair she spent so much time in, the chair that was as much a part of her as the books she read.

He fingered the thick paperback puzzle book sitting on the end table beside him. It was open to a page with a half finished puzzle. He picked it up and a card slid out from underneath it and fell to the floor. Leaning over, he picked it up. It was a birthday card.

His birthday card!

He'd forgotten he was going to be turning forty in a couple weeks. He opened it and read the verse and the scrawled handwriting below it, telling him how much he was loved, how proud she was of him, how important he was to her, and how much she missed him and suddenly the tears came and wouldn't stop.

Esther Patterson drew her final breath three days later at 6:42 p.m. As her frail body sunk with the last exhalation, John looked down from where he stood beside her bed and studied the woman who'd raised him and his sister all by herself. Until a few days ago, he'd never given much thought to the sacrifices she'd made for him and his sister: going without so they could have nice clothes, good food on their plate, a yearly weeklong vacation in the woods – albeit, in a tent – birthday parties, Halloween costumes, prom dresses and tuxedoes, and a decent Christmas every year. Now, it was all he could think about.

He gripped the bed rail, digging his nails into his palms, and felt his sister's hand settle over his. "I should've come home more often, should've written and called regularly, told you I loved you and that you were always on my mind," he muttered. He turned his head and locked eyes with his sister as the steady whine of the heart monitor filled the stilted silence. Her tender tearful gaze coming back crushed him. They both knew the score. He was a self-absorbed son-of-a-bitch, an angry-at-the world asshole, but she loved him anyway.

The doctor came into the room and shut the heart monitor off. After a quick verification that Esther had passed on, he left them alone. Finally, Peg tugged at John's sleeve and said, "You okay?"

John shook his head. "Yeah, I think so. So, I guess we have some things to figure out," he said, staring at his mother.

"Actually, most of it's already taken care of. I would've told you earlier, but I didn't think you were in a good place to hear it."

"Oh, really?" John said, surprised. He glanced up at her, taken aback, not liking the fact she'd presumed to know what he wanted or didn't want to hear. Moreover, he was pissed she'd taken it upon herself to make all the arrangements, effectively excluding him.

Peg looked off toward the window and was quiet a moment. "You know, you really need to stop assuming things, John."

"Assuming what?" he said, fighting to keep the annoyance out of his voice. On top of that, his leg was killing him and the lack of Sanjay's herbal medicine wasn't helping. He felt his body tighten and its urge or—rather need— for the little white pills was overwhelming.

"Oh, come on, we both know what I mean," Peg said, and sighed. She walked over near the window and nibbled a fingernail. "I really don't want to do this."

John sucked his lip, wondering what that meant.

Why do women always talk in riddles?

"Do what?"

She turned back, and with a constrained voice, said, "Argue!"

"Who said anything about arguing?" He fired back, letting go of the bed rail and waving his hand.

"It's in your tone, and could you please lower your voice?"

"Christ, Peg. I just made a simple comment, okay?" he said. "And it's not like I have a lot to say in the matter, anyway. You're the one who has been here with her. You know what she wants more than I do."

"Well, for your information, she's the one who's made all the arrangements."

He blinked. "Are you serious?"

She nodded. "Once I knew she was...well, you know...I started looking into things and found out she had it all organized."

"When…"

"Five years ago," she said, drifting back toward the bed. "Apparently, she went to a lawyer, drew up her will, bought a plot and a stone and prepaid for her funeral. There's also a letter addressed to each of us from her. The lawyer gave them to me."

John's mind was a whirlwind of questions. "Have you read…"

"No, not yet," she said. "I was thinking we'd read them together sometime before you have to go back." She paused. "By the way, when would that be?"

He sized up her enigmatic expression, trying to discern whether she was being sincere or sarcastic. "I get back when I get there." But in the back of his mind, he could just hear his boss, Ken, telling him he'd had to find someone to take his place, meaning he would essentially be out of Nepal for good.

Peg nodded, then walked around the bed and put her hands on his shoulders. "I love you, so let's not fight, okay? Mom wouldn't want that. Not now."

"Yeah, you're right." He forced a smile. "Just let me know what I can do."

John buried his mother four days later in a small countrified cemetery outside of town. It had all gone as his mother had planned, closed casket, no calling hours, a short service at the Episcopalian Church and a brief moment at the gravesite. That, in a nutshell, was his mother. She didn't like being fussed over, and so she'd made things as quick and as painless as possible for her children.

John stood in the living room, looking over the room that suddenly felt empty and abandoned. On the old marble-topped pedestal table was a metal framed black and white picture of his mom, sister and him. It had been taken when he was a toddler. He went over and picked it up, studying the vibrant young woman with dark wavy hair who was sitting at a picnic table holding him on her lap. It had been taken in the woods. The adoring look in his mother's large, brown eyes stared back at him. For a moment it was as if she were right there in the room with him. He chewed his lip as he gazed into the remembered past. His mom had been the one constant in his life, the one person he could always count on to have his back. At length, he set the picture back on the table, and as he did so, the faded black and white photo slid a bit under the glass. There was something behind it. He took the picture back up, knitted his brow and studied the edge of the frame where a telltale edge peeked out.

Another photo?

He turned the frame over and removed the back panel, revealing a small wallet sized snapshot. Turning it over, he looked down at a picture of his mother sitting beside Bob. But it was the baby in Bob's arm that made him blink. He flipped the photo back over and saw a date written on the back with his name scrawled below it.

What the hell? Why would Bob be holding me?

It didn't make sense. Then again, Bob had always been a good friend of the family, so perhaps it was nothing. Still, it left him at odds. He tucked the photo in his shirt pocket, buttoned the frame up and set it back on the table. He'd ask his sister about it later. Right now, he had something else on his mind. He went to the kitchen, snatched the letter-sized envelope off the counter along with a beer from the fridge and opened the back door to the house - his home now, his sister had informed him.

Popping the tab on the can of Coors, he took a sip and surveyed the flowering lavender hyacinths, daffodils and yellow tulips in the back yard. In the far corner of the pie-shaped lot, a thick, gray willow was coming to full foliage. A gang of squirrels was skittering in its hefty crown. One of them was busy robbing the resident bird feeder.

So many memories here. The swinging hammock under the willow he'd laid in as a child watching for shooting stars was gone now, but when he closed his eyes, he could still see it. And then there were hunting night crawlers in the flowerbeds and chasing fireflies. The drone of crickets and sitting around the makeshift fire-pit as it crackled, spit and hissed into the warm summer night. Later there was the fort he and Billy McMasters built on the edge of the woods hemming the property. Many a night, they'd retreated to it, listening to Skynyrd, Zeppelin, and Clapton on the radio.

At length, he pulled out one of the wrought iron wire chairs from the patio table and sat with his beer in hand. The beer wasn't doing much to ease his body's nagging need for Sanjay's remedy, but it was better than nothing. He sucked down a gulp and thought about the drive he'd taken earlier that morning through the old neighborhood visiting his old haunts: the high school where he'd played tight end for the Rams, the creek where he and

Billy had fished for trout. Later, he ended up out at the pavilion at Stagecoach Park where he'd said his last good-bye to Vanessa Hall, his high school sweetheart. She was heading to college back east. They made plans to keep in touch, but it never happened

He took another gulp of beer, stretched his legs in front of him and crossed his arms over his chest. Those days were long gone, and his life was on the other side of the world. What was he going to do with a house? His sister already had one, and he was loath to sell it. That left what...renting it out? A landlord, he was not! He sighed. Well, he'd get things figured out soon enough. Right now, he needed to get the damned prosthetic off his leg. He leaned over and unstrapped it and as he did so, the letter slipped out of his pocket. He picked it up and a moment later had it open in front of him.

John

Because we really never know when the good Lord is going to take us home, I wanted to take the time to tell you how much I love you and the joy you've given me throughout my long life. You have been my strength when I lost hope over the years. There's not a day that goes by that you are not on my mind. I think about what you're doing, whether you're having a good day or not, and where you are and if you're safe. And yes, John, I can see you shaking your head. But I'm your mother and it's my job because, you see, from the moment you were conceived, I have loved you. You are the very best part of me, my magnum opus.

And to you, my wanderlust boy, who tested me every minute of every day, telling me what you thought I needed to know, you cannot know how my heart swells with pride when I tell people you're a guide for the tallest mountain in the world. Yet I worry about you. When I don't hear from you, especially two years ago when you seemed to drop off the face of the earth, I was so afraid something had happened to you. You know, you could've told me you'd lost part of your leg. Oh yes, I found out all about it, and I know you've climbed that mountain, too!

More than anything, though, I've missed you over the last few years. I know it's unfair to say so, but I can't help it. You were my little troublemaker, always getting into some kind of mischief. Even now, as I write this here in bed, I half expect my door to come bursting open with this little blond-haired boy flying in, all excited about making a touchdown, or some big snake you caught. You grew up all too fast for me. Remember, you are not an island. Life is too short, too precious to go through all alone. Find someone to share your life

with and make beautiful babies. Yes, I went there.
I'm your mother, deal with it! And finally, treat the
people who matter in your life as I have treated you
- with kindness, compassion and love. It's the best
and only advice I can give.

All my Love,

Mom

Chapter 4

Michelle

Cornwall, Canada – May 23rd

Michelle pulled onto the 417 and headed west for
Ottawa. Her father's birthday was tomorrow and her
extended family was getting together at her brother's
newly-acquired camp on Lac a la Perdrix. As she fell in
line with the weekend traffic heading into town, she
ruminated about the inevitable conversation she was going
to have with her brother. He'd been relentless about her

moving north—pressing her to make a decision. She'd have a brand new house with no mortgage, be close to her nieces and nephews, spend weekends at the lake, share holidays with family and friends and do things with Dad.

He'd also sent her a gazillion shots of the log cabin chalet on the shores of the lake buried deep in the southern end of Laurentides National Forest. He said there were all sorts of trails she and the kids could hike and snowshoe on. And last but not least, he had connections and could get her whatever job she would like at Mannington. He was throwing it all out there.

Typical Charles J. LeConte modus operandi!

She couldn't deny she was tempted by the offer—who wouldn't be—but her life was rooted in Cornwall. She had a best friend there who'd stood by her when the world turned into a mess, a job she liked that kept her sane on days she wanted to get in a car and drive until she ran out of road. But even then, leaving had never been an option. Not really. Not with her mother and Adam lying in

Woodhaven Cemetery, gone forever but never forgotten. She knew someday she'd move on and maybe end up someplace new, but not now. It was still too soon.

She wished CJ could understand that. Yet she could appreciate his wanting family around. They were young when their mother died, and they dealt with it in separate ways. Michelle had been fifteen when it happened, and even though she was a year younger than her brother, she'd tried to take on the role of a big sister. But CJ was running with a bad crowd, breaking into houses, looking for drug money. It took all of their father's pull with law enforcement contacts to keep him out of Laurencrest.

Eventually things came to a head and CJ was found unconscious and near death from hypothermia in the park outside of town. He'd OD'd on a bad hit of heroin. That had been the turning point.

Six years later, he graduated from the University of Toronto. Six months later, he landed a junior management position at the Mannington Lumber Corporate office in

Ottawa. By the time he was thirty-two, he was vice president of the eastern region and a welcome guest at the Mannington mansion.

That was where he met Monica, the daughter of Edward Mannington. Once he married into the prestigious family, he lacked for nothing. He would never admit it, but Michelle knew his worst fear was that his past would catch up to him. Perhaps that was the reason he'd brought their ailing father to live with them and now wanted her there, too. It was all about circling the wagons in case everything went to hell. Michelle shook her head, pitying him and turned the radio on.

Ten minutes later, she was tapping her fingers on the steering wheel to the beat of Katy Perry's "Roar." The song was one of Cam's favorites. As she sang along with Katy's driving voice, Cam's suggestion of getting out there echoed in her thoughts.

Cam was right, but she just couldn't see herself going through a long line of dates looking for Mr. Right.

And as far as money went...well, she was managing financially – albeit paycheck-to-paycheck. She was quite certain if she was in a tight spot, her boss, Don, would step up to the plate and float her a loan. She'd been with Tyler Construction going on eighteen years now and had become an invaluable member of their little family. At least that's what Don had told her time and again since Adam had died. She attributed that sentiment to the big marshmallow wanting to brighten her world after it had crashed down around her.

Yet, sometimes he looked at her in a way that made her feel he wanted more. She shrugged it off. He was just concerned about her, worried about her being alone. She smiled as she thought of the suggestion he'd made last week about her getting a dog. But a dog deserved to be a priority, not a means to an end because you were lonely.

She arrived in Ottawa around noon, turned north onto the Montee Paiement Highway and drove into the vast Laurentides National Forest. As the towering maple woods, and sparkling lakes passed by, she understood what had lured her brother here. It was like entering another world, apart from the busy city life.

She rolled her window down, and let the resinous scents pour in around her until she came to a twisting forest lane that led to Lac a la Perdrix. She turned left and ten minutes later, pulled up in front of a gated entrance. She read the name on the metal plaque attached to the wrought iron bars bent together and splayed out on top like a crown of a tree.

LES MAPLES.

She pulled her cell phone out. "I'm here," she said.

A moment later, the gate swung back and she drove down a narrow, paved driveway that bent around the trees and snaked through the secluded wooded estate. As she went, flowering purple and white crocus lifted their heads to her on the side of the road. Beyond them, in the deepening understory, sprouting green ferns and seedling trees reached up to catch the splintered sunlight raining down. The only sign of the human hand, save for the road, were the wrought iron poles with decorative lantern heads passing by in forty-meter intervals. Michelle grinned in amusement as she motored along at a leisurely thirty KPH, trying to imagine what was waiting for her at the end of this dreamy Kinkade-like painted lane.

The prime real estate reeked of Mannington money.

The road took a sharp bend to the right and swung back on itself for some time until at last, the trees parted and the chalet came into view. She stopped her car and gazed at it in wonder, taking in the massive two-story rustic log structure sitting amongst a triad of towering spruce. The pictures her brother sent her didn't do justice to the size of it.

"Well, you certainly spared no expense here," Michelle muttered as she drank in the expansive wrap-around porch facing the lake. She turned the car off and got out as the front door of the camp opened and her niece came spilling out with her nephew trailing behind. Michelle took a deep breath and braced herself. She loved her brother's children, but after Adam had died, they reminded her of all she'd lost.

"Tantie M, Tantie M," her niece, Kate, squealed as she ran up to her and wrapped her arms around Michelle's legs. "You're here, you're here."

Michelle smiled as she looked down at the wiry six-year-old girl whose long, dark brown hair had been pulled back into a ponytail. Although it had only been four months since she'd last seen her, Kate had seemingly spurted up another inch.

"Yes, I am, and I'm so happy to see you," Michelle said, then turned to her nephew, who'd come loafing up from behind. She eyed the reserved young man who considered himself older than his eight years of age.

"Hi William," she said, careful not to call him the nickname he hated.

The boy pushed his dark-rimmed glasses up onto the bridge of his freckled nose and shot her a diffident smile. "*Bonjour* Tante Michelle."

Oh, William, you're way too young to be so serious.

"Well, are you just going to stand there, or are you going to give me a hug?"

William shrugged, then finally joined his sister and stepped into her arms. As he did, Michelle closed her eyes and held the children tight to her breast until she could bear it no more.

Kate grabbed her hand as CJ came out of the front door. "You wanna see our new camp?"

"I sure do," Michelle said as CJ walked up wearing khakis and a Mannington Company forest green shirt with a monogramed yellow M on the left breast pocket. She pulled her brother into a hug. "Quite a shack you got here, or should I say a hotel? You could host half of Ottawa here."

CJ shot her one of his winning smiles and laughed. "Oh, I don't know about that, but it has lots of room for family." He let go of her, gave her a knowing look, then added, "How was the trip?"

Yes, CJ, I get the hint.

"It was okay."

"Good, good," he said, "Well, let's get you inside and settled. I'm sure you're anxious to see Papa."

"Always. How is he?"

"Excited to see you," CJ said. He looked off and she could see him turning something over in his head. Finally, he turned back. "You know, you should phone him more often."

Michelle came to a halt and bristled. "Are we really going to do this right now...in front of..." She glanced down at the kids who were looking up.

He shrugged, "Just saying, is all."

"Right," Michelle said. How often she called her father, which was plenty, was none of his business nor was she going to be held to his appointed schedule. She shook her head. "Let me get my bag," she said, prying her hand away from Kate. When the little girl frowned, she turned to her. "Auntie M needs to get her stuff, honey."

She opened her trunk as her heart thumped and stared down at her overnight bag. This was not a good start to the weekend that she was sure was going to go downhill from here. But it was her father's birthday, and she wasn't going to be the one to ruin it. Collecting herself, she pasted a smile on and pulled her bag out.

"Okay, I'm ready for the grand tour," she announced to the kids as she shut the trunk and joined her brother, following the kids across the paved drive. As they walked side by side, she looked out over the sparkling deep blue lake that was lapping against the rocky shoreline. With the exception of a few canoes, not a boat could be seen anywhere, which surprised her, seeing how the sun was shining down from a clear blue sky.

"Looks like everyone is out on holiday," she said in the awkward silence between them.

"How's that?" CJ said, looking straight ahead.

She watched the kids race into the house, letting everyone inside know she'd arrived. "Well, there's hardly anyone out on the lake. Beautiful day like today, I would think people would be out waterskiing or something."

CJ shot her a thin smile as he stepped up onto the porch. "You'd think so, except motorboats are banned from the lake. Keeps things quiet the way I like it. One of the reasons I bought here." He opened the front door and waved her in ahead of him.

"*Bienvenue chez Les Maples.*"

Louis, or *Sparks* LeConte as her father was affectionately called by those he'd commanded in the fire department, was turning seventy-five tomorrow. He met Michelle at the door and drew her into his arms after she set her bag down. Michelle lingered in his embrace for a moment, then pulled back and looked up into her father's soft, slate gray eyes.

"How's my pearl?" he said.

"I'm good, Dad," Michelle answered as CJ stood nearby. "How are you feeling?"

"Right now, perfect," he said with a wink. He tilted his head toward the cavernous Great Room behind him. "What'd'ya think of all this?"

Michelle took in the sunlit Great Room with its large fieldstone fireplace anchoring the far end. The room, which was modestly furnished with Mission style furniture and a large leather sectional couch, could contain most of her home's entire downstairs. She eyed the family heirloom Oriental rug that stretched over a polished oak plank floor, and the oil painting of the St. Lawrence River at sunset that hung over the wooden mantel crowning the hearth. Her grandmother on her mother's side was a talented woman and had painted it shortly after she'd come to Cornwall back in the twenties. The muted slate blue and tan traditional Kashan rug had been brought back from Turkey by her uncle after WWII.

The kids came running back into the room with Monica trailing behind wearing a cream-colored cashmere sweater, designer jeans, and a pair of Prada heels. Michelle stifled the urge to roll her eyes as she watched the woman saunter in as if she walked on water.

"*Bonjour* Michelle," Monica said as she joined them. She smiled and gave Michelle one of her practiced arms-length hugs. As she did so, Michelle inhaled a subtle whiff of jasmine, vanilla and tonka bean. "How was your drive?"

"It was good," Michelle said. Kate tugged at Michelle's shirt and she looked down at her niece. "What, honey?"

"I made you a picture. You want to come see it?"

"Kate, what have I told you about interrupting people?" Monica said.

The girl frowned and bowed her head. "I'm sorry, Momma."

"It's okay. She's just excited," Michelle said. Kate had a budding talent for drawing, no doubt inherited from her great grandmother. "I'd love to, right after I get settled in."

Louis took the cue and scooped the little girl up in his arms. "How about you help your grand-père out in the kitchen, hmm? You, too, William."

As the kids went with her father, Michelle nodded toward the fireplace. "This place is amazing."

Monica glanced at the room nonchalantly. "We like it well enough. But you must be exhausted. Here, come and sit," she said, leading the way toward the couch.

"Actually, I'd like to get to my room and freshen up if that's all right," Michelle said.

"But of course. Then you must come down and join us," Monica said. She turned to her husband. "CJ, why don't you show your *sœur* to her room? I believe there are fresh towels in the closet, too."

After lunch, they all sat around the dining room table chatting about the comings and goings of their lives as the kids played in their rooms. Dominating the conversation was the designer line of clothing Monica was going to start in the fall, and CJ heading the new expansion of Mannington Lumber into the lower forty-eight. As her brother spieled off the details of the new state-of-the-art lumber mill, Michelle felt like an outsider in her own family. Her world was so far out of orbit with theirs, she might as well have been living on the moon.

She eyed her father sitting across from her from time to time, wondering what he thought of this new world he'd been injected into. Her father had always been a man of modest means and needs. Certainly, living in his son's world had to overwhelm him, albeit in the attached apartment to the sprawling estate in Gatineau Park. He traded a few glances with her, giving her the impression he felt the same way she did. Yet, she knew he was proud of his son. CJ had come a long way from where he'd started after their mother died.

The conversation drifted back and forth, from her job to the kids and all the extra-curricular events they were involved with. William had finished the school year with straight As and had joined a local junior chess club while Kate was taking art and dance classes. Finally, the topic of future plans came up.

CJ turned to Michelle from where he sat at the head of the table. "So what's on your plate this summer?

Already, CJ? Fine!

"Getting ready for a trip. Cam and I are going abroad."

Eyebrows flew up around the table. Monica, who sat beside her, said, "Really? Where? I know some wonderful hotels in Paris and London. I'd be more than willing to look into them for you."

Michelle eyed her father and turned back to Monica with a smile. "Thanks, but I'm going to Nepal."

Silence.

CJ leaned forward, his jaw dropped. Finally, he said, "You're going where?"

"Nepal. Cam and I are going to Mount Annapurna. It was on Adam's bucket list," Michelle said, pushing her plate away. She glanced at her father, hoping he'd not be against it. He stared back at her with a stunned expression but remained silent.

CJ sat back and cleared his throat. "Let me get this straight, 'Chelle. You're going halfway around the world to a Goddamned mountain. A third-world country, at that! Who came up with this harebrained plan? No, wait…let me guess. Cam?"

Monica shot a searing glare down the table. "Language, CJ!"

He pressed his lips together. "Pardon, Mon, but this is crazy." He turned back to Michelle. "You need to think this through, 'Chelle. If Cam wants to go there, that's fine. She's always been a bit of a vagabond. But you-"

"Shut up," Michelle barked back, glaring at him. Even though she'd half expected CJ's objection, she hadn't expected the fierce recoil in her body. "And it's not a harebrained plan, nor is it up for debate, Charles. I'm doing this."

"Matter of opinion," CJ shot back.

"Your opinion, not mine," Michelle fired back.

CJ took a deep breath, shook his head and turned to their father as if looking for support. But Louis just sat there and said nothing for a moment until Michelle noticed a subtle upturn on his lips.

He's happy for me!

She relaxed and smiled at her father. "We'll be with a group, and there's a guide with us at all times. We've done our research on this, Dad, so don't worry. We'll be fine."

Monica leaned into her. "Well, I say, go for it."

Michelle blinked as she watched her sister-in-law give her brother one of her famous the-subject-is-closed expressions. Of all of the people she thought would come to her defense, Monica was the least expected.

Michelle and her father sat on the porch with wine glasses in hand, watching the sunset over the lake. She looked out over the still-dark waters mirroring the deepening blue sky above and watched a pair of mallards skim over the surface before plowing in for a landing. The sound of the distant splash traveled across the lake and tumbled over the soft murmuring of the TV inside. She pulled her sweater tight around her, warding off the cool evening breeze and soaked in the honeyed scent of the flowerbeds.

Her father set his wine glass down, stretched his legs out in front of him and cleared his throat. "This is nice."

"Yes, it is," she answered and sipped her wine. "That was quite a dinner. I don't think I could eat another bite."

"Your *frère* is quite a cook when he puts his mind to it." He was quiet a moment, then said, "CJ means well."

"I know he does," Michelle said and crossed her legs.

"He's just concerned," her father said.

"And I appreciate that," Michelle said, knowing it had more to do with CJ judging her choices. Part of her couldn't help wanting to remind her brother about his own past decision making, back when he'd put their father and her through hell, but that was childish and would do no one any good. She drained her wine glass and set it down beside her. At length, she said, "So, what do you think about my going? You were pretty quiet at dinner."

Her father rubbed his neck. "I don't think it matters what I think. If it's something that's important to you, then do it."

"Adam would want this for me, I think," Michelle said, eyeing him.

He shot her a knowing smile. "I know. Just be careful."

Michelle extended her hand toward him and when he took it, she said, "I will." She looked back out over the water, trying to decide if she should bring up the subject of CJ wanting her to move. She knew her father would love having her close by. The question became, would he remain neutral when CJ eventually brought it up? Finally, she said, "CJ wants me to move to Ottawa."

"*Oui*, I know."

"I'm not ready."

Her father squeezed her hand and let go of it. "You do what you think is best." He took his glass up, drank the last of his wine, and got up. "I'm going in for a refill. Can I get you another?"

Michelle looked up at him. He was smiling down at her with one of his patented I-love-you expressions, which crinkled his careworn face and softened his eyes. "Yes, I would love another. And Papa?"

"*Oui?*"

"I love you."

He took her glass and as he went to go inside, CJ came out the door with a tumbler in hand. "Hope I'm not late to the party," he said.

"No, just going in for refills," Louis said. He ducked inside and left them alone.

CJ strode up to the railing and peered off into the darkening sky that was just being pricked by stars. Michelle got up and joined him. "Good job on dinner. The steaks were awesome."

"Thanks." He took a sip of his drink. "Nice here, isn't it?"

"Yes, it is."

He pointed to a jut of land wading out into the lake far off to their left. "There's a pretty little cove behind those trees about a kilometer down the trail at the west end of our property. Maybe tomorrow morning you'd like to take a walk over with the kids." He took another sip of his drink, glanced at her and said, "So...have you given any thought to my offer?"

Michelle closed her eyes.

Here we go.

She took a deep breath and looked up at him. "*Oui.*"

"And?"

"I'm going to pass for now, CJ."

He shook his head and glanced back at the front door. "You know *he* isn't going to be around forever."

"I'm well aware of that," Michelle said. "And it's not like I said never. But right now, I'm just not ready to make that kind of a move. Papa understands, why can't you?"

"Right," CJ scoffed. He downed the rest of his drink and stiffened his shoulders. "Papa doesn't say anything because he doesn't want to press you, but down inside, he wants you here. Believe it!" He looked away then turned back. "You know, it's about time you start thinking about others beside yourself, 'Chelle. He needs you close by, not 100 kilometers away. Time to get off the pity party."

Michelle stiffened. "Pity party?"

CJ set his jaw. "You know what I'm talking about."

Just then, her father came back out. Michelle had all she could do to hold her anger from spilling out as he joined them at the rail. He handed Michelle her glass of wine and placed his hand firmly on CJ's shoulder. Leveling a back-off-and-let-it-be gaze at his son, he said, "Ah, it's good to have the two most important people in my life here beside me. A toast…to family get-togethers, and birthdays. May there always be plenty of them."

"Happy birthday, Papa," Michelle said, fairly sure he'd heard them arguing.

CJ straightened his shoulders and nodded. "*Oui*, Papa, may there be many more."

The following morning, Michelle took the kids for a walk out to the cove her brother had pointed out. As she walked along the shady wooded trail, she ruminated on the comment CJ had made the night before. She wasn't on a pity party. She'd lost her husband forever. How dare he minimize how she felt! Still, there was a small part of her that wondered if there was some truth to what he'd said.

When would the ache in her heart become bearable? And what if it went away completely? What would that say about her?

That she'd moved on and forgotten him?

She couldn't even imagine that happening, but she wondered what it might *look* like years from now, after the visceral memories had faded to echoed whispers.

"*Tantie* M, look," Katie cried, pointing to a disturbance out in the water a short distance from shore. "It's a beaver."

Michelle came to herself and strode up beside her niece and nephew, who were standing at the water's edge. She watched the animal do a barrel roll and come up a few meters away. "I think that's an otter, honey," she said, noting its slender body and graceful antics.

They watched the animal play around for a few moments before it finally slipped away into the water's depths. Katie said, "Do you think she has babies?"

"I don't know," Michelle said. "Maybe."

William said, "I saw on TV otters can stay underwater for up to five minutes."

"That's a long time," Michelle said taking Katie's hand. "Well, come on. We still have a ways to go to the cove, and we don't want to be late for your *grand-père's* birthday party."

They turned away from the water and followed the footpath meandering through the wooded land surrounding the lake. As they walked under the leafy canopy, Michelle saw delicate golden honeysuckle flowers and purple touch-me-nots among the lacy fern, which Katie ran out to take a closer look at.

But William kept his eyes to the ground as he walked along the edge of the path, looking for little creatures among the leaf litter. As she watched the kids explore their world, she battled the surging reminder of things that would never be.

Katie came back with a handful of flowers and a shining smile on her little round face. Holding them up to her, she said, "I picked these for you, *Tantie* M."

Michelle looked down at her niece then smiled and dropped to a knee to take the hastily arranged bouquet of touch-me-nots. "For me?"

"*Oui!* You're my favorite tante in the whole world. I can't wait until we're all together all the time."

Just great, CJ! You had to promise them things you had no business promising. Now I'm going to look like the bad guy. Thanks a lot!

"Why, these are so beautiful. *Merci*, Katie. I'll put them in water as soon as we get back."

"I'm gonna get some for my Mere now," Katie announced, and ran back off to get more.

When Katie was out of earshot, William said, "Why don't you want to come live in Ottawa?"

Michelle blinked. *What?* "Where did you hear that?" she said, stifling the sudden heat in her voice.

"Last night I heard Papa tell my *mère* you didn't want to move to Ottawa. Don't you want to be a family? I know we're not the same as…"

"William," Michelle said, pulling him to her and hugging him fiercely, "Of course I want to be a family. It's just not a good time for me to move right now. There are things your *tante* needs to work through."

She felt William's hands tighten around her. "Okay, *Tante* Michelle. Maybe when you come back from Nepal you will have worked through them and feel better and be happy."

Michelle pulled back from William, disheartened, and studied his somber expression as he looked back at her. Was she giving people the impression she was depressed? "William, do you think I'm sad?"

He shrugged. "Sometimes. You never laugh like you used to before...you know."

His words sank into Michelle and gathered at the pit of her stomach. He was right. She hadn't heard the cheerful, carefree giggle that came from deep inside her in a long, long time. At last she ruffled his hair playfully and said, "Then I shall have to work on that." She forced a smile. "Do you remember the game we used to play when you were little?"

"You mean the 'sounds-like' game?"

"*Oui*. You say a word and I come up with a word that sounds like it, then you come up with a word that sounds like the word I said."

He smiled, and it lit up Michelle's heart. "Okay."

"You start first," Michelle said, taking his hand and starting off. She called Katie back to them and ten minutes later, they were deep into the game, giggling and laughing as they wandered down the path.

Chapter 5

John

Oak Creek, Colorado – May 27ʰ

John sat on the stoop of his mother's home, eyeing the wallet photo of his mom, Bob and him, then glanced at the brown bungalow across the street. Bob Murphy's house. Should he show him the photo perched between his fingers right now? He wasn't sure. He looked around him. The neighborhood was quiet. People had gone off to work and the kids were at school.

Ignoring the urge for one of Sanjay's little white helpers, he took up the cup of coffee beside him and sucked down a gulp. His sister would be arriving with the real estate lady anytime now. He sighed, knowing Peg wanted him to stay in town, to be an uncle to her children, but he knew he wasn't uncle material. Besides, all the memories would be more than he could handle. No, it was best to close this chapter on his life. Sometimes, you just couldn't come home again.

He looked out over the front yard, watching his mother's purple and red tulips and yellow daffodils sway in a soft breeze. The bird feeder was swinging gently off the limb of the maple that had stood guard over the driveway since before he was born. The old gray giant was coming into full foliage now, putting out leafy buds. His mother had used it as a backdrop for family photos over the years—his graduation at Oak Creek High, a prom picture of him and Vanessa, and Peg's going-away-to-college photo that still hung on the wall over the TV. And in the fall, when it dropped its leaves, he'd pile them up high in the front yard and dive into them with his friend, Ted, who'd lived a few doors down. Ted had moved on a long time ago to the East Coast somewhere. Bangor or some such place.

Across the street, he heard a screen door clap shut. He looked up and saw Bob in his bibbed overalls, wearing a Denver Rockies baseball cap. The man who was heading for his flowerbeds had lived across the street from them for the last forty-odd years, and he was a fixture in the Patterson household. John had looked up to him in his youth, listening to tales of a world far away when they were out hiking or fishing or hunting. There, in the wilds outside Oak Creek, the old fair-haired army veteran would look down at John with deep blue eyes, the way a father would a son, as he mused on a world of magical mountains and vast gray oceans.

At the time, John thought nothing of Bob's involvement in his family. Bob was simply there, like the sun rising every morning, a constant, nor did John think it strange the way Bob looked at his mother, Esther. It was just the way adult friends looked at each other. After all, Bob had been married during those years when he was growing up. But now looking at the picture in his hand and through the lens of time, John wondered. He thought about Bob's being at the hospital when he arrived and then how the man had acted at calling hours... how he had lovingly touched John's mother's face with a trembling finger and laid a rose in the casket beside her.

John tucked the photo away, dusted off his jeans and hoofed it across the street. "Hey."

Bob tossed his hand spade on the ground next to the raised flowerbed and looked up. He held John in his gaze a moment, then cleared his throat. "Hey yourself."

John glanced over the manicured lawn and flowering shrubs as he debated bringing the photo up. "Yard's looking good."

"It's getting there," Bob said, getting up off his knees. He took his gardening gloves off, slapped them over his leg and peeked over at Esther's house. "So, you home for a while, or are ya heading right back to the mountains?"

John followed Bob's glance back to his home and scratched his neck. "Going back in a couple weeks, I think." He looked at Bob and saw a subtle change in the man's craggy, sandpapered face. A light, caramel brown beard with a touch of gray in it was just starting to show. They stood in the awkward silence a moment, neither of them seeming to know what to say next. Finally, John nodded toward the house and said, "I guess Peg's gonna put it on the market."

Bob nodded and looked away. "Yeah, I guess that's the only thing to do, what with you going back to Nepal, is it?" When John nodded, Bob sighed and continued, "Sort of sad when all you've worked for your whole life is tallied up in a real estate deal, but that's the way of it." He looked away. "Your mom was a hell of a lady. I'm gonna miss her."

"She thought a lot of you, too. I want you to know I appreciate all you've done for her over the years," John said.

Bob nodded. "Thanks, means a lot. She thought the world of you. Talked you up all the time to anyone who'd listen."

John looked down and shuffled his feet. The opportunity to ask about the photo yawned in front of him. He was about to pluck the photo out of his pocket when Bob said, "How's Peggy doing? Didn't have much chance to talk to her at the funeral."

"She's getting by," John said, doubling back. "The grandkids are having a hard time. They loved their grandma."

"That they did," Bob said. "They were over here two, three times a week keeping her busy."

John nodded, envisioning his mother fussing over his niece and nephew. His mother was a doter and had been since he was born, making sure he was taking care of himself—that he was eating enough in Nepal, wearing sunscreen in the summer and dressing appropriately in the winter. He smiled. He could just imagine what she was like with her grandchildren. Feeding them all kinds of naughty, sweet things his sister wouldn't approve of.

Finally, he said, "They'll miss her apple pies the most."

"Yes, your mom made a mean apple pie," Bob agreed. "Your mom was a good woman, John, and my best friend."

John put his hand on Bob's shoulder and squeezed it as his sister's car came around the corner. "Hey, look, I guess we're having a family get-together at Peg's this Saturday. If you want to join us, I'm sure she wouldn't mind."

Bob smiled. "Thanks, John. I'd like that."

John shut the front door behind him and locked his mother's house up as Bob Murphy swung his old Ford pick-up out of his driveway and pulled up in front. Climbing in beside the man, he popped a couple of Advil and buckled himself in. Not that the over-the-counter pain remedy would do him much good. What he needed was the numbing effects of the opioid that lived in a little gray bottle beside his bed in Pokhara. He wondered, not for the first time, if he could've snuck it on the plane with him. And if he'd gotten caught he'd have missed seeing his mother one last time because he'd have been thrown in jail. He didn't need to be reminded that the Nepalese government didn't toy around with drug offenses.

Bob glanced at him as he pulled away from the curb and headed down the street. "Good day for it."

John nodded. "It is," he muttered. He didn't really want to attend this so-called family gathering Peg had thrown together, but he figured he owed it to his sister. She had been the better of the two of them, looking after their mom. For her, family came first and connections were important; for him, not so much. He didn't know why he felt this ambivalence toward his family, but he never cared to explore it. It just was what it was. He looked out the window at the passing homes with their neatly tended front yards, white picket fences and waving American flags on the porches. A slice of old Americana, a part of him he had left behind a long time ago. For the most part, nothing had changed, save for the loss of Dan Gowan's old gnarled oak tree and Carl Lyman's breezeway addition. People in this quiet neighborhood seemed to have been frozen in the generation of Eisenhower, holding to the ways of the grand old party of Lincoln.

What was really on his mind was Bob. Last night, as he'd lain in bed, he'd thought about the man's behavior at the funeral and toward him the other day, and as the night wore on, the ember of suspicion he'd ignored over the years ignited. Bob had been more than just a good neighbor and friend to the family, more than just a father figure, who having no children of his own, delighted in spending time with John when he was growing up. Finally, he said, "So, you and my mom, were you, um…more than just friends after your wife died?"

Silence enveloped the cab. Finally, Bob eyed him sidelong and said, "And if we were?"

"I suppose it's none of my biz, but I'd like to know."

Bob tapped his fingers on the steering wheel. "We were best friends, John. And yes, I loved her. Can we leave it at that?"

"I guess," John said as Bob came to a red light and downshifted. As they waited for the light to change, John's cell phone vibrated in his pocket. He pulled it out and saw a message from his sister asking him to pick up a bag of ice at the store on his way. He shook his head and said to Bob, "You mind stopping off at Kelly's? Peg needs ice."

"No problem," Bob said. The light turned green and they started off. They left the old neighborhood behind and connected with the main route leading through town. The old homesteads and tree-lined streets steadily morphed into one- and two-story brick buildings with colorful wood-clad storefronts. Signs for The Stampeding Buffalo Bar and Grille, Jamieson's Pharmacy, Barber Realty, and Haskins and Johnson Esquire passed them by. Bob pointed out the new library and the ever-popular Sander's Coffee House.

"Took long enough, but Sanders finally discovered Oak Creek," he said as they passed the flapping entry canvas canopy over Sander's front door. He drove past it and John could see the place was hopping with teens and young couples. "Won't be long before Star-Mart comes a knocking, I suppose. Although why we need them around town, I don't know," Bob said, coming to Kelly's. He pulled into the lot and hunted for a place to park. "They're plenty busy today. You want me to go in and get it?"

"No, that's fine," John said as Bob craned his neck around while driving down a long line of parked cars. At last he saw a truck pulling out, and he quickly filled the space left behind.

"Well, at least let me buy," Bob said opening his driver's side door.

John got out, joined the man and they zigzagged their way around the parked cars to the front door of the brick and mortar building. Kelly's had been a landmark of Oak Creek since before he was born, and it hadn't changed much, save for the band of ribbon windows that now ran along the front of the building, displaying posters of the week's best buys written in big black and red letters. Even though he'd been home now for three weeks, the shock of the modern world suddenly hit him. Then again, when he'd arrived back on familiar ground, his thoughts were focused on his mother. Now, everything around him in this sleepy little town vied for attention. From the breeze carrying barbeque from the firehouse fundraiser, to the music of Tim McGraw drifting out from Sander's Coffee House to the strip mall across the street, teeming with cars and people going here and there, the gas station down the road advertising pizza for $2.99 a slice and beer for $5.99 a sixer, and the whitewashed steeple of the Emmanuel Baptist Church peeking over the trees, he was overwhelmed, and he found himself longing for the simplicity of the tiny bucolic mountain villages of Nepal.

Once inside Kelly's, they headed for the back of the store, passing people in the aisles who were picking canned goods off the shelves. John grabbed a bag of ice out of the freezer case and looked up to a familiar face looking his way. For a moment he was shell-shocked. Vanessa Hall. Holy shit! He hadn't seen her since the night before she'd left for college. They'd been inseparable the last two years of high school; him practically living at her house. Her father joked he should've been able to claim John as a dependent on his taxes.

But as inseparable as they'd been, their aspirations went in separate directions. Vanessa had her sights set on medical school, wanted to be a surgeon like her father and although she said she loved him, she had to follow her dreams. He pretended to look away as she neared him, but he couldn't stop himself from furtively glancing at her. She was wearing dark blue medical scrubs, and she'd lost a few pounds since high school, accentuating her soft birdlike shoulders, cheeks and jaw. Short thick auburn hair brushed her ears. Soft green eyes hid behind delicate wire- framed glasses. She hadn't aged a day.

"Oh, my God…John Patterson?" she said, almost as if she didn't believe it was him. She set the can of whatever she was buying in her cart.

As she took a good long look at him, he caught a whiff of fragrant floral cologne and it took him back to when they were together. "Hey Van. Long time."

"It has been," she said. "I heard about your mom. So sorry about that."

"Yeah, it was a bit unexpected," he said, wondering if she'd been at the funeral. He hadn't seen her.

"You doing okay?"

He shrugged as his heart pounded. Why was he feeling like this? "Getting by. I see you're wearing scrubs. You a big-shot doctor now?"

"No, just a P.A. here at the clinic."

John nodded, and for a moment they stood in the awkward silence, staring at each other. Finally, he turned to Bob and cleared his throat. "Umm...this is Bob, my neighbor across the street. You remember him, right?"

Bob put his hand out. As she shook the man's hand, John noticed her ring finger was bare.

"So, you live around here?" John said.

"Yep. Over on Maple Drive," she said as a blond-haired man came around the corner.

John felt his stomach twitch as he eyed the young man coming their way.

"This is my son, Jason," Vanessa said. "Jason, this is John and his friend, Bob. You remember me telling you about John, right?"

Jason turned and smiled, and as he did, all the spit left John's mouth. It was like looking in a mirror and seeing himself twenty years ago. Suddenly, the memory of him taking Vanessa to bed before she left for college coalesced into a moment of undeniable clarity.

Finally, he said, "Hi, Jason."

The kid stared back. "Hey."

John glanced at Van and felt the room close in around him, caging him in as he fought for something more to say, anything to hide the shock racing through him. He shifted the bag of ice he was carrying into his other hand, trying to avoid the appraising look Vanessa was giving him.

Finally, she spoke up. "Jason just got accepted into Michigan State's medical program."

"Is that right?" John said, thankful for being rescued while the questions piled up. If Jason was his son, Vanessa would've gotten in touch with him... wouldn't she? He scraped his memory. Had she called or written and he'd ignored it, thinking what was the use—he was in Nepal back then and she was in the States. They had gone in the opposite directions twenty years ago. He tried to tell himself he was imagining things, but try as he might, he couldn't escape the sobering thought he had a son who was standing right in front of him.

Bob said, "Looks like you're following in your mom's footsteps."

Jason smiled. "Actually, I'm into forensics, which is a little bit different, but yes, I guess I am."

"Congratulations," Bob said. "Your mother must be very proud of you."

"She is," Vanessa piped up. She turned to John and peered down at the bag of ice he was carrying. "Well, it looks like your ice is melting, so we'll let you guys get on. So nice to see you again, Bob."

"And you as well," Bob said. To Jason he said, "Good luck and study hard, young man."

"I will," Jason said. He turned to John. "Nice chatting with ya."

"Same here," John said. "Van, take care of yourself."

"Will do. Maybe we could get together for coffee sometime…you know, catch up."

"Sure," John lied, wanting to get the hell out of there.

Bob turned into Peg's looping driveway and parked behind a string of cars. As Bob set the parking brake and turned off the engine, John sat, his mind awash with the chance meeting he'd had with Vanessa and its implications. He looked out at the sprawling cedar-clad contemporary home with its clerestory windows. Peg had married well and lived a life a world apart from him. He opened the door and got out. Bob followed with their ice, and they headed for the front porch where his sister's husband, Stu, was waiting for him.

"Come on in," the man said, taking the ice from Bob. He led them down the hallway into the spacious kitchen where Peg was rifling through the refrigerator.

She turned around with a bowl in her hands, set it down and walked over to John. "I was beginning to worry about you."

John looked around, saw the gathered crowd outside on the back deck and felt his body stiffen. He shrugged. "Traffic, and the store was busy as hell, sorry."

"No matter, you're here," Peg said as his nephew, Tommy came rushing in through the open sliding glass door. He rushed up to John, calling out his name, and wrapped his little arms around John's waist.

John tousled the boy's short blond hair. "Hey there, champ. Having fun?"

"Yeah, we're playing on my new trampoline," the boy said, looking up at him. "Come out and see it! It's really neat."

"He'll be out in a minute," Peg said to Tommy. "You go out and play." To John, she said, "You want a beer? How about you, Bob?"

"Sure," John said.

"Thanks, and thanks for inviting me," Bob put in.

"No, thank you for coming. You were so good to our mom," Peg said, going back to the refrigerator. She pulled out a couple bottles of Coors and handed them to John and Bob. "There's plenty of food outside, so help yourselves."

"Nice home," Bob said, looking around at the sprawl of glass-faced cabinets. "That maple?"

"Yes. We wanted to keep the kitchen airy and light," Peg said.

Bob nodded, went over and ran his hand along the oatmeal hued granite countertop. "Your mom loved to cook and bake. She must have been tickled pink in here."

Peg smiled. "You don't know the half of it. Come on, let's all go outside," she said, and led them out onto the back deck.

John pulled the sliding glass door shut behind him and stood off to one side, nursing his beer. At the far end of the cedar deck was his uncle Ed and his wife Margret with their son, Ed junior and daughter-in-law, Julie. Aunt Lucy sat at the table next to them with members of his mother's bridge group. The younger grandkids were bouncing around in what looked like an MMA fight cage in the back yard. Aunt Lucy's teenage daughters floated on rafts in the large kidney-shaped pool. Helen, the woman who picked him up at the airport, was talking to his other uncle, Michael and his wife Ellen by the barbeque pit that was sending up mesquite aromas into the puffy, cloud-ridden sky. When Michael spotted him, he waved him over.

John liked Michael. The man was a straight shooter and told it how it was and at six-four and two-seventy never had to be called twice to the dinner table. He strode on over and put his hand out to Mike.

"Hey, manning the goodies, I see," John said. To Helen and Ellen, he nodded a hello.

Mike sucked a gulp of beer and chuckled. "You know me. Don't want to see any casualties." He grabbed a pair of tongs, and as he turned a couple of steaks on the grill, added, "I was just telling Helen here a few stories about your mom when you were growing up."

"I bet," John said and smiled at the ladies.

Mike turned back to John as Stu joined them, and said, "You remember how she used to give you that 'vacant look', as if there was nobody home upstairs when we were talking with our friends, which generally amounted to nothing good, then later on she'd nail us to the wall."

"Yeah, I called it her Betty White look. She was dumb like a fox."

"Damn right," Mike said. "And then there was that time when one of her co-workers told her she'd made a mistake and button-holed her in front of the boss. Bad move. She hauled off and whacked him."

Helen's jaw dropped and John heard her gasp. Ellen just smiled.

"Yeah, I was like thirteen at the time. She came home pissed and scared. Thought she was gonna get canned. I'd never seen her mad like that before. Now I know where certain people in the family get their tempers," John said.

Mike cocked his brow and eyed John as he worked the grille. "Yeah, we know. Turned out Chet, I think that was his name, apologized to her afterward. Well, the steaks are just about up. You take yours well done, right, John?"

"Right, unlike you who likes to chase it around the plate," John said.

"Okay, I'm gonna call the gang to the buffet table in ten," Stu said, "So why don't you guys go over with Helen and have a seat and I'll bring it over when it's done. And someone needs to rein in my wife. She's been going non-stop since we got up."

"I'll get her," John said. He glanced over at Bob, who was chatting with Ed. All his life, he had taken the story of how his father had died after he was born at face value, and why wouldn't he? His mom was an honest woman, had drilled the importance of telling the truth into him no matter what the consequences were. Your name is the most important thing in your life, she'd had told him. Protect it at all costs. If you ruin it by telling lies, you'll never get it back.

But now, looking at Bob, remembering how the man looked at his mother at the funeral home, a niggling thought began to grow in his mind. Was there more to the story of how dear old dad had died than what he'd been told. He walked over to his sister and pulled her aside.

He put aside his running into Van and what that could mean, and said, "You got a minute?"

Peg turned to him. "Sure, what's up?"

"You remember anything about Dad?"

She narrowed her eyes. "That's out of the blue."

"I know, but do you?"

She pursed her lips. "I was only two at the time, so I'm afraid I know as much as you do. Why are you asking about this now?"

"This is why," John said, pulling out the photo and showing it to her.

Peg looked at the picture a moment, then gave it back nonplused. "What about it?"

John eyed her intently. "What about it? Really?"

"It's a picture."

"Of Bob holding me! Don't you think that's odd?"

"Not really. I mean Bob and his wife, God rest her soul, have been a part of our family like forever."

John shook his head, glanced at Bob again. "Never mind."

She tilted her head and eyed him. "Are you okay?"

"Yeah, I'm fine."

After dinner, John sat with Stu, Peg, Mike, Helen and Ellen around the table, swapping stories about Esther. The memories that came flooding out from around the table had them in roaring in laughter amid the grief. As John listened to the tales, he mused on the picture in his pocket, then Vanessa, and finally whether he'd made a grave mistake leaving home to chase his dreams. His mother would've scolded him for these thoughts, but there was no going back, and to tell the truth, he wasn't sure he wouldn't have still made the same decision. He looked around, watching Peg's children, Tommy and Terry, and as he did so, thought of Vanessa's son.

He clenched his fist and for the third time, did the math in his head. Jason was what, maybe twenty-one or two? That would make him a serious contender as the boy's father. The question in his mind was, did he want to know the truth if Vanessa would tell it?

While he mused on that, his niece, Terry, snuck over and tapped him on the arm. He eyed the little blond-haired girl, who ingratiated herself to him the most. She looked up at him with her china blue eyes and put her arms up. He smiled and plopped her onto his lap.

As she wriggled around, she looked down at his leg. The cuff of his pants had pulled up, offering her a good look at his prosthetic foot. "What happened to your leg?"

John rolled his pant leg up a little further so she could see the entire prosthetic, much to her mother's chagrin. "I had an accident," he said.

"Does it hurt?" she said.

John shrugged. "Sometimes."

His niece was quiet a minute and he could see her turning thoughts over in her head. Finally, she said, "I'm sorry. Maybe the doctors can give you medicine and make the pain go away."

John smiled and pulled his niece close to him. "I have medicine, but you know what?"

"What?" Terry said, wide eyed.

"You're all the medicine I need."

"Really?" When John nodded, she added, "Mommy says you're going back to the mountains. Why? Don't you like being here with us?"

John felt the sting of her words all the way down to his gut. "Of course I like being here with you. It's just that I work over there and people depend on me."

"You could find work over here," she persisted.

John swallowed, trying to think of a way to get out of this painful conversation. "Maybe someday I will," he said, not believing it for a minute. "Right now, your uncle needs to go to the bathroom." Which was a lie, but one he had to give. Otherwise, he'd be forced to make another one he didn't want to make.

The little girl slid off his lap, and as he headed for the back door to the house, he had a strong feeling that once he left, he'd never see her again, and that bothered him a lot.

Chapter 6

Michelle

Cornwall, Ontario – May 29th

Michelle walked into the rear entry vestibule of the Tyler Construction office building and tossed her hardhat into the field equipment bin. As she shucked off her muddy boots, Don came trailing in behind her. Their morning site visit at the Eastman Office Park complex outside of town had run longer than expected due to being cornered by the client's rep and the architect. More changes to the project scope, meaning another late night at the office doing a take-off and estimating the additional cost. Nothing she wasn't used to dealing with. Change orders were an inevitable part of every project, and profit boosters to the bottom-line, providing they weren't a deduct or, worse yet, a result of someone at Tyler not doing their job.

But as Don hung his jacket beside her, her thoughts were far away from that. Instead, they were ruminating on a difficult moment they'd had in the car after he picked her up this morning. He'd sensed she was struggling with what to do about her ailing father. As close as they'd become over the last two years since the accident with her husband, he knew she was on the edge of a transition, and had said as much. But it was the tender look he gave her that spoke louder than words. It was more than just a supportive gaze, and it had left her anxious. The last thing she ever wanted to do was to hurt him.

At last, she said, "Looks like another late night."

"We'll see," he said, untying his Timberlines and setting them on the mud tray next to hers. "First thing we need to do is get a hold of Darren and get a price on the additional steel. Have Peter take care of that. I'll deal with George on the H-VAC. You and Ed and Molly can tackle divisions four through nine. Don't go crazy trying to needle everything down. Just nail the big-ticket items. The rest, I'll throw a generous number at and see what sticks. I'll meet you in the large conference room...say in ten?"

"Okay. You want me to order lunch?"

He hesitated, pulled on his beard and glanced at her with a crooked smile. "Sure, why not? The usual, but let Lisa do it."

She'd seen that smile on his face before, and with him pulling at his beard along with it, sensed there was something afoot. "I don't mind..."

"'Chelle," Don said, shoving his foot into his office shoes. "Please?"

Michelle shook her head, her sudden suspicions growing by the moment. "All right, all right!" She grasped the pull bar on the interior door, pulled back, and as an afterthought, eyeballed him and said, "You know, you've been doing that pulling thing on your beard a lot lately...like you do whenever you're nervous about something or trying to keep a secret."

"Am I?" he said, darting his hand away from his face.

"Yes, for the last week," she said, and went in with a smile, leaving him behind to sort her observation out.

She went into her office, opened the lower file cabinet drawer under her desk and tossed her purse inside. Grabbing her mug, she started for the kitchenette, fairly sure she'd run into Lisa and Molly on the way. Her two twenty-something office clerks had heard Don was bringing on that new guy, what was his name...Gerry, Larry, Harry something ending in "arry"...to run the Tyler housing division.

She'd met him briefly after the man's job interview and had to admit the rugged dark-haired guy with hazel eyes was handsome, but he was nothing to get all wide-eyed about. Her chief interest as office manager was whether he'd be a distraction. It was bad enough Peter turned heads without adding another to the mix.

She came to the end of the hall and turned the corner to find the main office area strangely quiet. Panning her gaze around the room, she found no one there or in the kitchenette alcove.

What the…?

The phone rang and she picked up. "Tyler Construction."

"Is Don Tyler around?"

"May I ask who's calling?"

"Trent Woods from Centria Metal Panels."

"Hold on and I'll see if he's available," Michelle said. She put the man on hold and rang Don up in his office. But her call went to voice mail. She frowned. Don had just come in with her.

Maybe he's in the bathroom.

Switching back to Mr. Woods, she expressed her apologies and put him through to Don's office.

"Okay, now to find out where everyone is," she muttered and stalked back down the hall feeling perturbed. As she went poking and peeking in through open office doors, she discovered that not only was Don away from his office but also, Peter, Ed and Henry. In fact, all the project managers' offices were empty. She eyed the large conference room door. It was shut, which was unusual when there were no meetings scheduled. Suddenly, Don's pulling on his beard along with the hush-hush conversations and diffident smiles coming her way over the last week came to a head.

Okay, what's going on?

She walked up to the conference room door, drew breath and pushed in.

"HAPPY BIRTHDAY-ANNIVERSARY!"

Her breath caught as she looked out over the motley dressed crew that made up the family of the Tyler Construction Company. Don came forward toting a pair of hiking poles in one hand and a pair of binoculars in the other. Along with everyone else, he'd changed into a fleece mountain vest and khaki hiking pants.

"We know your birthday isn't 'til next week," Don said, "but today's also your anniversary here at Tyler. And it's a big one. Eighteen years! So, seeing how you have a big trip coming up, we all thought it would be right and proper to celebrate everything at once."

"I don't know what to say," Michelle said, trying to collect herself while Don put his arm around her. She looked at Peter and Ed in their slipshod hiking attire and grinned. It was like watching a warped version of Ace Ventura and Uncle Buck in Deliverance.

"Just promise us you're coming back," Don said.

"She better come back," Peter called out, "She's the only one who knows how things work around here."

Everyone laughed.

Michelle rolled her eyes. "Don't worry, I'll be back. And Peter...stay out of my office, and especially my computer. The last time you were in there, it took me a week to straighten things out."

That was followed by a loud, "Oooo" from the crew. Don spoke up. "Who's hungry? We have a few of 'Chelle's favorites here. The guest of honor goes first though."

He took her hand and led her to the buffet on the conference room table that had been pushed to the side of the room. She eyed him as they went over to it and tried to tell herself the look he'd given her this morning was no more than a look he'd give his own sister. Except, there was a twinge in her gut that was telling her otherwise. Had she been seeing that hopeful gaze and denying it over the last few months? She didn't know, and with everyone talking at her at once, she didn't have time to examine it.

She smiled, grabbed a plate and silverware, and helped herself to a chicken leg, salad greens and a cookie, then looked around for a place to sit. Henry came to the rescue, soda in hand, and directed her to the door leading out to the attached warehouse. He opened it and she walked in to see that an open area had been culled out within the material supply bay. Above it, hung a huge white banner with the slogan, MICHELLE - NEPAL OR BUST written in big, bold blue letters. A makeshift plywood bench to the right of her held several brightly wrapped gifts.

She eyed Henry. "Really?"

"Hey, I'm just the messenger," he said with a wide toothy grin. He took a drink of his soda and nodded toward three picnic tables with white tablecloths draped over them that were placed under the banner. "The table in the center is yours I believe."

She sighed, wanting to disappear. It wasn't so much she didn't appreciate what people had done for her, but because she didn't like being the center of attention and never had. There was just something about being out on the stage alone with unsaid expectations ringing in her ears that left her feeling exposed and vulnerable.

She turned to Henry. "So, who's responsible for this?" she said, having a good idea who it was.

"All of us. It was a team effort," Henry said.

Michelle nodded. "Uh-huh. Okay, have your secrets," she said as Don came in behind her with a heaping plate of food. He popped a bacon-wrapped scallop in his mouth and licked his fingers.

"What'd'ya think?" he said.

"I think someone overdid things, is what I think," she said, eyeing her boss sideways only to realize her reply had nicked him. "I'm sorry, that came out wrong." She dipped her head. "It's nice to be thought of. I just don't do well being on center stage."

Don brightened. "It's okay, neither do I."

Which was a lie of course. Don was a natural on stage and people gravitated to him. But she wasn't going to argue the point. She tilted her head toward the table. "Shall we?"

They took their seats next to each other as the rest of the crew filed in. Someone fired up the office intercom and "Sway" came squawking out of the warehouse speakers above. Michelle glanced down the table at Lisa. Obviously, someone had been doing their homework on her taste in music.

"Michael Buble. You guys thought of everything," she said, pointing upward.

"What's not to like?" Lisa said, lifting her fork and waving her hand to the beat of the song.

"So, what's it feel like being an old timer?" Ed said from down the table. He gave her one of his classic, wicked grins that usually ended up cornering someone into doing something entertaining at their own expense.

"Hey, I'm not that old," Michelle fired back, and smiled. "And, no, I'm not going to give any speeches, Mr. Caron, so just forget it."

Don leaned toward her and whispered, "You realize you've just signed your own death warrant."

Michelle groaned. "Don't start."

Don chuckled and as they ate, the conversation around the table drifted to a mix of business and her upcoming trip until finally, Don cast a glance at Molly that sent the woman into the office. A moment later, the music was cut off, and he stood up and tapped his fork on his soda bottle. Everyone went quiet.

"I want to raise a toast to someone who epitomizes the Tyler family's service to our clients and our community. She came to us eighteen years ago, fresh out of college, with a desire to learn and be the best she could be for us, and that continues to this day. She is a shining example of what it is to be a professional in anything you do. She is also my voice of reason when I get ahead of myself, always keeping me balanced and looking at things from the other point of view. Michelle, I thank you from the bottom of my heart for everything you do."

"Here, here," Henry said, and they all drank to her success.

But Don wasn't through. He cleared his throat and when she saw him take a deep breath, her body tensed. *What are you up to?"*

"You are my friend first and always, Michelle, and now I'm hoping you'll be my partner," Don said.

Michelle felt the room shrink around her as she tried to make sense of what she'd just heard. *Partner?* She swallowed and looked up at him unbelieving, trying to comprehend what he'd just done. And there was that look again that sent a wave of panic through her. How could he have put her in such a tight spot in front of everyone?

Her heart drummed as she fought the urge to ask him just what the hell he was doing. Everyone stared back at her expectantly, and it was a good thing she was sitting because were she standing, she was sure her legs would give out from under her. "I…I'm not sure what to say," she said, trying not to trap herself into a commitment.

"You could say yes," Don said, raising a brow and eyeing her with that compelling expression she found hard to say no to.

She forced a smile, refusing to believe he would intentionally put her in such a tight spot. He was a spur-of-the-moment type of guy, who thought on his feet too often for his own good.

At last, an idea came to her that seemed good. "I'm flattered, Don, I am, but I don't have anything to invest."

He looked down at her in his knowing way, as if to say, *I can wait*, then said, "You've already invested in this company, 'Chelle, and you'll continue to do so. That's enough for me. All I need from you is a dollar to make things legal when you're ready."

Michelle's mind spun. At last, she said, "I…I'll look into it."

"Good enough for me," Don said.

That's good, because that's all you're going to get, right now. We're going to talk after we're done here.

Molly spoke up, "Who wants cake?"

"And there's presents to be opened," Lisa piped up.

A minute later, the music was back on and cake was being passed out. Ed set a chair next to the gift bench and after everyone had finished up, Michelle was ushered over to it. She sat as Don came forward and took the first gift off the table. He handed the present wrapped in a blueprint sheet to her and stood nearby as she opened the card.

"This is from Peter," she said and after she read it out loud, tore the paper away and held it up for everyone to see.

Peter said, "It's an emergency bright stick just in case you get lost at night on the trail."

Michelle rolled her eyes. "Oh, geez, thank you for your confidence." She set it aside as Don handed her the next gift from Henry, which was a collapsible shovel.

Following these were hiking socks, a new fleece, gloves, a solar stove from Peter, a head lantern from Ed, and a host of gag gifts that included, not least of all, toilet paper (just in case).

Michelle set the last box with her gifts on the couch in her living room, kicked off her shoes and tossed her purse beside them. It had been a long, long day, working late on the change order notwithstanding. She flipped on the TV, went to the kitchen and poured a tall glass of wine. As she stood by the breakfast bar sipping the grape, she thought about the conversation she'd had with Don after the party. In fact, it was all she'd been thinking about since he'd ambushed her with the proposal. The man was totally clueless about the spot he'd put her in, which was totally who he was. But the offer, so far as she could see, was just an offer to be a business partner. So why was her gut shouting at her to run the other direction?

Don was a good man; no, he was better than a good man. He'd been there for her and given her all the time she needed to start putting her life back together after the accident. A life she was still trying to put back together, a life that didn't have room, at the moment, for anything other than friendship.

She took her wine glass up and drifted back into the living room where David Letterman was doing his top-ten list recitation. As the late-night host wound down to his number one answer, she went over to the boxes containing her birthday gifts and smiled. Everyone had gotten all dressed up in hiking gear for her party. The Tyler clan was good people. That they'd gone out of their way for her birthday meant a lot. She set her glass on the coffee table and pawed through the gifts again. Some of them, the socks and thermal underwear sets, were duplicates of things she'd already bought for the trip, but she hadn't had the heart to say so. The emergency stick though was definitely going with her along with the new fleece with Tyler's logo on it. As for the stove and the collapsible shovel, she'd stow them away for a future camping trip.

She tucked them back in the box, set it aside, and taking up her wine glass, sat and put her feet up on the coffee table. Thank God tomorrow was Saturday. She could sleep in and take the weekend to decompress before heading back Monday to finish up the estimate. Sipping her wine, she dug through her purse and pulled her phone out to check on messages. When she tapped her password in, the phone buzzed in her hand repeatedly. Cam had blown up her phone. She read the texts that wondered where she was and flipped her head back. They'd planned a dinner date at Pierre's she'd forgotten about.

She'd have to call her back in the morning and apologize. She tossed the phone on the coffee table, feeling bad she'd accidentally blown her best friend off only to tip her purse over in the process, dumping an envelope on the floor. Don had given it to her earlier in the day. She bent over and picked it up, remembering how he'd shoved it in her hand after the party was over. Said not to open it until after she got home. She eyed the sealed business sized envelope with her name scrawled across the front of it and felt her body tighten.

"He asked you what?" Cam said, sitting across the table from her.

"To be his partner," Michelle said, picking up her drink of water. She took a sip, set it down and added, "Said I epitomized Tyler, that I was the shining example of professionalism, and his voice of reason."

"Holy shit. I'm so happy for you."

Michelle nodded, forced a smile and looked away toward the oil painting of Upper Canada Village on the wall beside them. "I didn't accept yet," she said turning back.

Cam's eye's widened, and she leaned forward. "Excuse me, umm...hello, anyone home?"

"It's a huge step, Cam. I'm not just going to go winging it here."

Cam frowned. "Well, of course not. It is a big step. But holy crap, these kinds of offers don't just fall into your lap every day. What did he say?"

"He didn't have a problem with it, at least not that I saw," Michelle said, and took another drink of water. "He gave me a bonus, too."

"Oh? That'll come in handy for the trip."

"I'd say. It was ten grand" Michelle said as the server came to take their order.

Cam almost blew her sip of wine across the table. She swallowed hard, took a breath and said, "Ten thousand? This just keeps on getting better." She smiled at the server and said to him, "When the time comes, she'll be taking the bill."

Michelle grinned. "Maybe I should've waited with that piece of information until after you ordered."

"Damned straight," Cam said, then laughed.

They gave the server their order and after he left Michelle looked off, staring aimlessly toward the bank of windows facing the golf course. Finally, she said, "I think Don has more in mind than just making me his business partner."

Cam tilted her head and shot her a quizzical expression. "How do you mean?"

"He gave me the look...you know, the look guys give when..."

Cam stared back. "Are you sure?"

"Not entirely, but it seemed that way, and he's been very attentive lately."

Cam grinned. "So, he has the hots for you. Wow! And if he..."

"I don't think so," Michelle said, cutting her off. "But outside of you, he's my best friend. I don't want to hurt him."

Cam's knitted her brow. "So don't!"

Michelle rolled her eyes. "That's easy for you to say, but it's a bit more complicated than that."

"How so?"

"Umm… well…if I accept the partnership, and he has plans for me, what then? I'd be cornered into an unpleasant situation if things went south. And then, there's my father. I may not be going anywhere for the foreseeable future, but who knows what can happen. I don't want to hem myself in, and if I take the partnership, that's exactly what I'm doing. I'd be tied down here.

"Which is what I thought you wanted," Cam said. "Not tied down, but to stay here."

"Yes, it is, but only for the time being. In the long run, I have to think of my father. He's still alive."

Cam nodded. "I guess…but…walking away from an opportunity like this…"

"Yeah, I know."

"Well, do what you want," Cam said, sitting back. "But opportunities like this don't come along every day. Just saying."

Michelle nodded and sipped her water.

Chapter 7

John

Pokhara – June 6th

John's flight touched down in Pokhara under cloud-heavy skies. As the twin turboprop passenger plane extended its flaps and skimmed over the bumpy runway, he stared aimlessly through the tiny window. He was home, if that was what it was. To be truthful, he wasn't sure where he belonged anymore, and for the first time in his life, felt rudderless and alone, despite the fact that he had family back in Oak Creek that wanted him there. In his mind's eye, he saw Peg and the kids, still felt their hugs around him as they said their good-byes at the airport. Had he made a mistake coming back to Nepal? Honestly, he didn't know. What really niggled at him, though, was Bob and Vanessa. All through his transpacific flight back to Nepal, he ruminated over their actions and the things they'd said.

Was he Jason's father, and if so what should he do about it? He turned the thought over and over in his head. No matter how it played out, he didn't see a happy ending to it, because were he to be in the same situation as Jason, he was pretty sure he'd walk away and not look back. One didn't just show up after twenty years and say, hi son, how's life? Not in his world! Which brought him to Bob. He exhaled, felt his gut twist and turn as the haunting possibility that Bob was more than just a neighbor across the street, who'd devoted so much to him growing up. He closed his eyes, drawing back memories from the past, memories of when Bob and his mother interacted with each other. Little nuanced smiles back and forth between them, innocent hugs and pecks on the cheek, a brush of hands on each other's shoulder and back, whispered secrets between them when no one else was looking.

He'd always accepted the story his mother had told him about how his father had died. There was no reason not to, but now the story was crumbling away, and with it, little holes he'd always ignored were begging for answers. The irony of the unthinkable possibility swirling in his head made him squirm. Could his mom have lied to him all these years – well maybe not outright lied, but certainly omitted details. Details he now felt compelled to find out. As soon as he was settled back in, he was going to start investigating, and the first stone he'd go about turning over was one, David Patterson, his father.

At length, he reached into his pants pocket and dug out his cell phone, powered it up and typed his passcode in to see if Mick had messaged him yet. He'd texted him this morning in Kathmandu, asking if he'd be willing to pick him up when his flight came in and had yet to get one of

Mick's standard clipped replies. That was Mick though –
long on face-to-face conversation, sharp and to the point on
the written. As the screen lit up, the phone pinged. Sure
enough, it was Mick.

Out front.

He texted back that he was down and would be out
shortly.

The plane pirouetted ninety degrees and coasted
along the tarmac to a line of idle twin turbo aircraft. When
it came to a stop, his traveling companions scrambled to get
their belongings together as the cabin crew of one, a short
dark Nepalese woman in an out-of-place blue and white
button down western uniform, went to the hatch door.
When a knock came to it from outside, she pulled the bar
latch and the door flopped down, letting in the humid,
sticky air. It wasn't much better than the cabin's feeble
attempt at air conditioning. He waited for everyone to
deplane—because it was just damned easier—then grabbed

his pack and shuffled out behind them under the watchful and sympathetic eyes of the female attendant.

He gave her a passing glance as he went by and descended the portable stair.

Yes, I don't have a fucking leg and no, I don't need help. I can get off just fine. I'm not a Goddamned cripple.

He looked up at the brooding skies, felt a spritz of tiny raindrops pelt his face. It was getting to be that time again in Nepal when rain would rule the skies. He hiked his pack up onto his shoulder and, without looking back, walked toward the L-shaped masonry and wood-framed terminal building, ignoring the comings and goings of the airport crews rushing about.

With no checked bags to collect, he was in and out and heading towards Mick's blue Ford EcoSport, which was parked down the terminal access loop. He slapped the rear quarter panel, letting Mick know he was there and opened the back door. Throwing his pack in, he shut the door and hopped in front.

Mick blew out a cloud of smoke and notched the stub of his cigar in the corner of his mouth. He nodded toward the takeout cup sitting in the console's cup holder between them. "How was the flight?"

"It was crap," John said, wrinkling his nose. "That coffee?"

"Yup," Mick said puffing away, and pulled out into traffic, coffee cup in hand.

John gulped a mouthful of caffeine and rolled his window down, rain be damned if it came. "I need to eat."

Mick plucked the cigar from his mouth and set it in a dish that was seemingly glued to the dashboard. Slurping a swig, he said, "Where to? Sanjay's?"

John waved his hand in front of him, wondering how Mick smoked those God-awful things. "Sure, whatever." They were quiet for a moment until John finally added, "Hey, you mind putting that damn heater out before I choke to death."

"Oh, yeah, sure. I was about done with it anyways," Mick said and grabbed it from the dish and tossed it in his cup.

John turned the radio on and a reedy Asian melody of flutes and keyboards trailed out. "So what's been going on around here since I've been gone?"

Mick tapped his fingers on the steering wheel in tune with the music as they hit the main arterial going into town. "Well, the sherpa are in a snit over the government's lame response to their demands concerning all the shit that went down on the mountain. No surprise there. Can't say as I blame 'em. The ministry's been hosing them a long time, and the new guard isn't having it."

"I bet," John said. He'd been hearing rumors going on over the years regarding the younger sherpa guides' disapproval of the elder sherpa kowtowing to the big-time outfits and Nepalese authorities. "Think they'll boycott the mountain next year?" he added, not believing they would.

Mick shook his head. "No way. But I'll tell you one thing. They're gonna be real ornery to work with. They want their fair share of the mountain, and eventually they're gonna get it cause, let's face it, they can shut that mountain down if they want. No sherpa...no summit, and that's just plain bad for biz."

John couldn't argue with that. Without his sherpa, he couldn't even think of attempting any of the high peaks, let alone Everest. He chewed his lip as Mick went on.

"The big burr in the ass here is the sherpa demands on the gov's take on permits. They want thirty percent. The boys in the ministry came back with five. That went over like a fart in church."

"Yeah, but they need us as much as we need them," John said.

"Yup, that's why we need to throw our weight behind them to get what they want from the gov. Otherwise..." Mick shrugged.

"Right," John said. He fell quiet as Mick negotiated the maze of streets through town. Turning back to the window, he watched the sea of humanity swarming the streets among the comings and goings of cattle, motorbikes and rickshaws. Mick hadn't said anything about John's loss, but then John didn't expect him to. Neither of them were any good at delving into things that mattered, especially when it came to love and grief. It was just better to ignore them and move on. Finally, he said, "So you all done wrapping up spring treks and climbs?"

"Pretty much. Team one just summited Ama Dablam, and last I heard, they're on their way down. Teams two and three are breaking camp at Annapurna as we speak. Team four is on the Circuit. Should be back in a couple weeks, and that's it." He sighed and shook his head. "Been a hard season."

Understatement of the year!

"You got that right," John said, drifting into his own thoughts. He sucked on his coffee and kept his gaze pinned to the throngs of people going here and there outside his passenger side window. It seemed that no good deed he'd done the last five years had gone unpunished. Life was beating the shit out of him, and it seemed to be having fun doing it.

Mick went on in a drone.

John caught only the tail end of Mick's comment. "What?"

"I said it feels like '96 all over again."

John blinked in surprise and looked at him. "You were here in '96? You never told me that."

Mick shrugged. "Never occurred to me to. It was my first year on the mountain. Hell of a baptism, huh? Never been around death much and it shook the hell out of me. Especially when it happened to those guys. I was in awe of them. Hall was revered up here and so was Fischer. But then I don't need to tell you that. Or does being the best of the best mean anything on Everest." He eyed John knowingly then looked away. "Everything went wrong:

missing O2 bottles, the storm, a decision gone wrong, a dead man walking four hours to camp four. It was surreal, and what was really the shits was Hall's wife being pregnant with their first kid. She was three or four months along at the time or she'd have been on the mountain with him."

John had heard the story before, of course, but now it suddenly hit home. A vision of Greg Madden on the South Col looking upward when they were on their way down the mountain came to his mind's eye. It had been three years ago, but the events of that day were burned into his memory forever. Frank pointing up to the snow-laden ridge, telling the kid his father, Steve Madden, lay up there in the snow. It was like a bad B-budget movie being resurrected every so many years: same story, same mountain, just different characters. And now he realized he'd played a part in it, a bit character in the ongoing story of Everest's appetite for men and, yes, women.

"...Anyway, people are nervous on the mountains – all of them," Mick continued turning off the main arterial and heading for Sanjay's. "Even on the trails. People've been cancelling treks. Worried about avalanches and landslides," Mick said, then hit the brakes and laid on the horn.

John looked up to see a motorbike weaving in and out of traffic.

Mick stuck his arm out the window and waved it in the universal WTF gesture then shook his head. "Idiot!" He stepped on the gas and a moment later, they pulled up in front of Sanjay's. He put the car in park, sat back and turned toward John. "You okay?"

It was an open-ended question, veiled in the deniability of intruding into John's loss of his mother. John nodded. "Yeah, I'm good," he lied. "Let's eat."

Mick slapped the steering wheel and smiled. "All right then."

John followed Mick into the café and headed to a table near the back. On the way, Mick grabbed a copy of the Himalaya Times off the rack near the front door. As usual, the café was humming with the latest Nepalese tunes. John combed his fingers through his hair and pulled out a chair. As he sat, Nabin came shuffling out of the kitchen carrying a large tub of dishes. When the young man saw them, he set the tub on the front counter with a thud and came running to them like a puppy.

"Namaste, Mr. Patterson. Where have you been?" Nabin said, his dark eyes wide and his lyrical voice full of excitement. "We've been worried about you. We haven't seen you in long, long time."

John stretched his legs out in front of him and laid his hands on the table. Despite his mind being elsewhere, he was touched. He reached out and bumped fists with the boy. "Hey, Nabin. Missed you, too. How's that piggy bank coming along?"

Nabin smiled and bowed. "Getting there."

"Glad to hear it," John said. He turned to Mick, who was checking his cell. "He's saving up to go to Guide School."

Mick looked up and nodded.

"Something to drink?" Nabin said, pulling out his menu pad.

"Yeah," John said, "Bring us a Thermos of lemon tea."

Mick put his phone on the table and jabbed his thumb at John. "He'll take lemon tea. I want a pot of the good brew."

"Ah, butter tea," Nabin said with a knowing smile. "Sure." He glanced back and forth at them. "You want menu?"

John bent his head toward Mick, and when the man put his hand up, he turned back to Nabin. "Won't be necessary. We'll take our usual poison."

"Okay. But we have special today. Chicken Curry and side of Momos. Very good. You will like."

"Thanks, but we'll pass, son," Mick said, and as the boy turned to get their tea, Mick added, "Oh, and a plate of *Pukala* for me."

John rolled his eyes. "How do you eat that shit?"

"Same way you drink that watered-down fruit juice you call tea," Mick retorted and laughed. "One of these days, I'm gonna toughen that tender American stomach of yours."

"My stomach is just fine," John said and grabbed Mick's newspaper. He took out the middle section, leaving the rest for Mick, and opened it to the last page where the local job opportunities were. In the past, he'd worked construction jobs during the summer between expeditions to kill time and keep busy, but having been out of the loop over the last three years, his regular go-to gigs had probably dried up. That left what...odd jobs working for peanuts? Before his life went all to shit, he could've lived with it, but now with all the medical expenses he'd incurred from losing his leg and his emergency trip back home, he needed the money.

As he skimmed down the ads written in Nepalese, he heard Mick pick up the front section and turn pages beside him. A moment later, Mick's voice floated over the top of his page. "Construction's hit the skids this year."

John pressed his lips together. "So I see."

"I hear the Golden Monkey's hiring."

John lowered his newspaper. Mick's face was buried behind the front page. When the man lowered it, John said, "Doing what?"

"Bartending, I think," Mick said and turned back to his paper.

John wasn't sure how he felt about serving guys he once drank and caroused with, but his options were limited.

It was hard enough for a westerner to land a good paying job in a closed society that protected its own, let alone going in as damaged goods.

Nabin came back with their teas and Mick's platter of fried water buffalo meats and set them on the table. "You want me to pour for you?" Nabin said.

"No, that's all right," John said, setting his paper down. He filled his cup as Mick folded his section up and set it aside. Taking a sip, John dismissed the boy and said to Mick "Pay any good?"

"You mean at the Monkey? Haven't a clue," Mick said then leaned forward and looked at him hard. "Hey, you strapped for cash? Cause if you are, I can——-"

"No, I'm fine," John said cutting him off. "Just used to getting paid what I'm worth." But the look on Mick's face told him he wasn't buying the bullshit. The man didn't press it though, which was just as well. John returned to his newspaper, scanning down the page as Mick dug into his appetizer. There was only one construction job, and it was roofing. Something he wasn't suited for anymore, and of which he had zero chance of landing. He shook his head and folded his paper up just as Mick's phone buzzed.

Mick picked the call up. "Yeah? Oh, hi Binod. How's it going? Right...right...and Greg and Adam? Good...good. So, what's up?" He switched the phone to his other ear and frowned. "What? Christ! You tell him we have a contract! And? Of course he did. He's killing me." He sighed. "Tell you what, put him on."

Mick rolled his eyes at John, covered his phone with his hand and shook his head. "Fucking Kamal, always trying to nickel and dime me. Unfortunately, he's the only game in town up in Thorung, and he knows it."

The mention of Greg Madden caught John sideways. He pricked his ears as Mick put the phone back to his ear. The man stabbed a chunk of steak and said, "Yeah and Namaste to you, too, Kamal. What's the problem?"

As John watched Mick listen to the man on the other end of the phone, a thousand questions about the young and reckless Madden kid swirled in his head. As he fought to keep his patience in check, waiting for Mick to end the call, he saw Mick scowl and grit his teeth.

"Yeah…yeah, I know Kamal…the cost of supplies goes up when shit happens on the mountain…but hey, that's not my problem…We have a signed agreement, and a very good one I might add." Mick paused as if to get ahold of himself, and said, "But in the interest of friendship, I'm listening. Uh-huh, yeah… what? Forty-five hundred a night!"

Mick balled his fists as his eyes darted back and forth across the table. "No, I'm not going there with you Kamal…Yes, I know you're *it* up there, but I'm not going to be held hostage…Oh, you can do that, and maybe next trip I'll have my boys pitch tents and by-pass ya. How's that?" he snapped. After a brief pause, Mick went on. "No, no…I'm not angry with you. Yes, Sāthī, you and I, right…Okay, I'll hold." Mick put his hand over the phone again and shook his head. "He's thinking on it." He sipped his tea, and after a moment said, "Right, yeah, I know Kamal. You understand my position here though, right? Good. Yes, we'll work something out next trip…You have my word on it, and thanks for the break. Good health to you, too. Namaste."

He ended the call. "What a guy!"

John nodded, bit down on the urge to interrogate Mick about the Madden kid right off, and said, "Tea house owners. Nothing's ever easy with those guys."

"Just business. All part of the dance," Mick replied.

"Well, I'm glad I never had to deal with that shit," John said and sat back.

Mick took a bite of his appetizer, and as he chewed, curled his lips and said, "Yeah, one of the perks of being a lowly guide. You leave the dirty work to the uppers like me."

John couldn't help but laugh as Nabin brought their lunches out. "You got that right. And it's expedition leader to you, Popeye," he said as he unwrapped his silverware. Nabin set their dishes down, and after thanking the boy, he sent him off. Digging into his lunch, he speared a chunk of roast pork and popped it in his mouth. "So, tell me about Greg Madden."

Mick stirred his food around his bowl, mixing the strips of meats with the savory broth, and looked up. "From what I've seen and heard from Binod, he's not bad. Has an easy way about him with the clients, too, and he knows his shit."

"I bet," John said, and popped another bite in his mouth. "You just better hope he never has to make a decision that really matters."

"You can't condemn a guy for one mistake, John. It's how you get better."

"Or dead," John muttered. He looked up, swallowed, and stared across the table at Mick. "You weren't there," he said. "But hey, not my biz."

"No, it's not," Mick replied. "And you're right, I wasn't there. You want some advice?"

"Not really," John said, "But go ahead."

"We've known each other, how long...fifteen years? And yet, after all this time, I don't know shit about you, except for one thing."

"What's that?"

"You're an angry son of a bitch, Shanks."

"Am I?"

"Yeah, you are. You've had a bug up your ass since I've known you. I don't judge you. You're a good friend, and you are who you are. But one of these days, you're gonna pay a heavy price if you don't dig it out."

"That so?"

"Yeah. My brother was a lot like you. Pissed at the world. After a while, it rotted him out from the inside."

Mick rarely talked about his deceased brother except in passing. John just assumed it was a private matter and let it be. Besides, he didn't need to know the details beyond what Mick told him about the suicide. But now, Mick was pointing the finger at him. The man had hit too close to the mark for comfort, and what was worse, deep down he knew he was right.

But he had no idea how to let go of the seething contempt he had for all the wrongs that had befallen him over the years. He sucked his lip. "Thanks for the insight, Freud. I'll keep it in mind."

An awkward silence passed between them, and for the next five minutes they paid attention to their meal. Finally, Mick looked up and said, "Just being straight with ya."

"Yeah, I know," John said, and shrugged. "Don't sweat it. It's what friends are for, right? Pointing shit out?" He forced a grin.

But Mick didn't smile back. "Friends who give a damn, anyways."

John sat back and set his fork down. All these years, he'd considered Mick just a drinking buddy whom he shared professional common interests with. A man who did him favors now and then, asked about family and so on, and vice-versa. It never occurred to him Mick might think of him as a *real* friend—someone who really gave a shit, someone he could trust. He didn't know how to respond, except to say, "Thanks, Mick. Means a lot."

The Golden Monkey's roots to the surrounding industrial district of Butwal went back over a hundred years or so it was said. It was hard to determine anything as absolute fact when it came to nailing down the origins of anything in Nepal. Then again, John wasn't interested in the Monkey's history and how the building had been handed down from generation to generation of the Gorkha family, which he'd heard ad nauseam since he'd first entered the pretentious neighborhood establishment. He liked it because it was a regular watering hole with regular people who were straightforward and left you alone if that's what you wanted.

He pulled up in front of the Monkey, found a place and parked. As usual, the Monkey's wrought iron tables and chairs outside were filled with the noonday lunch crowd. The potent aroma of garlic and curry permeated the air along with the lyrical Nepalese voices. But he wasn't there for lunch today. He snatched yesterday's newspaper off his passenger side seat and got out. In the light of day, the Monkey's salmon hued stucco façade above the brownstone masonry knee walls took on a deeper earthy tone. Today the columns, with their carved golden Tamarin bases under the sweeping blue canopy, were muted. He hoofed it to the front door and went inside. The long familiar room was humming with patrons sitting in dated wood and vinyl backed booths eating their lunches. A broad flat screen TV behind the bar pumped out the latest music videos.

John took a deep breath. Coming here asking for a job left him feeling like he'd slid down the ladder to rock bottom. But he needed something to see him through until the Circuit started up. He glanced down at his leg, saw how the pant cuff hung empty around the steel prosthetic, and not for the first time, felt like he was less than. A cripple, handicapped. And what if the Circuit didn't work out? In his heart, he knew Andersen was throwing him a bone, and it wasn't because they were kind-hearted. They were looking out for their interest. Letting go of a recognized hero was bad PR, at least for the short term. It would only be a matter of time until they'd be looking for ways to ease him out unless he could prove himself and make it near impossible for them to let him go.

He gritted his teeth and tromped ahead, his footsteps clacking on the polished wood plank floor. Determined not to run into one of his drinking buddies, he found a place at the end of the bar. Then again, what did it matter? If he got the job, he'd be facing them soon enough. Sliding onto a stool, he ignored the framed newspaper article about the high-altitude rescue on Everest with his picture in it.

"Hey, Ajay," he said leaning in over the bar, "the boss around?"

Kiran Gorkha, who was the head of the large Gorkha family, ran the Monkey and he was a hands-on type of guy, mingling with his patrons, asking about their health and families. And if you were a mountaineer, so much the better. Mountaineers brought in the business. Add the fact that John had become legend, and it was no surprise Kiran sent him a bottle of his best rice wine on birthdays and such.

"Sure. Something wrong?" Ajay said, clearing away empty glasses and wiping the bar.

"No, no. Just need to talk to him a minute," John said, setting the newspaper in front of him.

"Okay," he said. "You want a drink while you wait?"

John thought about it. A little patronizing might help his chances. "Yeah, why not? Whatever you have on tap."

The kid nodded and headed toward a closed door at the other end of the bar.

As John waited, he pulled out his phone and went on line, looking up drink recipes in case Kiran decided to quiz him. He had a pretty good idea he knew enough to get by should it come to that, but it couldn't hurt to have one last refresher. While he was searching, his phone chirped. He looked at the number. It was Frank.

Christ, I'll deal with you later!

He let it go to voice mail and went back to the previous screen just as Kiran's large, round body came swaying down behind the bar.

"Namaste, John. What can I do for you?" The man said as he brought John's drink. He set the beer on a napkin in front of John and wiped his puffy hands on the soiled white apron wrapped around his body.

John closed out of the website and put his phone down. Forcing a smile, he said. "Kiran. Namaste. Timi lai kasto chha?"

"I very fine, thank you," Kiran said then laughed. He leaned back against the rear counter and considered John with a speculative gaze. "So, what on your mind today, John ji, or are you here to practice your Nepalese?"

John let all pretense fall away and drew his folded newspaper in front of him. Tapping the want ad with his finger, he said, "Not at all. I'm here to fill your bartending job."

Kiran wrinkled his brow. "You want bartend? Why? Expedition company not pay you enough?"

John took a gulp of beer, half expecting this question, debating how he would answer if it came up. He didn't want to appear desperate nor did he want to come off nonchalant. He took a drink of his beer and looked Kiran in the eye and said, "Actually, yes I'd like the job, and Andersen pays me just fine. I just like to keep busy in the off season, but with things as they are…" He glanced down at his leg then back up at Kiran to see if the man got his meaning, and went on, "I can't exactly work my usual gig in construction."

Kiran nodded then stepped forward and splayed his hands on the bar. "I don't know. You big deal around here."

Meaning Kiran was worried how it would look having the local hero tending bar. With Kiran, as with many Nepalese men, appearances were everything when business was involved.

But John smiled. "You think too much of me. I'm just a regular here, but if you're right, I'd probably pull more business in."

Kiran ran his hand over his bald head and as he did, John got the impression he was trying to figure out a way to say no without saying it directly. The man looked away, pressing his puffy lips together, then turned back. "I looking for regular full-time bartender. I hire you, what happen when you go on expedition?"

John's heart thumped. He had no idea how to answer the question. How could he have overlooked such an obvious objection? Then again, he'd always been used to the seasonal work construction offered him. He took another drink, trying to figure out a solution, but in his heart, he knew there wasn't one. At last, he sighed and said, "I guess you got a point there."

Kiran eyed him and there was sympathy in his gaze. "Certainly there are other things you can do, yes?"

"Right," John said, grabbing his beer and polishing it off. "It was a thought." He dug a 500-rupee note out of his pocket, threw it on the bar and got up. "I guess I'll be on my way. Thanks."

Kiran nodded, "Sorry."

"Don't worry about it," John said. He got up and started off. Suddenly, Kiran spoke up behind him. "John ji, wait. I have idea. I need bartender now, but you could fill in until I find someone, say around time you leave for expedition, one time...hmm? It don't pay much, though. What you say to that?"

John turned back to the man. "How much is not much?"

Kiran rubbed his chin appraisingly. "One-twenty-five a week, plus tip."

The man was right. It wasn't much, but what did he expect? "When can I start?"

"Tomorrow. You stop by, say five o'clock. Fill out paperwork," Kiran said, collecting John's empty glass and rupee note. The man headed back down the bar to his office, then stopped and looked back at him. "You know how to make drinks, right?"

"Of course," John lied. "See you tomorrow." He headed for the front door to go home, but changed his mind when a waiter passed by him with a platter of chicken curry. He hadn't realized he was hungry, so he found a table near a window looking out at the street. As he waited to be taken care of, he woke his phone up to see Frank's voice message blinking on the screen. He debated whether to call him back.

The last time they spoke, Frank was hot on him to press Andersen into ponying up a donation for a Sherpa fundraiser he was working on. That was the last thing John wanted to talk about right now. On the other hand, there was the matter of Frank not telling him Greg Madden was back in the mountains, and worse yet, that the kid was working for Mick's outfit, and on the Circuit no less. Yeah, sure, Frank and the kid's mother had a thing going on, but still...after all that had happened three years ago, he deserved a heads-up. And to think Frank had actually referred the kid to Mick. Frank knew Andersen had moved him to the Circuit, knew how he felt about what had happened on the mountain. It was a damned insult.

The waiter came to the table and he ordered the chicken curry along with another beer. As he sat there thinking about whether he should call him back, anger roiled in his gut. But it was more than anger. Something else he couldn't quite nail down. His finger hovered over Frank's number as he tried to sort out his thoughts. With Frank, you had to think things through when you went after him or he'd take your words and use them against you like a club.

Damned Buddhist bullshit logic!

It drove him nuts because every time he'd ever confronted Frank, the man had left him questioning himself. Because in the end, whatever they were arguing about, he had to concede Frank had a point, which only dug into him, making him feel like a teenager. But this was different, he told himself. The two of them had gone through some serious shit that just couldn't be forgotten, shit that drew them together. Frank owed him an explanation, so he pressed the send button and prepared himself to launch into the man.

Frank picked up on the third ring and before he could say anything, John said, "Yeah, what's up?"

"Hey, John. I heard about your mom. You all right, guy?"

What the hell you think, Frank? My mother just died. Of course I'm not fucking okay.

He bit down the urge to repeat aloud what he was thinking, and said, "I'm doing,"

"There anything I can do?"

Yeah, tell me why I had to find out the kid's here from Mick.

"No, not really," John said, and looked out the window. He tapped his fingers on the table. "So, I hear the Madden kid is here," he said and waited to see how Frank would answer.

"Yeah, he…umm…he's been coming over yearly on visas. Works with the Hillary Trust," Frank said.

"That so?" John said. "Doing what?"

"Helping them manage projects in Sagarmatha."

"I see, and does managing projects include trek guiding in Annapurna?" John said as the waiter came to his table with his lunch.

"Well, no."

"Uh-huh. Seems he has a lot of free time."

"He has a fair amount of it, yes."

"And thought he'd try his hand guiding," John said, and sucked a gulp of beer. "Interesting how he got hooked up with Mick, seeing how Mick operates out of Pokhara."

"Yeah, I was surprised to see Greg was in Pokhara, too. Apparently, he finished the project he was working on in Khunde and decided to check out the Annapurna region."

Humph…Not nearly as surprised as me, believe it!

"So you talked to him?"

"Yeah, he called me shortly after the Holi Festival. Said he was looking for a gig before heading home."

"That so?" John said, trying to rein in his temper.

"Yeah. I thought of Mick, so I gave his office a call."

John bristled, tightened his grip on his phone. "And it never occurred to you I just might have a problem with that? Jesus Christ, you know how I feel about that shithead. I don't want him anywhere near me. And now he's right here in my Goddamned back yard, and thanks to you, on the fucking Circuit. Christ!"

"Look, John. I—"

John ended the call before Frank could go on and slammed the phone down on the table, startling the couple sitting across from him. He looked past them, glaring at nobody and everyone. The one person who should know better, the one person he'd risked his life for, had given a chunk of his body for had betrayed him. He eyed his lunch sitting in front of him, resisting the powerful urge to sweep his hand across the table and dash it all over the floor.

Chapter 8

Michelle

Cornwall, Ontario, Canada – June 9th

Michelle sat in the passenger seat as Don drove to the site of the Medical Center they were building. As they drove through town in the early morning traffic, she went through the change orders in her Pendaflex folder, reviewing them for the client to sign off.

Don glanced over at her. "Everything in order?"

"I believe so. You sure about this number here on the additional site work drainage? Looks a bit low to me. I mean, in the past we've used a higher number on the per foot of trenching."

"We'll be okay. There's more than enough slush in the addition number to cover it."

Michelle frowned. In all her experience, she'd never seen a project where an addition to the design of this magnitude happened at this stage of the game. Not that she was complaining. This Add was going to be a boon to the company. "I wonder why they suddenly decided the original site design wasn't sufficiently large enough. Didn't they take all their needs into account in the beginning? Seems like they weren't thinking things all the way through."

Don shrugged. "They always wanted it, but didn't think they had the dollars for it."

"Then why didn't they put it in as an Add Alternate? I mean, you always get a better number that way. Even I know that. Seems shortsighted to me."

"I agree. Not very smart on the architect's part."

"Unless the owners told them not to. My guess is that's what happened. Labrador and Caron Architects are pretty sharp. I can't believe they missed this. Makes no sense."

Don turned off of Ninth Street and headed down McConnell Ave, heading north. "They did seem to have a plan ready to go right off the bat."

"I bet the owners found some money and didn't want to wait to go through another bidding process."

"All the better for us," he said and shot her a smile. He was quiet a moment, and then added, "So, have you been giving thought to my offer?"

"You mean the partnership?" Michelle said, not really wanting to have this conversation right now.

He shifted in his seat and cleared his throat. "Yeah."

Her gut tightened. "Some. You know, I was uncomfortable the way you sprang that on me."

"So you said when you reamed me a new one," he said and smiled. "And I am sorry. Like I said, I was just caught up in the moment."

"I know, and it's not like I don't appreciate the offer. I'm flattered, but it means big changes for me," she said as they stopped at a traffic light.

He eyed her with a confused look on his face.

"You're thinking it's a no-brainer, but it's not, at least not for me."

"How so?"

Michelle debated what, if anything, she should tell him about her brother's offer to her to come live in Ottawa. At last she said, "A partnership is a big step, and I have a very busy life these days. My father has health issues, and I don't want to be in a situation where you're depending on me for something and I can't be there. It's not fair to either one of us."

"You know there would never be an issue with that," Don said.

"You say that now, but you can't know the future."

He started off driving again. "How long have you known me?"

"A long time."

"And in all that time, have I ever giving you crap over taking time off?"

"No, but being a partner is sort of like getting married and buying a house. You get tied down." *What'd I just say? Shit, nice choice of words, ding-dong!*

"I never thought of it that way," he said and grinned. "Kind of like the sound of it."

Michelle rolled her eyes, but her insides were churning. He'd been making subtle hints over the last few months that he was interested in taking their relationship in another direction. She'd been trying to convince herself she was overthinking things, but in her gut, she knew it was true. And lately, he'd taken to being more demonstrative in action toward her, pulling her in for hugs and touching base with her out of the office more. She liked Don a lot, maybe even loved him in some ways, but that wasn't enough to take the relationship a step further.

"Stop."

He twitched in his seat and glanced at her. They drove for a minute in silence, and she could sense him working up to something. Something, she was sure she didn't want to hear. At last he said, "Look 'Chelle, I'm not going to lie to you. You're a beautiful, intelligent, compassionate woman who's been through a lot. And..." he broke off and she saw him swallow, "And I kind of would like to see if there's anything worth exploring with us."

There it was. Her heart pounded. She scrambled for words as her stomach did flip-flops. "I...um, exploring...hmm... you mean date?"

"Yeah, something like that," Don said.

"I suppose…sure, but I haven't been on a date in years."

"Well, neither have I." He smiled. "We'll both fumble through it together."

"Uh…yeah, I guess." She took a deep breath. *Well I copped-out on that, didn't I? Thank God for this trip coming up. It'll give me some space and maybe he'll re-think things. Right! Who you kidding? It'll just make him want me more than ever, and then what do I do?*

Two days later, Michelle pulled into Cam's driveway. She snatched up her purse and canvas bag sitting on the seat beside her and got out. Today was her best friend's birthday, and she'd made reservations at Danielle's, a fashionable bistro located in Glen Walter. Their table would be beside the window on the cantilevered deck overlooking the seaway. She was running late, but then she and Cam always seemed to be running behind. Such was the nature of their jobs.

She walked to the front door, half expecting Cam to come rushing out to hug her after telling her best friend the other day about Don's proposal. The door remained shut though. At least that's the way it appeared. When she came to it, she saw it was ajar. It was unlike Cam to be cavalier regarding security, even in the upscale neighborhood she lived in.

She wrinkled her brow. "Cam, it's me," she called out as she pushed the door open. There was no answer save for Merlin who came bounding into the living room from down the hall. She set her bag and purse down on the couch and petted the dog. "Cam!"

"I'm in the bedroom," Cam called out. Her voice sounded anything but upbeat.

Michelle's body tensed. "Everything okay?" she said as she padded down the hallway with Merlin trailing behind. When she came to Cam's bedroom, she found her lying on top of the bed curled around her body pillow. Beside Cam on the night table was a bottle of Xanax. The top was off of it. Her cellphone sat by the table lamp.

Cam looked up as Merlin hopped on the foot of the bed and lay down.

Michelle's breath caught. Had someone died? Cam's mother's face flashed before her. After Adam died two years ago, his mother's health had been steadily declining. Michelle swept up next to Cam and sat on the bed. "What's wrong?" she said, putting her hand on Cam's shoulder.

Cam shrugged. "It's been a really bad day, 'Chelle."

She waited for Cam to continue and braced for the worst. When Cam remained silent, she swallowed and said, "What happened?"

"I had a patient die on me," Cam muttered. "I did everything I could, but it wasn't enough."

Cam had lost patients before. It was something she said you grew to accept. She rubbed Cam's shoulder and choosing her words carefully, said, "He was a friend?"

Cam nodded. "He's been a patient with us for years. I took him on after Dennis retired. He's a St. George grad, class of '58. When he saw I went there too, he took right to me and over the last seven years, we got to know each other pretty well...too well. I knew it was a bad idea, getting close to a patient, but I couldn't help myself. He was such a nice man."

"I'm sure he was. Anyone that gets into your heart is special."

"Yes, he was very special, and I failed him."

"I don't understand," Michelle said. "Failed him, how?"

Cam shook her head. At last she said, "He didn't look good when he came in. Said he was short of breath and achy. I was thinking pneumonia or bronchitis, and was about to refer him to the hospital when he went cyanotic on me."

Suddenly it all made sense to Michelle. "Are you saying…?"

Cam nodded. "Yeah, he died right in front of me."

Michelle reached down, pulled her best friend into her arms and held her tight. In all the years she'd known her, Cam had always been the strong one. She fought to find words of comfort, but everything that came to mind sounded trite.

"His poor wife, she was waiting outside for him," Cam muttered into Michelle's shoulder.

"Oh, my God," Michelle said, trying to wrap her head around the words.

"Why didn't I see the signs right off? It was so obvious and I…"

Michelle bit her lip. She knew all about recriminating guilt. Had been living with it for the last two years, a dark inner journey that hounded her, stalking her in the bitter watches of the night. She questioned everything, played things over and over again in a maddening loop. What if she'd gotten gas that day instead of pressing her luck to get to work because she was running behind? Adam would still be alive. But the hard truth was, there was no turning the clock back. It happened and no matter how she played it, the answer was the same: it was her fault.

"I screwed up," Cam said. "All the signs for the widow maker were there, and I didn't see 'em." Cam looked away. "You know what's really pathetic? I couldn't even look his wife in the eye afterward. I had to have one of the other doctors tell her. Real nice, huh? She deserved better."

Cam pulled away as the condemning silence gathered around them. Finally, she said. "I'm sorry."

"For what?" Michelle said.

"For ruining dinner tonight."

Michelle reached out and took Cam's hand. "Cam, don't worry about it. Now what can I do for you?"

Cam shook her head. "Thanks, but…"

"But nothing. I'm gonna check out the fridge and throw together something for us to eat," Michelle said. She stood and put her hand out to her best friend. "You go have a soak in the tub. I'll scramble us up something."

"Okay, boss," Cam said, grabbing her cellphone. She picked it up and handed it to Michelle. "Mind putting this on charge out in the kitchen?"

"Of course. Now go on with you."

Michelle turned off the burner and set the pan with their omelets off to the side as Cam shuffled into the kitchen with Merlin padding along ahead of her. "Feel a little better?" she said, noting her friend was barefoot and wearing a T- shirt and a pair of tattered jeans.

Cam raked her fingers through her damp hair that hung limp and straggling on her shoulders. "Some."

Michelle pulled a couple plates down and dished out their dinner as Cam stepped beside her.

"Smells good," Cam said. "That bacon I see?"

"Yeah, and some red peppers and cheese and some seasonings. Go sit."

Cam looked her square in the eye. "You're the best."

Michelle searched the gaze coming back. "And so are you." She grabbed their dinner off the counter. "You know, I don't have to work tomorrow. Why don't I stay the night?"

"You sure you wanna be around me?" Cam said, taking a seat. "I'm not good company right now."

Michelle eyed her sidelong as she grabbed forks out of the drawer. "I'm your best friend, and that's what best friends do, remember?"

A tiny smile came to Cam's face. "I guess I said something like that to you once, didn't I?"

"More than once," Michelle said. "Tell you what, after dinner, why don't I whip us up a couple of chocolate shakes and we can go in and watch the tellie just like old times?"

Michelle looked down at her best friend who had laid her head near her lap and was facing the TV. From the soft drone of her breathing, Michelle knew she was close to falling asleep. She grabbed the remote beside her, and as she turned the television off, Merlin lifted his head from where he lay on the floor in front of them. For as long as she'd known Cam, she'd never seen her unglued like this. She pulled a lock of hair away from Cam's face, and as she did, Cam snuggled in tight to her and mumbled.

"Hey sleepyhead," Michelle said, "Why don't you head off to bed, and I'll clean up out here?"

"Mmm...what time is it?" Cam murmured.

"It's after ten."

Cam turned her head upward and blinked. "Ten?"

"Uh-huh," Michelle said and got up. She put her hand out to her best friend. "Up you go."

Cam sat up and rubbed her eyes. "I feel like crap."

"You'll be okay," Michelle said, wanting to believe it. "Go on in, get changed and go to bed. I'll see you in the morning."

She watched Cam shuffle out of the room and down the hall with Merlin trailing behind, then scooped up their glasses and went to the kitchen. As she rinsed them out and set them in the sink, she heard Cam's pager ping on the counter where she left it. Was Cam on call? She looked upward and sighed.

Just great! That's the last thing she needs right now.

Wiping her hands with a dishtowel, she picked the pager up and looked at the number. It was the office's answering service. Reluctantly she took it and the cellphone down the hall to Cam's room.

"Hey," she said through the closed door. When Cam answered from inside, she pushed in. "You have a page."

Cam sat up in bed and put her hand out. "Thanks."

Michelle handed her the pager and watched Cam check the number. "I have to take this in private. Sorry," she said.

"I know. I'll be down the hall if you need anything." She gave her the cellphone and shut the door behind her, hoping whatever it was could be handled over the phone. If not, Cam would be out the door in minutes. She decided she should wait on the couch to see how things shook out before heading to bed, and stole down to the living room. As she sat on the couch with her eyes closed, she thought about Adam, about all the things Cam and her had endured during that first year, trying to pull each other out of their mutual hell. She'd never had a true appreciation of how hard it must have been for Cam to stand by and watch her beat herself up when she was going through her own loss. How did Cam find the strength to keep them both going when all Michelle wanted to do was die?

Cam called off from work the following morning, and Michelle spirited her and Merlin off on a car ride along the St. Lawrence. As she drove with her best friend beside her, Michelle remembered the things Cam did for her after the accident. And what she'd discovered mattered most was just Cam being there. That had been what had sustained her during those days. It was Cam who badgered her into seeing a therapist and it was Cam who got her out of the house, taking her to movies, plays, festivals and on long walks in the woods and along the seaway. Simple things. Quiet times, just being with her sister-in-law, her best friend.

Cam had been her salvation. But what had she done for her? Cam had lost her big brother, her partner in crime, her protector, her big *lug*.

She turned off Highway 2 and parked alongside of the surging waters of the seaway, and there they sat under a brooding sky watching the tankers churn their way down the broad channel toward Lake Ontario.

Finally, she said, "May I make a suggestion?"

"What?"

"Write her a letter, tell her how much you cared about her husband. Tell her things you talked and laughed about. Let her know you were as shocked as she was and that you are having a hard time dealing with it, too. Let her know she's not alone in her loss."

"I'm not very good at writing letters, 'Chelle."

"Write it from the heart. The heart always knows what to say." Michelle paused. "When are calling hours?"

Cam turned to her. "I think, Friday."

Michelle reached out and took Cam's hand. "Why don't you go? You don't have to go through the line. You can just leave the letter next to the guest book."

"I don't know," Cam muttered.

"Well, it's up to you," Michelle said as the memory of Adam's wake came tumbling back. She squeezed Cam's hand, and when her friend looked back, she went on. "Remember when the driver of the truck who ran into Adam showed up at the funeral home?"

"Yeah, I umm…wasn't very forgiving, was I?"

"It was a hard day for all of us. But you know something, when he put his arm around me, telling me how sorry he was, I believed him. He was just in the wrong place at the wrong time. And there's something else I never told you, we still keep in contact. He writes me every once in a while, asking how I'm doing. Tells me he thinks about me every day."

Cam drew back. "Really?"

Michelle nodded.

Cam was quiet a minute. "You think I should go, don't you?"

"Doesn't matter what I think, Cam. Matters what you think."

"I guess," Cam replied, and knitted her brow.

Michelle let her sit with that a minute, then said, "You hungry?"

"I could eat."

"Good, 'cause I need breakfast," Michelle said. She turned back to the dog sitting in the back seat. "You hungry, Merlin?" Merlin looked up, bright eyed with his tongue lolling out, and barked. "I guess that's a yes!"

Chapter 9

John

Pokhara – June 12th

John looked out his bedroom window at the slate-gray clouds as he buttoned his shirt. He was supposed to be at work down at the Golden Monkey in twenty minutes. Well, that wasn't going to happen, and at the moment, he really didn't care because his chances of ever getting back to Everest were in the toilet, waiting to be flushed. He glanced down at the torn, crumpled newspaper scattered around his feet. In bold, black letters the headline announced Andersen had elevated (none other than kiss-ass wonder boy) Phil Grantham to head up their Everest Team.

His team! The team *he* built. He gritted his teeth, tucked his shirt in and stomped out of the room.

What he wanted was to call his director of operations, Ken Wentworth, and ask him why the hell he had to learn about this from the paper. Didn't the man owe him that? But in his heart, he knew Ken wasn't the enemy, and probably had nothing to do with Andersen making Phil's promotion public. In fact, Ken had fought to keep him with Andersen when the mucky-mucks had wanted to cut him loose despite his heroics on the mountain three years ago. But still...

He grabbed his keys, locked up, and as he stepped out onto his porch, a loud rumble swept down the land from above followed by a chill breeze. Out over Phew Tal, it was raining, and it was coming his way fast, rousing the waters. Already, he tasted rain in the air and felt the first spritz on his face.

He stepped off the porch and strode to his car, which was parked in the front yard, and by the time he pulled up to the Golden Monkey twenty minutes later, it was pouring. He parked around back and got out, cursing under his breath. It wasn't so much that he minded getting wet—he'd weathered Everest, for God's sake. But instead, it was the added indifferent nip of an ungrateful world.

He clunked into the tiny vestibule leading to the Monkey's kitchen, shook the rain out of his hair and shut the door behind him. The potent odor of garlic and curry wafting in the air announced it was dinnertime at the restaurant and bar. He hung up his Colorado Rockies baseball hat as the incessant scolding of the Monkey's lead cook, Rajan Thakuri, came rattling through the door ahead.

Rajan had been with the Gorkha family for over ten years, and he ruled his disorderly realm like a tiger reigning over a jungle. The rotund Nepali with a fleshy pear-shaped face looked up and shot John a passing glance. He watched Rajan put a sprig of parsley on a favored local dish of seasoned cauliflower and potatoes as he marched past him to the dining room.

The Monkey was hopping; then again, it was a Saturday night and the Real Madrid game was on. That, and the slicing rain was driving people indoors. He strode through the raucous crowd watching the soccer match and went to the men's room to put himself together. As he did so, he recognized a few of the regulars he had no name for sitting at the mobbed bar along with a couple of local Circuit guides.

Brad Dorfer and Dan Coates were Kiwis, and to his way of thinking, overly full of themselves. When they weren't trying to blow smoke up his ass about their latest conquests, they were trolling the long-legged tail coming off the Circuit. Just now, they were sitting near the end of the bar drinking down beers and watching the match on the flat screen mounted above the liquor shelf.

Just wonderful. I gotta listen to those assholes BS the babes all night.

They looked his way as he passed them by. "Hey, John," Brad piped up.

John grunted a curt hello, and pushed into the dated wood-paneled restroom that carried a faint reek of stale beer and urine. As he stood in front of the urinal, he wondered, not for the first time, how he ended up guiding on a track that was best fitted for old men and women. After he zipped up, he stared into the chipped and clouded mirror above the vanity. He was a world-class alpinist for God's sake, not a God damned trail bum. Except there was one little problem below his knee reminding him he wasn't that man anymore. He bent over, lifted his pant leg and checked the elastic sleeve around his prosthesis, then went out to meet his waiting bar flies.

After he logged in to the cash register, he relieved Ajay and made an assessment of what the patrons were drinking. Chhaang appeared to be the preference of the night, although there were more than a few imported beers: Heineken, Bock, Irish Red, and of course, Budweiser.

Sadly, no Coors. He grabbed a bar towel, threw it over his shoulder, and drifted down behind the bar. As usual, Ajay had kept things tidy and organized underneath the bar with the exception of a lonely glass sitting in the sink. He rinsed it out as a certain pretty waitress squeezed through the mob and set her tray of empty glasses on the service bar.

Dhani Thakuri was one of Rajan's five daughters and she had the most alluring brown eyes. The thing that struck him was she didn't know how attractive she was, and had no idea what her smile was doing to the young bucks hitting on her. Furthermore, she made it no secret she favored him over the local boys (hanging near him during her breaks), and that irritated her father. As a rule, John wouldn't care who thought what of him, but Rajan had considerable influence with the Gorkha family. The last thing he needed was for Dhani to mess things up before he was back on Andersen's payroll.

"I need three bottle Red Irish, one glass white house wine, and…" She paused, looked at her slip and went on in her stilted English. "Double bodka on ice."

John ignored the engaging smile she was giving him and pulled a wine glass down. As he set it on the bar and opened the cooler door, she leaned over the bar.

"What wrong, John?" she said. "You look unpleasant."

He shook his head as he poured wine into the goblet. "Nothing, Dhani."

"Oh, okay," she said as he went to the beer cooler to fill the rest of the order. When he turned back with the beer bottles in hand, he came to a sudden stop. The room shrank as he eyed the young, light brown-haired man standing beside Dhani.

Jesus Christ!

"John?"

John came to himself. "Hi, Greg."

"Wow," Greg said. The kid shrugged, as if not knowing what more to say for a moment, then finally spoke again, "How ya been?"

Yes, I'm working a bar and I'm doing just fucking ducky.

"Doing. And you? I heard you were in town."

"Yeah, guiding for High Trails," Greg said, as Dhani looked on with a quizzical expression. "You know him?"

"Yup," John said, setting the bottles on Dhani's tray. He turned away, went to the liquor shelf and closed his eyes. The one person he never wanted to see, much less in this place, was Greg Madden. At length, he mastered himself and took down the bottle of vodka and grabbed a tumbler under the back cabinet. "So, what can I get for ya?" he said, turning back to the bar. It was then he noticed the woman standing close to Greg. She was tall, dark-haired and obviously European, and eyeing him like low hanging fruit.

Dhani's glance strayed to the woman and then to John. It didn't take too many smarts to see the appraisal going on behind his waitress's eyes, and he suddenly felt like a shit even though he had no designs on Dhani.

He filled the tumbler with ice, poured the vodka and sent Dhani on her way. But as she went, he caught her glancing back.

Greg said, "A couple Buds and a Sprite would be great. By the way, this is Felicia, and this here," he said, waving at a chisel-faced Nepali beside them, "is Binod, my trekking leader."

So, this is the Nepali Mick is so high on. Hmm...

John nodded to the Nepali, but his eye lingered longest on the woman who had a smile that just wouldn't quit. "Nice to meet ya," he said, guessing she'd just come off the Circuit with Greg.

Greg turned to Felicia and Binod. "This guy here is arguably one of the best mountaineers in the world."

Yeah, right after your hero, Frank.

He grabbed Binod's soda and went for their beers. When he came back with their drinks, he said to Felicia, "You need a glass?"

"Oh, no thank you. I am fine," she said, with a heavy Spanish accent. "So, you and Greg climb together?"

Not again in this lifetime.

"No, we just met on a climb," John said.

Greg leaned into Felicia. "It was more than that. I owe this man my life."

Felicia's large, brown eyes widened, if that was possible, and Binod's brow rose as he sipped his Sprite. Felicia said, "Really?"

Greg nodded as he took her beer and handed it to her. "It's a long story, but he risked his life to come after me. If it weren't for this man here, I'd still be up on Everest. I owe him a debt of gratitude I'll never be able to repay."

John was taken back by Greg's admission, and he tried to reconcile it with the brash young kid who'd totally screwed up on the mountain three years ago. The way the kid said it sounded genuine and sincere. Had the kid possibly manned up? At last he said, "Well, I wasn't alone."

"True enough, but it was you who got us down the mountain," Greg argued.

"Who's 'us'?" Felicia said, darting glances between them.

"My team leader, Frank Kincaid," Greg said. "We were all in pretty rough shape, but John kept us alive until help arrived." To John's astonishment, Greg went on to tell her how the blizzard had trapped them overnight near the South Col, and how John had devised a small snow shelter they hunkered down in to wait out the storm. "Like I said, if it wasn't for John, we'd be dead." He raised his bottle of beer to John and took a drink.

"He exaggerates," John said, and earned an admiring gaze from the woman on Greg's arm.

Binod said nothing, but his star-struck expression and widened dark eyes told all.

"Don't believe him," Greg said, eyeing Binod and Felicia. He took another swallow of beer, laid a thousand rupee note on the bar. "Anyway, I don't want to take up your time. Looks pretty busy in here."

John nodded. "No problem."

Binod dipped his head. "It was good to meet you, John-ji. Mick talk about you sometime," he said as a waiter came up to inform Greg his table was ready.

"Yeah, you too," John said.

Greg put his hand out to John. "If you have a chance later on, come find us."

"*Si*, please," Felicia echoed.

John hesitated to take Greg's hand for a moment as he considered the offer. He had to admit the kid had done a hell of a thing, confessing what really went down on the mountain, but he just couldn't see himself sitting at a table with a man who had cost him so much. At last, he shook

Greg's hand, and said, "I'll see how it goes. Enjoy your dinner."

As Greg and Felicia melted back into the crowd, he heard Brad Dorfer call out to him from down the bar. He ignored the man and took the order of another who filled the hole in front of the bar.

After the Monkey closed its doors for the night, John cashed out, marked the liquor bottles and began wiping down the bar. As he did so, he thought about meeting up with the kid. He hadn't known what to expect if they were ever to run into each other again, but shaking hands and stopping by the kid's table for a quick drink sure wasn't it. He planted his palms on the bar, leaned forward and pursed his lips as he ruminated on why he'd joined Greg, Binod and Felicia. Sure, Greg had spoken highly of him, told the truth about what happened on the mountain and apologized, but that wasn't reason enough to forget and move on...was it? Apologies, no matter how genuine, weren't going to restore his leg or get him back on the mountain. Still, he had to respect the kid for laying himself out in front of Felicia and Binod like that. Maybe that was why he'd dropped by their table or maybe it was Felicia. She certainly was easy on the eyes, and her infectious laughter still echoed in his ears.

And then, as if on cue, Dhani came through the kitchen door and stepped behind the bar. She shot him a lingering smile as she collected her purse then turned and walked back out. He felt a pang of guilt he told himself he didn't deserve...or did he? It was fairly obvious she was crushing on him, and though he hadn't been encouraging her, he hadn't exactly shut her down either. And why was that, he wondered. He shook his head, knowing the answer; that he liked the attention. It felt good knowing he was in someone's dreams at night, even though she was out of bounds. Sometimes he really didn't like himself, let alone understand the things he thought.

At length, he finished closing down the bar, and as he was about to head out, heard Dhani arguing with her father though the kitchen door. He came to an abrupt halt and backed away, but he couldn't not hear Rajan's deep booming voice rattling off a string of heated Nepalese. In a way, he was glad he didn't know the language beyond a rudimentary understanding because the gist he was getting coming through the door was Rajan telling her to stop moping around, and then some kind of ultimatum. The next thing he heard was Dhani's shrill voice along with his name being mentioned, and then the back door slamming.

I'm screwed. Wonderful!

He set his jaw and pushed through the kitchen door. Rajan was standing at the prep table going through the weekly food order and had his back turned to him. As John marched to the back door, the man looked his way and frowned.

You got something to say? Say it!

But the man just grunted and went back to his order.

Yeah, what I thought.

John grabbed his Rockies hat off the hook and let himself out into the warm, damp night. The rain had abated, but he knew it would be back in spades in the morning. He slid into his beaten sedan and pulled out of the lot and around the restaurant to the main drag leading to the lake road, which led to home.

A few blocks away from the Monkey, he passed three guys arguing with someone near a dark alley. He didn't think much of it until it suddenly occurred to him Dhani had just left the Monkey, and it might be her they were arguing with, or rather harassing. His body stiffened. Slowing to a crawl, he stopped, rolled his window down and listened to the halting conversation. When he heard Dhani's agitated voice, he backed up, not needing to know Nepali to understand the menacing tone of the men harassing her.

He got out, slammed the door behind him, and marched up to them. "Dhani, get in the car," John said, staring the three men down.

She broke free of them and skittered away to the safety of his sedan while John appraised the men before him. To his left stood a thin, scrawny kid with a hatchet face who was glancing from John to his buddies and back to John again. The punk was in no itching rush to get into a fight, and he paid him little mind. The man to the far right, who was older, lean and tall, darted a knowing glance at the man in the middle who was staring at John with a sullen expression. John sensed that he was an opportunist, quick to jump in if the fight was going their way. The large, stocky man in the middle with a scar across his square jawed face was the man that held John's attention. The man's hands were down at his sides, his fingers flexing.

John sucked a breath as his mind went into overdrive.

Fuck, he's armed.

He gauged the distance between him and the three potential assailants then glanced back at his car as a light went on across the street. He'd never make it. Then again, he'd never run from a fight before and he wasn't about to now.

Screw it. You want some of me, be my guest. Everyone else does. Just know ya better make your first shot stick, grease ball 'cause if you don't, I'll feed your teeth to ya.

But the big man in the middle only stared back, his dark cold eyes measuring him, as if committing his face to memory. Translation: not today, but we'll meet again.

John backed away to his car. Once he was inside and the door was shut, he turned to Dhani. "You all right?"

She nodded, but by the way her hands shook in her lap, he knew otherwise.

"You know those guys?" He said to her as he pulled away from the curb.

She shook her head.

John nodded and wondered how her father could've allowed her out alone on the street this late. He came to a traffic light and stopped. "Where do you live? I'll take you home."

She cleared her throat, and when she spoke her voice cracked. "Not far. A few blocks up." She was quiet for a moment then added, "Please, not to say anything to my father about this."

John was taken back. "What'd'ya mean?"

She looked off. "I told him my sister pick up me and we go her apartment for some time."

He switched the radio on as the light turned green and drove ahead. He wasn't going to judge her for lying, nor did he want to get into her business with her father. "Next time, come to me if you need a ride, okay?"

"Okay. I pleased you help me very much."

"Don't mention it. Now where'm I going?"

It was after two in the morning before John got home. He tromped in, grabbed a beer out of the fridge and plopped on the couch with his laptop. After tonight's shit-storm trifecta of events, there was no way he was going to get any sleep, at least not for a while. As he booted up his computer, he thought about the confrontation he had with the scum-balls threatening Dhani. He'd been unarmed and outnumbered, but damn it, he wasn't going to wait for help that might never come. Besides, after finding out kiss-ass wonder boy, Phil Grantham had taken his place on Everest, he'd been itching all day to lash out at something, and if it had gone south, well tough. At least that's what he told himself.

He sucked down a long gulp of beer as his homepage popped up on his laptop. The fundraiser for the Sherpa was the chief story on the page. He perused the article, and as he did so, remembered his last conversation with Frank. It hadn't ended well. Then again, did he care? He took another gulp, opened his email page and saw a slew of new emails, two of which he was interested in and one he'd been ignoring. He deleted the ones he didn't care about.

Clicking on the first one, he opened it and read Ken Wentworth's apology for how the news came out regarding Phil taking over the Everest team.

He typed back a quick message to Ken, letting him know they were still good and shot it off. The second message from Ken was a client list. He hovered the cursor over it a moment then dropped it down to open Frank's note.

John

After you hung up on me, I felt bad because I consider you to be one of the finest men I know. Actions always speak louder than words, and yours have always shown that. Again, I'm sorry to hear about your mom and my thoughts are with you. If there's anything I can do, please don't hesitate to reach out.

Regarding Greg, I know you're angry with him being on the Circuit, but I can't control what he does any more than anyone else. As for my giving him a reference with Mick, I did it to steer him away from you and Andersen.

I doubt you'll ever want to see him, but he's not the same kid who was over here in 2011 and he truly wants to make amends for what happened. I leave it up to you. Anyway, there it is.

Sincerely, Frank

P.S.: There's a ticket to the fundraiser in your pox box in town. I hope you'll attend.

John sat back. He hated to admit it, but Frank was right about Greg, but that didn't mean he was interested in seeing the kid again. He sipped his beer, divided in thought about Frank's explanation and the offer of a seat at the fundraiser. Did he want to go and sit among men he'd climbed with, endure the pitying looks they'd be giving him? He was no charity case, and he refused to be treated as one. Yet, there was a part of him that yearned to be among the brotherhood of men who climbed, who understood the language, and the life of a man who loved the mountain.

He sighed. Truth to tell, he thought as much of Frank as Frank thought of him. He just couldn't see how to bridge the yawning gap between them. At length, he chewed his lip and opened the second message from Ken. This one was forwarded from Andersen's site, and had a very preliminary itinerary for his first Circuit trek in October and a list of client names. He scanned down the document indicating the teahouses they'd be staying in, along with the contact person. Also, there were detailed descriptions of allowable expenses and monetary limits along with a list of standard equipment, (porter and sleeping bags, hiking poles, etc.) and outfitter clothing available to the clients. Everything was spelled out precisely, including his contract fee, which was a tenth of what it had been on Everest.

He grunted.

You sure like to know where every damned rupee's going, don't'cha, Andersen? Goddamned penny pinchers.

He drained the rest of his beer. *Okay, let's see who I'm dragging along on this Disney ride through the Mountains.*

Name	Address	Age	Dietary restrictions	Medical requirements
Mark Drummond	Detroit, Mich.	32	None	None
Brian Blackwell	Portland, Ore.	28	None	None
Daniel Mondes	Los Angles, Cal.	55	None	None
Scott Humphries	Flagstaff, AR.	29	None	None
Nick Diamond	Columbus, Ohio	44	None	None
Vic Sacco	Los Angles, Cal.	38	None	None
Camilla Legault	Cornwall, Ont.	44	None	None
Michelle Bonheur	Cornwall, Ont.	42	None	None

Huh...no Europeans. Unusual.

He closed out of the email and drew his cursor over the trash icon next to spam folder bursting with junk mail. As he was about the click on the trash icon to empty the folder, a twitch in his gut stopped him. He rolled the cursor away and opened the folder to reveal 114 messages. He scrolled down them, not knowing why he was wasting his time, but he couldn't help himself.

Then he saw it: a message from the Bureau of Vital Statistics in Oak Creek. He'd contacted them shortly after he got back, along with several other agencies as well as Googling his father's name and looking for information on him. He opened the mail and read the brief statement:

Mr. John Patterson,

We have reviewed your documentations regarding your relationship to David Patterson and have found your credentials to be acceptable for your request for information regarding Mr. David Patterson. You will need to open the attached link, provide your name, a password in the required fields. Please allow five minutes for our system to confirm. Upon confirmation, you will be directed to the record you requested.

John clicked on the link and when it opened, input his information. As he waited for the system to confirm his identity, he sucked his lip. When the Bureau of Vital Statistics banner loaded on the screen, he scrolled down to the link directing him to the file. He opened it and stared ambivalently at the death certificate. He blew out a breath, took a swig of beer and scrolled down the certificate, reading the pathologist assessment of his father's mortal injuries sustained in a vehicular accident. Alcohol had played a part in his father's death. He frowned, then again found he wasn't surprised. He scrolled back up the document, looking for a date. When he found it, the room shrank around him.

Date of death and time: July 12th, 1968 at 22:32 hours; a year and a half before he was born.

Chapter 10

John

Pokhara – Aug 19th

John opened the door and looked over the lake, which was burning off the morning mist, sending spirals of steam upward into the ubiquitous gray world, just as Mick pulled up in front of his porch. It had been three days since he opened the email from the Bureau of Vital Statistics, and a million things were swirling in his mind. Who was his father? Bob Murphy's face flashed before him. He pulled the picture of his mother and Bob holding him out and stared at it once again. Could it be him? He chewed his lip. The man's continued presence in his growing-up years was hard to ignore. But more importantly, why had his mother never told him about his father? He thought his mother was honest, steadfast and forthcoming, but now that sacred trust had been shattered. Who was he? And who was she? And what else had she lied to him about? A harrowing thought of being adopted had been rambling through his head since he read the death certificate, and it frightened him. He'd been trying to push it away, but the idea wouldn't let go and the more it insisted on wanting answers, the more he felt alone and lost in a life built on lies.

He eyed Mick, sitting in his car, waiting for him to get in, and took a deep breath. The last thing he wanted to do was to hop on a plane at the crack of dawn for Kathmandu to attend Kincaid's fundraiser for the Sherpa, but he'd been roped into it, and it was too late to pull out now. He sighed, being 8,000 miles from home, there was nothing more he could do at this point, so he sucked it up, pocketed the photo and tromped down the stairs to his ride.

"Morning, Shanks," Mick said as John opened the back door with his duffle bag slung over his shoulder.

"Is it?" John said, and threw his pack onto the back seat littered with piles of food wrappers and tattered High Trails paperwork. "I need coffee."

Mick lodged the stub of his unlit cigar in the corner of his mouth. "There's a Thermos in the back seat. Should have some left in it."

"I don't think so," John said, hopping into the passenger seat. He shut the door and pointed ahead to no place in particular. "There's a joint up the road, stop there."

"You're a picky bastard, you know that?" Mick said, eyeing him cockeyed as he pulled out onto the main road.

"So, I've heard. Drive."

Mick shook his head and went quiet as he drove along the Panchase Marga that followed the ragged shore of the lake. Traffic was light this time of the morning, a few cars, a truck or a bus, here and there trundling up the road. As they went, Mick chomped on his unlit cigar while passing clusters of the hardy lake folk walking along the shoulder of the road, some heading into the city to find a day's work. A few of them waved at John and Mick as they passed by. At length, they came to an insignificant, whitewashed building with a ragged canvas canopy over the front door. *Bakery* was written in blue block letters on the side of the building.

"Pull over there," John said, gesturing to the gravel lot that flanked the building. Mick pulled in and John got out and went inside. As he ordered his morning coffee, he glanced up at the portable black and white TV behind the transaction counter. At the moment, it was tuned to a local news station. He watched the screen flicker with a video of the widespread flooding in Surkhet and in the

Sindhupalchowk district and then saw the massive landside in Mankha. Thousands of people were being displaced across the country and hundreds were dying. It was being deemed as one of the worst monsoons to hit Nepal in fifty years.

He shook his head as the clerk brought his coffee to him. As much as he loved this land he'd adopted twenty years ago, the cruelty it exacted on the people eking out their lives in the hill lands saddened him. But right now, he was angry—angry at his mother, at Andersen and at the world in general. He dug into his pocket, handed the clerk 500 rupees and was about to head for the door when he glimpsed a familiar face on the TV. He stopped and stared at the young man smiling back on the screen.

Nabin, what are you doing on TV?

He asked the clerk to turn up the sound, listened to the stream of Nepalese coming back and felt the wind go out of him. Nabin was dead, struck by a bus that had swerved to miss a speeding motorbike darting in and out of traffic. John put his hand to his head, trying to wrap his mind around the news. Other than chatting with the kid waiter at Sanjay's Internet Café over the last two years, he didn't know Nabin all that well. But he liked him. Nabin was one of the few people who, in his opinion, had an honest heart. Now there was one less in the world.

He gritted his teeth, sighed and stalked out the door into the humid morning air heavy with the threat of rain.

As he got in, Mick out the car in gear and pulled back out onto the road. "All good?" he said looking over at him.

"Yeah, peachy fucking good," John said and stared off over the mist-laden trees passing by his passenger window.

Mick parked in the lot alongside the Pokhara Regional airport and they got out and walked into the terminal. The airy lobby was humming with a cacophony of lyrical Nepali voices as people went here and there on their errands. Mick nodded to a long line in front of the Buddha Airlines ticket counter and they took their place at the end of it. As they waited under the fluorescent lights to get their boarding passes, Mick eyed him. "Eh, you wanna tell me what's going on?"

John hitched his duffle bag higher on his shoulder and snuffed. "Not really."

Mick shook his head and went quiet, but his discerning gaze remained. The line ahead of them moved up and they followed along. At last, Mick cleared his throat and said, "I hear Frank got big time news coverage for this little party of his."

"Did he?"

"Yeah, CNN, THT, NEP and I hear rumors of BBC and even Xinhua. A lot of big boys," Mick said. "I wonder how he pulled that off. He's not exactly connected."

"Couldn't tell ya," John said. But he had a suspicion Greg Madden might've had something to do with it. The kid was running with the boys from the Hillary Trust, and they certainly had influence. Yet, he had to grudgingly concede Frank was doing good work.

Mick said, "It was nice he sent you a ticket."

"What a guy," John said as the line moved up again.

Mick chewed on his answer for a minute, then cleared his throat and said, "So, you two still aren't talking?"

"Nope," John said, hoping it would shut down any further discussion. It worked. That didn't mean it was over for Mick, though. Sooner or later he'd start talking again, because that was Mick. The line shrank ahead of them, and at last they found themselves first in line. After they got their passes, they headed to the crowded concourse. John nodded toward the men's room. "Gotta hit the head. Be right back."

He marched across the threadbare carpet, passing people waiting for their flights and went into the vacant, tiled room. Standing before the urinal, he closed his eyes, glad for the silence, but he couldn't escape the unbidden image of Nabin's smiling face coming at him in waves.

An hour later, they stepped into the Yak and Yeti's lobby and checked in. The flight had been a bumpy ride and had set down at Tribhuvan International Airport amid a heavy downpour. John opened the door to his room and tossed his duffle bag on the made bed. The room accommodations were better than he was used to. He panned the room, taking in the pastel pictures of the Himalayan range and Dubar Square on the beige muted walls. A fluffy red and white comforter covered a king size bed. Three plump pillows were stuffed into crisp white pillowcases. A large widescreen TV sat on a cherry lowboy dresser and a plate glass table with two cushioned chairs sat near the window.

He kicked his shoes off, went over and sat. Glancing at the open folder describing the amenities of the room along with a menu for the Sunrise Restaurant, he wondered how much Frank had dished out for this event. Quite a bit, by his reckoning. He pulled his phone out along with his keys and wallet and plunked them down on the table, then sat back gazing aimlessly out the window. He didn't want to be here. His head wasn't in it. He thought of Nabin, remembering of the last time he saw the kid who insisted on calling him Mister Patterson. It wasn't right. The boy had his whole future ahead of him snatched away.

At length, he got up and lumbered into the bathroom. As he stood before the mirror, pulling the tie out of his damp hair, he thought of the many times he'd put his life at the mercy of the mountain and had come back in one piece. How would it have been for his mother if he'd drawn the short stick like Nabin had? He'd never thought about that before because he'd always been living life in his head, doing the things he wanted to do without consideration of what would happen if it all went south.

He stripped his shirt and pants off, started the shower and stepped under the hot spray. As it pelted his back, he leaned forward and pinned his palm against the tiled wall. How did he get to this place in his life? How had everything suddenly turned against him? He set his jaw and snatched the bar of soap off the shelf.

When he stepped out of the shower his phone was chirping in the other room. He grabbed a towel, wrapped it around his waist and thunked out to get it.

"Yeah?"

"You almost ready? I need to eat," Mick said on the other end.

"Tell me something I don't know," John said.

"Hey, I haven't eaten all day," Mick crowed.

"Okay, hold your Johnson, I'll be there in ten." He ended the call without another word, toweled off, threw on a fresh shirt and pants and clocked out of the room toward the elevator. When the doors opened on the first floor, Mick was waiting for him. He followed him down the hall to the Sunrise Restaurant where they were met by a hostess, who led them to their table. As they followed her, John glanced around the busy dining room and in a far corner saw Terry Hobbs, Ken Wentworth, and next to them was Frank and then, lo and behold, Phil Grantham. From all appearances, Frank and Phil seemed to be getting on pretty good.

He bristled.

What the hell?

But he resisted the urge to go over and make a scene, and followed Mick to their table. When they were seated, he glanced back at the men and saw Frank huddling up with Phil, about what, he didn't know and didn't care, or so he told himself. He looked off toward the tall window looking out on the manicured lawn beside him, clenching his fist and scowling.

Mick said, "You wanna be alone? I can move to another table."

He turned to the man, who was staring back at him across the table. "No. I'm just in a mood, is all. I'll get over it."

"Right."

"You see whose over there," John said, jabbing a thumb in the direction the meeting was taking place. "Any idea what that's all about?"

Mick glanced toward the men and turned back. "Oh, it's Frank and Terry! I'll have to drop by and say hi before they leave."

"Yeah, right," John said. "But what's all that about? Looks like a Goddamned ladies day convention over there."

"No clue," Mick said. "But if I had to guess, they're debating what to do about next year."

"Uh-huh," John said, trying to master the muddled and mixed emotions raging inside him. He didn't care whether it was just a meeting to discuss the situation on the mountain or raising money for the Sherpa or any other

Goddamned thing. "Looks like Frank's getting cozy with wonder-boy."

Mick picked his menu up and narrowed his gaze on him. "Hey, let it go. You'll get back there."

John sucked his lip, and picked up his menu. But he suddenly lost any appetite he had. In fact, the thought of eating nauseated him and the subtle scent of fried potatoes and onions wafting from a couple's table behind them wasn't helping. At last he said, "You're damned right."

The waiter came to their table and Mick ordered. John tossed his menu on the table and ordered a cup of masala tea.

After the waiter left, Mick said, "That's it?"

"Yeah, that all right with you?"

Mick shrugged and shook his head. "Okay. You know, this is me you're talking to, not some numb nuts."

"I know."

"Well then? Come on Shanks. It's more than just Frank and what's his name having a chat over that's getting up your ass. Out with it."

John sat back wanting to talk as Mick leaned forward, but he just didn't know how or where to start. He took a deep breath. "Life just sucks right now, is all."

"I get that. But you'll get back in the game."

"It's not that," John said.

"Okay, go on," Mick said, folding his hands on the table.

John shifted in his chair, feeling cornered. He sure as hell wasn't going to get into the messy feelings he had toward Frank. Nor did he want to bring up Grantham's mooching his place on the mountain. That left Nabin, except he was afraid if he started talking about the kid, he might end up choking on his words.

He eyed Mick. The man was waiting for an answer. He supposed he owed him one. At last, he took a deep breath, gritted his teeth and said, "You know the kid who works at Sanjay's?"

"You mean Nabin?"

"Yeah."

"What about him?"

John tamped his feelings down for the kid, stiffened his jaw and said, "He's dead!"

"What?"

"Hit by a Goddamned bus," John said, spitting out the brittle, cold words.

Mick shook his head. "Christ. I liked that kid."

John looked off again, staring at nothing. "Me, too."

John entered the Khumbu Room and glanced around. The hall was packed with people all dressed to the nines, many of them he knew. He looked down at his sweater and slacks that had seen better days and felt like an outsider. Then again, he really didn't care anymore. He sucked a breath and followed Mick through the gathered crowd, past circles of men engaged in idle chatter about politics and the issues surrounding the fall climbing season.

One of the men looked up, giving him a discerning nod. Did he know the guy? He tried to place the large, wind-burnt face with a thick mop of swept back brown hair, but couldn't. Not that he was going to strike up a conversation with the man. No, he had other things on his mind. He turned away and went back to rehearsing what he was going to say to Frank when he saw him. The so-called Lion on the mountain was going to know how he felt about him at long last. There would be no holds barred this time. He didn't care if Frank knew the Andersen EBC team leader or not; he was tired of being betrayed and someone was going to hear about it. He tromped to one of the empty pedestal tables that were scattered around the back of the room and stood beside it, gazing out at the crowded room.

Mick turned and called back to him. "You want a drink? I'm heading to the bar."

"Sure, whatever," John shot back and fell into nursing his sour mood, and as he did so, saw a fair-skinned woman in a dazzling crimson sherpa traditional dress, making her way through the crowd. He watched her as she drifted from circle to circle of guests and dignitaries, and found himself suddenly mesmerized.

Mick stepped beside him and set their drinks on the table. "They only had Walker and Dewars, so I gotcha an upgrade.

John looked down at the bottle of Bud, then back up at Mick's beaming grin. The man's face was colored from the too-tight tie and the jacket that looked like it was about to burst at the seams trying to hold in his generous body. "How did you even get into that jacket?"

"What'd'ya mean?"

"Your suit. It's a bit snug on ya."

"Says the man swimming in a sweater and slacks. You could've rented a suit, you know."

"What, and ruin my rep? By the way, who's that?" John said, pointing toward the dark-haired beauty, who was making her rounds.

Mick turned and looked in the direction he pointed.

"Over there," John said.

Mick studied the crowd and then suddenly whistled under his breath. "Damn, that's a honey."

John elbowed Mick. "You know her?"

Mick turned back to him, took a sip of his drink. "No, but I'd like to. Look at her. Jesus, I think I'm in love."

"Down boy," John said and grinned in spite of himself. He turned back to find her laughing at something one of the men around her said and he was having a hard time looking away. He wasn't the only one having a difficult time either. The men around her were falling all over each other. And why shouldn't they? She was downright gorgeous.

He grabbed his beer. Taking a pull from the bottle, he gritted his teeth and turned to Mick about to excuse himself when Ken and Terry walked up to them, drinks in hand.

"John! Long time, no see. How are ya?" Terry said, and held out his hand.

John took a deep breath, eyed the Andersen Expedition owner and dialed back the impulse to turn and walk away. "I'm doing, you know," he said shaking Terry's hand. "Just trying to get back in the game. Hey Ken."

"John, good to see ya here," the man said.

John forced a smile. "Couldn't keep me away," he said to his operations manager. "So, any word on the mountain for next year?"

Mick picked up his drink. "Think I'll go mingle. Catch ya later, Shanks."

"Yeah, I'll be around," John replied, and turned back to Ken. "So, what about it?"

Ken sipped his drink. "You mean Everest?"

John nodded.

Ken looked at Terry.

"Things are sort of up in the air right now, but I think we'll have a go of it," Terry said. He paused and looked off. Finally, he said, "So, I heard your mom passed. Sorry about that."

"Thanks. It was umm...unexpected."

They were all quiet for a moment as the words hung around them. Finally, Ken said, "If you need more time, let us know. I can back your first trek up a couple weeks."

"No, that's fine," John said. He paused, and seeing an opportunity to bring up his future on Everest with Terry, cleared his throat and added, "So, umm...I hear, Grantham's filling in for me 'til I get back."

Terry shot Ken a knowing look and stared off. "John, you know I respect you, you're a hell of a mountaineer, but—"

"But what?" John said. "Look, I can do it. People climb that mountain every year with a disability."

"I know, but those are clients, John. We make allowances for them. You're a guide. They expect..."

"A whole person, yeah, I get it," John shot back. He pressed his lips together, fighting the urge to go on a rant. "Terry, I need the mountain, not that cow pasture of a trek you're sending me on. I'll die out there if you leave me on it."

Terry nodded. "I hear ya, John. Tell you what, why don't we see how you do on the Circuit for a bit and we'll come back to it?"

"Come back to it when?" John said.

"What about a couple years?"

"A couple years! Are you kidding me? Come on, Terry, cut me some slack here."

"Best I can do, John," Terry said and shrugged. The man pressed his lips together and eyed him. "You could always look elsewhere. I hear Mountain Madness is looking for someone."

"What, and start all over at the bottom?"

"John, we're trying here," Ken put in, "but you've got to give a little too. Two years is not the end of the world, and if you get to where you need to be, you'll be back on the mountain. In the meantime, we need time to prop you up with folks so everyone's comfy."

Bullshit!

"Two years, then. Fine," John said. He took a slug of his beer and for good measure, added, "I'm holding you to it."

"You do that, John. Believe me, I'd love to have a healthy John Patterson back on the mountain more than you know," Terry said. "Look, I gotta mingle a bit here, but I'd like to see you at our table if you want."

With Grantham sitting across from me? I'll pass.

"Thanks, but Mick's saving me a seat with High Trails."

"Okay, stop by and say hi to folks though," Terry said, and patted John's shoulder.

John sat back, crossed his arms, and listened to the long litany of speeches from the Nepalese Travel Ministry dignitaries who were falling all over themselves to congratulate each other, as the sherpa contingent sat quietly listening behind them on the stage. To John's way of thinking, it was just a big love fest, each of them trying to outdo the other. He turned to Mick, shook his head and rolled his eyes.

Finally, Frank got up and took his place behind the lectern and as he did so, looked back at a large screen dropping down behind him. The lights dimmed and John wondered what the man would say, whether he'd join the self-congratulatory back patting of the men before him.

The screen lit up with a picture of Da-wa's family standing outside their home in Nunthala. The sherpa's three adolescent children were in front of Da-wa and his wife, and Da-wa's brother and sister stood to the side. That slide was followed by sixteen others in a slow progression, each showing the families of those who gave their lives on April

18th and as each slide passed, Frank read their names out:

"Mingma Nuru Sherpa.

"Dorji Sherpa.

"Ang Tshiri Sherpa.

"Nima Sherpa.

"Phurba Ongyal Sherpa.

"Lakpa Tenjing Sherpa.

"Chhiring Ongchu Sherpa.

"Dorjee Khatri.

"Then Dorjee Sherpa.

"Phur Temba Sherpa.

"Pasang Karma Sherpa.

"Asman Tamang.

"Tenzing Chottar Sherpa.

"Ankaji Sherpa.

"Pem Tenji Sherpa.

"Ash Bahadur Gurung."

Frank turned back to the people in the room, cleared his throat. "Namaste. People who know me know what I'm about, so I'm not going to talk about politics or what should or shouldn't happen. Instead, I want to talk about the men who risked their lives every day to make a better life for their families and their community. I want to talk about the men who included me in their way of life and introduced me to their loved ones. Men who accepted me as part of their world, brought me into their homes, fed me, laughed with me, taught me their language, their ways, and told me their hopes and dreams for the future. These men will never have the chance to see their children grow, never have a chance to teach them the ways of the land and of the mountains, or have the chance to grow old with their wives, their brothers and their sisters.

"These are men who are fearless, men who risk their lives so men like me can provide adventure to people around the world. They know the dangers all around them, yet they do a job no one else wants to do on the mountain.

They ask nothing more than a fair wage and respect, and when tragedies like what happened on April 18th occur, that their families are provided for by men like us."

John sat forward and nodded as the words soaked into him. This was the Frank he respected and admired, saying what needed to be said. He glanced at Mick and saw him nodding as well, while the rest around the table seemed to be taking things in stride. Then again, they were only interested in their own needs: the thrill of the climb, and of course, the money that went along with it. They didn't live with these people like he and Frank did, didn't take the time to really know them. The sherpa were merely a means to an end. That Frank was cutting through all the bullshit and telling it like it was, hit him where it mattered.

Wow!

Frank paused and looked around the room, then went on. "It is little to ask for, that we should open our hearts and our wallets and give back what they deserve. We, as mountaineers, profit handsomely from the labors these men provide on the mountain and so we are in their debt. And we, who are Nepalese, benefit from the enormous permit fees men pay to climb these mountains, and so we are all in the debt of these men's families, and also the communities in which they live and support through their sacrifices.

"The land in which they live is raw, and while beautiful, exacts its toll on the men and women who make their lives upon it, and if we are to move forward in bringing its majesty to those in the world, it is imperative we work together to both make the labors these men and women do safer and also to protect their families and communities when tragedies happen, because they surely will, no matter how hard we try. But we must try because the cost of not doing so is too high."

As Frank turned back to the sherpa contingent on the stage, John ran his hands through his hair as his heart thumped. The man he loved and hated had nailed it, and all the anger he was harboring towards him fled, leaving him star-struck.

He glanced around the room, assessing the passive expressions on the faces of those who made their living off of Everest and the Sherpa people.

Yeah, he's talking to you, assholes.

He turned his gaze back to Frank and watched him bow low to the sherpa men and women. As he did so, he said, "To my extended sherpa family behind me, I offer my undying loyalty and support in this endeavor. Nga kayrâng-la gawpo yö. Thank you."

The room was silent for a long time after Frank finished as if none of those assembled knew what to do with the charge Frank had just issued. Finally, John found himself getting to his feet and he put his hands together in one solitary clap, followed by another and then another, until the whole room joined in with applause.

Chapter 11

Michelle

New York City, New York – Sept. 28th

Michelle boarded the 330-300 Airbus at JFK International Airport and found her seat midway down the wide-bodied cabin. Stowing her carry-on bags in the overhead compartment, she turned to Cam. "Thank God, I was able to get an aisle seat or I'd be a raving lunatic by the time we arrive in Hong Kong."

Cam gave her a slanting glance and slid into her seat. "You'll be fine. And we have a nice big bottle of Xanax to keep you from being locked up in the luggage compartment."

Michelle laughed, took her seat and peered out the little window as the cabin crew went about shutting overhead compartments. The plane pushed back from the gate and Michelle buckled her seatbelt as the intercom came to life. She listened to the standard rap about emergency information and closed her eyes.

As if I need to hear this.

"You okay?" Cam said.

"Yeah, I'll be fine," Michelle said.

The plane taxied out to the runway and as it did, Michelle tried to redirect her overactive fear of being trapped in a flying tin can for sixteen hours. Her grip on Cam's hand tightened.

"Umm…you're cutting off circulation, dear."

"Oh, sorry."

"It's okay." Cam said. "Just breathe."

"Right." Michelle opened her magazine and turned the page.

Cam plucked a book from her backpack and opened it. "So, back to Don."

Michelle shut her magazine and frowned. "You're not going to leave this alone, are you?"

"No, I'm not" Cam said. "You've convinced yourself you have to walk away from his offer, but the reality is, you don't want to."

"That's not it at all. I had every intention of telling him last night."

"But you didn't," Cam said, and gave her a knowing grin.

Michelle shook her head and blew out a breath. "I just put it off, that's all. I'm going to tell him when I get back."

"Right, you keep telling yourself that," Cam said peering down at her book. She was quiet a minute then added, "He's a good catch 'Chelle. You could do worse."

"I don't want to get into a relationship that can't go anywhere...wait, what did you say?"

"You heard me."

Michelle rolled her eyes. "You're relentless, you know that? How many times do I have to tell you I'm not a good fit for Don or anyone else right now?"

"You don't know that, 'Chelle. Doors are opening for you. You're overthinking things. Just relax and see where things go," Cam said, alluding to all the things Don could offer her; money, stability, intelligence, kindness and of course a body and looks to die for. But it was more than that, and Michelle knew it. Her best friend would never admit to it, but she wanted her freedom back, wanted not to worry about Michelle anymore.

The plane pirouetted and came to a stop. The pilot's voice came over the intercom. "Cabin crew, prepare for takeoff."

The jet engines powered up, and the plane shuddered as it accelerated down the runway. Michelle felt her body press back into her seat as the aircraft lifted off, gaining altitude in a hurry. Turning back to Cam, she said, "I don't want to hurt him."

Which was the truth. And to be honest, she'd enjoyed the couple of dinners she'd had with Don that Cam insisted were dates. But having enjoyed dinner with him was as far as it went. There just wasn't anything else there that made her think more could come of it. What that something was, she didn't know, only that she hadn't felt it.

"So don't," Cam said. "Just be honest with him. Tell him you can't make promises. Then the decision is his."

Michelle chuckled. "As if."

"As if, what?"

"Never mind. Read your book."

"You know you want to," Cam said, fixing her with a lopsided smile before going back to her book.

They landed in Kathmandu the following day after thirty hours of traveling. The only thing Michelle wanted was her feet firmly planted on the ground. She peered out the jetliner window into the deepening gloom as the plane taxied toward a ghostly brick and mortar terminal right out of the '40s.

Cam pulled her cellphone out of her bag. "Well, we're here."

"Thank God! My legs feel like concrete."

Cam powered up her phone, yawned and scrolled down the screen. "I think maybe we should upgrade to business class on the way back?"

"I wish."

"What'd'ya mean, money bags?" Cam said.

"I don't have that kind of cash."

"Umm...the bonus you just got?"

"Oh, that," Michelle said and smiled.

The jetliner pulled up next to the terminal, and came to a stop, the clicking of seatbelts clattered around the cabin. A moment later, aisles surged with passengers pulling down stowed bags from overhead compartments. Michelle's chest tightened. "I hate this part."

Cam pulled out her Andersen baseball hat from her bag, balled her hair up and snugged it over her head. "You know, you should just close your eyes and relax. We'll be off before you know it."

"Not fast enough," Michelle muttered. She leaned to the side and peered down the crowded aisle to see if anyone had started moving. After what felt like forever, the line of passengers started off. She saw her opening and jumped up to grab her carry-on from the overhead compartment. Cam chuckled behind her, which she didn't find funny at all.

After going through customs and getting their visas, they walked through the crowded terminal to a broad vestibule with a full height glass wall to their right. Behind it, a sea of dark faces pressed up to the glass. But the view out the front door was what sent Michelle's heart racing. She eyed her best friend and swallowed hard as the front door opened up into a dense mob under the black of night. The cacophony of voices calling out in broken English and Nepali drummed in her ears. She gripped her bag and followed Cam into the warm, humid air and the surging crowd.

Cam looked back over her shoulder "Look for a guy in an Andersen shirt."

Michelle nodded as she tried to control her rising panic. Everywhere she looked, a blur of men vied to carry her bags or give her taxi service to wherever she wanted to go. One of them reached for her luggage.

Cam turned and shooed the man's hand away. "We're fine, thank you," she said, backing him down. To

Michelle she added, "Come on, let's get into the open so the Andersen guy can find us."

How are we ever going to find our connection?

A thin Nepali man, in a white button-down shirt two sizes too big for him, reached for her luggage. "Kē ma timrō lāgī lāgna sakchu?"

Michelle pushed past him and bumped into a small brown woman wearing a long red sari. A small child was in her arms. The woman switched the child to her other arm, knotted her small round face into a scowl and turned away.

Embarrassed, Michelle called after her. "I'm sorry."

"Hey, I think I see him," Cam said up ahead.

Out of the mob, a robust Nepalese man came forward wearing a black shirt with an Andersen logo placed over the left breast pocket. Behind him, another man wore a black T-shirt with a silkscreened picture of a mountain. The word, EVEREST, in large white block letters was underneath it.

Thank God!

The man with the Andersen shirt put his hand out. "Namaste, welcome to Nepal. Here, allow me to take your bags."

He led them through the throng to a sea of cars, motorbikes and buses in front of the terminal. "This way, this way," the Andersen man said in a lilting voice over the incessant ruckus of blaring horns.

Five minutes later, they came to a dark blue Andersen transport van that looked like it'd just come through a demolition derby. Its side door slid back and a short dark-haired Nepalese boy wearing a pair of designer sunglasses jumped out. He flicked the filtered cigarette in his hand away and motioned them to get in as the Andersen men loaded their luggage in back.

Michelle shook her head as she got in. *Sunglasses at night! Really? Okay. The boy can't be more than twelve.*

The kid shut the door behind them and hopped into the driver's seat. Michelle's brow went up. Cam shrugged as they pulled out of the lot and headed down the terminal loop road.

The following morning, Michelle and Cam went down for breakfast in the hotel's café. In the light of day, this new world opened up like a flower, dazzling her eyes with its exotic décor of bamboo-paneled walls, ceiling-hung prayer flags and large colorful porcelain statues of Hindu gods and goddesses. A waft of curry, garlic, thyme and ginger seasonings stirred her appetite. Lively Nepalese music murmured above. She glanced around the room.

The café was crowded with older men and women dressed in colorful t-shirts and khaki shorts. Others were in hiking attire. Nepalese, English, Spanish, Italian and Chinese languages competed with each other. Cam found a table near the edge of the courtyard that looked out at the large round pool with a burbling fountain in the middle. Blackbirds were perched on a wrought iron rail, waiting for their chance to scour vacated tables for scraps of bread or whatever was left behind.

Cam parked her luggage by the railing and tossed her pack on one of the four chairs, then sat and pulled her cellphone out. Her fingers danced on the screen. "Got a text here from the Andersen rep. He'll meet us here at eight."

After Michelle rolled her luggage beside Cam's, she set her pack beside her and glanced at her watch. "That only gives us like forty minutes. Hope they serve fast around here."

"Well, I saw a buffet when we came in," Cam said.

"Where?"

"Over there," Cam said, nodding toward the far wall on their right. "Guess you missed it." She went to her phone and scrolled down. "Hmm...says here the trip to Pokhara is 143 kilometers. We should get there before noon."

"You really think so? Judging from last night's ride to our hotel, we might not get there until next week."

Cam laughed. "Guess you have a point there." She opened her menu and scanned down it. "Oh my God!"

"What?"

"They have waffles."

"Really?" Michelle said, and opened her menu as well. A color photograph displayed a golden-brown Belgian waffle topped with whipped cream with a side of sliced strawberries.

"I'm getting one," Cam announced, tossing her menu to the side. Michelle looked up as Cam leaned back in her chair, one arm casually stretched out on the table while panning the room. "So, you text Don to let him know you got here alive?"

Michelle turned back to her menu. "No, and stop already."

The waiter came to their table with glasses of water. "Namaste," the man said, and pressed his hands together in a prayerful manner. "Something to drink?"

"Yes, coffee. Black, please," Cam said.

Michelle ordered green tea. After the waiter left, she said, "I thought I'd be jet lagged, but I'm not."

"Neither am I, thank God."

Michelle sat back and cast a glance around the room, taking in the ongoing foreign chatter, the coming and goings of the staff and the view of the city beyond. She shook her head. She was really in Nepal.

Cam smirked. "What?"

"I can't believe we're here." Michelle said.

"I know," Cam replied, smiling and looking around. "It's like we stepped into another world."

Michelle couldn't agree more as the waiter came to their table. It was good to be here with her best friend in this land Adam had always wanted to see.

At eight sharp, the Andersen rep showed up with a couple of Nepalese boys. "You ready?" he said dipping his head to them.

"All set," Cam said, tossing her napkin on the table.

The rep pointed to their luggage. "This is yours," he said.

"Yes."

He nodded to the two boys.

Michelle watched them collect their bags, then pushed her chair back and followed them out of the hotel to an awaiting transport van. She boarded it behind Cam, with the Andersen rep following. As the door shut behind her, her gaze drifted over the faces of the men who would be their trekking companions. As she did, the crosstalk in the bus came to a halt.

An attractive young blond man with smoky blue eyes said, "You must be the rest of our motley crew. Scott, and you two would be?"

Cam hitched her daypack up on her shoulder and shot Michelle a furtive glance. "Hi Scott. I'm Cam and this is—"

"Michelle, nice to meet you," Michelle interjected as Scott's gaze lingered on her best friend.

Scott smiled back at her. "What kinda camera ya packing?" he said, nodding toward her bag.

"Nothing spectacular. Just a Cannon Rebel T5."

"Cool. I carry a Nikon DSLR," he said, pointing to the camera with a monster telephoto lens on the seat next to him. "Maybe we can compare notes later on?"

"Sure," Michelle said, fairly sure she wouldn't understand half of what he'd say.

The man across the aisle from Scott got up, his head scraping the bottom of the mini-bus ceiling. He gestured toward their packs. "Nice to meet you. Can I help you two with those?"

Michelle felt her eyes widen as she stared at the hulking behemoth in front of her.

"Oh, you're a doll, but I'm okay right now," Cam said as the bus pulled out into traffic. She patted his arm, looked back at Michelle with googly-eyes. "We should find our seats."

The man stepped aside as she passed. To Michelle, he said, "First time in Nepal?"

"Yeah. You?"

"Been here a few times," he said. "Nothing like it. By the way, I'm Mark. Where ya from?"

"Cornwall, Ontario. And I'm Michelle."

The man behind Mark slid over in his seat. Shaved smooth up on top, he wore a pair of rimless Cavalli sunglasses even Bono would be proud of. He put out his hand to Michelle. "Nick Diamond. Cornwall, lovely town! I have friends down river in Lancaster. Haven't gotten there in a while though."

"You're Canadian?" Michelle said.

"Nah. American."

"Where 'bouts? By the way, love the glasses," Michelle said.

He shrugged. "Thanks. Something to keep the glare down. Anyway, I'm from Dublin, suburb outside of Columbus."

"Ohio, right?" Michelle said.

Nick nodded.

"What about you, Mark?" Michelle said and lost her balance when the bus made a sharp right turn. Mark's hand struck out and grabbed her arm, steadying her.

"You okay?" Mark said.

Michelle laughed. "I guess I should probably find my seat, too."

The bus vibrated over the bumpy road as it sped up. "Might be a good idea," Mark agreed. "And, Detroit."

"I'm sorry," Michelle said.

"You asked where I was from," Mark said.

"Oh, yes." The bus veered right, almost sending Michelle tumbling into Scott. She regained her balance and shuffled back toward Cam. On the way, she passed a pair of twenty-something jocks. Clean-shaven with short dark hair and broad noses, they could easily pass as twins. One of them had a large ugly tat of a bat on his arm. The other had a tat of a snake that slid down his neck under his t-shirt. Both of them gave her the up-and-down.

"Hi *boys*. I'm Michelle," she said.

The one with the bat tattoo, who she decided to call Bat Boy, smiled. "Dan."

"Vic," the other one said.

Michelle smiled. "Nice to meet you." She passed them, her pack conveniently swinging out to whack Bat Boy on the shoulder.

Cam winked at her and gave her the thumbs-up as she tossed her bag on a pile of packs on the rear seat of the bus. In the seat next to the pile was a young man whose attention was glued to his smartphone. He looked up, his long frizzy red hair jutting out in all directions.

"Hi, I'm Michelle."

"Brian."

"Where you from?" Michelle said, sitting sideways on the seat with her back against the window.

"Portland."

"I hear it's a beautiful city."

He shrugged. "It's all right," then went back to staring at his phone.

She waited to hear if he would say more, but he didn't. *Oh well.* She turned around and looked out the window at the passing buildings that sprang up out of the urban landscape like rangy weeds. Large billboards clung to their sides advertising Coca-Cola, Western Union and Nikon. Power lines hung on utility poles like balls of tangled fish line. People were everywhere. Motorbikes wove back and forth on the road beside them.

It was a little after seven that night when the bus pulled up in front of the Annapurna Grande. Michelle lifted her head off her daypack she'd pressed against the window.

She rubbed her neck as the door to the mini-bus swung opened.

The Andersen man got up and cleared his throat. "Welcome to Pokhara. If you wish, you may leave whatever luggage you don't need on the bus as we'll be boarding again day after tomorrow for trailhead in Besisahar. Please to head to restaurant inside while I get you checked in. I will give you coupon for dinner. Okay, we go in now."

Michelle gathered her things and joined Cam who was already out of her seat. "I don't know about you," she said, "but all I want is a long, hot shower, a firm mattress and a soft pillow."

Cam glanced back, yawning. "I hear that." She swung her pack onto her shoulder and set off behind the men heading toward the front of the bus.

Michelle waited for Brian to pass by, then straggled along behind him. When she stepped out into the fresh air, she caught sight of a tall longhaired blond wearing a Colorado Rockies baseball hat. He strode for the lobby front door, his wavy locks poking through the hole in the back of his cap. She heard a prominent click-clack when his foot met the pavement. He turned his narrow wind-burnt face toward the departing trekkers, his steel blue eyes measuring them. Over his shoulder, he carried an Andersen Expedition duffle bag that hung from his shoulder. He came to a halt in front of the Andersen man, said something, then glanced her way before ducking into the hotel.

Chapter 12

John

Besisahar - Oct. 5th

John stepped off the bus in the mountain settlement of Besisahar as his clients collected their gear. The treacherous ride through the hills on the aged and failing highway skirting the Seti River gave his clients a fair dose of what living in rural Nepal was all about. Life in this hard yet pristine beauty of the mountain foothills was an uncertain thing, which a few of them would soon find out.

He watched his party plod off the bus one by one as Orsen pulled their gear and packs down from the top of the bus. For the most part, they appeared fit and able, but the woman named Michelle, he wasn't sure about.

Cam, or Blondie as he thought of her, was Michelle's traveling companion. The long-legged blonde with mercurial hazel eyes walked with an air of confidence. She put him on edge because he was fairly sure that at some point, they'd lock horns. He wasn't one to candy coat words and was damned if he was going to censor everything that came out of his mouth. He pegged her as type-A, with lots of attitude. Maybe that wasn't fair; he didn't really know her, but it's what his gut was telling him.

As for Michelle, she was the Yin to Blondie's Yang. She carried her slender body uncertainly, like a field mouse, alert and anxious despite the perpetual open smile and innocent, laughing dark brown eyes. The minute he saw her getting off the bus the night before, flags went up. She was going to need a lot of looking after.

Mark, Nick and Scott were stand-up straightforward guys, which he liked, and it didn't hurt that they were experienced alpine hikers who knew how to take care of themselves. The gym jocks, with their smirking grins, rolling eyes and bored expressions he'd leave to their own devices. They'd soon find out who was boss up here, because no matter how fit they thought they were, when it came to high altitude hiking, it didn't matter. Altitude sickness didn't discriminate.

He leaned against the side of the bus and crossed his arms as they sauntered past. *Yeah, you punks have no idea of the ass-kicking you're headed for.*

Finally, there was Brian, a quiet, polite kid who'd kept to himself. John wondered if he should be worried about him as well. The kid nodded to him as he stepped down onto the pavement with his backpack slung over one shoulder. At least he had top-of-the-line hiking gear, not that it meant anything.

Once everyone was off, John hitched his pack up on his shoulder. "Okay, we're gonna spend the night here so everyone has a chance to look around and relax and get a good night's sleep before we head out tomorrow to Chamje. I'll go check us in while you grab your gear and follow Kembe inside. He'll be coming 'round with menus and taking orders. After we're all set, I'll hand keys out. Rooms are upstairs." He eyed Michelle and Blondie. "This is not the Hyatt Regency, so don't expect much. The head is a shared one at the end of the hall upstairs. It's a western can, but keep TP and umm..." He cleared his throat as Cam stared back, "whatever out of it. All trash goes in the bucket in the room, understand?"

When nods followed, he went on. "Okay then. Chow's at six, so if you go wandering 'round stores and shops, make sure you're back by 5:30. After chow, we'll have a sit-down to go over Circuit details." He turned and narrowed his eyes on the smirking gym jocks. "It's mandatory. Alright?"

He didn't wait for a response.

The following morning, bright blue skies shone with a wisp of cloud off to the north. John tromped out and took in the chill crisp air and waited while his party filed out of the teahouse behind him. The awakening mountain settlement was quiet. Morning mist gathered in the tall rhododendrons. In the distance, a dog yapped. Black birds flitted back and forth between the branches and the montage of rambling rooftops. A whiff of burning juniper and cedar floated on the breeze. He waved the waiting bus toward them for the two-hour ride to Syange where they would start their hike in earnest.

The bus pulled up and opened its doors.

"All right, let's get this party started," he said, stepping beside the bus.

Scott's fist soared upward. "Yeah!"

John shook his head as his clients walked ahead, carrying their packs. As they passed him, his eyes fell on Michelle the longest. He nodded to her as the memory of their conversation the other night flashed before him. After hearing the regular drill on the Circuit, she'd followed him outside, plying him with questions. Not anything he didn't expect, except for the way she was looking at him. The way she was looking at him right now, as if she could sense the unbridled anger that was simmering right below the surface. That, and the fact that she was wearing a diamond encrusted gold wedding band. The setting looked like it had come out of the distant past, and it stirred his curiosity. Where was her husband?

Kembe climbed down from loading their gear on top of the bus and walked up. "All set."

"Okay then," John said. He turned and stepped inside the bus with his two sherpa guides following. The driver shut the door, and a moment later they were creeping

320

along Besisahar's empty main street crowned with fluttering prayer flags.

Michelle and Cam plopped down in the second row seats. He watched Blondie fuss with her hair as Michelle stashed her camera case under her seat. Behind them sat Scott with Brian opposite him on the other side of the aisle. Mark and Nick filled the next row, with the gym jocks in the row after them.

John threw his pack on the floor and nudged it under his seat, then sat with a thunk, putting his back against the window.

Michelle leaned forward, crossing her arms on top of his seat back. "Looks like a good day to be out on the trail. "

He tossed her a smile as the back and forth of the bobbing bus bounced her around. "Yeah, I think so. You ready?"

"I am," she said. "This is an amazing country. You live here long?"

He crossed his legs, setting them across the length of his seat. "A few years." He looked off, put his hand to his mouth and coughed, not so much because he had to, but because he didn't know what more to say. When he turned back, Michelle was staring ahead. He watched her a moment, seeing tiny twitches tug the corners of her mouth. Finally, he said, "So, you're from Canada. Where 'bouts?"

She blinked. "Cornwall. Born and raised there. You?"

"Colorado. Little po-dunk town outside Denver called Oak Creek. First time out of the country?"

"Yes, not counting the U.S of course."

"Well, you certainly dove into the deep end of the pool, didn't you?"

Michelle shrugged. "Yeah, I guess I did."

"Takes a lotta stones to come halfway 'round the world your first time."

"Well, it was Cam's idea," Michelle said and sat back, leaning her shoulder against her friend who was looking out the window.

"What?" Cam said, turning to her.

"I was just telling John, coming here was your idea."

Cam shook her head and eyed Michelle. To John, she said, "She never goes anywhere, so I gave her a little push out the door."

Michelle rolled her eyes. "A little push? More like you tossed me out head first."

"Well if you're gonna do something, go all the way, or what's the point?" Cam said. She eyed John speculatively. He wasn't quite sure what to make of what she was thinking, and truth to tell, he didn't care.

He reached down and pulled a water bottle out of his pack. "Right," he said, "as long as you know your limitations." He glanced at Michelle and saw her eyes dart back and forth between the two of them.

Cam's gaze sharpened on him. "So, how long have you been guiding, John?"

He shrugged. "About twenty years or so."

"That's a long time," Cam said. "You must know this land pretty good."

"I do all right," he replied. He took another swig of water. "So tell me, why come all the way here to hike, I mean besides getting out of the box?"

"One of the partners where I work came here last year," Cam said. "Said it was life altering."

John nodded. *Did he? Life altering. Hmm...You want life altering? Finding out your father really isn't your father. That's life altering! But whatever.* He capped his water bottle. "He recommend Andersen, did he?"

"Yes, he did. Funny, he didn't mention anything about you."

"Well, I wasn't on this particular hike last year." *And I have no intention of ending up here permanently.*

"Oh, so you do other treks then. Where 'bouts?" Cam said.

"Everest," John said. The words came out automatically and he regretted it the minute they were out.

Michelle's eyes widened.

"Oh, the EBC trek," Cam said. "I heard that's a pretty demanding hike."

Tembe and Orsen donned a hint of a smile as they tossed a knowing look at John.

"It's a shag, but nothing most people can't handle if they're prepared," John said, wondering if he should tell them what he really did. But that was over the top, and he didn't want to go there. Besides, there would be an endless barrage of questions coming back, which he really didn't want to answer.

"What's EBC," Michelle said.

Scott, who was working his smart phone leaned over. "Everest Base Camp."

"Oh." Michelle went quiet for a moment, then added, "Did you ever…"

"He did. Summited five times!" Scott put in, looking up from his phone. He showed Michelle something on the screen and eyed John like he was a God. "We're being guided by a world-class mountaineer!"

Great. John looked away, but not before he saw his esteem rise in Cam's eyes.

Cam said, "Really?"

John hesitated and blew out a breath. There was no denying it now. Finally, he turned back to them and said, "That's what it says, so I guess it's true."

Michelle's jaw dropped as the bomb hung on her shoulders. Her large dark brown eyes studied him, "So you're a mountaineer?"

"What are you doing here?" Cam said.

John glanced at Scott. He hadn't intended on telling them about his leg, but it was only a matter of moments before Scott would dig that information up. He looked down at his feet, feeling trapped, then pulled the cuff up around his prosthetic.

Cam leaned forward to get a look. No one said anything for a minute as they stared at the gunmetal gray of his artificial limb.

Finally, Michelle said, "How?"

"Frostbite." John muttered. He turned back to Michelle, "Don't worry, it's not anything you have to worry about. We're a month or so away from when the heavy snow hits the area." He paused and cleared his throat and said to Cam, "So, what do you do, for work that is?"

Cam smiled. "I'm a GP."

"Which is?" John said, swaying his head side to side.

"General practitioner. Doctor."

He blinked, dumbfounded. *What? No shit.* "And you, Michelle? What do you do?"

"She's a partner in a construction firm," Cam put in.

"Cam, I haven't decided yet," Michelle protested, and looked upward.

"'Chelle, you'll take it, trust me," Cam said.

John listened to them go back and forth about Michelle's future a minute. It was clear, Michelle didn't want to discuss the decision she was going to have to make, which he could sympathize with. Sometimes you just wanted to be left alone to make up your own mind without having someone yelling in your ear about it.

As the bus rambled though the forest passing gushing waterfalls, the lively banter and the clicking of Scott's camera grew to a staccato. The narrow ribbon of broken road alongside the Marsyangdi River provided a breath-taking view of the upthrusted snow-capped mountains beyond the ragged treed landscape. Occasionally, the bus slowed to a crawl to squeeze through tight spots where sections of the road fell away into the fast-running river. This was the Nepal most people never saw, the Nepal that refused to be tamed by man's feeble attempts to civilize it; the Nepal John loved because it was here, in the beauty of the surrounding mountains and the sturdy people who eked out their lives, that he felt most at home.

The memory of Frank's speech at the Sherpa fundraiser echoed in his thoughts. The man had told it like it was, not the way politicians like to candy coat things. If only Frank hadn't been such an asshole on the mountain in 2010, meddling with his sherpas. If only the man hadn't tried to even the score by throwing him a bone for saving his life on the south summit, he could've seen him becoming a friend. But the past was the past and there was no going back, nor was there any forgiving.

He closed his eyes, fell into the rhythm of the back and forth rocking of the bus as it trundled along. As he did so, he slipped into ruminating on all the things life had slapped him in the face with. It seemed there was no end to being left with the short end of the proverbial stick. Why had his mother lied to him all these years about a father who was never his father? Why did he have to lose his leg doing the right thing on the mountain he had no business going back up on? And all to save a kid who'd put his and Frank's life in danger.

It just keeps getting better, he thought as the bitter taste of Andersen's replacing him on Everest with that opportunistic asshole, Phil Grantham. The thought churned in his gut. Now he was just a glorified tour guide, and to top it all off, there was Vanessa and her son. Last night, he'd had his phone out with the intention of Googling her, to see if he could find out about her, but when it came right down to it, he chickened out. There was no use in learning the truth about Jason. What could he do about it? That's what he'd been telling himself, trying to convince himself over the last month. But the truth was, he wanted to know. Maybe he'd screw his nerve up and try again tonight. Maybe....

He shook his head and before long, he was drifting into sleep and suddenly he found himself standing on a snow-covered ridge high above the clouds. In front of him, Frank stood in a faded orange parka and snow pants. The man was jabbing his finger wildly toward a man sitting in the snow.

"Holy shit! What the hell? You gotta let him go, Frank."

"How long a line do you have?"

"What?"

"How long a line, John?"

"Umm...twenty-five feet maybe."

"We'll daisy chain 'em together. That should do it."

"Are you nuts? If that ridge gives way, you're dead. Give it up, man. I know you're into the kid's mother, but it's not worth it."

"Look...I never asked you to come, John. You wanna leave...go! I'm staying and if I die, then so be it."

"All right, let's do it."

"Good! Greg, it's Frank...don't move!"

"I thought...it was my father. I really did, Frank. Oh God, I screwed up."

"Happens, Greg. Don't worry about it. Right now the only thing that matters is getting you down. Gonna throw you a line. Want you to clip onto it then slowly get up."

"I...I'm done...got nothing left. Just leave me."

"I'm not going anywhere! You hear me? Grab the line when I throw it. Grab it, damn it...grab the damned line! All right, good....Now get up slowly and step into the same footsteps you took getting out there."

"The ground's moving, Frank. Run! Run, God damn it!

Suddenly, a hand wrapped around John's arm, gripping him in the blinding white miasma. "John, John!"

Shuddering, John gasped and opened his eyes to find Kembe's round, dark face in front of him. John licked his lips, ran his hand over his face then glanced up to see

Michelle and Blondie bending over the back of his seat staring down at him.

"You were having a bad dream. You okay?" Michelle said.

"Yeah, yeah, I'm fine." He blew a breath out, trying to calm his thudding heart. He hadn't had this nightmare in months. Why now? He ran the back of his hand over his mouth, feeling embarrassed in front of Kembe who was looking on with obvious concern. "Really, I'm good Kembe."

The sherpa went back to his seat, but Michelle and Cam remained, peering down at him. Was that pity in their eyes or was it compassion? It didn't matter, he didn't want anything from them or anyone else. He glared at Cam. "What?"

Cam shot him a *whatever* crooked smile and sat back down. But Michelle sat back with a frown. She pressed her lips together as if debating whether to say something and as she did so, regret reared its head. He turned away, wanting to disappear. But there was nowhere to run.

He gritted his teeth and stared ahead, watching Taral drive while talking on his phone. The wiry Nepali flicked the ashes of his lit cigarette out the window and steered the bus around a sharp bend in the road toward the Marsyangdi River. They'd been flanking it for some time. Crossing it was no less dangerous than riding alongside it on an uncertain narrow road. Taral downshifted as he brought the bus around the final turn that led to the banks of the shallow rushing glacier-fed waters.

John heard whispers and muttering behind him. *Yes, we're going to cross it by driving through it.* He took his water bottle up and drank as Taral eased the bus over the grassy bank into the water. The bus plowed into the shallows, rocking back and forth as its tires crawled across the rutted bottom.

Scott's camera clicked away.

John glanced across the aisle at Kembe and Orsen, who were sitting in their seats with eyes closed, earbuds plugged in and hands folded across their laps. The same couldn't be said for his clients. He glanced back at Michelle, who was leaning across Blondie, joining her friend who was staring wide-eyed out the window. Mark, Scott and Nick had their faces to their windows as well, along with Brian. Even the wise-ass gym jocks seemed taken aback. He watched the two of them darting anxious glances at each other.

Humph...Not so bored now, are we?

The bus jerked to the right, tilted and came to an abrupt halt leaning into the rushing water. John sat up straight and looked back across the aisle at Kembe and Orsen. Both men's eyes were open and alert. The sherpas got up and went ahead to Taral. The three of them dropped into their native Lhasa tongue, speaking quietly while pointing here and there. Taral grabbed the stick shift, ground the gears. The bus lurched upward, then slid back down again. Kembe pressed his lips together and shook his head. Orsen turned to Kembe and Taral, said something and nodded toward the door.

Turning back to John, Orsen broke into English. "We need get out and push."

John squashed the urge to sigh, got up and turned to their clients. "All right, you heard 'em. Everyone out."

One of the gym jocks, Vic, he thought his name was, blinked and stared back at him. "You mean into the river?"

John tossed him a sarcastic smile. "Yeah, into the river. Time to give those pecs a work out."

Michelle and Cam broke into smirks, despite their wrinkled brows and stiffened shoulders. They got up and dutifully filed past John to the open front door with Brian, Mark, Scott and Nick following behind. Mark shot John a sidelong glance as he passed him, winked and said, "We got this."

Vic shook his head and sneered as he gathered his gear. "What the hell. This is crap."

"Yeah, what kinda country is this anyway?" Dan said, echoing his partner's sentiment.

John took a deep breath, swallowed the angry retort sitting on his tongue and stomped out of the bus, hopping into the icy, thigh-deep water slushing against the transition panel. The current was strong and the footing uncertain underneath for anyone who had two healthy strong legs, let alone having to deal with a prosthetic. He gritted his teeth and waded back to where Mark, Nick, Scott, Kembe and Orsen stood with their hands on the rear quarter panel, bracing themselves against the surging river. What he didn't expect to see was Blondie and Michelle between them, ready to pull—or rather push—their weight.

Nice!

Kembe pointed to the bottom of the rear bumper as Vic and Dan came sloshing up beside them. Tapping Mark and Scott on the shoulder, he said, "You, here please. When bus start up, you lift, okay?" When Mark and Scott nodded, Kembe turned back to John and the rest of them. "Everyone push when I say."

When everyone was in position, Kembe banged his fist hard on the side of the bus. "Garaurh!"

A second later, John heard the rear tires grind into the riverbed, sending the roiling river water around him into a frenzy. As the bus jerked forward, he put his hands and shoulder to the metal, pushing with all his might along with everyone else as Mark put his powerful arms to the underside of the bumper along with Scott. As they lifted, John felt the bus creep forward, climbing up out of the rut until it finally spurted ahead, leaving him face down and sputtering in the water.

Someone reached out and grabbed his arm. Struggling to his feet, he shook his head, mopped the water from his face and found Cam looking back at him with a lopsided grin. For a moment, he didn't know what to do or say.

At last, she said, "You're welcome," and turned away.

Shivering, he watched her slosh through the water and join up with Michelle by the open door of the bus.

Chapter 13

Michelle

Syange - Oct. 6th

Michelle dug her hiking pole into the gravel road and came to a stop under the canopy of oak, Tibetan cherry and rhododendron. She'd been hiking along this winding road through the forest for the last hour and a half. With every step she'd taken since leaving Syange, she'd found something new to dazzle her eye. Snippets of the grand, snow-covered mountains in the distance peeked in through the trees shedding their leaves. Long stone-built walls with engraved Tibetan writings on them Orsen called Mani walls, and of course the ever-present prayer flags that hung in the clacking branches overhead.

Adam would have been in heaven here, and she could almost see him standing beside her. Suddenly, she felt her heart quake with the thought, and she tucked the vision away in a secret part of her heart. It was like that sometimes, memories lurking and waiting for their chance to strike out, to remind her of all she'd lost.

Kembe, who was bringing up the rear, came up beside her and looked out at the dense woodland. They stood there awhile, side by side, Michelle watching him drink in the landscape. The sturdy sherpa, whose stout, powerful hands were crossed over his stomach, turned to her. "Is beautiful, yes?"

"Stunning," Michelle muttered. She took a drink from her CamelBak.

"Back home, where I live, we have lots of nice trails where we used to hike, but nothing like this."

Kembe turned to her and smiled. "Maybe you bring family next time you come and you show them."

Michelle eyed the round-faced sherpa who was looking back at her. She forced a smile, knowing he wasn't aware of how close he'd hit to the hurt in her heart. "Well, I should get moving. Don't want to keep people waiting on me."

Kembe nodded and waited for her to start off.

The road went on, up and down, past the towering chir pine that stood sentinel at the side. Every once in a while, Kembe would remind her to take a drink, keep her hydrated. She peered ahead to where Cam was walking alongside Scott.

Eventually, the road dipped down and they came abreast the fast running gray Marsyangdi River flanking the steep, treed land on the other side. Back home, these tors would've been considered mountains, but against the backdrop of the Himalayas they were no more than molehills.

She stopped, took another drink, immersed herself in silence where the world wasn't yelling at her, pushing in and telling her how to feel, what to say; to get on with life. Except, she hadn't figured out yet how to *really* get on with life. Sure, she'd done all the dutiful things—thrown herself back into work, took care of her home, attended parties, let Cam drag her out for dinner or drinks and outings on the St. Lawrence, but it was a sham and she knew it. She wore the mask of the brave survivor, because that was what she did; used it as a shield to ward away the pitying glances in the beginning and now to prevent them from returning.

She glanced back at Kembe who was walking behind her. He pointed out a mountain coming into view on her right. "Take picture, maybe?"

She looked in the direction he was pointing and saw the snow-capped massif reaching up into the deep blue. A shock of brilliant white gleamed on its vast shoulder as the mid-morning sun kissed it. "What's it called?"

"Manaslu, also called Kutang. It very popular with climbers."

She took her camera out and brought the viewfinder up to her eye. As she took the picture, she suddenly thought of John. He'd made a living getting people to the top of mountains, and now he was a trail guide. It was obvious he wasn't happy dragging them around a trail, but that was his job and she hoped he'd get past it because despite his sullen looks, she wanted to like him.

She put her camera away and turned to Kembe. "Can I ask you a question?"

Kembe smiled. "Of course."

"Do you know what happened to John, how he came to lose his leg?"

"It was frostbite."

"I know," Michelle said. She searched for words. "What I mean is, how did he get frostbite in the first place?"

Kembe shook his head. "I not know. I work Circuit then."

"I see," Michelle said, disappointed.

"Why you ask?"

"I was just curious."

The sherpa knitted his brow and considered her a moment. Finally, he said, "Do not worry. John will make sure you be okay."

The party stopped at the settlement of Jagat, and there they entered one of the ragged stone-built teahouses that huddled near the cliff bank overlooking the ribbon of the river far below. They'd been walking at a steady pace for the better part of three hours amid the thick, spindled pine forest. Michelle shed her pack, set it against one of the worn four-by-four wooden posts holding up the teahouse porch roof and tossed her hiking poles beside it. Arching her back, she stretched and went inside.

The rectangular main room was just like the one she'd eaten in the other night. Faded, wood-paneled walls, exposed timber rafters and creaky, dust-covered plank floors. Slanting rays of pale sunlight sprayed through yellowed curtains across the hodgepodge of trestle tables. The heady aroma of garlic and cilantro permeated the room. A stream of Tibetan conversations poured out of the kitchen along with the clanging of pots and pans and the hissing of a cooking fire.

Kembe came beside her and led her though the room to a narrow hallway that went out back to the rest of the party. She glanced over her trekking mates and their sherpa porters who were sipping tea around a rickety old picnic table.

The two gym rats were sitting off by themselves in plastic lawn chairs, listening to their music through their ear buds. Brian was on a knee in front of the table, rifling through his backpack. Scott was talking up a storm to Cam at the end of the table, gesturing to his camera and showing her pics on its screen display he'd taken.

Michelle pushed through the door, looked to her right where Mark and Nick were jabbering back and forth and pointing here and there toward the muted hills. They turned around as the door clapped shut behind her. "Hey, ya made it," Mark said, and shot her a wide grin. She waved back to him and Nick.

"You know us Canadians, we're in no hurry, and I'm the poster child for being the slowpoke," Michelle said, calling out to them.

Orsen came up to her and politely nudged her toward a chair. "You like tea?" he said, grabbing a glass mug off the tray on the table. He set it front of her and shoved a pitcher of cream on the table her way.

Michelle smiled. The sherpas were so accommodating, always looking for a way to be of service. Cam had mentioned earlier how it was interesting that the sherpas bent over backwards for the two of them, as if maybe they thought Michelle and Cam needed it because they were women. Maybe that was true and maybe it wasn't. At the moment, Michelle didn't mind being catered to. She let Orsen pour her tea and sat back, glad to be off her feet for a bit. John was leaning up against a low, crumbling rock wall at the far end of the terrace that hemmed the property in from the steep drop-off on the other side. At present, he was on his phone, talking with someone.

He pocketed his phone and looked up with that penetrating gaze he had, taking in the goings-on around him. His gaze fell on her last. He pushed away from the wall and strode toward her in his long, loping gait.

"How ya doing?" he said, standing beside her and looking down. A dim smile spread across his long, wind-burnt face that was just now showing the promise of a strawberry blond beard.

She sipped her tea, feeling like she was being appraised on whether she had the right stuff to make it in this mountainous land. Was it concern for her wellbeing that was behind John's demeanor and open-ended question, or was it chauvinism? It wasn't the first time she'd been on the receiving end of a look that conveyed the latter. She preferred to think his inquiry was the former.

"I'm great," she said, looking him dead in the eye, having a good idea her late arrival was imminent in his thoughts.

"Good," he said, nodding. "There's no great rush, just don't want to fall too far behind, eh? We have long days ahead of us. You don't wanna be slogging in the dark." He patted her shoulder, and headed for the teahouse.

From the corner of her eye, Michelle watched him go in as the Diamox fizzed in her fingers. She set her mug down and flexed her hands as Kembe brought out a dish of fried potatoes. The presence of their savory aroma brought people to the table. Cam broke away from Scott and found a place beside her.

"You two looked pretty chummy over there," Michelle said as Cam grabbed a plate and heaped a pile of potatoes onto it.

Cam unwrapped the napkin around her silverware. "He's a nice kid."

"Who is quite interested in you," Michelle put in, and raised her brow.

Cam rolled her eyes. "Pfft, you read too much into things, 'Chelle."

"Maybe, but you have no idea what you do to some guys."

Cam glanced down the table where Scott was fiddling with his camera and sucked her lip in. Turning back to Michelle, she struck a naughty look in her eye and shrugged. "He's not bad looking."

"Oh, my God," Michelle said, and laughed in spite of herself.

Cam nudged Michelle with an elbow and tilted her head toward Nick, who was staring out over the low, stone-built wall. "I think he likes you."

Michelle crunched her face up. "Cam...really? I'm not interested in a vacation romance."

"What's wrong with that? It's a good way to get your feet wet again, before you hook up with Don," Cam said though a mouthful of potatoes. She washed it down with a drink of tea, and added, "Might be a lot of fun."

Michelle rolled her eyes. "I'm not getting my feet wet, and I'm not hooking up with Don."

"Uh-huh," Cam said, obviously not believing her. "You keep telling yourself that."

Michelle got up and went over to Brian. She hadn't talked much to him. Then again, he pretty much kept to himself. There was a brooding undercurrent to him that reminded her of her brother, CJ, before all the drugs and the upheaval of their mother dying. Back then, she was young and going through her own stuff, trying to make sense of the world. Now, looking back through the lens of the past and her own struggles with depression, she knew the subtle signs she'd missed. And since that day on the bus, she had a good feeling that Brian was struggling with something. Perhaps that was what had brought him here to the other side of the world. She didn't know, but she had a strong feeling he was running away from something.

"Hey."

He looked up with a thin smile. "Hi."

"I noticed you sitting alone and thought maybe you'd like a bit of company."

He studied her a moment, as if he didn't believe she was talking to him, or for that matter, interested in talking to him. Finally, he shrugged. "Sure, if you want."

Michelle sat on the edge of the bench next to where he was going through his pack. "So, we haven't had a chance to talk much."

Brian dug a bottle of pills out of his pack. "Well, we've been pretty busy."

"Yeah, we have. So, you came for the mountains?"

"Yep."

She watched him uncap the bottle and dash out a caplet. The pill was too large for the Diamox tabs she was taking, so that left her wondering what it might be for. As he popped it in his mouth, she spied the label on the bottle, but the writing was too small to make out what the medication was. "Allergies?"

He popped the pill, downed it with a pull of water from his CamelBak, and shoveled the bottle back in his pack. "Something like that."

Michelle looked off, wondering what more to say to move the conversation along. "So you mentioned you come from Portland. You live there or go to school there?"

"Both...well, sort of. I graduated in August," he said and zipped his pack up.

"What's your degree in?"

"Computer Sciences." He stood up, and as he did, winced and rubbed his hands together as if trying to bring warmth into them. "Umm…you're from where again?"

"Cornwall, in Canada."

Brian nodded. "Uh, that's right. Sorry, I forgot."

"That's okay," Michelle said, watching the muscles around his chin tighten. "I'm constantly forgetting things. She glanced down at his legs, saw him bend one leg up behind him then the other. "Your knees bothering you? Those down-hills can be tough on them."

Brian shook his head. "Just stretching them out." He took up his mug. "Think I'm gonna grab another shot of tea. Nice talking with you."

"Yeah, it was," Michelle muttered to his retreating back. As she watched him walk away, a red flag waved in her thoughts.

Three hours later, Michelle slogged into Bagarchhap with Cam beside her. For the last hour on the long winding trail, her mind spun with questions about John and Brian and about her future. Her life had become a comfortable existence, her days moving in the familiar circle of work, tending things around the house, paying bills and sleeping. That was, until Don had upped the ante. She shook her head, wondering how she'd gotten trapped into making a lose-lose decision. But she wasn't going to do anything she didn't want to.

"That's a sight for sore eyes," Cam said, breaking into her thoughts as they stood before the gated building to the mountain settlement. Michelle cast her gaze upon its sturdy, whitewashed block walls and prominent pagoda-styled roof. Beyond it, a colorful two-story wood framed Annapurna Guest House peeked out. The teahouse's pink walls and blue-trimmed windows gleamed in the sunlight.

"Our home for the night," Cam said, and she strode ahead through the broad gateway opening, turning the barrel shaped, embossed, bronzed prayer wheels as she went. Michelle tagged along behind and when she came to the guesthouse, followed the signs around back to a flagstone courtyard dotted with terracotta urns, white plastic lawn chairs, and tables. A canvas canopy swayed above. In the distance, the thwack of an axe echoed down the mountainside.

John, who was standing in the center of the courtyard, said, "Our digs for the night. Go on in and Kembe will bring your keys around."

Michelle unsnapped her daypack, shrugged it off her shoulders and collapsed her hiking poles. "I'll be glad to get out of these boots," she said to Cam as they carried their gear inside and dropped it in the dimly lit hallway. She took her fleece pullover off, tied its sleeves around her waist and crouched beside her pack. As she stuffed her gloves and hat away, Cam bent down beside her.

"You okay? You've been quiet for a while now."

"I'm fine, just tired," Michelle said, which wasn't entirely a lie. She dug a brush out from the pouch in her pack and ran it through her hair.

"Okay. Just checking in."

"Thanks," Michelle said as Mark, Nick and Scott passed them by. When Nick smiled down at her, she waved back.

Cam's gaze followed Nick as he passed them by, then whispered to Michelle. "You see that? I wasn't kidding, he likes you."

Michelle shook her head. Sometimes she wished she could be more like Cam, able to rebound from bad things and to just live in the moment, taking what came and letting it go when it was over. Not that Cam was shallow. She was just good at hiding her junk behind a smile and sucking up what life threw her—like shutting away the pain of losing a brother. But she wasn't wired like Cam; she couldn't contain the memories in a safe place and wing it.

Getting to her feet, she pulled the green and orange buff up around her neck over her head. "I don't know about you, but I need something hot to drink." She straightened her shoulders, pushed the door open and strolled into the dining room. Their party was sitting at a long table near a band of windows flanking the courtyard.

John nudged his chair over giving her his seat, then pulled a chair up beside her. "You hungry?" he said as Cam sat next to Scott.

"Famished," she said as Kembe brought her a mug.

John reached over beside him and grabbed a large metal Thermos on the table and set it in front of her. As she poured ginger tea into her mug, he pushed a menu her way. "So, how ya feeling?"

"Tired but good, thank you."

"Good, glad to hear it."

Michelle wrapped her hands around the warm, welcoming mug and brought it to her lips. After she took a sip, she added, "I love these mountains. They fill you right up; make you forget about the rat-race back home."

"So, what's the rat-race like back home?" John said.

Michelle eyed him. "Stressful, compared to the life you live here."

"Life's just as stressful here. Trust me." He eyed her and was quiet a moment. Taking a sip from his mug, he added, "So, you work in construction. What is it you do, again?"

"I put together bids and manage the office."

"Sounds like you do more than that," John said leaning forward. "You've been offered a partnership, right. That's no small thing."

"Well, I haven't taken it yet."

"Why not? Sounds like a golden opportunity."

"That's what I keep telling her," Cam piped in from across the table.

Michelle ignored her and turned to John. "It's complicated." Now it was her turn to be quiet. She looked out the window and saw their refracted reflections looking back, felt his discerning gaze on her, as if he was uncertain of what to make of her. She didn't like the direction the conversation was going, so she turned back to him. "So, tell me, what was it like standing on top of the world?"

John considered her question a moment then said, "The first time, it took my breath away."

"Literally, I bet," Michelle said and grinned.

John chuckled, wrinkling the weathered skin around his deep blue eyes and Roman nose. "You could say that."

It was the first time Michelle had heard him really laugh and she liked the sound of it. It had a full and robust tenor. "So, it was everything you thought it would be then?"

John nodded and as quickly as the laugh had come, it was swallowed up with a somber expression. "More," he replied.

"I can't imagine looking down at the whole world, seeing everything laid at your feet," Michelle said.

John shifted in his chair. "It changes your life." He cleared his throat, brightened and said, "So you took the plunge and came to Nepal."

Michelle sipped her tea as the men bantered back and forth down the table from her, talking about the trail, sports back home and what f-stops to use on their cameras. "Yes, I did," she said, sensing he didn't want to talk about himself either. Then from the corner of her eye, she noticed John's gaze drift down to her hands.

"That's quite a ring on your finger."

She turned to him, knowing his interest in her ring probably had nothing to do with its history. Sooner or later, she'd expected someone like Mark or Nick to bring up the ring. She looked down at Adam's heirloom that had been passed to him through the family and forced a smile. "It was handed down to me."

"It looks old."

"It is. It came through the French and Indian war," she said, watching him dart his eyes back and forth over her ring.

"Interesting." He paused and shifted in his chair. At last, he pressed his lips together and cleared his throat. "Okay, before I forget, let me check your vitals," he said, pulling out a small journal and a pen from his pocket along with a little black device.

Michelle watched him play with the instrument. "What's that do?"

"It measures oxygen saturation in your body," he said. He attached it to her finger and took her pulse. "How much water did you get through today?"

"Almost three liters."

"You need to drink more than that tomorrow, okay? We're going to start getting up there pretty soon. You don't want to get dehydrated, trust me."

"Okay."

He jotted her answer down in the book. "Any headaches? Shortness of breath?"

"Nope."

"Good." He took it off her finger, read the results and entered it in the book. He shot her a tight smile. "Okay, you're looking good. If you'll excuse me, I have to take care of some business with our host."

He got up and strutted across the room toward the transaction counter, leaving her with more questions than answers.

Chapter 14

Michelle

Bagarchhap, - Oct. 7th

The following morning, they left under scudding clouds. Michelle looked up at them as she trundled along at the rear end of the party, wondering if they were going to run into rain. It was cool out with a slight breeze that played with the collar of her jacket. Some distance ahead, Cam and Scott were poling along and chatting together, looking pretty chummy with each other. Her best friend was certainly having fun with the striking young man. Michelle wondered if Cam's off-handed comment about Scott looking good was really off-handed.

Kembe came beside her as she poled along the gritty trail that had left the crumbling paved road they'd been on the last four days.

"Lots to see today," he said.

"Oh?" Michelle replied as she stepped up onto one of the embedded rocks scattered along the track. She hopped down and plotted her next step, enjoying the rocky obstacle course laid out before her. After walking the road for so long, this was a welcome change; she had a sense that they were really getting into the wild. She turned and glanced back at him. "Tell me about it."

Kembe's round face smiled and there was a glint of mischief in his dark eyes. "Ah, you will see. I don't want to spoil for you."

Michelle grinned back, liking the sherpa's easy-going playful manner. "Okay, have it your way."

She turned back to the trail and poled along in silence, sometimes taking a picture. It seemed there was something marvelous to look at in every bend in the trail: a tumbling waterfall, a towering wall of rock, or a snow-covered mountain peeking over the rising shoulders of the land. It was the world at its glorious best! In the distance, she heard the sound of bells drifting toward her. Another cattle train! She smiled, loving the lilting musical sound of it coursing through the trees. The trains carrying supplies up and down the trail had become a regular thing over the last two days. She plodded ahead and around a sweeping bend of the track and saw instead a column of donkeys heading toward her. She moved off to the side, giving the gentle beasts carrying their loads a wide berth as they marched forward, their hooves clip-clopping on the earthen path.

As they plodded past her, their heady scent brought back memories of when she was little and her parents took her and her brother to her grandfather's farm, back when life was simple and uncomplicated. She stood there waiting for the train to pass, reliving visions of riding her grandfather's pony through the woods that bordered the farm.

Kembe tapped her arm, rousing her back to the present. The column of donkeys had swelled out to five or six animals abreast, overtaking the rutted shoulders of the trail. She moved up a few more steps onto the sloping flank and dug her hiking pole into the leaf litter. Peering ahead, she couldn't see an end to the long file of donkeys, which had suddenly come to an abrupt halt. A dozen defiant animals stood unmoving in front of her. She turned to Kembe. "What now?" she said.

Kembe stepped beside her and leaned back onto the trunk of a large gnarled oak. "We wait."

Michelle pulled her camera out, and as she snapped a few pictures of the unruly animals, a distant sharp whistle downwind strafed the air. Following it were loud claps, vocalized grunts and slashing verbal outburst. The vanguard of the train pressed forward on the lingering donkeys and a moment later, the traffic jam broke loose. When the last animal passed them by, she hopped back down onto the trail, wondering how far she had fallen behind the rest of the group.

To her surprise, she met up with them ten minutes later at the rim of a steep ravine. As she came among them, John looked up at her from where he sat next to Orsen on a low stone parapet overlooking the gully. He smiled, but it seemed forced as he got up and came to her.

"Hey, how ya doing?"

Michelle tossed a defiant smile back at him. "Doing good." Which wasn't a lie. "We got caught up in that train back there."

"I know," John said. "It was a long one."

"You can say that again," Cam piped up, marching up to Michelle and John. "Hey girlfriend. Didn't mean to abandon you back there."

Michelle shrugged. "Don't worry about it. I had great company," she said, tilting her head toward Kembe, who was standing beside her. "You look like you're ready to head out."

"Pretty soon, yes," Cam said. "But why don't I hang back with you? I'm in no rush."

Michelle eyed Scott, who was darting glances back at Cam. The young man was totally gone on her best friend, and she knew if Cam hung back, Scott would as well. That made for three's a crowd, and she didn't want to be a third wheel. Besides, she was perfectly content having Kembe as her hiking companion.

She waved Cam off. "Thanks, but I'm good. You go on ahead."

"Are you sure?" Cam said.

"Positive," Michelle replied, unhitching the vest clasp of her daypack.

As she slid out of it, John put his hand out. "Here let me take that." He turned to Kembe. "Take everybody down the hill with Orsen and we'll catch up after she has a breather."

Michelle regarded the tall blond Andersen guide. *Well, I wonder what this is all about?*

Fifteen minutes later, she and John geared up and started down a rocky switchback trail toward the bottom of the wide ravine. As Michelle poled her way down the narrow zigzagging path with John following close behind, she thought back to her time alone with John up at the rest area. She'd expected him to say something about her needing to pick up the pace, but he had only reminded her to keep drinking. She dug her pole into the ground as she came to a jumble of boulders and looked down the sweeping wooded landscape. One wrong step could lead to a tumble of several meters.

John tapped her shoulder. "Take your time."

"Planning on it." She debated her next steps through the plunging v- shaped crotch between two large rocks. Beyond them was a big step down onto another that sloped toward the receding edge of the trail. There was no good place to plant a pole to brace her against a fall. Her other option was to climb up and around the leeward boulder, then slide back down to the path on her ass. She didn't like that choice either.

"Relax and lean back as you step through and down," he said. "You can do it."

Right!

She chewed her lip, stepped ahead and, leaning back as John instructed, skidded down through the wedged opening onto the path below. John slipped down behind her like a cat. She looked over her shoulder at him. "You get around pretty good."

"Meaning what?" he said, eyeing her.

Michelle was pretty sure he didn't care for her reference to his prosthetic leg. She closed her eyes, regretting her comment. "Sorry, I wasn't thinking how that would come out."

He nodded and put his hand out for her hiking poles. "Here, let me make an adjustment on those. They're a bit short." After he extended them, he handed them back. "There, that's better. Remember to keep your knees relaxed and your poles in front of you as we go down."

She eyed him. "You probably think I'm in over my head."

He shook his head. "Not at all. There's no shame in being a slowpoke. Better safe than sorry." He pointed ahead. "You ready?"

She took a deep breath. "I am."

"Let's go then."

For the next ten minutes, the two of them walked down the rocky trail in silence under the gold and crimson canopy of the forest. As they went, she felt his eyes on her, as if he was debating something. She came to a stop and sucked a drink of water from her CamelBak. "I thought this morning we might run into rain, but it appears not."

"Which is a good thing," he said. "Although we might see some later tonight."

She took another draw of water and wiped her lips with the back of her hand. "Can I ask you a question?"

"I guess," he said.

"You were born in the States, right? How'd you end up here?"

"That's a long story," he said and started ahead.

"I have time," she called after him.

He turned back and studied her as if trying to make up his mind about going forward with an answer. At last, he shot her a crooked smile. "You really wanna know?"

"I do," she said digging her pole into the ground and tossing a smile back at him.

He shrugged and swung his hand out, showing her the way ahead. "Okay. It's not anything to speak of, but I guess if you really want to know." He pulled a chocolate bar out of his jacket pocket and tore the wrapper off. After taking a bite, he said, "I came here twenty years ago after hooking up with Andersen. At the time they had an opening for a tent man on Ama-Dablam, setting up camp and—"

"Ama-Dablam?" Michelle said.

"Yeah, it's a mountain southeast of Everest. Tactically, it's a more difficult summit. Anyhow, I saw the chance to get into the big leagues, so I jumped at it."

"And Andersen, how did you get hooked up with them?" Michelle said, poling along beside him.

"I saw an ad in the paper right after I graduated high school," John said, popping the last of the candy bar into his mouth. "I was looking for a summer job before heading to college, and having logged a lot of time in the Rockies growing up, I couldn't resist. I got to hang out with guys like Lowe, Takeda and Weiss, who were running a summer clinic on Mt. Elbert. It was only supposed to last the summer, but Lowe took a liking to me and put a word into the mucky-mucks at Andersen. Next thing I knew I got a full-time job offer. My mother wasn't happy about it when I told her I wanted to put off school for a couple years. She had nightmares about me ending up alone in a yurt. Turns out she wasn't so far from the truth." He chuckled, but it was a sour laugh. "Anyway, one thing led to another, and here I am."

"Don't you miss your family?" she said.

He was quiet a moment. "I get home now and then."

She chewed his answer over. Obviously, he wasn't close to them. "I don't think I could move that far away from home."

John shrugged. They walked for a moment in silence. Finally, he said, "You have brothers and sisters?"

"A brother. CJ. He's a bit of a control freak, but I love him. He has two children, a boy and a girl. They're sweeties. What about you? You have brothers and sisters?"

"A sister, Peg. She's the family go-to person whenever something needs to happen."

"My mother was like that," Michelle said.

"She passed?"

"Yes, fifteen years ago come November. My father is still with us though. He lives with my brother and his family in Ottawa. What about your parents?"

"They're gone." He paused and looked off ahead. "So, you enjoying yourself here?"

"Yes, very much. So, umm…you live in Pokhara?"

"Careful, there's a tripper right there." he said, pointing to a thin tree root leaping out over her path.

"Thanks, that would not have gone well," she said and stepped over it. She glanced at him. "So, Pokhara?"

"Oh, yeah. Umm…yes. I have a rental down by the lake."

"The Lake?"

"Yeah, Phewa Lake, south of the city."

"Ohhhhhh," she said as her feet went out from under her. As her back thunked the earth, her breath caught. She blew out a breath and looked up at the waving tree branches overhead.

John bent down beside her and put his hand out. "You okay?"

She assessed herself. Nothing hurt except her pride. She chuckled as she took his hand and got to her feet. "Well, that was graceful, wasn't it?"

He brushed the leaf litter and dirt off her backside. "Oh, I don't know. I think I'd give you a 9.5 on it," he said and winked.

"You're a stinker!"

"I've been called worse," he said.

They walked on a little further without a word and as they did, an urge to confide more about her life to this man she barely knew grew in her mind. Perhaps it was the safety of anonymity, the telling of her sheltered thoughts to a complete stranger, that begged her to let them out. She didn't know, but she suddenly found herself opening her mouth. "So, I bet you're a bit curious about me being here and all."

"Outside of your telling me your girlfriend pushed you out the door, the thought has crossed my mind," he said. "But I don't want to get into your business."

"That's alright, I don't mind," she said. "My life's not all that exciting, at least not like yours." She glanced back and when she saw him looking on impassively, she held her tongue and frowned.

He cleared his throat. "Well?"

"Oh, sorry. I was thinking how to put things," she lied. She took a deep breath, and said, "So, umm...I was married as you've probably guessed."

"I did notice the ring."

"Well, the reason I'm here with Cam instead of my husband is that my husband died a couple years ago in a car accident."

"I'm sorry to hear that," he said.

"It hit me pretty hard as you can probably imagine, and for a long time, I didn't go anywhere. It was Cam. She's my sister-in-law, too, by the way, who finally got me out of the house. Then last year, she came up with this idea of coming here, fulfilling her brother's bucket list. I loved the idea and here we are."

John nodded and behind his steel blue eyes, she could see him turning things over.

"Cam and I go way back. We were besties in high school and went to the same college together," she said. "I don't know what I would've done without her after my mom died." She paused, remembering life in the tiny apartment she shared with her mother and brother, then went on. "I was fourteen when she passed. My parents were divorced and my father did the best he could, taking care of my brother and me, but it was hard on everyone because of his long hours at the firehouse. He was a commander there."

He studied her a moment, and for the first time she felt like he was really seeing her. At last, he said, "It's good you have a friend like Cam. They're hard to come by."

"Yes, they are," she said and went quiet, wondering whether she had said too much, and what he was thinking of her.

"My mom passed recently," he said, breaking into the silence between them.

"I'm sorry to hear that," she said. "Were you here when she passed?"

"I was here when she got sick, but luckily I was able to get home before she..." He broke off, took a breath and went on. "Anyway, my mom's like your father, raised me and my sister by herself."

Michelle turned to him as they walked, saw him battling some hidden memory. "So your father had already passed?"

"Yeah, but I don't remember him much."

She went quiet a moment as his answer played over in her mind. The two of them shared much in common, but she could only imagine what it felt like growing up, wondering about a mother or father you never knew. It seemed to her that John would've been close to his mother, but yet here he was.

Finally, she said, "Your mom? Did you get along with her?"

"Oh, yeah, although you probably find that hard to believe, me living half a world away," he said.

"Not at all," she fibbed.

He narrowed his eyes on her and she could sense his skepticism as they came to another switchback. Guiding her around it, he led her down another descent through the trees until at last they came upon the rest of their party.

Chapter 15

John

Chame, Nepal – Oct. 8[h]

The next morning, John led his clients out of the village under a molten sun as it beamed down from the blue dome of the world. Reaching into the breast pocket of his jacket, he picked out a chunk of chocolate he bought on the way out from the Annapurna Guesthouse shop. They'd left Chame an hour before and were headed for Manang where they'd have their first acclimatization day. As he walked, he thought about what Michelle had told him about her journey through life, and he couldn't help comparing his own life to it. She'd been through some tough shit, and yet she seemed to take it all in stride, or at least that's the way she presented herself. He'd been dead wrong about her. She wasn't timid or unsure of herself. She was a survivor. And what was more, she'd surprised him even more last night when she engaged with the men, playing cards, swapping stories and telling jokes around the table.

Perhaps that was what scared the hell out of him, because he was pretty sure if he got too close to her, he'd find himself revealing things he'd rather not talk about now or ever. He set his jaw, fighting the long-forgotten feeling of wanting a woman for more than just a tumble in bed and marched forward, following the long line of tourist trekkers heading for Thorung Pedi and beyond.

He passed a small farmhouse whose ragged rooftop ridge dipped in the center like a swayback horse. It was like many of the farms that had seen their fair share of years. Its leaning hand-lain chimney, racked windows and crumbling stone foundation were a testament to the hard winters. He eyed the improvised, bright blue nylon tarp over the roof and breathed in the crisp tang of mountain air laced with earthen pungency. In so many ways, this broken yet resilient home reflected his life.

Behind him, he heard his client's co-mingled voices talking about the mountain along with the ting-ting-dinging of cattle bells. He glanced over his shoulder and saw them walking in pairs, engrossed in conversations about the land and things going on back home. But his glance fell most on the soft-spoken, chocolate-haired Canadian.

The Apple Trail, as the Circuit was called, stretched before him like a thin brown ribbon through the rising landscape. Today would be an arduous hike, descending a steep, giddy trail into a valley scraped of all vegetation. Here, they would cross the river once more before heading back up in elevation. But the views of the soaring Paungda Danda rock face were worth it for his clients, and there was no great rush to get to where they were going. Not that Dan and Vic would appreciate it. They were more interested in the destination than the journey.

Well, they'd better start listening to him if they were going to get to where they wanted to go. He chuckled to himself over their choice of lightweight fleece tops and baggy shorts. Yes, it was seasonably warm, but the weather could change on a dime. Soon enough, they'd be regretting their choices, but it was none of his business.

An hour later, the trail spit him and his clients out into the tiny village of Mungji, which was no more than a scattering of pieced-together homes and trailside trinket shops geared to lure the wide-eyed tourists. A little ways through town, he stopped and had them take tea at a small café whose bowed exterior plank walls hadn't seen a lick of paint in years. A weathered, wood trestle table with a tattered tablecloth and splintered benches sat under its porch roof. After the brief lunch of seasoned potatoes and momos, he checked in on everyone's health, donned his pack and led them back out on the trail again.

As he plodded along, Mark and Nick came up and joined him, and they chatted about the weather, the mountains, children and their lives back home. Mark was single and worked in forestry management, regulating tree harvesting at Timber Creek, north of Detroit. This required lots of traveling back and forth from where Mark lived. Nick was divorced and taught Mechanical Engineering at Ohio State. He had two boys, James who was studying architecture at Pittsburgh University and David who was studying structural engineering at Syracuse University.

As John listened to Mark and Nick, his mind drifted back to his conversation with Michelle, thinking of her story. She'd laid herself out there to him, and for a moment, he almost had a mind to tell his own story to her—how he'd decided not to go to Colorado State University to study Conservation and Land Management, how Vanessa had suddenly changed her mind and announced she was heading east to study medicine, away from him and the future they'd planned together.

He'd always thought the decision she'd made had to do with her dream of being a doctor or more to the point her mother pressuring her to get away from the kid from the other side of the tracks. But meeting Van's son had given him pause to think otherwise. Yet why would she have run from him if she were pregnant? It didn't make sense. No, it had to be her mother. The woman had never liked him, and he knew it. But he'd thought Van had loved him and that she would've fought back harder. But she hadn't even batted an eyelash. That had been the first cut in the long line of slights, but who was counting?

At last he turned to Mark and said, "You like your job?"

"Actually yeah, at least most of the time," Mark said with a smile. He sucked a drink of water from his CamelBak. "You?"

"For the most part, I guess," John lied, knowing his answer was less than it could be.

Mark nodded and was quiet a moment, then said, "But you'd really rather be on Everest, I'm guessing."

"You could say that," John said.

Nick smiled. "I hear you. So, I take it this is just something to tide you over until you're ready to get back at it?"

"It has been on my mind," John said. The conversation was wearing thin. He glanced over his shoulder at Vic and Dan, wondering if they were drinking as much as they should.

Nick jabbed his thumb back in their direction. "They're gonna be in a world of shit, if they don't start hydrating better and paying attention to their body."

"You think?" John said.

"I tried to tell 'em, too, but they weren't interested in listening," Mark said. He pulled a bag of trail mix out from the vest pocket of his hiking jacket and tore into it.

Popping a handful of trail-mix into his mouth, he offered the bag to John.

John put his hand up, waving off the offered treat. "Well, I'm not gonna drag their sorry asses all around this Circuit if they get jacked up."

"Hope they got good traveler's insurance," Nick put in.

That got a chuckle out of Mark and a smile from John. "They don't start paying attention, they're gonna need it," John said.

That night, John sat on his cot in his darkened bedroom above the teahouse kitchen in Pisang. Beside him, a tiny window looked out over the veiled mountains displaying a glittering, star-spattered sky. Below him, the muffled voices of the kitchen staff trickled up into his room. He untied his laces on his boots, yanked them off and tossed them aside. His leg ached tonight, and he winced as he rolled down the sleeve of the prosthetic, revealing reddened skin around the stump. He set the artificial limb aside and rubbed the tender area around it as the memory of talking with Michelle and hearing about her family replayed in his mind.

He peered out the window, trying hard to ignore the unsettling notion that he might be a father. But the thought wouldn't let go. He knew he was overthinking things, but until he found out one way or another, he'd be a slave to a rambling mind. At length, he huffed, pulled his cell phone out of his pocket and woke it up. It was time to stop procrastinating about it and put it to rest.

He connected to the Internet and in the search field typed Vanessa's name. The screen flashed and a list of entries came up with her name, or rather several entries that had the same name but were different women as far as he could tell. He scrolled down through them, read the thumbnail lead-ins, searching for snippets that matched up with the young woman he'd once loved. On the second page one rang true, except for one thing, a hyphen after her maiden last name with an attached last name he didn't recognize.

The memory of meeting Van at Kelly's flashed before him. She hadn't been wearing a ring on the finger that mattered. If this person on the web page was indeed her, she'd been married at some point, which might mean her son had someone else as a father. But that all depended on when she'd gotten pregnant, not that having a child out of wedlock mattered all that much anymore.

His finger hovered above the hot link on the screen as he chewed his lip. With a deep breath, he tapped the link and watched the phone load the page.

Summary

Vanessa Hall-Ambose is 44 years old and was born on 8/17/1970. Currently, she lives in Oak Creek, CO, and previously lived in Gainesville, FL. Sometimes Vanessa goes by various nicknames including Vanessa Hall and Van. She currently works as a General Physician at South Routt

Medical Center. Her ethnicity is Caucasian, whose political affiliation is currently a registered Independent; and religious views are listed as Lutheran. Vanessa graduated from the University of Florida and is now divorced. Other family members and associates include, Tim Ambrose (ex-husband), Jason Hall-Ambrose (son), Michael Hall (father), Vivian Hall (mother) and Michael Hall II (brother). She has a reported annual income of $120,000 - $159,999 and a current net worth value of $275,000 - $299,999.

John pursed his lip and felt his body relax. The kid's last name was Ambrose. He wasn't a father, unless the boy was adopted, which he couldn't believe. He stared at the link a bit longer, unable to stop from reading more about the woman who'd left him behind. After a while, he tossed the phone on the bed.

Screw it! What am I doing and why do I care?

John woke the next morning to the sounds of people getting around in their rooms. He ran his hand over his bristled face, hitched himself up on his cot and turned his eyes to the window. A dreary slate sky stared back. As he watched the heavy clouds slowly drift overhead to the east, Michelle's face flashed before him. He held the vision of her thick, dark, curly hair and butter-soft brown eyes for a moment, then shook his head. A long day was ahead of him, so he reached over the cot and dragged his prosthetic up beside him.

A moment later, a knock came to his door. He pulled a fleece over his head, tucked its tails into his pants and pocketed his cell phone. "Yeah?"

"You up?" Orsen said on the other side of the door.

John cinched his belt and stepped into his boots. "Be right out."

"Hō. Umm...we have small problem—sick client."

Damn it! "Who?"

"Vic. His friend, Dan, say he spend a lot of time in toilet room last night. I think something he ate not agree with him. Maybe he stay back from acclimation hike, what you think?"

Wonderful, he's got the shits. "I'll be down in a minute," John said. "In the meantime, make sure he's drinking."

"Hō."

John heard Orsen's thudding footsteps recede from his door. He'd warned the brash young know-it-all last night about ordering the yak steak, but the kid insisted on having it. Now he was paying the price for it. He'd have to leave Vic here and have him deal with not getting properly acclimated for tomorrow's long haul. Problem with that was, they had a significant elevation gain ahead of them after they reached Manang. He rifled through his pack and took out a bottle of Imodium.

"Fuck it," he muttered as he went for the door. "He put himself in this situation, he can deal with the consequences."

He tromped down the stairs and into the main dining hall. His clients were sitting at the far end of the room near a ribbon of paned windows looking out upon the fast running Marsyangdi River. As he joined his clients, Orsen came beside him and leaned in close. So, what's you want to do?" he said, his voice just above a whisper.

John grabbed a mug off the tray in the middle of the table, pasted a smile on and bid everyone a good morning save for Vic, who was absent. He eyed Dan, who sat at the far end of the table, picking at his breakfast of eggs and pancakes before turning back to the sherpa and taking him aside. "I'm gonna have a chat with the other half of the Testosterone Twins."

Orsen nodded. "You want me to hang back?"

"If you wouldn't mind."

"No problem," Orsen said, and strode across the room to the transaction counter.

John grabbed the Thermos sitting next to the tray of mugs and poured tea for himself as Kembe brought out a platter of cakes and honey along with a bowl of seasoned fried potatoes. The sherpa set them on the end of the table. John inhaled the aroma of garlic and his mouth watered as he drifted along behind his sitting clients who were jabbering back and forth about the hike ahead. He forced a smile at Cam and Michelle who looked up as he passed them by.

"You ready for your acclimation hike?" He said to them.

Cam set her fork down. "Think so." She took her napkin and wiped her mouth. "So, how far are we walking today?"

"A couple miles up into the hills," John said, appraising their heavy, long-sleeved fleeces and dark blue thermal tops peeking out around their necks. Good, they were listening to him. Dan, not so much. He slid into the chair next to him. "So, I hear your buddy had a rough night of it."

Dan leaned back in his chair, crossed his arms and stared at him. "Yeah, you could say that."

John pulled the bottle of Imodium out of his pocket and set it on the table. "This'll help. Directions are on the bottle."

Dan looked off, then turned back. "Yeah, thanks. So what now?"

"We're gonna hold Vic back from his acclimation hike," John said.

"No big deal, right?" Dan said. "I mean, it's not gonna keep him from going on, is it?"

"Actually, it might," John said. "Everyone should be on this hike to help their body adjust to altitude. Life isn't going to get easy going forward for him without it." He glanced at Dan's plate then. A small stack of pancakes were barely touched. "Not hungry?"

Dan shrugged.

"Headache?"

"Nothing a little Advil won't cure," Dan said eyeing him.

John stared back, took in the dull eyes and dismal expression. *A little Advil, my ass.* "What about Vic? He have a headache, too?"

Dan leaned forward and took a bite of pancake and nodded. "Big time.

John sucked a gulp of tea and ran his tongue around the inside of his mouth, trying to decide if Vic's headache was due to dehydration. The last thing he wanted to deal with was the kid developing AMS. At last he said, "The headaches you're feeling right now are from not drinking like you guys should. You don't realize it, but the air up here siphons the water right out of you. You two have a long, difficult walk ahead of you, and if you don't drink like you should, you're gonna be hurting units later on." He got up and gave Dan's black cotton T-shirt and puffy, tan, nylon sleeveless vest a good look. "And that shirt you're wearing—not good. This isn't a fashion show up here. The weather is fickle in these mountains. Grab something warmer, and for God's sake, get your thermals out and put 'em on."

Chapter 16

Michelle

Manang, Nepal – Oct. 10ʰ

Michelle sat across from Cam at the long breakfast table, readying herself for a very long day on the trail. At the far end of the table, Brian sat by himself nursing a glass of mango juice and writing in his notebook. He wrote in it every morning. When she commented on it, he told her he was recording his trip. She eyed him, wishing he'd join her and Cam, but she wasn't going to push him. In a corner of the room, Vic and the Bat Boy, Dan, sat huddled over a table. The cocky, dark-haired jock with the snake tattoo was having a hard time of it, and he'd missed his acclamation hike yesterday. She shook her head, wondering why they'd signed on with Andersen if they already thought they knew everything. Well, they were finding out going it their own way wasn't working out very well. Maybe they'd sit up and take notice of John's suggestions going forward, but she didn't have a lot of hope of that.

As for Mark and Nick, they hadn't come down yet and neither had John, but Kembe and Orsen were busy bringing out breakfast and setting it out on the table. She pulled her camera out as the two sherpas buzzed about them and reviewed the pictures she'd taken over the last few days. The last two were of the Paungda Danda rock face. She turned the camera so Cam could get a look at the colossal scalloped bowl of burnt umber rock that soared up into a muddy, gray overcast sky.

Cam spooned up a bite of porridge and pointed to the serrated ridge that'd been kissed with snow. "Wait 'til the folks back home see that," she said, and fed herself.

Michelle eyed Cam. Her best friend was working on her second bowl, wolfing it down as if she hadn't eaten in days. "Hungry, much?"

"Actually, yeah, and you should carb up. We have a long day today," Cam said as Scott stepped up to their table.

"Mind if I join ya?" he said, looking over Cam's shoulder.

Cam regarded him with a more-than-friendly smile and scooted over toward Michelle, making room for him. "Morning."

Michelle's suspicion that Scott had been visiting Cam's room the last couple of nights grew when she saw Scott sidle up nice and tight to her best friend. When

Cam made no move to put space between them, the suspicion was confirmed.

Okay...I guess we're cradle robbing!

Scott grabbed an empty bowl from the middle of the table and ladled up a helping of porridge. "How'd ya sleep?"

Michelle saw Cam struggle to stuff a smile. "Like a baby," she said. "You?"

Scott shot Cam a wink that was so obvious it was embarrassing. "Can't complain," he said and plucked a slice of sourdough toast off a plate and buttered it.

Michelle averted her gaze to the viewfinder of her camera, not sure where to look. *Oh, my God! A little discretion, maybe?* She cleared her throat and set her camera down. "So, umm...Scott, Cam tells me you develop computer games. What kinds?"

Scott drizzled honey over his porridge. "MOs and RTSs."

"Which is?" Michelle said, pulling her mug of tea over and cradling it her hands.

"Multi-player and real time strategy games, like *Team Fortress* and *Age of Empires.*"

Michelle lifted her hand and swiped it over her head. "Wooph!"

"They're action games where you become one of the characters defending something or try to kill a dark lord or whatever," Cam said.

"Oh. So I take it there's money in that field," Michelle said, and sipped her tea.

"Oodles of it," Scott said and shoveled a spoonful of porridge into his mouth. After he swallowed, he went on, "Take *Warhammer*, for example; it grossed 170 million dollars last year. If you're on the ground floor of all of that, you can buy an island in the Bahamas and fly in on your own personal Gulfstream jet."

"I imagine it's a pretty competitive field then," Michelle said. "Have you sold anything?"

Scott picked up his toast and bit into it. "Not yet, but I'm close," he said, and washed it down with a gulp of tea.

"Morning," Mark said dropping his pack on the floor next to the adjacent table. He grabbed a mug off the tray and poured himself tea as Nick filed in behind him.

"Looks like a good day for a hike," Nick put in.

"That it does," Mark said, pulling up a chair.

Cam picked up the honey bowl and offered it to Mark. "You know when we're leaving?"

Mark spooned a dollop into his tea. "No idea, but my guess is pretty soon."

"And you'd be right."

Michelle turned around to see John standing behind her. "Oh, hi."

He flashed her a quick smile then looked them over for a moment before bidding everyone at the table a good morning. "Okay, we have a long hike today through some outstanding country to Yak Kharka, so gas up and get your water when you're done." He glanced over to the two boys from LA, pressed his lips together and stalked over to them.

Michelle watched him as he took a seat next to them and heard a long, muttered conversation drift back. The gist of it, from what she heard, was if Vic continued to worsen, he was going to send him back down to Besisahar with Orsen. At length, he got up and came back and sat on the other side of Cam. Pulling an empty plate to him, he loaded it up with fried potatoes, eggs, and toast. As he gulped his breakfast down, he asked everyone how they were feeling and if their sherpa bags with all their non-essentials for the day had been set outside their rooms.

Michelle stared down at her plate of half-eaten breakfast, knowing she should finish it off, but she wasn't hungry. When she looked back up, John was staring at her. She pursed her lips. *Yeah, I know, force it down.* She took up her fork and dug in, much to the dismay of her disgruntled stomach.

Twenty minutes later, they were out under clear blue skies, hiking upward toward the village of Gunsang. Michelle eyed the faint tract lines burnished into the rising flanks of the scrubland, following them with her gaze as they crisscrossed each other before slipping out of sight over the domed mount. As she poled alongside Cam in the middle of the strewn-out party, John walked beside them, glancing back from time to time at the boys from LA, bringing up the rear with Kembe.

Michelle pulled her buff around her ears, warding off a stiff chill breeze riffing over the hill land. "You're worried about Vic?" she said to John.

He turned to her as they walked and was quiet a moment. "Keeping him back a day and having him lose an acclamation hike isn't going to go well for him. But there wasn't much I could do about it. We'll see."

Cam pointed to an icy peak piercing a whiff of clouds. "What's that mountain over there?"

"That would be Tilicho Peak. There's a stunning glacier-fed lake at its foothills. Unfortunately, the path to it entails a hell of a climb, which I doubt those two boys behind us could deal with, so we'll be bypassing it. When we stop for lunch in the village, there's a teahouse with pictures of it."

Michelle frowned at the thought of having to miss seeing the lake, but she didn't say anything. "Would you send Vic back down if he doesn't improve?"

John considered her then smiled, which she knew was meant not to worry her, should she run into trouble. "As one of my friendly competitors on Everest would say, 'One day at a time. All you can do'."

Michelle saw she wasn't going to get a straight answer, so she let the matter drop and the three of them walked in silence for some time, ascending a steep, dizzying incline up into the barren rock and stone-strewn landscape. As she plodded along, she looked out over the vast brown lands stretching out to the feet of the great snow-covered massifs beyond. Before her were small homesteads with tiny hemmed-in planting fields. As she walked on, she thought of how this land exacted much from the people who lived here, people who greeted her with smiles and hospitality, people who didn't know they were poor by Western standards.

At last she came to a halt and took a well-deserved breather. As she sucked a drink from her

CamelBak, John and Cam stopped beside her, doing the same. John turned and peered down the trail at the two boys who were grinding their way up toward them with Orsen following. The expression on his face left little to the imagination. He was making up his mind and his decision wasn't going to be liked by the kids. She felt a twinge of sympathy for them, then remembered they'd put themselves in this situation.

She took another pull of water from her CamelBak and gazed up the unforgiving slope. "How much further?" she said.

"Another forty-five minutes to an hour," John said.

Michelle furrowed her brow and shot him her best I-don't-like-you-anymore playful gaze. "You said that twenty minutes ago."

"Did I? Hmm..." He winked at Cam who stood nearby poking at the ground with her poles. Her best friend was barely out of breath and was obviously anxious to get moving again. For a moment, they all looked at each other, and as they did, Michelle saw Cam adding two and two together and getting the wrong ideas about John and her. Michelle narrowed her gaze at her best friend.

Don't you dare go there, girlfriend!

But Cam flashed her a Pollyanna smile and said, "Think I'm gonna move on ahead if that's okay, 'Chelle."

Oh, you are in so much trouble.

"Sure, go ahead, I'll be fine," Michelle said. She glanced at John, hoping he wasn't getting the gist of Cam's subtle hint. To her relief, he'd turned around to get another look at the boys coming up the trail. She watched him turning thoughts over in his head, saw the lines at the corners of his mouth deepen, the subtle flare of his Roman nose and the intensity in his deep blue eyes. She'd never met a man like him; he was such a contradiction she didn't know whether to like him or be afraid of him sometimes. Yet, there was something about him, a veiled goodness that went deep and she couldn't help but be drawn to him.

Finally, he turned back to her and pointed out the mountains, giving them names— Gangnapurna and Annapurna III—and telling her about the routes to their summits, what the hazards were and the rewards once you made it to the top, and as he did so, Michelle's thoughts turned to his leg and what had happened to him. From all that she had seen so far of him, he was a careful man, unyielding in his attention to detail. How then, barring something unforeseen, had he lost his leg to an accident?

She debated bringing the matter up. She didn't want to sound like a nosy tourist, but listening to him tell her about the world he lived in got the better of her. She cleared her throat. "Can I ask you a personal question?"

He shrugged. "Ask away?"

She glanced at his leg. "How did that happen? I know you said frostbite, but there's more to it than that, right?"

He looked away and was silent a moment. "You're right, it is a personal question."

"You don't have to answer."

"I know I don't." He paused again and considered her discerningly. Finally, he said, "But I will. Let's walk."

He waved her forward, telling her about a competitor guide named Frank Kincaid and how they'd had run-ins on the mountain over the years. But one thing was clear, he respected the man.

"So, Frank was involved with this woman, who was the mother of one of his clients?" Michelle said. "I didn't know family members came to base camps."

"Well, they don't, not as a rule, anyway. And yes, he was umm…between the sheets with her, so to speak. Anyway, the kid, who was a decent alpinist, was troubled upstairs," John said, poking a finger at his temple.

"Apparently, the kid's father had died on the mountain when he was a baby, and when he found out his father's body was still up there, he decided he wanted to get a peek at the old man. Not a good idea, going hunting up in the death zone, and definitely not a good idea when there's a fu…freaking storm barreling down on you.

"Anyway, base camp radioed up the weather had taken an abrupt turn. A blizzard was heading straight for the mountain. We were in the death zone. Not a good place."

"What's the death zone?"

"Anything above 27,000 feet. Up there, you have limited oxygen. Stay too long without supplemental oxygen and you're dead. And we were running low. So…there we were on the balcony, a small ledge on the mountain, switching out O2 and trying to get a bit of water and food down us, when Frank's sherpa radios down the kid's gone off line and is up on the ridge looking for something. The kid's mother goes nuts on the radio back at base camp as

Frank tries to talk him back down. When the kid doesn't answer, Frank throws his hands up, tells the kid he's gonna have his sherpa leave him there. The mother loses it and begs Frank to go up and get him."

"Oh my God. What did he do?"

"What do you think? He loves the woman, so he gears up and starts off. I think he's nuts. You don't go back up into the death zone trying to pick someone up. It's a death sentence. But off he goes."

"What did you do?" Michelle said, feeling like she already knew.

"What any good idiot would do. I went along with him. Seemed like a bad idea at the time, but what the hell, I didn't have anything better to do." He sighed. "Anyway, we found him and somehow got him off the ridge. Problem was the storm was raging down below and we were going to be walking right into the teeth of it. By the time we hit the balcony on the way down, it was barreling at eighty, ninety miles an hour with visibility near zero.

"So we dug in, exhausted, knowing we couldn't get much further down, praying we could weather the night. What I didn't know was that Frank had run his O2 down to almost nothing and had shut if off during the night, probably hoping it'd be enough to get me and the kid down to camp 4. When I woke and saw him lying there motionless, I figured he was dead, but I checked him anyways and the old bugger was still alive. So I shot him up with dexy. That seemed to work, but I knew it wouldn't last long. If we didn't get moving down the mountain, there'd be nothing left to do but leave him there."

John shook his head. "We were screwed every which way to Sunday. But, it was what it was, and I did what I had to."

"Which was?" Michelle said, and felt her eyes bulge at the thought of leaving someone to die.

"I stayed with him," John said. "I had the kid and I snuggle up tight to him to keep him from going hypothermic, and we prayed for a miracle. Six hours later, I looked up to see the tarp we'd covered ourselves with during the storm being pulled away, and in front of us stood Frank's sherpa and two of his team. They got us on our feet and we headed down. It wasn't 'til I got to camp 4 that I realized my leg had been exposed during the night, and the rest, as they say, is history."

Michelle came to a stop as John walked behind her and turned to him, seeing a man of principle and deep conviction. The casual way he spilled out his part in putting his life on the line to save not only the young climber who'd made a foolish decision, but also the life of a man he clearly stated he wasn't a fan of reminded her of Adam. Her husband had been like that, a man of service who wasn't interested in anything but doing the right thing.

At last she said, "I'm glad you made it back. I would hate to be here with anyone else but you."

He studied her as she stood before him, his gaze searching her as if he was wanting, needing to believe her.

Then he smiled and said, "Well, you're stuck with me, so I'm afraid you have little choice."

A little ways after they crested the top of the foothill they came to Tenki Manang, a vibrant little village of stone-built homes with flat roofs. Many of them bore rooftop staffs with narrow vertical banners waving in the wind. Bands of yellow, blue, red, green and white ascended the staffs. Michelle poled her way alongside John, who hadn't said a word since the telling of his story. But he was ever watchful of her, as if he was making his mind up about something. From all Michelle had seen and sensed so far from him, she had a good idea trust didn't come easy for him.

She took a drink from her CamelBak as she walked the zig-zagging trail and thought about what she'd said to him after he told her what happened on the mountain. At the time, her words had just spilled out, an outpouring of admiration for him and what he'd went through, but now the more she thought about it, the more she wondered if she felt more than just admiration. What was it about this brooding, solitary man that intrigued her? Yes, he was angry, but it was more than just losing his leg that stoked the silent rage inside him. And more importantly, why had she found herself wanting to be near him? She wasn't sure, were he to make an overture to her, to become more than just a guide that she might just go there.

And if she did, what then?

She felt a flash of heat come to her cheeks as the sudden thought coursed through her. It had been a long time since she'd felt the quickening of interest with a man. It startled her, and what was more, she couldn't say she minded the unexpected feeling.

At last she said, "Are we taking tea in the village?"

"That's my thought," John said. He glanced back at Vic and Dan who were bringing up the rear with Kembe. Vic was stumbling along with his head down.

"He doesn't look too good to me," Michelle said.

"To me, either," John answered. "So, how ya feeling?"

"Pretty good," Michelle said, taking out her camera. "What are those tall colorful banners called?"

"They're Tibetan dharchoks," John said. "You hungry?"

"I could eat a bite."

"Good," John said as he pulled his cellphone out and stepped away a few feet. Michelle brought her camera to her eye and as she snapped a few pictures of the village, she heard John tell Orsen to meet him and Kembe off to the side while the clients were having their tea and snacks. It didn't take a lot of smarts to know what the meeting was about. Vic. John was going to send him back. She scolded herself for not feeling bad about it.

After a short break in the village, the party moved back out onto the trail, having left the Marsyangi Valley. From then on, they would trek through another basin called the Jarsang Khola Valley. Once there, they came across the first snow cover on the trail. Michelle looked up into the bright blue dome of the world and gazed at the towering ice-laden massifs hemming in the valley. For a moment she was overwhelmed by the vast panorama. Not even her camera could take it all in or could it captivate the totality of how small and insignificant her presence was in this world.

Everything she had seen and read prior to going there had not prepared her for this moment. She dug her hiking pole into the snow and came to a stop. This was what her husband had yearned for, to be there with her, drinking in the majesty of the world they lived in. This was his dream, a dream that had been passed down to her, to celebrate what he could not. Suddenly, her throat tightened. It wasn't supposed to be this way. They were supposed to see this together and share the memories as they grew old.

Cam came beside her and stood. "Wow!"

"I know," Michelle muttered.

"And it gets better the farther we go."

Michelle couldn't imagine anything getting better than this as she stood between the giants reaching up for the sky. "Adam would've lost his heart here."

Cam nodded.

They were quiet a minute as trekkers from another party passed them by, some of them, bidding them a Namaste or a hello. More than a few stopped and aimed their smart phone cameras at the mountains. When they were alone again, Michelle looked down the trail to where Kembe was walking alongside Vic and Dan and then turned her gaze ahead toward Brian, who was poking along beside Scott.

It was time—time to let go of Adam. She reached inside her fleece and unclasped her husband's ID tag that hung around her neck. She hadn't intended to memorialize Adam here; she had intended to place his tags on the monument at Thorung La Pass, but this place, this heaven on Earth just felt right.

Cam looked at her with a puzzled expression as Michelle opened her hand, revealing the tags she'd worn every day since they'd lost him. "Adam's tags," Cam said.

Michelle stared down at them, felt the weight of them in her hand and the weight they bore on her heart. "I wasn't going to say anything about what I was going to do, but I think I owe it to you, to include you in on this."

Michelle felt Cam's gaze on her as she kissed the silver tag.

Good-bye honey, but not forever.

"Include me in what?" Cam said.

Michelle detected wariness in her sister-in-law's tone. She gathered her courage and looked up and said, "I'm going to bury Adam's tags here in this spot, a spot he would've loved. Will you help me make this gift to your brother? I know he would've wanted this."

Cam stared down at the tags in Michelle's hand a moment, then looked up. "I think so, too. Where do you want to put them?"

Michelle pointed to a waist-high stone monument with a dharchok on top a few yards away. "Over there, next to that shrine. That way he can see the whole valley and the mountains."

That night after supper in Yak Kharka, Michelle, Mark, Scott and Cam sat around in their coats playing crazy eights and drinking Nepalese wine. Sitting next to them was Nick, who was nursing a mug of ginger tea. Brian had since retired and so had the gym jocks. The conversation at the moment revolved around Dan having made the mistake of staring at a yak when they'd come into the settlement. Michelle could still see Dan leaping up onto one of the fieldstone walls as the beast came charging. At the time it hadn't been funny, but looking back on it from where they were sitting, they found it rather amusing. Even Dan had grinned about it afterward.

"Okay, deal the cards," Mark said to Cam above the banter. He'd just gotten beaten for the third time, and his competitive nature was showing up.

"I'm getting there," Cam said. "Keep your socks on."

Michelle picked up her hand after Cam dealt and saw three 8s. She suppressed a smile, feeling good about her chances of going out quickly. Mark frowned after looking at his cards and so did Scott. Cam pursed her lips as she went about organizing her hand. Scott laid the first card down and for the next couple of rounds, everyone followed suit until Mark ended up having to go to the deck and start drawing cards. He ended up with a fistful by the time he was able to change suit.

As the game went on, one of the sherpa porters came over and sat watching them play. She glanced over at the round-faced young man who was maybe in his mid-twenties. Bibek was his name and he was her porter.

As the cards fell on the pile, she could see the sherpa's sudden interest. She smiled at him. He'd been very attentive to her over the last couple of days during their meals, clearing her empty plates away and asking in his barely broken English if she wanted more to eat or drink.

She followed suit with the card Mark had laid on the discard pile and looked down at her remaining card. It was an eight.

"One card," she called out.

Groans went around the table. Scott played his card, then Cam. That left Mark to decide his card. The man eyed Michelle and knitted his heavy brow, picking between the two cards in his hand which one to play. At last, he laid his

426

ace of hearts over the ace of spades, changing the suit. Michelle grinned and laid her eight down.

"I'm out."

Cam rolled her eyes and tossed her cards onto the discard pile. "You are so lucky! Okay, I'm heading up to bed." She eyed Scott sidelong and got up—his cue to drop in later on, no doubt.

Michelle darted glances at Mark and Nick and saw knowing grins. Everyone knew what was going on. "Okay, see you in the morning. Don't let the bed bugs bite."

As Cam retreated toward the hallway, she raised a hand and waved.

They all looked on with smirks on their faces, except Scott, who for all intents and purposes, was clueless. Finally, Mark cleared his throat and sat back, giving Michelle the evil eye. "Well, I guess it's down to the three of us then. Okay, deal, Annie Oakley."

Michelle gathered the cards and as she went about shuffling, looked over at Bibek. "Hey, you want to sit in?" she said to him.

Bibek's dark brown eyes brightened and he nodded vigorously.

"Okay, Bibek, here's how you play."

She dealt a practice hand and they went a few rounds until he got the gist of it. When she was satisfied he had a good grasp of things, she collected the cards, shuffled and dealt. Twenty minutes later, Mark had a handful of cards and so did Scott. She had three left and Bibek was down to one. As she was sitting to Bibek's left, she was the one who had the responsibility to block him from going out, but she didn't have an eight, so that left things to chance. Mark laid down a ten of diamonds, which fortunately she had a ten of hearts to change the suit or she could follow the suit and hope Bibek's card was a club or a spade, unless of course he had an 8. She looked up from her cards and studied the young sherpa's poker face.

428

You sure catch on fast.

She chewed her lip and laid the ten down.

Bibek frowned and reached over, pulling her jacket sleeve up. "You have cards up there?" Everyone laughed as he sat back and reluctantly drew a card and then another and another. By the time he found a heart, he had a dozen cards in his hand and there were smiles all around. The game went on and again the sherpa got down to one card, and again Michelle blocked him from going out. By the time they'd gone through the deck four more times, Michelle had stymied Bibek two more times. He was clearly getting frustrated, albeit in a companionable way.

After a dozen more rounds, Michelle looked down at her hand. She had two cards: an eight and a deuce of spades. Bibek had a single card once again. It was her lay. Mark had played a nine of spades. If she used her 8 that would leave her to depend on the lay of cards on the next round, but if she played the deuce, she would be a sure winner. What to do? She looked at the young sherpa, who was leaning over the table, anxiously awaiting her decision, then played her eight.

Bibek shot his head back and squeezed his eyes shut. "You're killing me!"

Mark burst out with thundering laughter and Scott could barely contain himself from spitting a mouthful of wine all over the table. Nick was wrapping his hands around his chest laughing as well.

John, who was busy doing paperwork over in the corner of the room, looked up and came over. "What's so funny?" he said, casting his glance around at them.

Mark managed to bite down his laughter. "She just blocked Bibek for the fifth time."

"Oh," John said. Obviously he'd never played crazy eights. "Well, I'll leave you to it then."

As he started back to his table, Nick piped up, "How's the kid, Vic, doing?"

John turned and shook his head. "Not good."

"You gonna send him back down?" Mark added.

John pressed his lips together and nodded. "Yeah, with Orsen in the morning."

Nick said, "His buddy going with him, too?"

"No, he wants to stay on," John said and sighed. "Anyway, enjoy your game."

Michelle watched John walk back to his table with a slump in his shoulders. He hadn't made the decision lightly.

.

Chapter 17

Michelle

Yak Kharka - Thorung Pedi, Nepal – Oct. 12th – 13th

Another annoying headache woke Michelle up. She'd been dealing with them on and off over the last three days. She sat up in bed, rubbing her temples as light poured through the small window in her cell-like, plywood-clad room. She looked outside. It was a clear day in Yak Kharka, and from the eaves of a nearby stone-built teahouse, she spied a waving prayer flag banner. What was it John called it? Dharchok? Yes, that was it.

She pushed her heavy comforter aside and got up, feeling as if she hadn't slept at all. John had said this would be a common theme the higher they went. High altitude often disrupted sleep. She reached up to the windowsill and dragged her water bottle down. Uncapping it, she took a drink, dispelling the stale, dry taste in her mouth. She wanted a shower, and more importantly, to wash her hair, but that wasn't going to happen anytime soon. She snatched her deodorant out from her daypack and ran it under her arms then brushed her unruly hair. At least she wouldn't stink or look like she'd just got out of bed, not that it mattered to anyone. Certainly not to the guys; either that, or they wouldn't say.

Outside her room, she heard doors opening and shutting, and the voices of other trekkers getting about their business. She wondered if Cam was one of them and pricked her ears. But she couldn't tell. Besides, it was a little early for Cam to be getting about, now that she had a bed warmer to keep her company at night. Michelle smiled in spite of herself. Her best friend had returned to old habits. But Scott? Really? He had to be at least a dozen years younger than Cam, if not more. Not that it was any of her business. Cam was just being Cam and probably looked at it as just a fling and nothing more. Michelle was pretty sure Scott wasn't seeing it the same way. Should she say something?

She gathered her things and stuffed them into her sherpa bag, content to let the matter go and checked her cell phone for messages from back home.

Hey 'Chelle

Been thinking about ya and

hoping you're having a great time

over there. Everyone here says to

say hi. BTW Peter had to get into

your computer to look up

something. LOL We hope to have

it operational by the time you get

back. Stay safe over there and

keep sending pics back. They're

awesome.

Don

PS: Miss you bunches 🖤.

Michelle sighed. Peter! She shook her head and

popped a message back. What niggled her was the heart

emoji. She chewed her lip. She had tried not to send Don

any mixed signals before she came here, but obviously

she hadn't been successful. Or maybe she was just

overthinking things again like Cam always accused her

of. One thing was for sure; she'd have to put things to

rights with Don when she got back home before they got out of control.

She pocketed her phone, grabbed her toothpaste and brush and started for the door. When she opened it, Cam was just coming out of her room with Scott trailing behind. Michelle flipped them a smile. "Morning."

"Morning," Cam replied as Scott set her sherpa bag outside next to her door. Cam pulled her door shut. "Scott was just helping me with my bag. They're such a pain to get zipped up."

Of course they are.

"If you need help with yours, I'm sure Scott wouldn't mind."

"I'm not done packing mine yet and I'm sure Scott wants to get to breakfast," Michelle said, not wanting to put him out.

Scott shrugged. "It's no trouble at all."

They all stood looking at each other for a moment in the awkward silence. Finally, Cam smiled at Michelle and said, "Well, I'm heading down. See you there?"

"Yes, you will," Michelle answered and struck off down the hall to the bathroom. On the way, she ran into John who was busy stuffing his sleeping bag into his backpack.

He glanced up at her as she took in the black T-shirt hugging his broad shoulders and muscled chest. Up until now, she hadn't paid his tall, well-defined body much thought. She averted her gaze, bid him a good morning and ducked into the bathroom, hoping he hadn't gotten the idea she was checking him out. Except, she had to admit she didn't mind what she saw. With his hair pulled back into a ponytail and his strawberry blond beard having filled out, he reminded her of Greg

Allman, who she used to listen to all the time when she was in college.

When she went down to the dining area, she saw John sitting with Vic, Dan, Cam and Orsen over in the corner of the room. The two boys from L.A. looked glum. Vic was hunched over in his chair as John and Cam spoke quietly to him. A sherpa bag was sitting off to the side on the floor near them along with another bag that was being stuffed by Orsen and Dan with what appeared to be Vic's belongings.

To be honest, to one extent or another, everyone was dealing with headaches, restless sleep or lack there-of, and loss of appetite. "Vic's oxygen saturation is veering into dangerous territory," Cam had said the other night. "John and I agree, he needs to go down. Hopefully, he'll listen to us."

It appeared to Michelle they had finally gotten through to him. Again, she felt bad for Vic, but she reminded herself that a lot his problems were on him. Had he listened to John on the way up, he might not be heading back down. Then again, this could've happened to any one of them because as John noted, altitude didn't discriminate. You could do everything right, and still run into problems. Even Sir Ed, he said, had suffered from Acute Mountain Sickness, and this was after his historic ascent of Everest.

Michelle found a seat next to Mark and Nick. Scott and Brian sat at the next table. Scott was playing with his camera while Brian wrote in his journal. Scott looked up, shot her a lopsided smile, as if he'd gotten his hand caught in the cookie jar, and went back to what he was doing.

Don't worry, Scott. I'm not going to ruin things for you. I just hope you don't think anything will come of it with her. I love her to death, but she doesn't do the long-term exclusive thing.

Mark glanced over toward the quiet meeting being held in the corner as he forked a mouthful of fried potatoes. He washed them down with a slug of tea and said,

"Probably for the best. He's a hurting unit right now. Hopefully, Orsen gets him down okay."

"I hope so, too," Michelle said, grabbing a plate and spooning up a couple potatoes and some eggs. Kembe brought her a mug of tea and set it in front of her. She thanked him and reached into her pocket, taking out a bottle of Advil. Popping a couple of caplets, she downed them with a sip of tea. "Looks like a nice day out there. Sleep well?"

Mark nodded. "Not bad. Yourself?"

"Spotty. It's hard to get comfortable on those cots."

"Yeah, I know what you mean," Nick piped in. "How's the headache?"

"It's there," Michelle said. "And yours?"

"Ditto," Nick replied. He buttered his toast and took a bite. "I guess there's a big storm down south of us in India. Hudhud, they're calling it, 'an extremely severe cyclonic storm.' Winds over 185 km/h, flooding and power outages in some of the port cities. Over a hundred deaths already, they're saying. Good thing we're not down there."

"That's terrible," Michelle said, and forced a bite of potato down. "So, I guess we hang here today, or are we heading up to Ledar as planned?"

"John said it's up to us," Mark said. "It's only an hour and change there, and the views of the mountains are much better, but he didn't want to push anyone if they didn't want to go."

"Well, Ledar gets my votes," Nick said.

"Mine, too," Scott put in. "What about you, Brian?"

Brian looked up. "Sure, why not?"

The meeting over in the corner broke up and John came over with Cam. Dan hung back with his friend as Orsen zipped up Vic's sherpa bag and handed it over to Sherpa Porten.

"Okay, Vic's gonna head down with Orsen and Porten in a couple," John said. "He should be fine once he gets down. How's everyone feeling?" He eyed Michelle the longest. When everyone gave him the thumbs-up, he went on. "Good. So are we up to heading onto Ledar, or do ya want to hang out here?"

Everyone looked at each other, as if to confirm they were all on the same page, then Nick said, "Let's do it!"

"All right then. We'll head on up after breakfast. Get your gear ready when you're done with chow and set it out by your door for the boys."

They left the teahouse shortly after 9:00 a.m., joining in with the steady stream of trekkers heading up the trail. It was a cool but comfortable morning under a patchwork of puffy white clouds. A thick veil of mist was gathered around the upper flanks of the great snow-covered massifs and a blazing sun rained a fiery shower down on their shoulders. Michelle poled along with her feet crunching through the thin snow cover, passing by lowly yaks grazing out in the surrounding fields. The sound of their bells dinging and clinking serenaded her as she walked. The mountain air carried a faint whiff of dung along with the headiness of earth and stunted grasses poking their heads up out of the white landscape.

She turned to Cam, who was walking beside her. "So, he's gonna be okay, you think?"

"Once he's down in altitude, he should start feeling better," Cam said. "I noticed you and John are getting a little chummy."

"We talk. He's not as aloof as you think he is. In fact, he's really a pretty nice guy under all that swagger. And don't get any ideas. It's not going any further than chatting between us. Speaking of which, I see the way Scott looks at you. Be careful, Cam. Scott's a sweet guy, don't lead him on."

"What makes you think I'm leading him on? He's fun, and besides, what if I want it to be more?" Cam said, and stared back side-eyed.

"Uh-huh."

"What's that supposed to mean?" Cam said, titling her head.

"Nothing," Michelle answered, suddenly wishing she hadn't brought the subject up.

"What, I can't be serious with someone?" Cam pressed. Again the side-eye came back at Michelle.

"Not saying that at all," Michelle said. "It's just—"

"What?"

"Nothing."

"You mean he's too young for me. I do have him by a few years—"

"More than a few, Cam," Michelle said. "How old is he, mid-twenties?"

"Twenty-nine."

"Okay, fourteen. I guess it's not that bad, but seriously, what more could you be talking about? Dating, really?" Michelle said. "You live 5,000 kilometers away from him. You gonna fly back and forth to Arizona?"

"Maybe. Keeping my options open," Cam said flashing a crooked smile. She turned serious then. "Look, I know you've seen and heard this all before, but I like him. He's not like all the bozos I've dated. When he looks at me, he doesn't see my boobs or my ass, he sees me."

"Well, I have to agree with you there. So, what then?"

"I don't know. Just gonna have some fun."

"Right."

"What's wrong with that?" Cam said, furrowing her brow.

"Nothing."

"Right...nothing!" Cam said. "I don't see the problem here. Scott's well aware of the situation and has no expectations? We're here, halfway around the world, and you're sitting on the fence."

"Meaning?"

Cam rolled her eyes. "You could have any guy here you wanted. And I don't mean a roll in the hay either, although, I'd highly recommend it."

"Cam!"

"Oh please, 'Chelle," Cam said. "Relax, enjoy, have some fun for God's sake. You know, I see Nick looking at ya. I think he likes what he sees."

"I'll take it under advisement," Michelle said as John's face flashed before her.

"You do that," Cam said.

Michelle walked off the long cable-stayed suspension bridge crossing a deep gap between the dark brown and umber hills. As she brought the tube of her CamelBak to her lips for a drink, she stopped and regarded the view ahead. Rising from behind the hills was a towering white-capped mountain reaching for a fading blue sky. In the distance, she saw the trace of a village, small wood and stone-clad buildings blending into the vast brown landscape so much that they were barely discernable.

Kembe walked up beside her and nodded toward the mountain. "Annapurna. Take picture maybe?"

Michelle took her camera out, handed the sherpa her poles. "How about I get a photo of you in front of it?"

Kembe shrugged abashedly, but when she vigorously waved him on, he walked ahead, finding a broad flat-topped boulder a little off the trail. As he scrambled up on top of it, Michelle looked back at her party who were strung out along the track. John was walking ahead with Nick, Scott and Cam poled along several meters behind them and Brian was just coming over the bridge. Nick was bringing up the rear with Dan. She turned back to Kembe who stood at ease on the rock and struck off toward him. "You look like the King of the Mountain," she quipped as she snapped his picture.

The sherpa smiled back, then hopped down. "How 'bout I take picture of you?"

Michelle shrugged. She wasn't a fan of having her picture taken, but why not. She handed him the camera and he helped her up onto the rock as Brian came parallel to them on the trail. The young man from Portland glanced their way as Kembe snapped away on her camera. She waved to Brian and caught his attention. They'd had a few friendly words this morning since leaving Yak Kharkha.

"Hey, Brian. You want a pic of you?"

Brian stopped walking, looked over and paused a minute before answering. "Yeah, sure."

Michelle climbed down from the boulder and waited while the redhead made his way over to them. "It's quite a view, isn't it?" she said to him as he set his poles against the rock. She watched him take in the vast deep cleft of the valley before them as if he was committing it to memory.

At last he said, "Yeah, it is." He swung a leg up and heaved his thin body onto the rock, standing with his back to her and facing the mountain.

"Oh, that's perfect," Michelle said, and snapped his picture. "You look like you're contemplating your next great adventure. Okay, turn around and I'll get another one so the folks back home can see you."

When he turned, his face was tight and his expression somber.

"Come on, smile!" Michelle said.

At last, Brian turned his lips up, but it felt forced to her as she took the shot. She didn't get it. Here he was, living the dream, and yet he looked like he was lost—sad almost. What was going on with him, she wondered as he jumped back to the ground? When he landed, he lost his balance and Kembe snatched his arm to keep him from falling. As he did so, Brian grimaced.

"Are you okay?" Michelle said as he straightened up.

"Yeah...just a twinge in my arm. Old football injury...nothing to worry about," Brian said as he flexed his hands, opening and closing them.

Why don't I believe him? Michelle thought as the memory of his flexing his arms and legs a few days ago flashed before her. In fact, now that she thought about it, he'd been doing this flexing a lot. And then there was the medication she'd seen him take in Jagat, and had continued to take on the trail when he thought no one was watching him. He'd told her it was just for allergies, but questions were running around in her mind.

What could she say, though? She was pretty sure he wouldn't appreciate her cornering him, trying to get him to talk. And going to Cam and telling her what she saw would only provoke her best friend to go and ask him questions, because that's what Cam would do. No, not until she was absolutely sure, was she going to say anything. In the meantime, she was going to keep a wary eye on him.

The party filed into the small village of Ledar. The tiny outpost village sat on a prominent knoll overlooking the deep cleft in the valley and mountains beyond. The Ledar Guest House was a quaint two-story wood-framed building with a sloping tin roof and broad fixed windows facing the panoramic view. A modest rooftop terrace snuggled up one side of the second story with plastic tables and chairs scattered about.

Michelle opened the front door, entered into the sunlit dining room and tossed her pack on a pile of others huddling around a potbelly stove. The spacious room was vacant, save for their party and their sherpa porters, who were sitting at the far end of the room apart from the rest. She spied Bibek pointing to playing cards he'd laid out on the table before his friends. She smiled. He was teaching them crazy eights.

Cam and Scott looked her way as she came beside them. "What a beautiful walk that was," Michelle said pulling her buff down around her neck. She pulled a chair out and draped her jacket over the back of it. Across from her, Dan sat with his back against the wall and a little way down from him was Brian, who was digging through his daypack. She watched the rail-thin redhead from the corner of her eye pull a medicine bottle out and pop a pill.

"Outstanding!" Scott said and turned to Michelle. "Can't wait 'til the sun gets behind the hills. Join me later on with your camera and I'll show you how to get the most out of it."

Cam said, "Just make sure that camera of yours isn't pointed at me, mister."

Scott frowned, than glanced at Michelle. "She says cameras make her look fat. I call bullshit on that."

Michelle chuckled. "I agree."

"Says the woman who refused to sit for class pictures," Cam said.

"That was different," Michelle said. "I was fat."

Cam huffed. "You were never fat in your whole life." She took out her lip balm, ran it over her lips. "I need to find whatever they're calling a bathroom here. Be right back."

Michelle and Scott watched her walk away. "I know what you're thinking," Michelle said to him. "Don't go there."

"What, me?" Scott quipped as they took their seats.

Michelle groaned. "Yeah, you." She pulled a comb out and ran it through her hair, which she was sure looked like hell. As she did, she saw Dan typing on his phone. "You talking with Vic?" she said.

"Trying to. Service sucks up here."

"I'm sorry for your friend. It must be hard leaving him behind."

Dan shrugged, but his tightened lips betrayed him. "Shit happens."

"Well, I hope he'll be okay."

"Yeah, me, too," Dan said as Kembe brought mugs over to the table. Dan put his phone away. "Hey, you have any Advil?"

"Yeah, sure," Michelle said. She got up and went over to her pack as Mark and Nick came drifting in. The guys were talking shop back home in the States as they went past her, but the furtive glance she got from Nick made her wonder if Cam was right about him being interested. She dismissed the thought and bent down beside her pack.

As she unzipped its side pouch, John stepped beside her. She looked up at him. "I'm getting some Advil for Dan."

John darted a glance at the kid, then squatted down beside her. "Your key," he said handing it to her. "Room's upstairs, down the hall, first door on the right."

She took it from him and stuffed it in her pocket, unsure of how to read the look in his eyes. "It's quite a view out there."

"That it is," he said, gazing out the window. He turned back to her. A quiet, awkward moment followed, and as it passed, she sensed something bothering him behind the guarded mask he showed to the world. She'd seen that look before in her own bathroom mirror.

Something was troubling him. Finally, he brightened, cleared his throat and stood. "Well, gotta get the keys around."

"Right," Michelle said, and smiled. As he walked away, she watched him, wondering what it was about him that was drawing her to him. He wasn't like any man she'd ever been attracted to, had none of the gentle manners she looked for; not that she had a lot of boyfriends.

She got up, went back to the table and handed Dan the bottle of Advil as John went around handing out keys. When he was finished, he called everyone's attention.

"Tomorrow is a big day, people," he said. "We make for Thorung La High Camp, so I want to go over a few things while we're all together. First of all, the views you're going to have on this leg of the Circuit are out of this world, so take your time and enjoy them. Few people have the pleasure of seeing what you're about to experience over the next two days. But in order to enjoy them, you need to take care of yourself and listen to your body. As you know, I've been harping on all of you about staying hydrated; well it goes double for tomorrow," he said eying Dan. "We have a 750 meter elevation gain ahead of us, meaning we'll be ending up at about 5,000 meters or about 16K above sea level. I'm not going to lie to you. Some of you are going to be miserable for the next forty-eight hours, but you can go a long way in making it less so if you carb up and drink as much as you can as we go. Also, get a good night's sleep tonight. We'll be leaving bright and early. 5:30 a.m.! Set your alarms. Don't make me come knocking on your doors. I'm a grumpy man in the morning."

That earned a few chuckles from Michelle and Nick. Scott, Cam and Mark grinned. Brian and Dan looked on impassively.

"Also, I know we've had warm weather so far, and I get it that you might be thinking of packing your parkas in your sherpa bags. Don't go there. Seriously, people! The weather up here, as I've said time and again, can change in a heartbeat. Don't get caught with your shorts down."

Cam and Scott exchanged furtive glances.

Michelle rolled her eyes. *Really?*

"One last thing," John said. He cast his glance at Michelle and then at Dan. "We're short one guide here, so I'd like to keep us from getting too far strung out on the trail tomorrow. That means we're only going to go as fast as the slowest person. Enjoy your lunch. I'll be around to check on everybody afterward."

That night, they all sat around the potbelly stove warming their hands and feet. Michelle yawned, pulled out her camera and scrolled through the photos she'd taken of the mountains with Scott's help. He really knew his way around a camera, too, and the things he showed her about light and shadow, and f-stops brought a whole new depth to the shots she'd taken.

"That's a nice photo," John said as he passed behind her.

She turned around. "Thanks. I'm learning all these new things about photography I never knew before." She brought her camera to her face and focused it on him. In the soft, golden light raining down from the overhead lamps, his long, bearded face and straggled blond hair gave him the look of a rugged frontier man living off the land.

He let her take the picture, then headed for the door and went outside. Through the window, Michelle saw him gazing out into the black of night. She set her camera down and got up. Maybe it was intrusive, but she felt compelled to join him.

"Where ya going?" Cam said.

"Just outside. Thought I'd take in the stars." Michelle said, as a troop of trekkers came rambling in. Germans from Munich. One of them had a guitar strapped over his back.

Cam nodded and went back to talking with Mark and Scott as the troop settled in.

Michelle let herself out the door and stood under the canvas of night not far away from John. He glanced back at her from where he stood at the edge of the stone terrace.

"Getting a bit crowded in there for you?"

"A little," Michelle fibbed. She listened to the sounds of yak bells dinging in the distance. "I'm not crowding you, am I?"

"No, not at all," John said.

She drifted his way and stood beside him. "Not a lot of stars out tonight."

"No. Clouds are gathering. Might get a bit of snow by morning. So, you ready for tomorrow?"

"Yeah, I'm looking forward to it," Michelle said looking out at the half moon cresting the veiled mountains beyond.

"Good."

"You're worried about me, aren't you? I saw the way you looked at me earlier when you were going over things…things about going only as fast as the slowest."

John shook his head. "You'll be fine. It's Dan I'm concerned about. I'd hoped he would have gone back down with his buddy, Vic, but he wanted to stay on. Guess I can't blame him. Trip like this doesn't come along every day for most people."

Michelle nodded. "You didn't care for either of them, did you?"

"Not a fan, no. But they paid to be here, and it's my job to give them what they came for."

"A job you're not fond of."

John side-eyed her. "If you mean I'd rather be on Everest, then you'd be right. But this isn't all that bad a gig." He rubbed his hands together. "Land's nice and the company's not all that bad."

"Oh, gee, thanks," Michelle said, tagging him on the arm.

John chuckled. "You know what I meant." He was quiet a minute, then added, "Have you decided if you're going to take that partnership yet?"

"Tell you the truth, I haven't thought much about it. My boss...he's hinting at more than just a business partnership."

"I see, and you're not interested in that, I assume?"

"No. I mean, I like him a lot...more than like. He was there for me big time when my husband died. Gave me all the time off I needed, looked after me, and all. But as far as anything more than friendship; I just don't feel it. Besides, I have an aging father in Ottawa who would love to have me close by."

"What's keeping you from going?"

Michelle glanced up at him. "My husband and mother. They're both buried in Cornwall and...well, I just haven't had the heart to leave them. Does that sound weird?"

"You're asking the wrong person. I have no idea what normal looks like."

"Neither do I," Michelle said as the sound of singing erupted inside the guesthouse. "Can I ask you a personal question?"

"Another one?" John quipped. "Go ahead."

Michelle tried to frame the question in her mind so she didn't sound like she was a therapist. "Are you upset about something?"

He bent his gaze on her. "What do you mean?"

"I don't know. You just feel angry to me." When he furrowed his brow, she sucked a breath. "I'm sorry, I probably shouldn't have said that...I should go."

But as she turned to go back in, he gently grabbed her arm. "No, stay, it's okay. And you're right. You ever try to do the right thing, and when you do, the world shits on you?"

She nodded. "At times, yes."

"But hey, that's life, right?" He looked down at her. "You, of all people, should know that."

"I don't know about that, but I'm beginning to see that carrying the past around like a ball and chain hasn't worked out very well."

"You sound like Frank. I told you about him."

"Right."

"So, your past, what about it?"

Michelle was quiet as she considered what she should say. At last, she took a breath, steeled herself, and said, "I blame myself for my husband's death. I ran out of gas the morning he died. I called him to bail me out, and on the way, he was hit head on by a truck going the wrong way."

"But you couldn't have known..."

"No, I couldn't. But I kept thinking, if I'd only gotten gas the night before on my way home from work like I should've, none of it would've happened. But I was in too much of a hurry to go see the new camper we were going to buy." She shook her head. "Do you know that since that day, if my tank gets less than half full, I will go out of my way to find a gas station to fill up?"

John nodded.

"Anyway, I'm sure you don't want to hear any more of my ramblings."

"Your ramblings are just fine," John said and winced.

She reached out and touched his arm. "What? You okay?"

"Oh, it's my prosthetic. Rubs a bit on me after a long day on my feet."

"Well, why don't we get inside and put our feet up? By the sounds of it, they're having a pretty good time in there."

"It does seem that way." He darted a glance back toward the window where the Germans were leading a sing-a-long inside. He turned back to her and for a moment they stood face to face. Finally, he said, "Thanks."

"For what?"

"For the company and the talk."

"Soon enough, you'll want me to be shutting up," she said. He broke into a crooked smile then averted his gaze out over the moonlit hills that were silhouetted against the black of night.

Chapter 18

John

Near Phu Village, Nepal – Oct. 13ᵗʰ

John closed the door to his room behind him, shutting out the light coming from the hallway lantern. Ahead of him, soft pale moonlight poured in through the tiny window at the foot of his cot. Creeping through the deep shadows, he came to his cot and sat, looking out at a pale moon frosting the shoulders of Annapurna. The conversation he'd had with Michelle on the terrace and what followed when they went back inside was on his mind. He could still see her dancing around and singing with Cam like high school seniors at the prom. There was no pretense to her, no pity or judging in her eyes. She just accepted him as he was with seemingly no expectations. And then there was the way she'd looked at him on the terrace. Did she know what she was doing to him? How she was stripping away the veneer of indifference he'd shown to the world over the last twenty years?

He flopped back on the cot, planting his head on a lumpy pillow and looked up into the dim shadows streaking across the paneled ceiling. He'd had his share of hooking up with women over the years without a single thought of things going any further than a romp or two. It was safer that way for them. He liked his own company too much, and sooner or later, things would get messy. At least that's what he told himself. But now he wondered because he was pretty sure if Michelle were to live in his world, he would be hard pressed to walk away from her.

He let out a scornful laugh into the darkness. Once again, life was screwing with him. Nothing new there, except this time it was taunting him, dangling a woman in front of him who was good, a woman who'd gone through horrific loss and had come out the other side still intact. A woman who wasn't broken like him, a woman he could trust. She deserved a man who had a future, a man who could walk beside her. He was neither of those things. He was a dead end.

A pulsing, beep-beep-beep roused John. He sat up in the twilight lit room, groped for his cell phone and turned the alarm off. 5:30 a.m. flashed on the screen. For a moment, he stared into the inky darkness mindlessly, then finally flipped the heavy down comforter away. He hadn't slept well last night. He'd tossed and turned, ruminating on a decision he didn't want to make but knew was the right thing to do. Michelle deserved no less. And there it was—

doing the right thing. Always the right thing, even when you were getting screwed up the ass. But he'd never known any other way. Stand up, show up, and be counted on to do what's right had been drilled into him by his mother.

He reached over the side of the cot and dragged his pack and prosthetic up beside him as a tap came to his door.

"Yeah?"

"It's Kembe. Boys are all up and ready when clients have gear out."

"Right, I'll be right down," John said groping around in his pack. He pulled a tube out and slathered a handful of ointment on his stump. The limb ached, but it was what it was. He'd manage. What he didn't care for was Andersen's insistence of doing this huge 750-meter elevation gain in one day, especially with people who'd never hiked high altitude trails before. 500-meter gains were more than enough. He'd see how things went, and if he wasn't feeling the love with it, he'd duck his clients into one of the small mom and pop teahouses on the way.

He pulled the elastic sleeve of the prosthetic over his stump and ten minutes later, pushed through his door and went downstairs with his pack slung over his shoulder. The dining room was quiet when he tromped in. One of the teahouse staff was starting a fire in the potbellied stove. He set his pack down beside it and found a mug on the transaction counter at the end of the room. As he poured his morning tea, Michelle came in and dropped her pack beside his.

"Morning," she said hanging her jacket on the back of a chair.

"Morning it is," he said stirring a dollop of honey into his tea. As she joined him, he tried to ignore her smile and the deep brown eyes looking back at him. "Your gear out by the door?"

"Yep, all ready to go. How'd you sleep?"

"Good, and you?"

She yawned as she pulled a mug off the counter and poured tea. "Not bad. Last night was fun."

"Yes, it was." He sucked a gulp of tea then cleared his throat. "Well, I got to get around here."

"You're not eating?"

He smiled. "Already did."

She glanced around the empty room and eyed him doubtfully.

"I grabbed a bite in the kitchen," he lied. "They'll be bringing out breakfast in a few. Eat up." He went over, grabbed his pack and marched outside, looking for something to do, anything to put some space between them.

An hour and a half later, he led his clients out on the trail under a brooding sky. He took the lead, leaving Kembe to bring up the rear with Michelle and Dan. As they filed out of the tiny outpost into the vast barren land of rock and stone, snow and ice, John's thoughts drifted toward the future. It didn't look bright. If he couldn't convince the mucky-mucks at Andersen to get him off the Circuit, all his hopes to get back on the mountain would melt away like a spring thaw. And then what? Go home, and do what? Working a dead-end job at some bar or whatever? The alternative was ending up to be a glorified tour guide, a has-been. Irrelevant or worse yet, looked upon with pity! He didn't know which was worse.

He ruminated about that as he walked along, content to be by himself until eventually his thoughts gave up and he was left to deal with the trail before him. He glanced back at his clients as he trod up the long, steep, snow-covered slope. They were strung out more than he would've liked, but not enough to worry about. Another group of trekkers was moving up behind them at a fair clip. It wasn't long before they were passing him. He eyed them as they went by in their shorts and lightweight jackets and shook his head.

Idiots!

But that wasn't any of his business. He put his face to the soft buffeting wind and strode on in no great hurry, picking his steps on the snow-dusted trail. An hour and change later, he came to the top of the crest and a short time later, gathered his clients for a well-deserved break in front of the long cable-stayed bridge over the Kone Khola river.

Mark and Nick, who were standing beside him, looked up as a gust of wind strafed their collars. "Looks like we got a bit of snow in the air," Nick said.

John looked up as well. Tiny flakes were swirling and dancing in the air. He pulled his buff up and tied it back around his head then cast his gaze around his circle of clients. They were winded, but no one seemed the worse for what they'd just gone through. He gave them fifteen minutes to catch their breath, get a good drink from their CamelBaks and then struck off over the bridge, with Mark and Nick tagging along close behind.

As he stepped onto the riverbank on the other side, Mark spoke up behind him. "So, John…how long have you been here in Nepal?"

John shrugged. "Twenty years, give or take."

"And you live here permanently?"

"I do," John said starting off on the trail.

The two men joined him side by side. After a moment, Nick piped up. "Don't you miss the states?"

John shook his head. "Not really. Especially with the bullshit I hear coming out of Washington."

"I hear that," Nick said.

Mark chuckled, then said, "But don't you have family back in…Denver, is it?"

"Oak Creek, and I do. We're just not all that close," John said, not at all interested in discussing his family. "What about you guys? You said you both travel a lot?"

"I do, but I still get home every weekend," Mark said.

"For me, not so much," Nick put in. "Then again, I'm divorced and the kids are away in college." He paused and from the corner his eye, John saw Nick look his way. "Gets lonely sometimes though. Don't you ever feel untied? I mean, doing this job. You never really get to know anybody, do ya?"

John considered the man and paused. Nick was right. In all the years he'd been in Nepal, he had maybe a handful of people he considered friends, if that's what they were. Mick was certainly at the top of the list. Then there was Frank. He didn't know what Frank was; only that the man had become part of his world. At last he said, "Sometimes, that's a good thing. Keeps life simple, easy to manage."

"Maybe, but you end up alone at the end, I think?"

And there it was—alone at the end. He pushed the sobering thought away and said, "So, you an Ohio State football fan? You live in Columbus, right?"

"Not so much football. I do like basketball though. We went to the Final Four last year," Nick said as the falling snowflakes kissed their faces. He was quiet a minute as they walked, then said, "Sure is pretty up here."

"You got that right," Mark echoed and the conversation came to an end.

As John walked, Scott and Cam's voices coming from behind kept him company. At the moment they were trading family stories and laughing. In the beginning, he'd pegged Cam as a type-A diva with lots of attitude but over the last ten days, he saw a woman who lived in the moment, enjoying life with no apologies. He could appreciate that. Once, he felt the same way. What perplexed him was her choice of men to take up with. He would've figured someone older like Nick or Mark, not Scott who was a dozen years her junior. But again, that was none of his business.

The snow-covered trail stretched on and upward toward the great massifs beyond and as they walked, the banter died altogether and was replaced by the snow crunching under their feet. An hour later, the light falling snow had turned into a steady flurry and the air was growing cold. John looked up at the slate gray sky covering the land and got an uneasy feeling. They still had a good slog ahead to High Camp and if the weather worsened, things could become dicey.

Nick, who had moved ahead of him, stopped and tucked his hiking poles under his armpit. After taking a slug of water from his camel back, he said, "It's starting to really come down."

John looked back over his shoulder, checking on his clients. Cam and Scott had pulled their hoods up over their heads and were trudging along. Brian, who was behind them, had pulled his buff up around his head and was leaning into the soft gusting wind. Michelle, Dan and Kembe had their hoods up as well and were slogging along.

He checked his watch and did an approximate calculation of where they were on the trail. They'd been hiking the last five and a half hours. If the weather continued as it was, they wouldn't make High Camp at Thorung Pedi for another three or four hours, if that.

He shimmied his pack up on his shoulders and trudged ahead, anxious to get out of the elements that were quickly deteriorating.

An hour later, John and his party were in their parkas as the snow came punching down at them. Visibility was near zero. John turned around and squinted into the raging snowstorm, watching his weary clients struggle along through the drifting snow that was up to their knees. The trail was gone, buried by the accumulating white stuff falling from the sky like confetti in a ticker-tape parade. As they came and joined him, he took stock of them. Their faces were wind-burnt from the frigid, blustering wind. Kembe stared back at him. The sherpa knew they were in trouble.

Nick stabbed his hiking pole into the snow and looked into the whiteout. "How much further?"

John turned and studied the vanishing landscape, trying to gauge how far they had to go as the mountaineer in him kicked in. At last, he pushed his buff away from his mouth and said, "Not far." Which was a lie. He had no idea, but he had to keep them moving or they could all end up in deep trouble. He worried most about Michelle as he pulled his buff back up. She was stamping her feet and blowing into her gloves. She hadn't signed on for this shit. Finally, he turned back into the blustering snow-pocked wind, bent his shoulders into it and started ahead, ignoring the growing ache around his stump.

What he needed was a landmark, anything to give him a clue of where they were. But the white world ahead shrouded everything. He gritted his teeth as he plowed through the deepening snow and as he did so, the memory of the storm on Everest three years ago came roaring back. Although this wasn't Everest and his reasons for being here were not the same, the mess he was in wasn't lost on him. It was happening all over again! He was snake-bit.

Suddenly, behind him he heard Cam call out. He turned around and saw her pointing toward a deep blue speck in a drift.

"There's someone over there," she cried and slogged off the trail toward it.

Everyone stopped and looked on as she waded through the snowdrifts.

John didn't need to see whoever it was to know they were a lost cause. He sighed, knowing he was going to have to make a wretched decision that would not be accepted by anyone, least of all, Michelle, and he hated himself for it. He had a responsibility to her and to all of them to keep them alive. He walked out to the poor soul who had lost his or her way.

As he came beside Cam, he saw a woman curled up in the snow. Her ice-frosted nylon jacket was unzipped and her face was bright red. The woman was shivering and her breathing was labored. She was one of the women who was part of the group that had passed them by earlier, the group who was improperly dressed. Cam took her glove off and put her hand to the woman's neck, then looked up at John.

"She's going hypothermic. We've got to get her inside somewhere," Cam said as Michelle and the others gathered around them

John bent down beside Cam, chewed his lip and said, "I'm sorry, but—"

"You're not suggesting we leave her here, seriously?" Cam said, narrowing her eyes on him.

"There's nothing to be done," he said, and coughed. "I know it sounds cruel, but—"

"But nothing. I'm not leaving someone here to die!"

John closed his eyes. "Yes…we have to! I can't risk your life or the lives of this party for her, I'm sorry."

Cam looked down at the woman, as Michelle and the other's looked on wearily. "I'm not leaving her."

"Then you will die along with her. Is that what you want, because that's what'll happen." He paused, looked off into the storm raging about them then turned back.

"You think I like this? I don't! I hate it! But it's the way it is, and I'm not going to let you throw your life away needlessly."

He glanced at Michelle as he sucked a deep breath of the suffocating, frigid snow-filled air, then looked back at Mark and Scott and finally to Nick. They bowed their heads as they poked their hiking poles into the accumulating snow. At length, Michelle stepped forward. "I know you think what you're doing is right, but leaving her here to die, that's not you, at least not the man I believe you are."

John looked off to Kembe, whose dark, watchful eyes peered over his buff-wrapped face. As he considered Michelle's plea, he got up and went and pulled the sherpa aside. "Any idea where the hell we are?"

Kembe looked off and panned the shifting white landscape as John looked on with him. Then suddenly, the sherpa stirred and pointed to a faint dark dot some ways ahead."

A trail marker at last!

Kembe said, "I'll go check it out. Be right back." The sherpa turned aside and hastened for it.

"Well, are you going to help or not?" Cam said.

John turned back to her, then glanced at Michelle. "Screw it," he muttered. He shed his pack and gloves and took off his parka. "Here, put it around her."

Michelle gasped. "John!"

He ignored her, though, and went about digging his sleeping bag out of his pack. As he pulled it out of its compression bag, he said, "We'll get her into this."

Cam didn't need to be told twice. She turned to the dazed and dull-eyed woman. "Hey, hey, you're gonna be okay, but you need to help us here. Can you do that?"

The woman's eyelids flickered. Whether she understood Cam, John didn't know. He handed the sleeping bag to Cam as Michelle stepped beside him, stabbing her poles in the snow. When he got to his feet, she put her arms around him, rubbing his back and chest. He looked down at her as Mark and Scott joined Cam and unrolled the bag beside the woman. As they got the woman into it, Kembe came tramping back.

He blew into his hands and pointed back the way he came. "We not far from shepherd house. Maybe thirty minutes."

John shivered and rubbed his hands together as snow gathered on his fleece. "Okay, get Dan, Brian and Michelle to it and we'll be right along."

"I'm not going anywhere," Michelle said.

John stared back into defiant brown eyes. "Go!"

"No!" She fired back. "I'm not leaving without you."

John sighed. He was too tired and cold to argue. "Fine." He turned to Kembe. "Go on."

"Okay," Kembe said. "Here, you want my coat?"

"No, I'm good," John lied putting his gloves back on.

The sherpa eyed him doubtfully then turned away and led the kids off as Mark, Scott and Cam zipped the bag around the woman.

Mark got to his feet and handed John his parka back. "If you can clear a path for me, I'll carry her."

John hadn't expected to get his jacket back, but he trusted Cam knew what she was doing, so he went with it. As Michelle helped him back into his coat, he said, "That we can do."

John poled his way up the slope, following Kembe's tracks, and as he went, he stomped a narrow swath through the drifting snow, which Nick, Michelle, Scott and Cam widened as they followed behind him. The storm was now a blizzard comparable to any he'd ever seen on Everest. He came to a halt and squinted into the falling snow. Through it, he barely made out Mark's hulking body bringing up the rear. The giant of a man had his head down as he carried the woman they'd found over his shoulders like a sack of rice. Satisfied everyone was still with him, he turned back into the gusting, gritty wind lashing his face and stomped ahead, following Kembe's fading tracks until at last, he saw the muted dark outline of a lowly shelter.

Finally!

He turned and waved the others on and ten minutes later they were breathlessly pushing through the front door of the lantern-lit shepherd house.

John dropped his pack on the floor with a thunk and bent over, catching his breath as Michelle and Cam collapsed beside him. Mark pulled the woman off his shoulder and handed her over to Kembe as Nick and Scott shut the door behind them.

"I started a fire in the stove," Kembe said, as he carried the woman into the back room.

Mark blew out a deep breath and yanked his snow-caked hood off his head as Brian and Dan brought out old ragged, woolen blankets from the other room.

Cam sat on her heels and rocked back and forth, gasping, then yanked her gloves off. "Holy shit."

Scott sat beside her, blowing into his hands, then rubbed them over her arms and shoulders. He turned to John and stared back. As he did so, John could see the kid was scared, yet trying to be the man.

Finally, Cam got up. "I need to check on her. I don't suppose anyone has a thermometer on them."

"In Kembe's med pack," John said over his shoulder. He heard Cam rummage around in it. A moment later, she ducked into the other room with Scott trailing along like a puppy.

Michelle stretched her legs out in front of her on the floor. "I can't feel my legs."

John snuffed and slipped down beside her. "Here, let me take a look," he said rolling her pant legs up over her calves and removing her boots. He blew out a breath and put his hands around her legs, warming them. "You're just cold," he said. "Get over by the fire. Warm yourself up."

He put his hand out for the coverlet in Dan's hand. When Dan handed it to him, he draped the woolen wrap over her shoulders.

Mark said, "Well, that was fun."

John eyed him and smirked, knowing the big man was joking. "Right." He turned to Nick who was shucking snow off his parka. "How you doing?"

"I'll be better once I get some warmth into me." He panned the room and nodded toward the storage alcove. "What kinda things they keep in there?"

John unzipped his parka and pulled his buff over his head, "We'll take a look once we get our breath back."

Michelle said, "What's in those big burlap bags in the corner?"

"Dung. They use it for the stove," John said as it hissed beside him.

"Oh," Michelle said. She was quiet for a minute, then added, "I don't get it. How did she end up alone out there? I can't believe her trekking party just left her to die."

John shrugged. "My guess is they got strung out and she was last in line. They probably don't even know she's missing."

Cam came in with a couple large swathes of cloth and set them at the foot of the stove. "We need to get her warmed up. John, Kembe says there should be tea around here somewhere, and maybe some honey. Can you find them and put some water on to boil?"

"How is she?" Mark said.

Cam pressed her lips together. "We got her out of her wet clothes and back in the sleeping bag, but she's delirious and pretty cold, so not good. I think we got to her in time, though." She turned to Michelle and pointed to the large pieces of cloth lying at her feet. "'Chelle, can you get those warmed up for me and bring them in? Not too hot though, just nice and warm."

Michelle snuffed. "Anything else I can do?"

Cam shot John a furtive glance. He knew she understood they were in serious trouble. At last she said,

"Pray?" She turned and went back into the other room as he grabbed the head light out of his pack and put it on. He got to his feet and marched into the supply alcove. Clicking the light on, he panned the narrow beam of it over the stack of supplies stuffed onto the wooden shelves.

Sleeping bags...one, two, three...four of them...okay, better than nothing! What do we have here? Blankets, maybe six or seven more of those, couple lanterns, and oil, brushes. What's in this box; nippers, pliers, an awl, matches, a mallet? A bag of rice, potatoes, lentils, pots—kettle! Need that. And there you are...tea and, honey.

He scooped the bin off the shelf along with the kettle and a couple of mugs and went back out.

Nick held his cell phone up. "No signal."

"We'll just have to deal then. Keep checking though," he said, as he emptied his CamelBak into the kettle and set it on the stovetop to heat. He zipped his parka back up, went to the alcove and snatched a bucket.

Michelle looked up as he went for the door. "Where ya going?"

"Out. We're going to need water. Can you do the tea for Cam?" When she nodded, he pulled the door back and stepped into the blizzard. The white stuff was piling up and being sculpted into a sea of sprawling spiked drifts by the raging wind. He stared out into the blinding white and wondered if Orsen was caught in this shit storm as well. People were going to die today. He shook his head, scooped up a bucket of snow and went back inside to find Mark and Kembe digging around in the alcove, and hauling out sleeping bags and blankets. Nick was stoking the fire in the pot-bellied stove next to Michelle, who was up and warming cloths for Cam. Dan was going through the bin of potatoes, sorting the good from the bad. Brian was digging through his pack, looking for something.

He set the bucket of snow down and unzipped his parka. The room was warming up and smelled of dung smoke, but the warmth the stove was putting out was all that mattered. He eyed the two large burlap bags of dung chips. By morning one of them would be half empty. If they were pinned down another day and night by the storm, it would be empty. If they were pinned another day and night after that, they'd run out, and things would get cold, really cold. He banished the thought. Right now, the important thing was not to go into what-ifs.

Chapter 19

Michelle

Shepherd House – Oct. 13th – 14th

Michelle sat by Cam at the woman's bedside in the

lantern-lit bunkroom, watching her press warm compresses

on the woman's chest. The woman they'd rescued from the

snow lay still within her sleeping bag under the golden

spray of light shining down from the rafters. Cam sat back

on her heels, her brows knitted and expression grave as she

looked at the woman. Finally she said, "Well, this is all we can do for right now. Let's hope it's enough."

"You're doing your best," Michelle said, wanting to encourage her best friend.

Cam sighed. "I'm concerned she might have suffered neurological damage, and if she were to go into cardiac arrest, well...we'd be screwed. And there's something else." She glanced at Michelle and peeled back the flap of the sleeping bag, exposing the woman's arm. An ugly pale sheen went from the woman's fingers up past her wrist.

Michelle gasped. "Frostbite."

"Beyond frost bite. She's probably going to lose the hand." She reached over beside her and took up the mug of tea. "Warm this up for me. If she comes to again, I want to get some more of it down her."

Michelle took the mug and got up. "Hopefully she will, and we can find out who she is. You want some tea?"

Cam nodded. "Sure and find out where Scott is on warming up those compresses for me."

An hour later, the rooms had warmed up enough that their exhalations could no longer be seen as mist in the air. John had shucked his parka as had Mark, Kembe and Nick as they worked to make their shelter as accommodating as possible. Michelle stirred rice and cut up potatoes in the cooking pot as she watched them organize the supplies they'd pulled out of the alcove. Occasionally, John glanced her way, offering up a smile, as if to reassure her things were going to be all right.

Scott was peering out the small dust-covered window with Dan. Brian was standing beside them, taking inventory of various items stashed in a wood box John had placed on the built-in wood plank table. He pulled out a handful of metal dinner plates and as he did so, lost control of them, dropping them to the floor. John, Mark and Nick looked up from the far corner of the room where they were working on a little project Nick had come up with to get some heat from the stove into the bunkroom using scraps of sheet metal roofing left over from a former repair project.

"Sorry," Brian said, rubbing his hands together as if to warm them, but the way he was doing it, gave Michelle the distinct impression he was trying to wake them up. She set the ladle down and went to help him pick things up. "It's all right. I got 'em," he said, squatting down and waving her away. But when he reached out to grab a plate, his fingers trembled. He flexed his hands, making fists, then gathered up the fallen plates and placed them on the table. "Just the cold," he said shooting Michelle a crooked smile. "Think I'll put my gloves back on.

He stepped out of the room, leaving her to ponder what she'd seen. A minute later, after she went back to the pot, a tiny thunk hit the floor in the other room, followed by a shriek and curses. Everyone turned around and stared wide-eyed at the passage to the bunkroom. Michelle dropped the ladle and ran in, fearing something had happened to the woman they'd rescued, only to find Brian on his hands and knees, searching for something. Cam had turned around as Michelle and the others stood, looking down at the scattered pills across the floor and the prescription bottle on its side next to Cam's feet.

When Brian saw Cam pick it up and look at the label, he froze. She handed him back the bottle, and as she did so, Michelle got the sense Cam was bewildered by what she read. "Here, let me help," Cam said to Brian and joined him in gathering up the pills. When everyone except Michelle went back to what they were doing, she eyed the young redhead. "How long?"

Brian licked his lips as he folded his legs underneath him. "Almost a year."

Michelle's suspicions that Brian had a medical condition were confirmed and heightened.

Cam nodded. "You need to let me know if this happens again, understood?" She said, handing him her mug of tea. She watched him pop the pill and down it with a swig.

Michelle stayed quiet as Cam and her exchanged glances. Cam gave a subtle shake of the head. Not now. Whatever Brian had, it was serious.

The party ate their meager supper of rice and boiled potatoes seasoned with garlic as the storm continued its assault on their ramshackle shelter. Scott, Dan and Brian sat wearily beside Cam, playing cards next to the woman who had stirred briefly enough to tell them her name was Brenda. Nick, Mark, Kembe and John went back to working on Nick's improvised idea to spread more heat into the next room – something that looked like a funky metal duct that, as Nick explained, would spread the heat coming from the bottom of the stove to the bunkroom. Michelle didn't know if it would work, but she sure wasn't going to say anything. The project was giving people something to do to take their minds off what was going on outside. She scraped the dregs from the bottom of the pot into the stove and set the cast iron lid back into place. It was going to be a long night, but maybe when they woke up in the morning, it would all be over and they could get cell coverage and call for help. She fiercely held onto that thought, otherwise she'd spiral down to catastrophizing, which she was sure would do no one any good.

John sat back and rolled his neck. The man was dead tired. All of them were. She picked up the kettle and went over to him, and the guys.

"Can I get you refills?" she said as she glanced at the improvised duct, which Nick was just putting the finishing touches on.

John closed his eyes then opened them. "No, thanks."

"Me either," Nick added. "Okay, let's give this a whirl." He picked up the long L-shaped metal duct and went about attaching it to the stove.

Kembe shook his head.

Mark yawned and ran his hand through his hair. "I'm fried. I hope it works, but gotta tell ya, heat or not, it wouldn't make any difference to me. I could fall asleep standing up right now."

"Get to bed then," John said. "You, too, Kembe and Michelle."

"What about you?" Michelle said, as Kembe rolled his bag out on the floor near the stove.

"I'll be along, don't worry. Gonna help Nick finish this thing off here and stoke the stove before I head in. Oh, one last thing. I set up a can in the alcove over there in case anyone needs to go during the night," he said. "I know it's not pleasant, but it's what we got. There's a roll of TP in there, too, along with the bin Brian emptied earlier. Put the paper in the bin and keep it out of the bucket. Let the others in there know, okay?"

"Of course." She paused. "Hey, I just wanted to say, what you did out there today, that was good...and despite what you might be thinking…in the end, those things even out. I have to believe that, because if we live in a world where every good deed gets punished, it's not a world I want to live in. You're a good man, John. Don't let the bad things that have happened to you beat you down, and more importantly, don't ever stop being who you are, because if you do, the bad wins, and you're better than that."

She turned away and went into the other room. Cam looked up from where she sat on the floor next to Brenda. "Any change?"

Cam shook her head as Nick ducked out beside them.

"You should get some sleep," Michelle said. "I'll look after her for a while,"

"No, I'll be all right," Cam said.

Michelle glanced around the dim lantern-lit room. Brian and Dan were in their sleeping bags at the far end of the room with their backs to her. Mark was stretched out under a blanket with his long legs hanging over the end of the bed. He was already fast asleep and snoring. The other two bunks were empty with their bags open and waiting. Scott was lying on the floor in his sleeping bag nearby. His face was in shadow but Michelle could see him peering out at them. As he held Cam in his gaze, Michelle saw both adoration and awe in his dark blue eyes.

"Well, if you're awake, so am I," Michelle said to Cam. She folded her legs under her and as she sat, the headache she'd been too busy to pay attention to came slinking back.

"You okay? Cam said.

"Yeah, just a throbbing between the ears," Michelle said and reached in her pocket for her bottle of Advil. As Cam handed her a mug of tea, Michelle darted a glance at Brian. "So, what's going on with him?"

"I'm not sure I'm at liberty to say, 'Chelle."

Michelle downed the pills. "Is it that bad?"

"Bad enough. It's nothing imminent, but the sooner we all get out of here, the better," Cam said. As she took back the mug from Michelle, Brenda moaned. "She's back." Cam leaned forward over the woman. "Hey, Brenda, can you hear me? You're in a cabin with friends."

The woman's eyes fluttered open. "I…cold."

"I know," Cam said, taking her pulse. "You're gonna be okay."

"Where's Larry?"

"Is he your husband?" Cam said.

"My brother. He…he was behind me. I turned…turned around and he was gone. I went looking for him but I…I couldn't find him."

Cam glanced back at Michelle.

"Oh, my God, we must have walked right past him," Michelle said.

The howling wind roused Michelle out of restless sleep. She sat up in the cold dark and listened to it strafe the roof. The timbers creaked and whined as gust after gust slammed into the shepherd house. She wasn't the only one awake. In the other room, someone was stoking the stove. She unzipped her bag, slipped out of it and peeked around the corner. A soft, buttery, golden light from the lantern by Kembe's feet lit up his burnished round face. He looked over at her as he tossed dung chips in the stove.

"Hey," Michelle said just above a whisper. She grabbed her coat and padded in, careful to avoid the duct running on the floor Nick had fabricated.

He nodded, grabbed the cast iron poker off the shelf beside him and jabbed it into the mouth of the stove, stirring up the fire. At last he said, "You cannot sleep?"

"No," Michelle quietly said, and hugged her arms around herself. "It's really blowing out there."

"Yes, very bad storm. Worst I see." His gaze drifted to the window. "We be all right, though. You see."

Michelle followed his pensive gaze, and as she did so, saw John rolled up in his bag on the floor under the window. She thought about what she'd said to him, and it was true. He was a good man who'd just been beaten down by life. What those things were, besides the loss of his mother and his leg, she didn't know.

At last, she said, "Do you think people know what's going on up here?"

Kembe set the lid back on the stove. "Hō, they will come once storm lets up."

Michelle chewed on his answer a moment. "Brenda, the woman in there, she was looking for her brother when she got lost. I wonder how many others got lost. People are dying out there, aren't they?"

There was a long silence between them as the wind rattled the window. Finally, he said, "Maybe, hard to know."

Michelle looked at the sherpa, studying the deepening creases around his eyes and over his brow. "You're worried about your friend, Orsen, aren't you?"

Kembe set the poker down and glanced back at her. "He be okay."

She wasn't convinced he believed that, but she wasn't going to argue with him. She put her hands out toward the stove, warming them and said, "I suppose you're used to this kind of thing."

Kembe shrugged. "Way of life in mountains. You want I put on some tea or maybe you go back sleep?"

She snugged her coat around her. With the wind blowing, Mark's snoring and her headache, she knew sleep was impossible even though she was dead tired. "Tea would be nice."

Kembe set the kettle on the stove, plucked a mug off the shelf beside him and handed it to her. "Ginger or lemon?"

"Ginger, I think," Michelle said.

Kembe slipped around her and dug into the wooden bin sitting on the floor. As he rummaged through it for her tea, Cam poked her head around the corner. "Couldn't sleep, huh?"

Michelle shook her head.

"Me either," Cam said, drifting in with her coat on. "Damn, it's cold."

"Here, get by the stove. How's Brenda doing?"

"Sleeping at the moment," Cam said, stepping beside her. "I hope to hell we get out of here tomorrow. She needs more medical attention than I can give her here."

"Kembe seems to think people will be coming after the storm lets up."

"Good, let's hope it's sooner rather than later."

"Kembe looked up. "You want tea, too?"

"Sure, why not?" Cam said. She dipped her hand in her coat pocket and took out a bottle of Advil. "You want some?"

"If you don't mind." Cam tapped a couple caplets into her hand. "Well, this has been an experience, hasn't it? I don't think I'll ever complain about the snow we get back home again."

Cam popped her pills. "Ya think? I'll be glad to be back home."

"Me, too."

"Hey, I think something's wrong with Brian."

Cam and Michelle turned around and saw Dan standing in the pass-thru. Cam said, "What do you mean?"

"He's shaking like crazy."

"Oh, damn!" Cam said and ran past him.

Michelle followed along behind her with Kembe, bringing the lantern. Cam knelt down beside Brian, who was thrashing and convulsing in his bag.

"He's having a seizure," Cam cried over her shoulder as she rolled him on his side. When Michelle came beside her, Cam put her hand out barring her from coming any closer. "Don't touch him, 'Chelle. It'll pass. Look at your watch. I need to know how long this lasts."

As Michelle pulled her sleeve up around her watch, Scott and Mark stirred.

"What's going on? John said, suddenly behind them.

Michelle glanced over her shoulder. "Brian's having a seizure."

"Jesus," John said. "Is he gonna be all right?"

Cam kept her hand on Brian's shoulder to prevent him from flopping onto his back and looked back. "Hope so."

They all looked on, waiting for the storm to clear in Brian's head as the wind raged outside, slamming against the walls that shuddered under the unrelenting assault. Finally, the seizure let go of Brian and Michelle heard the release of everyone's collective breath.

John stepped up to Cam and stared down at Brian's still body. "What now?"

Cam turned Brian over. "Brian, do you know where you are?"

Brian blinked and stared out into space.

John kneeled down beside Cam and studied the boy's grimacing face. "He's got HACE."

"I don't think so," Cam said, and glanced at Michelle.

"Then what?" John said.

Cam chewed her lip and looked up. "He has MS."

Michelle gasped. "Oh my God. So the pills…"

"Yes. It's a drug called, Gilenya, a sensor activator in the lymph system, preventing your body from attacking the nervous system."

"MS?" John said, running his hand through his hair. "You got to be kidding me. Really? What's he doing here?"

"My guess is he wanted one last shot to see the world before it really takes hold of him," Cam said. She shook her head and Michelle saw pity in her eyes. "Can't say as I blame the boy." She got up and pulled people off to the side. "He should be all right once the aftershock passes, but I'll have to monitor him until then."

"So, he could have another one?" John said, glancing over to Brian. He rolled his eyes. "This just keeps getting better."

"John," Michelle said, placing her hand on his arm.

He met her imploring gaze. "Yeah, I know, I'm sorry. Okay, it is what it is."

Cam spoke up, "It's true, he may have another one, but my gut tells me this one came on because his body was overstressed by what he went through today, that and depending when he takes his meds, he may have missed his dose."

Mark eyed John and said, "My brother-in-law has epilepsy and with the right meds, it's pretty well controlled. What's the kid taking for it?"

"Not sure," Cam said. "I'll ask him later. For now, I'm gonna let him get some sleep."

"Which sounds like a really good idea," John echoed. "We're gonna have a really long day tomorrow if this storm doesn't let up."

Michelle was lying in her bunk, looking up at the rafters and contemplating all that had happened yesterday when a loud crack pierced her ears. She sat up along with Cam, Mark, Dan and Scott."

"What was that?"

Mark furrowed his brow and got up. Michelle slid out of her bag into the chill air and followed him into the other room. Kembe was up and peering out the window as John slept peacefully in his bag with his prosthetic lying beside him. Nick roused from sleep and pinned his elbow on the floor as he looked on. Suddenly, a deep rumbling vibrated through the floor, growing in intensity with every second. Kembe's body went rigid.

Michelle's breath caught. "What, Kembe?"

"Avalanche," he said. He turned his round face to them as his eyes bulged. "Everyone, get to the back room, now! Go, go, go!" he cried.

Mark's brow rose. "Oh shit!"

Nick scrambled out of his pack. Kembe shook John awake as the deafening thunder came steamrolling toward them. Michelle froze as the floor shook under her and watched John frantically fit his prosthetic to his leg.

He glanced her way. "Get in the other room, now!"

But her only thought was to help him, so she ran over and bent by his side.

"I said, get in the other room!"

"Not until you're on your feet!"

Kembe shouted, "Hurry! It coming."

The first wave slammed into the walls, shattering glass and shaking the building as Michelle helped John to his feet. Then another wave crashed in. Pots and pans flew off the shelves and table and the metal flue snapped off the stove, spraying gritty ash all around. As the house shuddered, the hanging lantern above them swayed back and forth, casting wild shadows across the room. Grit and dust rained down over their heads. Then everything went deathly quiet, save for their ragged breaths.

Finally, Michelle looked up and said, "Is it over?"

John stared up at the ceiling, his gaze sweeping over the wooden timbers and rafters. "Yeah, I think so."

Then all at once a loud crack pierced her ear and she looked up just as the timber snapped over their heads. Without thinking, she shoved John back as the world came crashing down on her.

Chapter 20

John

Shepherd House, Nepal – Oct. 14th

John shook his head, clearing the fog from his brain and looked up through a gaping hole in the roof to a muted gray sky. As his wits returned, he glanced around, confused, and saw roof debris scattered within a heavy pile of snow draped around the room. A sharp cough and a grunt pricked his ears. The last thing he remembered was Michelle, crying out and then bolting forward and shoving him.

Michelle!

He crawled on his hands and knees, felt a sharp stab dash up his arm as he got up. Kembe, Cam and Mark came rushing into the room. Nick was a few feet away, throwing off a section of roof planks lying across his chest. Scott and Dan stood gaping from the opening to the other room.

But where was Michelle?

He scrambled around through the fallen snow-covered timbers and torn roofing, tossing them aside in a frantic search as Mark and Kembe came beside him.

"Where is she?" John cried, his voice hoarse and alien to his ears.

Mark and Kembe dug in beside him and Cam, Nick and Scott joined in.

"There!" Cam said, pointing to an arm sticking out from under a large jagged section of torn roofing. John felt his body go rigid.

Oh, no…no, no, no!

Suddenly, her sacrifice came into razor sharp clarity and he threw himself onto the ground, tossing bits and pieces of broken timbers and roof planking off her in reckless abandon. A minute later, Michelle's still body lay in front of them, pinned down by a large framing timber.

Cam bent down beside Michelle, put her fingers to her neck, feeling for a pulse as John looked on, feeling more helpless than he'd ever felt in his whole life. The woman he'd once thought as timid and unsure of herself had saved his life. That was supposed to be him lying on the floor! He swallowed hard as he looked at the angry cut on her forehead and the nasty scrape on her cheek. She couldn't be dead. No! His throat tightened as his breath left him.

At last Cam said, "She's alive." She ran her hand through Michelle's hair and stopped at a spot just above the cut. Palpating the area, she turned back. "She's got a hell of a bump. I need a flashlight."

John let out a breath as Nick reached into his pocket and pulled a penlight out.

Cam grabbed it from him and checked Michelle's pupils. "Get me your med kit, Kembe."

"We gotta get that off of her," John said stepping over and straddling the timber pinning Michelle down.

"Stop!" Cam shouted, turning back as he grabbed ahold of it.

He blinked. "What?"

Cam pointed to the large splinter of wood stabbing through Michelle's down jacket. For a moment, John was confused at what he was looking at. "John," Cam said, rousing him. "We don't know if it's nicked an artery. If it has, and we remove it, she could bleed out."

"We can't leave it in there," John fired back as Kembe returned.

"Of course not," Cam replied, grabbing the med kit. She nodded toward the rest of the fallen timber. "Do we have anything here to cut that off from the rest of it?"

John tried to think, but his mind was a mess.

Kembe said, "Maybe. "Let me look. He tromped over the broken roofing to what was left of the supply alcove. A moment later, he came back with an old butcher knife. "It not much, but we try, yes?"

Cam looked up as Kembe kneeled beside John with the blade. "Hold on, wait! We need to stabilize this stake before you go hacking away. Anyone got a pocket knife on them?"

"I do," Scott said.

"Good, get down here beside me and put your hands around that, nice and tight to her jacket. Don't let the damned thing move, okay?"

Scott handed her his knife and wrapped his hands around the stake while she cut a large square of Michelle's jacket and undergarments away, exposing bare skin.

John watched as Cam checked the reddened area around the puncture wound.

At last Cam looked up, her expression guarded. "Okay, not a lot of blood around the penetration which may be good...or bad." She let out a breath, blowing a wisp of blond hair away from her face and nodded to Kembe, who held the butcher blade. "Nice and slow and steady."

Kembe put the blade to the base of the stake where it connected to the timber and drew back. Mark joined in with John and held the beam still. Five minutes later, the sherpa was no closer to making a dent in cutting through the connecting wood.

"It'll take forever to cut through it like this," John said.

Nick, who was looking on, said, "The blade needs to be serrated."

"I know that," John barked. "Wait, I saw a pair of nippers on one of the shelves. Maybe use them to notch the blade?"

"Good idea," Nick said. "Give it to me."

He took the knife and went to the alcove. Ten minutes later, he came back.

"Here, try it again," Nick said, holding the knife out to Kembe. He glanced at John. "Your hand, you're bleeding."

John looked down and saw a thin red line of blood running over the back of his hand. "It's nothing," he said, ignoring the pain running down his arm.

Cam sat back on her heels. "John, your sleeve...look at it."

He huffed. "We don't have time for this."

"Make time!"

Grudgingly, he peered down at a long rip in the sleeve. The fabric around the rip was slick and dark red.

"Take the damned jacket off," Cam demanded.

"Fine!" He unzipped his coat and as he pulled his arm out of the sleeve, another sharp stab took his breath away. Grimacing, he looked down at a long deep cut.

"Kembe, can you deal with that?" Cam said, eying John. She tossed the med kit to the sherpa.

Kembe nodded and gave the knife back to Nick.

As Kembe pulled John aside, Nick said, "Hopefully, this will work."

John watched the engineer from Columbus put the knife to the stake while Kembe tended to the cut on his arm.

As Nick worked the blade over the splintered piece, Mark put his large hands on the offending splinter above Scott's hands, making sure the stake piercing Michelle didn't wiggle around. For the next few minutes, Nick whittled away using the blade and nippers until finally the stake was freed from the roof beam.

"Good, good," Cam said. "Okay, now get that out of here."

Mark and Nick lifted the timber from Michelle and cast it aside as Cam had Scott continued to hold onto the jagged stake piercing Michelle's abdomen. Cam sat back on her heels, and John could see her thinking as Kembe wrapped his arm with gauze and taped it off.

"I see flakes in the air," Mark said.

John looked up through the hole in the roof. The sullen sky frowned overhead. *Wonderful!* "We need to get her into the other room."

"Wait!" Cam commanded.

"Now what?" John said as he scooted back over to Michelle.

"We can't just pick her up," Cam said. "We need something to put under her, a board or something, anything."

"Good luck with that," John said and waved his arm up at the open roof. "It's snowing again and it could turn into another blizzard any minute. She needs to be out of here, now!"

"What about putting a blanket or a tarp under her and using it like a litter?" Nick offered.

Cam panned her gaze around the debris strewn among the piles of gritty snow. "I guess."

John looked at Kembe. "What do we got here?"

Dan stepped up behind Cam. "Brian's thrashing around again."

"Shit! I don't have enough hands here," Cam said as Kembe went to the supply alcove. "Umm...roll him onto his side and make sure he doesn't hurt himself. If he doesn't stop soon, you come get me, okay?"

"Yeah...yeah." Dan said. He paused. "She gonna be all right?"

"If I have anything to say about it, yes," Cam said. "Now go!"

Kembe waved his hand at John and held up a large, ragged nylon tarp. "What you think?"

"It'll have to do," John said.

"Kembe, help me spread it out next to her," Cam said. When the tarp was lain, she went on, "Okay John... Scott, I want you both on the other side of her, and when I tell you to, I want you to carefully roll her onto her side, nice and easy and make sure that stake doesn't move. Mark and Kembe, take one end and we'll snug the tarp under her as they roll her onto her side."

They nodded and got in position as John and Scott bent down beside Michelle.

"Ready, one…two…three, and roll," Cam said.

As he rolled Michelle toward him, John bit his lip, hoping like hell he wasn't hurting Michelle while Cam, Mark and Kembe pushed the tarp under her.

"Okay, roll her back. Easy, easy," Cam said. She sat back on her heels and checked the stake piercing Michelle. "All right, let's get her into the other room." Cam got to her feet and motioned Mark and Scott to join her at the end of the tarp near Michelle's head. "Ready?"

When Mark and Scott nodded, they each lifted the end of the tarp, and slowly carried Michelle over the rubble into the other room. Once they had her out of the elements, Cam went back and grabbed the med kit. "I don't suppose you have any sutures or a needle in this goodie bag of yours?" she said eyeing John's pack and darting a glance at him.

John sighed.

"Thought so," Cam said.

"Wait a minute," Nick said. "They use nylon thread in sleeping bags. I bet we could snag a section or two from one of them if we're careful." He turned to Cam. "How much would you need?"

John could see Cam mulling over the suggestion a moment. Finally, she said, "Not a bad idea. All right...I'd settle for eight inches...but we need a needle. Anyone got one of those around?"

She didn't look hopeful and everyone was quiet for a moment. John put his finger up. "What about a hypo needle?"

"It's straight, though. I need something curved," Cam said, and drew out a shape in the air with her finger. "Wait a minute, you have a hypo needle?"

"Yeah. I keep a couple doses of dexy in my pack," John said. "Force of habit from my days on Everest. Better than nothing, though."

Cam sighed. "Well then, how do we attach the thread to the needle?" she said, reaching down and fishing the hypo needle out of the med kit and holding it up.

John thought a moment. "Thread it through the tunnel hole and crimp the end of the needle around the thread?"

"Easier said than done," Cam said and blew out a breath. She shook her head, and John could see her having doubts. Finally, she came to herself and poked around in the kit, pulling out a bottle of irrigation solution and a tube of antibiotic. An X-ACTO blade, Steri-Strips, latex gloves followed along with gauze, tape, scissors and alcohol. Finally, she said, "Okay, I guess I'll have to work with what I have. First thing we need are sponges." She picked up the roll of gauze and turned to John. "This won't be enough."

He knew she wasn't accusing him of wasting precious supplies, but he couldn't help feeling like a shit, knowing Kembe had spent most of the roll of gauze on his arm.

"How about a pair of our thermals?" Nick said.

Again, Cam mulled the idea over. At last, she sighed. "Those will have to do, I guess. Anyone have a pair they're not wearing?"

Everyone looked at each other. John said, "You can use mine."

"Are you sure?" Cam said, but John was already taking his jacket off. He stripped out of his fleece and pulled his upper thermals off.

"Now what?" he said.

Cam eyed him as if he'd lost his mind. "Okay, I need you to cut it into ten or fifteen six-inch squares." She turned to Kembe then. "Let's get something to put over her so she doesn't go hypothermic on us." To Nick, she said, "Do your thing with the nylon thread, and Mark, you help him, and see if you two can figure out a better way to thread this damned hypo. Oh, and one more thing, I need something for drainage and something to retract the wound."

"Like a hook," Nick said.

"Yeah, something like that, and something clean to set everything on," she said handing the hypo to Nick. She paused, then said, "And get some water to boiling, stat."

"Boiling water's a tall order," Mark said. "We lost the flue and if we build a fire, the place will fill up with smoke."

"Hello!" Cam said and pointed to the other room. "We have a hole in the roof in here."

"Oh, right," Mark said rolling his eyes.

"I'll get a pot," John put in, wrapping his thermal top around his neck.

"What do you want me to do?" Scott said.

"You stay right here by her. If she starts to come to, you keep her from moving around," Cam said. She bent down and checked Michelle's pulse again. "Let's hope she doesn't wake up while we're doing this. She won't be a happy camper." She paused. "Okay, I'm gonna check on Brian."

Scott looked up at her as she got to her feet. "You're leaving me here...alone?"

"Only for a moment," Cam said. "You'll be okay. I'm only a couple feet away."

John saw Scott nod, but the kid didn't look convinced. "Hey, Cam, why don't I switch with Scott?"

Cam shook her head. "He's got it, John. I need you to do what I asked, please."

John nodded, but he wanted to do more than just cut squares in his thermals and it was then that he realized he'd never be the same if he lost this woman who'd put her life on the line for him.

John kneeled beside Scott and Michelle as Cam studied the area around the stake. At last Cam looked up and called over her shoulder, "Nick, Mark, how we coming with things out there?"

"Almost done," Nick called out.

Kembe came over and set a slab of wood down by her side. "Maybe set things on this?"

Cam glanced down at it. "I guess." She set the items from the med kit on it along with the squares of blanket John had cut up. The fire Mark and Kembe had built in the other room hissed.

"John, check the water in the pot," Cam said. "It needs to be boiling."

He got to his feet and pulled back a tarp they'd used to close off the opening to the room with the collapsed roof. Snow was swirling and dancing in a whirlwind, accumulating around the corners. The fire hissed under the pot of boiling water. Gritty slush pooled around the fringes of the stove. He added more dung to the flames and came back. "Water's boiling," he said as a gust of cold air chased him in.

Nick and Mark stepped up next to Cam. Nick said, "Check this out and tell me what you think."

"Good. Set the tubing you cut from the CamelBak in it along with the X-ACTO blades and scissors," Cam said to John. "Okay, Nick, what did ya come up with?"

Nick bent down and handed her two small curved needles with the nylon thread dangling from them.

She looked them over carefully. "Not bad," she said, obviously impressed. "This isn't from the hypo. Where'd you come up with the wire?"

"It's the stems from my sunnies," Nick said. "I melted the plastic off the flared ends of 'em and crimped the metal around the nylon thread. Put a bit of a point on them, too."

"With what?" John said.

Nick pulled out his nail clippers and showed him a small file.

"Your sunglasses?" Cam said. "Huh. I never knew they made rims so thin."

"That's what $800 a pair gets ya," Nick said. "Anyway, I think it should hold, but just in case I made two of them."

"It's a little thicker than I'd like and looks a bit square, but I think it'll work," Cam said with the first smile John had seen since everything went to hell. "I think I like engineers. What about the retractors?"

Mark held up a pair of spoons they'd bent the handles back on.

"Super. Get them in the water," she said.

Suddenly Michelle moaned.

They all froze except Cam who moved around Scott next to Michelle's head. She shined Nick's penlight on Michelle's face. "Hey sweetie, we have a situation here, and I need you to stay still, okay?" To Scott she said, "Don't let her move. Put your hands on her shoulders, and hold tight. I'm depending on you."

"I'll do my best," Scott said.

"Do better." She went back to her place beside Michelle. "Okay, let's run through what's going to happen here. Depending how deep that wound goes, it could mean it hit her spleen. I won't be able to get to it if it did."

"What then?" John said as his breath ran away from him.

"I don't want to think about it," Cam said. "Now Mark, when I tell you to, I want you to slowly and steadily pull it up out of her, okay?" When the man nodded, she eyed each of them and went on. "After it's out, there may be a lot of blood and I don't need anyone panicking, understand? I'll take care of things." She paused and took a breath. "Okay, now once it's out, I'll need to do a little poking inside to make sure there's no bleeders. Hopefully it's a clean wound."

"And if not?" John said staring at her and having a hard time breathing.

Cam eyed him back. "Then we hope I can do something about it. Now, Nick, I'll need you here on my left next to the things I've laid out. When I ask for something, I need you to give it to me right away. Mark, Kembe, I'll need you to take hold of Michelle's legs and hold them tight."

"What about me?" John said.

"You'll be holding the light, and you shine it where I tell you. Once I've cleaned and checked the wound, I'll close her up. Nick, I need you to make sure to count the number of sponges I use and discard. I don't want to leave anything inside her."

"Right," Nick said.

"Okay, let's get this over with," Cam said, pulling on the pair of latex gloves. "John, get the tubing and the rest of the stuff out of the pot and set it on the board next to me."

John sucked a breath and got up. This was really going to happen. In the past he'd always prided himself in being calm and steady in difficult situations, but this went way beyond dealing with mountain sickness or frostbite. This was surgery in the middle of fucking nowhere in a shepherd house with a roof that had collapsed under an avalanche in the dead of a raging blizzard.

Give me one break, just one time here. Yeah, I'm talking to you up there!

He went out and fished the needles, tubing and cutting items from the water and brought them back to Cam. As he took the light, his hand trembled, spraying the light over the dimly lit room.

"She's going to be all right," Cam said to John.

He wanted to believe her as she sat on her heels and tilted her head back. At last, she came to herself, pulled her buff up over her nose and took the bottle of peroxide and doused the area around the wound. "Okay, Mark, just like we talked about; place your hand around that poker and pull up nice and slow and steady. Don't stop!"

Mark pressed his lips tight and lifted the stake inch by inch, and as he did so, blood pooled around the puncture wound.

"Sponge, Nick. Keep 'em coming," she said as Mark pulled the stake free of Michelle. A loud moan rasped from Michelle's lips and her body arched upward. "Hold her tight, damn it! I can't see. John, get the light over here…shine it right there. That's it. Another sponge, Nick…come on, hurry up, one more."

John watched the sponges soak up blood as Cam pushed them into the wound. She put her hand out and called for the X-ACTO blade. When Nick put it in her hand, she made an incision, opening the wound further. Dragging the sponges out, she called for the improvised retractors and slipped them under the skin.

"John, Nick, pull back on them, and John keep shining that light in so I can see what's going on." She dipped her finger into the wound and felt around. After a moment, she looked up. "I'm not feeling a bleeder. Pull back on the retractor a bit more. That's it, stop! Scott, can you check her pulse?"

John looked down into the exposed wound, felt himself get light-headed as bile trickled into his throat. He swallowed it down and summoned his resolve as Michelle jerked.

"Mark, Kembe, Scott, keep her still! Nick, sponge." She pushed it in with her finger and swabbed it around, then pulled it back out. "Okay, let's hope her spleen hasn't been nicked. What's her pulse, Scott?"

"One-twenty-eight, I think."

Cam turned her head to the side and paused, thinking. Finally, she said, "Shit, she's going into shock. I've done what I can." She glanced at Nick. "Tubing."

When Nick gave it to her, she inserted it. "Needle and suture."

Nick handed them to her and she held them up in the light.

"Here goes nothing. Nick, all the sponges out?"

"Yep."

"Okay, let's close her up. John, Nick, remove the retractors, nice and easy." She glanced at John then dipped the needle into the skin as he watched. Five minutes later, she backed the needle out and had Nick cut the thread away. "Let's hope Superman comes to the rescue and that holds 'til we can get her out of here"

As Cam bandaged the wound, John thought over all that had happened and all that was still uncertain. He peered up at Michelle's tight knitted face, seeing her grimace. If he could swap himself with her right now, he'd do it without a thought.

Chapter 21

Shepherd House – Oct. 14th - 15th

As night approached, the storm began to let up. John looked out through the tarp Kembe and Mark had draped across the pass-thru, surveying the wreckage in the other room. Half of the roof was gone and there was a section of the back wall that had come down with it. The issue right now was heat. With the stove out in the other room, all they had was their coats, blankets and sleeping bags. With Michelle and Brenda in their tenuous conditions, that spelled trouble. He pulled his phone out and looked for service. Still nothing. They couldn't hold out too much longer. He tapped Kembe on the shoulder and gestured Mark and Nick over.

"We need to get out of here soon before things get ugly," John whispered.

Kembe nodded. "I will go in the morning. Should be able to make Ledar by noon if storm is over," he whispered.

"I'll go with him," Mark added.

"Me too," Nick put in. "Less mouths to feed."

John looked up at the hole in the roof that was now the only way out of the house. It was going to be a trick getting up through it. "Okay. In the meantime, let's figure out a way for you to get out of here without bringing the rest of the roof down around our ears."

For the next hour, the four of them fashioned a raised platform out of broken timbers and plywood, using the built-in table against the interior wall and the stove as supports. With the roof just a little over seven feet and the height of the platform at three feet and change, they were left with something Mark could work with. He stood on it looking out over the snow swept world falling into shadow.

"Snow's up to the eaves. We're gonna need to carve a path out of here," he said hopping down. "I don't see how we can do it, though."

John panned his gaze over the broken debris and after he did so, he looked up to see Nick smiling. The man knew what he was thinking.

"Snow shoes," Nick said.

"Right," John agreed.

They sifted through the snow-laden piles and scavenged pieces of plywood as Mark went to work, cutting long swathes from an old blanket for bindings. By nightfall, they had three pairs of improvised shoes. John set them just outside the tarped-off pass-thru and gathered everyone around him.

"All right, here's what we're up against. It's gonna get cold tonight, so huddle together and use each other's body heat to keep as warm as you can." He eyed Dan and Brian. "Yes, that means guys need to get up close and personal with each other, so unless you want to freeze to death, put your pride aside and do it. Now, I'll be bunking with Mark and Nick will be with Kembe."

"I'll be with Michelle," Cam said.

Brenda, who'd been looking on as people were making choices, turned to her three choices and rasped, "I guess I'm with one of you young bovvers."

Scott glanced at Cam while Dan and Brian side-eyed each other.

"Well, don't all jump up at once," Brenda said.

"I'll bunk with ya," Scott said.

Cam winked at Scott, and flashed a grin at John.

John had to smile. "Well, that leaves Brian and you, Dan. Okay, the other thing is we've had to use the stove out there for a platform for Kembe, Mark and Nick to get out in the morning so they can go looking for help, so that means, raw potatoes tonight for dinner and whatever trail mix you might have squirreled away. Finally, if you have to go take care of business, do it before we bunk down for the night. And be careful not to ruin what we've spent the last three hours building out there."

The following morning came brisk and cold. John opened his eyes to the shards of bright light trickling in through the tarp walling off the outside world and found Mark's beard inches from his face. The fact that he slept all night with Mark's roaring right beside him was a testament to how tired he was. He cast a long look around the heavily shadowed room, holding his gaze on Michelle's cot the longest. The woman who'd saved his life lay still under the heavy covers he'd draped on her and Cam last night before he went to bed. The rest of them were still fast asleep, save for Kembe who was trying his cell.

"Still no service?" John muttered into the darkness,

The sherpa's head shook under the bright screen light spraying out onto his face.

John sighed. He'd sell his soul for just one break right now. At length, he jabbed an elbow into the Mark's side. "Time to get up, sleeping beauty."

Mark blinked. "What time is it?" he said, rubbing the sleep out of his eyes.

"Does it matter?" John said. "Come on, let's get around and see what we got out there." He peeled back the sleeping bag and groped around for his prosthetic as Mark sat up behind him. As he pulled the leg on and strapped himself into it, Nick stirred.

The four of them snuck out through the tarp to find a bright blue sky peering down through the ravaged roof. Tiny flecks of snow soared overhead, driven by the wind.

The men geared up as John bent down and filled their CamelBaks with the snow-melted water they'd scooped up the night before. He dropped a purification tab in each of their CamelBaks and counted what remained in his pouch. Sixteen left, meaning just under four gallons for seven people.

Nick tagged him on the shoulder. "You gonna be all right?"

"Gonna have to be," John said. "Okay, let's get you guys on your way."

Mark went first, by consensus, because they needed his strength to pull Kembe and Nick up through. The man raised his arms and leaned over the rim of the opening and as he did so, Nick grabbed his foot and gave him a boost through. The rafter underneath bent down and they all held their breath until Mark rolled away and it came back up. Mark tossed a braided rope they'd made out of one of the blankets down for Nick, who quickly scooted through. That left Kembe.

John eyed the sherpa. "Hey, you be careful out there."

"I will."

John put his hand out, and when Kembe took it, he said, "I'm not much on these kinds of things, but may Ganshe be with you."

The sherpa smiled. "It's Ganesh, and dhaniavaad."

"Right. Okay, off you go."

The sherpa perched himself on the platform as the rope came down. John gave him the thumbs-up, and a minute later he was on the other side.

So far so good. Let's hope these snow shoes work.

He fetched them from where they sat near the tarped opening and tossed them up along with the men's packs. Fifteen minutes later, Nick peered down through the hole. "Mark just stepped off into the drift and they're working!"

John let out a breath. "Great, see you on the back side."

"You got it," Nick said, and a moment later, he was gone.

For the next eight hours, the haggard group huddled under the blankets within their sleeping bags, save for the meager meal of boiled potatoes and rice John managed to put together and cook on the abandoned stove outside. He picked his cell out of his pocket and powered it up for the umpteenth time. Still no service. Putting it away, he went back to where he'd been sitting next to Michelle for most of the day while Cam checked in on Brenda and Brian.

Everyone was exhausted and most were fighting headaches. He sat on the floor with his legs spread out in front of him, and looked down at Michelle. She looked so small and vulnerable as she lay next to him, wrapped in her sleeping bag. He hadn't felt this helpless since he was a child. She couldn't die, not after all the cartwheels they'd done to save her life. But it was more than all they'd done;

it was the gut-wrenching fear that he'd never forgive himself. He glanced over at Cam, who was checking Brenda's pulse. The Brit had come through the woods and Cam was quite sure if they got her out of there within the next day, she'd make it. And Brian hadn't had another episode. Michelle was the one they all worried about.

How had everything gone to hell so quickly? In all the years he'd spent on Everest, he'd never seen such a cluster of events, not even the '96 disaster that had claimed the lives of Hall and Fischer rivaled this. Their one hope at the moment lay with Kembe, Nick and Mark. Hopefully, the heavens wouldn't open up again and vomit down the white death, which was how he thought of it now. At length, Cam got up and slid over next to him.

"She's strong," she said.

He nodded and looked off. "I'm sorry."

"About what?"

He spread his hand out and swept it around. "All this! You didn't sign up for it."

"Yeah, well…you didn't sign up for that either," she said pointing to his leg. She was quiet a moment. "Don't be too hard on yourself."

"Yeah, right." He arched his back and rolled his head side to side, stretching stiff and sore muscles. "Can I ask you a question?"

Cam crossed her legs, leaned to the side and dragged her pack over. "Okay."

"You being her husband's sister, what was he like?"

"Adam?" She paused. "He was the best. A brother I could count on no matter what. I wasn't easy to grow up with, but he never judged me. He was just there, keeping me in bounds," Cam said, pulling a flask out of her bag. "But you're not interested in how he treated me, are you?"

She was right. He didn't know what to say.

Cam tilted her head and studied him a moment. "You're in love with her, aren't you?"

John looked back at her. He didn't know what love looked like anymore, only that he couldn't breathe with the thought of Michelle dying on him.

She nodded. "Thought so. Anyway, to answer your question, my brother loved 'Chelle with all his heart, and he proved it every day. She was his shining star and there's nothing he wouldn't have done for her." She unscrewed the cap of the flask, took a drink then held it out to him.

"What's this?" he said and took a pull. Rum. He cocked his brow and ran the back of his hand over his mouth, then gave it back. "You've been holding out on me."

She took another pull and capped the flask. "Saving it for a good moment. Originally it was for celebrating my brother's dream, but now that's all gone." She paused and bent forward, pulling the flap of Michelle's sleeping bag back. As she checked the incision under the bandage, she went on, "You know, we were best friends long before she married Adam."

"I gathered that," he said.

She covered the wound and pulled the flap of the sleeping bag up over Michelle. "My turn to ask you a question. Why Nepal?"

"What'd'ya mean?" he said.

"What brought you here, of *all* the places in the world?"

"I don't know. I just sorta landed here."

She pursed her lips and eyed him skeptically. "Hmm…"

"What?"

"I don't think someone just *lands* here," she said. "Care to share?"

He looked off again into the deepening shadows around them and said, "I cared more than I should've for someone a long time ago, and I got shit on."

"What happened?"

"More like what didn't happen. We had plans. Least I thought we did. Then one day, she tells me, 'I have a dream of being a doctor and life waits for no one', and then walked away..." He cleared his throat. "A week later, she'd moved halfway across the country. When an opportunity came up to work with Andersen, I took it. I had nothing to keep me home and I couldn't see myself hanging back in Oak Creek."

"You had your family."

"Well, yeah, but I couldn't stay. Just too many reminders of her were there."

"Well, you certainly ran as far away as you could, didn't you?"

"I didn't run away, I just...wait, didn't Michelle tell you all this?"

Cam took another swig. "A little, but not all. But back to running. If you weren't running, what do you call it then?"

"I don't know...but it wasn't running! And it was a long time ago. Ancient history."

"Right," Cam said. She stretched her arms out behind her, leaned back and planted her palms on the floor. "Maybe ancient history, but it's still tailing you, isn't it?"

"No, not unless a certain somebody, who shall remain nameless, continues to bring it up."

She flashed him a sardonic smile. "Uh-huh. Is that what you think?"

"It is. And like I said, I left because I needed to put it all behind me," he said. "My mother always said, 'You can't live in the shadow of the past.'"

"I agree," Cam said, and took a pull of rum. She capped the flask. "Like I said, you ran. Nothing to be ashamed of; everyone runs once in a while, John. Fact of life. The question is, are you still running?"

"You don't give up, and like I said, I'm not running," he said, reaching for the flask. "So, if everyone runs, what are you running from?"

"That's a good question. I haven't quite figured it out yet."

John smirked and took a pull from the flask. "You're a piece of work."

"Aren't we all."

He glanced off toward Scott who was sleeping on the cot across from them. "The kid likes you a lot you know."

"Meaning?"

"Just saying," he said, handing the rum back to her.

"If you're worried about me breaking his heart, don't worry. The feeling's mutual."

"So, it's more than just a fling then?" John said, not believing her.

"Actually, yes. He treats me like a person and not some kind of trophy to hang on his wall. It's quite refreshing."

"I used to be like him, once."

"Yeah, I wonder what happened to that person?"

He looked down at the floor and was quiet a moment. "Yeah, me too."

They both retreated into their thoughts for a moment. Finally, Cam sat up. "So, what are you going to do about 'Chelle?"

The question caught him sideways and he blinked. "Nothing! It's not like I can do anything about it, even if I wanted to." He looked away, unable to endure her searching gaze. The woman had him pegged, and he didn't know what to do about it.

"You keep telling yourself that," she said, and chuckled.

"What?"

"Never mind.

"Well, she has someone at home waiting for her, right?"

She took another drink and ran her sleeve over her mouth. "Yes, but I don't think he's the one."

He wanted out of this conversation, but something inside him just had to see it through. "What do ya mean? If I remember correctly, you were the one encouraging her."

"You're right, I was, but now…I don't think so," Cam said. She paused. "He's good to her and can certainly provide for her financially. My guess is he loves her and she'd do well with him. But now, I'm thinking I might be wrong. I know—shocking, isn't it, me being wrong?" She chuckled. "But the more I think about it, the more I realize I was looking at things from my point of view."

"Which was?"

"I take care of me, first. Doesn't mean I can't love someone, but I've always had trust issues. But 'Chelle, she's not like me. She needs that spark. She's a romantic, and though I'm sure she loves Don on a certain level, I'm not sure it would ever be enough." She bent forward and all the sass drained from her face. "I can't believe I'm going to say this. But I can't deny it, either. She likes you and I think if you wanted to put yourself out there, you might be surprised."

"Really, and do what?" John said. The thought of Michelle liking him struck him where it mattered. "She lives half a world away. I think you value your opinion a little too much."

"Maybe, but I think I got this."

"You go on believing that."

"I will," she said. "What you don't know, Johnny boy, is that she talks to me, and the things she says about you and the way she acts when you're around speaks volumes. You ever notice the smile on her face when she sees or talks to you? Of course not, because you assume too much. Typical man. Anyway, that's beside the point. The real deal is what happened yesterday. She put herself in harm's way for you without a second thought, and now you're holding vigil over her like a lost puppy dog. Like it or not, there's an inseparable bond between you two. You can deny it all you want, and you can try and run away from it, but you'll never escape it."

"So you figured all this out by yourself, huh?"

"Tell me I'm wrong."

John opened his mouth, but nothing came out.

"I thought so. It's up to you. You can stay here and guide away the rest of your life if you want to, but you'll always be questioning yourself. I guess it comes down to whether you want to stop running away from life or— here's a thought—turn around and run *towards* something. I'll let you think about that. I need to check on Brenda and Brian again." She dug the flask out of her pocket. "Here, I think you need this more than I do."

Chapter 22

John

Shepherd House – Oct. 15ᵗʰ - 17ᵗʰ

John thought about what Cam had said. Had he been running? He didn't think so. He loved what he did, loved the mountains, the thrill of pitting himself against the snow and ice and the rewards of standing on top of the world. At least that's how he'd felt until now. But if he was honest with himself, he had to admit he'd just followed one thing that led to another, avoiding getting close to anyone until slowly it became a way of life and he'd ended up here, believing this was what he wanted.

He stared down at Michelle's pale, drawn face. She'd stirred a little while ago, moaning and muttering under her breath. She was running a fever and her body shivered. He watched Cam check the incision as Scott and the others looked on from their cots. When she covered it back up, she sat back on her heels. John didn't need to ask; he knew she was worried.

"She's going into septic shock, and I don't like that bump on her head. She needs a hospital, John" Cam said, looking up at him.

He looked off, unable to endure the sobering expression on Cam's face. His gut burned from the mess of emotions churning inside him. He needed to do something, anything, but the stone-cold fact was no one could do anything but wait and pray. Finally he turned back to Cam. "How long—"

"Can she hold out like this?" Cam said finishing his sentence. "I don't know, but I wouldn't want to be having this conversation tomorrow if help doesn't come."

Come on, Kembe. I need you to make it.

Scott got up and sat beside Cam. "Isn't there anything more we can do?"

"No, Scott," Cam said. "We're at God's mercy here, I'm afraid."

Dan said, "If anyone wants, I can start a fire and get us something to eat."

"Is that all you can think of...eating?" Brian snipped.

Everyone spun around at the sudden outburst and looked at the quiet, reserved redhead who'd kept mainly to himself during the trek.

"He's just trying to help, Brian," Cam said. She shut her eyes hard and grimaced.

John bit down the urge to lash out. He was still pissed at the kid for keeping his condition a secret, regardless of his understandable motive for being there. But blowing up at him would do anybody any good. More than ever, he knew deep down, they all needed to pull together.

"Brian, put a pin in it, okay?" John said. To Dan, he added, "Why don't you do that."

Dan rolled out of his cot as Brian rolled over putting his back to them. John watched Dan slip outside then turned to Cam. He knew she was fighting a headache. They all were. But it was more than that for her. He set aside his own mixed feelings and thought of her. Her best friend was in serious trouble and the fact that she'd been pressed to perform surgery on her in this shithole wasn't lost on him. He tapped her shoulder and pointed to her camel back. "You need to drink."

She nodded, licked her chapped lips and pulled her pack over.

Hours passed in relative silence, save for scattered mutterings. John pressed Cam to get some rest. As far as he could tell, she hadn't laid her head on a pillow for more than an hour in the last two days. Grudgingly, she went to her cot and snuggled in with Scott, but not before giving him strict orders to wake her if there was any change in Michelle. With everyone burrowed under their blankets, John dimmed the light on the oil lantern and took up his place beside Michelle.

"Hey, you got to hang in there, okay?" he said to her as he watched her body rise and fall under the pile of blankets. "There's a lot of people here, pulling for you." He paused, looking for something to say, anything to fill the dreadful silence. A crooked grin came to his face as he thought of what Cam had told him. "Guess what? Cam tells me we're linked, that there's some kind of bond between us now. I don't know. Maybe she's right. I'm not the sharpest tool in the shed when it comes to these kinds of things. All I know is you make me feel things I haven't felt in a long time."

The wind picked up and the tarp over the opening rattled. He got up and pulled the tie through its eyelet snug to the hook on the wall, then sat back down, thinking about all he'd left behind in Oak Creek. A life, he'd evicted himself from. At last he said, "Care to hear a secret? It's rich." He took a drink from his CamelBak and blew warmth into his hands. "My mother lied to me all these years about my father, said he walked away when I was little. Except the father she told me about, died before I was born." He reached over and drew his pack closer and unzipped the side pouch. "It gets better. I found a pic hiding behind a family portrait. I have it right here. I'll show it to you." He pulled a curled yellow envelope out and opened it. Digging out a faded black and white photo, he showed it to her then went on, "That's my mom there, and in front of her, that's our neighbor, Bob from across the street and there I am in his arms. So, what do you think? Dear old dad? Certainly looks like it to me."

He put the photo back and tucked the envelope away. "And you know what's really the shits? He was married at the time. So, that makes my mom an adulterer. The mom who told me to always tell the truth, to never cheat, to do the right thing. What am I supposed to do with that? I don't know." His throat tightened. "I don't know anything anymore, 'cept you have to pull through. I need to know you're still out there in the world."

The uncounted hours passed, and as they did, Michelle's fever rose. John looked on, watching her hover at the edge of consciousness then stretched tired achy muscles as he sat beside the woman who'd put her life on the line for him. Even though a gnawing ache ran through him, he refused to give in to his body's demand to close his eyes. He blew out a breath and glanced at Michelle's hand. The top of her glove had peeled down a bit, exposing bare skin. He reached over and pulled it up, and as he started to draw back, felt her fingers tighten around his. For a moment he had a mind to pull away then gave in and entwined his fingers with hers. It had been a long time since he'd held a woman's hand with his heart in the right place and he marinated in it as he watched Cam remove the dressing around Brenda's frostbitten hand across the room.

"I'm afraid you're going to lose the hand," Cam said to her just above a whisper. "I'm sorry."

"Not to worry, dear. Not your fault," Brenda said stiffening her angular jaw. The Brit was quiet a moment, and in the dim lantern-lit room, John saw her brows pinch together. Cam peeled back the gauze over the shriveled hand as the woman eyed the grim injury. Finally, Brenda looked up. "Not too pretty, is it?"

"No, it's not," Cam replied.

"Oh well." She paused then said, "You don't suppose my brother could still be alive, do you?"

"I think…I think until you know for sure, you should believe the best," Cam said, inspecting the hand.

The woman drew her face into a tight smile. "You're an optimist, aren't you?"

"Oh, far from it," Cam said. She glanced over her shoulder at Michelle. "The eternal optimist is over there."

"Fighting for her life," Brenda said. "So, you're sisters, I take it?"

"Sisters-in-law. 'Chelle's my best friend. Known her half my life. She's been through a lot."

Brenda shot her a pensive look. "Where's her husband?"

"She's a widow."

"Oh, the poor dear. I'm so sorry." She winced as Cam palpated the skin above her wrist.

"Good, you can feel that," Cam said.

"In spades," Brenda replied. She watched Cam peel off a strip of gauze from the roll. "That was very good of you last night, letting your husband keep me warm."

Cam chuckled and John felt a smile come to his face. "Oh, Scott's not my husband."

"Oh, I just assumed."

Cam went about dressing the woman's hand. "Don't worry about it."

"So you came here on holiday, then?"

"Something like that. My brother always wanted to see the mountains, so 'Chelle and I thought we'd fulfill his wish. Even left a little piece of him back on the trail. That was 'Chelle's idea. She's a sentimentalist."

"And you're a cynic?" Brenda said, cocking her brow.

Cam sat back and shrugged. "That's the scuttlebutt. There, all done!" She put the medical supplies back in the med kit and got up. "You let me know if you start feeling nauseous or dizzy, okay?"

"Of course, and thank you."

Cam reached over and patted her shoulder, then joined John by Michelle's side "Hey grumpy, you need to get some sleep."

"In a bit," John said, letting go of Michelle's hand. But it was too late.

"Holding hands, are we?" Cam said and shot him a sassy smile. "Don't worry, I promise I won't tell anyone." She blew into her hands, rubbed them together and put a hand to Michelle's forehead. "She's starting to burn up. I'd give anything for an IV of antibiotics right now." She looked back at him and her expression was grave. "She can't do another day and night here. If we don't get her out by tomorrow..." She shook her head.

After a meager meal of boiled rice and lentils, they all hunkered down for the night, again sharing covers to keep warm. To their good fortune, the cold had eased up somewhat and so had the wind. But their water was running low and so was the dung chip fuel used for the fire. Not only had Cam been right about Michelle's condition, another day and night without help and they'd be left without a fire and worse yet, viable drinking water. John's mind spun all night with all the what-ifs as the huddled mass slept around him.

When morning finally broke, peeking in through the cracks around the tarp, he got up and went outside. Above the broken roof was a pale blue sky. He sighed. If help didn't come today, Michelle would die. The thought of it consumed him, threatening to swallow him whole. He steeled himself, dragged the bag of dung chips over, and swept last night's dusting of snow off the pot-bellied stove. As he popped the lid off it and dumped the last of their chips into it, Scott pulled the tarp back behind him and shuffled out.

"We've used the last of the purification tabs, so we'll have to boil water for drinking now," John said, without looking up.

Scott rubbed his hands together as John pulled a dirty rag out of his parka pocket, struck a match and put a flame to it. "You think they made it?"

John dropped the lit cloth into the stove and watched the flames take hold. "I hope so, otherwise…" He forced the thought away. "Cam awake?"

"Yeah, she's with Michelle right now. Fever's getting worse, I guess." He snuffed and wrapped his arms around his belly. "What are we gonna do?"

"I don't know," John said, grabbing the pot and scooping a pile of snow into it. "Do me a favor?"

"Yeah, sure."

He nodded toward the alcove. "Dig a few potatoes outta the bag in there and cut 'em up for me. There's a bag of lentils in there, too. We need to eat."

"Right."

John watched him shuffle over to the alcove. Eating was the last thing anyone wanted to do at this point, but it was necessary. He put his hands over the opening on top of the stove, warming them over the fire burning inside.

"John?"

He turned around and saw Cam poking her head out through the tarp. Her face was pale. His heart crashed. *No!* He dropped the pot of snow and waited for the crushing words.

"She's burning up. I don't know what more to do. If help doesn't get here soon, she won't make it," Cam said and for the first time, he saw how scared this gutsy woman really was.

"They'll get here," he said, having to believe it. *They have to.* He picked the pot of snow up and put the lid back on the stove. As he set the water on to boil, a faint whopping sound drifted in the wind. He pricked his ears, wondering if he was imagining it or if it really was what he thought it was.

Scott popped out from the alcove, holding a pan of cut up potatoes. "Is this enough?"

John put his hand up to silence him, and as the thwapping sound grew, his heart lifted. A broad smile ran across his face and he turned back to Cam. "A chopper.

They're here!" He swept the pot off the stove, popped the lid and fanned the rising gray smoke. A moment later, the air crackled, and a large military transport chopper was blotting out the sky.

As he watched its side door slide back, Cam and Scott rushed to him and looked up at Kembe's familiar, round face smiling down at them. John glanced at Cam. Tears streamed down her cheeks as Scott dragged her tight to him.

Forty minutes later, the weary trekkers were speeding high above the snow-swept land. John crouched down beside Michelle in the deafening drone of the rotor blades and held her hand as Cam and the medical officer on board tended to her. Kembe sat nearby, looking on as the others huddled in back. The medic adjusted the oxygen knob on the bottle and placed the mask over Michelle's face as Cam inserted an IV needle in her arm. As the medic hooked Michelle up to the on-board monitor, Cam taped the needle to the arm, and pulled the blanket snug over her best friend's shoulders.

The medic turned the monitor on and as it lit up, concern etched itself on his heavy brow. He spoke into the mic attached to his headset. John turned the volume up on his and heard, "Seventy over fifty, BPM, one-fifty."

Cam darted a wary glance at John as the pilot up front, radioed in to CIWEC Hospital's emergency center. "Female...serious abdominal injury...request emergency team to be available on arrival...ETA, nineteen minutes."

The medic inserted an ear thermometer into Michelle's ear and read it. "Forty," he reported.

Cam chewed her lip and John could see her debating what to do next. Finally, she reached over and tagged the man on the arm. "You have adrenaline on board?"

The medic shook his head as the chopper jittered.

Cam tilted her head back, and though John couldn't hear what she muttered, he could see the word *damn* on her lips.

"What about paddles?"

"Hō, we have."

"What's wrong?" John said into his mic.

"Nothing," she said, and checked Michelle's pupils. But John knew there was something wrong and he prayed like hell it wasn't something that required adrenaline.

The chopper put its nose down and veered right, skimming past the snow-covered hills. ten minutes later, the city of Pokhara came into view. But Michelle was slipping away.

"Forty over twenty, BPM one-eighty," the medic called out.

"She's crashing," Cam cried. "Get that over here."

The medic shook his head. "We can't use on chopper. It affect controls."

Cam turned to the man and stared at him hard. "If I can't use them and she goes into V-fib, she could die! You want that?"

John sucked a breath as Cam's warning slammed into him.

The medic licked his lips and wrinkled his brow as he looked down at Michelle.

John reached out and grabbed the medic's arm. "You heard her. She'll die!"

The medic darted an anxious look at him and then at Cam. "I know." He shook his head, then got up and scrambled ahead to the cockpit. After a heated discussion with the pilot, he darted back and ripped a large plastic case secured with Velcro straps to the chopper wall. Bringing it back, he shot a hesitant glance toward the cockpit then opened the case and set an attached pair of dark rubber discs with handles to the side.

Cam stared at the heart monitor. "Come on 'Chelle," she cried and ripped her headset off. "Don't quit on me now, God damn it!"

Suddenly the pulsing green line on the monitor went flat. "Flat-line!" the medic called out and squirted a dollop of white cream on the discs.

"Charge to 200," Cam yelled, tossing the blanket aside. She ripped Michelle's top down the middle. Planting her palms on Michelle's chest, she thrust down hard several times then got off her. The medic handed the paddles to her. "Clear!" she cried.

When Michelle's body lurched up from the jolt, all the air went out of John's lungs. The trail of the green line on the monitor jumped then went flat again. "Charge to 300," Cam yelled straddling Michelle again. As she pounded on Michelle's still body, John's world spun.

"Ready," the man said, handing back the paddles.

Cam jumped off Michelle. "Clear!" She put the paddles to Michelle's chest and pressed down.

Again, Michelle's body lurched and so did the green line on the monitor. This time it didn't go flat. "Sinus rhythm," the medic said as the chopper descended toward the hospital landing pad.

John let out a breath and swallowed hard as the bird set down and the door slid back. Outside, a team of doctors rushed in. As they whisked their patient away, Cam ran alongside them.

All John could do was stagger off the chopper with Kembe's arm around him.

Chapter 23

John

Pokhara, Nepal – Oct. 17th

John and Cam rushed toward the Emergency Department doors that slid open as they approached. The waiting room was jammed with people asking attendants about loved ones. He marched past them to a pair of double doors and pushed through into a hallway littered with gurneys and wheelchairs holding victims from the storm. A nurse who was treating a man on a gurney looked up as he and Cam came in. She stepped away from her patient and blocked them from going any further.

"You go back, you not supposed be here," she said.

Cam said, "I'm a doctor. We just came in with the woman you took down the hall. I need to consult with the attending."

The woman considered Cam with a wrinkled brow, pressed her lips together and said, "You wait here."

John panned his gaze around the noisy hallway as his heart thumped. It was a war zone of moaning and crying refugees from the storm. The man on the gurney in front of him looked back, and as he did so, John saw the blackened skin on his nose and along the side of his long, brown face. The ugly black streak reached up to the man's eye. Another man sitting in a wheelchair down the hall had gauze dressings wrapped around his entire arm. A young Nepalese girl, maybe fourteen or fifteen lay crying on a gurney, her thin frail legs blackened with frostbite from her feet to her knees. Brenda was in a wheelchair beside the girl, trying to console her as a male nurse looked at her hand. And still there were more victims beyond.

"Holy crap, this is insanity," Cam muttered beside him as a nurse rushed past him.

Behind them, more were coming in. John and Cam scooted closer to the wall as a team of soldiers pushed a trekker on a gurney past them. They watched the team turn the corner and disappear from sight. But all John could think of was Michelle. He turned to Cam.

"She's gonna be okay, right? She has to be."

"I know. It's gonna be nip and tuck for a while though. We just have to hang on and hope."

"Yeah, I guess." He was quiet a moment, then said, "What you did in that chopper...you're pretty awesome, you know."

Cam flashed a tiny smile. "Thanks. She's my best friend."

John blew out a breath. "I know," he said and grasped her hand, holding it tight. "Where's that God damned nurse?"

"They're busy, John. You need to cut 'em some slack," Cam said as a Nepalese man in scrubs came around the corner with the nurse who went to fetch him.

"Hi, you are her doctor, yes?" the man said.

"*A* doctor. I'm her best friend," Cam said, letting go of John's hand. "There's a couple things you need to know. She's allergic to ceftriaxone, so don't give her that. I did a field suture on the wound, but it's very primitive and there may be other bleeders and debris in it I couldn't get to."

The man nodded. "Okay, I will let attending know. You go back to waiting room. We come get you once she stabilized, okay?"

"She's gonna be all right, though…right?" John said to the man.

"We doing everything we can," the man said. "You go. We come get you."

"Come on, John, let's do what he says. We're only in the way here," Cam said.

Reluctantly, John followed Cam out into the crowded waiting room, where Kembe, Scott, Brian and Dan were waiting by the door.

Scott rushed up to Cam and said, "Is she gonna be okay?"

Cam shrugged and took his hand. "It's a waiting game now.

They all sat in the far corner of the chaotic waiting room hoping for good news on Michelle. John couldn't think, couldn't breathe, couldn't feel anything as he sat there feeling more helpless than ever before. Kembe brought him tea in a Styrofoam cup. He took a sip and stared out into space. All he could see was Michelle lying still and in pain on the cot in the shepherd house. The memory of her grasping his hand consumed him. Losing her was not an option.

Cam stirred beside him and took his hand in hers. "She's gonna be all right."

He nodded. Patience had never been one of his better virtues, and this pushed what little reserve he had to the limits. He needed to do something, anything to take his mind off the terrifying visions playing over and over in his head. At last he got up and went outside into the cool autumn air and watched a flock of birds settle in the trees across the lot. For the past twenty years, he'd kept people from getting too close to him for precisely this reason. It was just too hard dealing with the feelings coursing through him. But now there was no turning back. He cared for her, more than cared, and he couldn't deny it any longer.

Kembe came out and joined him. They stood side by side for a minute listening to traffic passing by on the roads beyond. Finally, the sherpa said, "Ken been trying to reach you."

John started. He'd forgotten all about his phone with everything going on. He reached into his pocket, pulled it out and turned it on. There were dozens of missed texts and a slew of voice messages staring up at him. Most of them were from Mick. He dialed the man.

"Hey."

"Jesus, Shanks, you scared the hell out of me. You all right? People are pretty worried about you back here."

"I'm doing," John said, shuffling his feet.

"Where the hell are ya? You get caught in that storm? They're saying a lot of people died up there."

"Yeah, I imagine that's right. It was pretty damned ugly."

"So where are ya? Besisahar?"

"No, I'm back in Pokhara," John said, looking out over the trees.

"Pokhara?" There was a pause. "Where in Pokhara?"

John debated whether he should tell him, but knew if he said nothing, Mick would just bare down on him until he relented. At last he cleared his throat. "At the hospital."

"Jesus! Which one?"

"CIWEC. Look, I'm okay so don't get a head of steam and come rushing up here. They're pretty busy."

"Bullshit. What room ya in?"

"I'm not in a room," John said, and eyed Kembe. "I'm waiting for someone."

"Oh, that's good. For a minute there, ya had me worried." Mick paused again. "Wait, who got hurt? Kembe, Orsen?"

"No, a client. One of the women. Hey look, I gotta skate. I'll hit you up later, K?"

"Right."

The call ended, and John shoved the phone back in his pocket. The rest of the calls and texts could wait.

Two hours later the nurse came out and led John and Cam down the hall to the nurse's station were a couple of doctors were discussing something at the counter. As they approached, one of them turned around and came over to meet them.

"Hi, I'm Dr. Thapa. And you are?"

"I'm Dr. Legault and this is John," Cam said. "I'm her best friend and John is—"

"No need to explain. Why don't you come with me and I'll fill you in on your loved one's condition."

John followed the doctor, along with Cam, to a waiting room where they went over in the corner next to a table set with Thermoses and cups. As John stood by watching the doctor pour them tea, he fought to keep his anxiety under control, trying to console himself with the man's confident, composed behavior. If anything had gone wrong, certainly the doctor wouldn't be dragging this out.

Finally, the doctor looked up, offered them both a cup and said, "She is stable now and responding to antibiotics. We had to remove the spleen, but I expect a full recovery. What worries me a little is the bump on her head. Did she regain consciousness prior to coming in?

"A little," Cam said. "She was in and out of it with the cold and all, that and what I had to do to her."

"Understandable. You went through a very bad storm." He took a sip of tea, and went on, "We did a CAT scan, which did come out negative, but with concussion, you never know."

"Meaning?" John said.

"She could have some mental deficits. But like I said, one ever knows until the patient is fully awake." He eyed John. "Do not borrow trouble until it comes, okay? I'm sure your wife will be just fine. I just have to be clear."

Cam shot John a knowing glance and a quick devilish smile, which he knew was attributed to the doctor calling Michelle his wife. He didn't say anything though, which surprised him.

The doctor turned to Cam. "My assistant tells me you did the surgery in the field?"

"Yeah, we'd all taken shelter in one of the shepherd houses during the storm when the avalanche hit," Cam said. "It crushed part of the roof, and a beam landed on her, stabbing her with a broken piece of wood. We had no medical supplies except the med-kit we carried, I had to make do with what I had."

"So you operated in the snow?" the doctor said, widening his dark brown eyes.

"Not quite," Cam said. "Part of the house remained intact. We pulled her inside and did it in there, but it was anything but sterile."

"Hmm, that is amazing," The doctor said, shaking his head. He took another sip of tea and set the cup down on the table. "I'm curious, where did you get the suture?"

"Sleeping bags," John put in. "We fished the threads out.

The doctor nodded. "And the needle?"

"You wouldn't believe us if we told you," Cam said.

"I'm sure I wouldn't. Okay, I'll take you to see her now," he said, picking up his cup of tea. "We have her on some pretty strong pain meds, so she is pretty out of it."

He led them into Michelle's room and when he shut the door after them, John saw Michelle lying in bed surrounded by monitors, tubes and IVs. A long strip of white gauze was taped around the top of her ear and a small cut on her shoulder had been sutured.

The doctor put his hand on Michelle's arm. "Michelle, you have visitors."

Michelle's lids fluttered, and for a moment her eyes opened before they shut again. John swallowed. She looked even smaller in the hospital bed than she did on the cot in the shepherd house. Hesitantly, he crept up to her bedside and as he did so, the memory of seeing his mother fighting for her life not all that long ago flashed before him. He glanced at Cam, who'd moved up on the other side of the bed, as the doctor let himself out of the room. For the first time in a long, long time, he knew where he belonged.

Chapter 24

Michelle

Pokhara, Nepal – Oct. 19ᵗʰ – 22ⁿᵈ

Michelle opened her eyes and stared up at the ceiling, not quite sure where she was, only that she felt warm and dizzy. Everything she saw looked alien and out of place. Where was she? The sensation of floating and spinning in darkness was fading and with it, a dull ache grew in her side. The pain intensified, pushing a muted cry to the surface. Her body tightened and jerked, sending mind numbing jolts up her spine. Something sour trickled into her mouth as her stomach churned. She coughed and a moment later, there were voices entering the space around her. Her eyes fluttered as people went in and out of focus. Something strong and warm settled on her shoulder. She looked up and saw a thin brown face staring back.

"Michelle, Michelle, can you hear me?"

The voice echoed in her ears.

"I'm Dr. Thapa. You're in the hospital. You've been in an accident. Try not to move, okay?"

Accident? Hospital? Where?

Suddenly, the memory of being impossibly cold flushed through her, and she felt her body shiver. She inhaled deeply, which hurt even more. Her body tightened and the urge to bend forward overpowered her as a hot, sour taste spilled into her mouth and out over her lips. She felt a warm, soft sensation brush her lips and chin.

"She's coming off the Duromorph," a melodic voice said.

"We'll switch her over to Hydrocodone for the next twenty-four then to Codeine after. Michelle, can you hear me?"

She turned toward the voice and focused on the thin dark face with kind, dark eyes. The voice was coming from him. She nodded as she gasped for breath.

"Good. You be all right. We give you some more pain medication. You will start to feel better soon, okay?"

Michelle nodded again, and before she knew it, the ache melted away and blissful darkness returned.

The hours passed uncounted, or was it days? She didn't know. She blinked and took in the sunbeam shining through the window into her room. A new room or so it seemed, with soft pastel colored walls and bright blue curtains. She looked at the surroundings and winced. Gone were the banks of monitors and the harsh overhead lights she remembered from the one time she'd been awake long enough to notice them. She rubbed her temples. Her head hurt and there was a gnawing ache in her side. Outside her door, she heard the lyrical Nepalese voices of the nurses.

"Hello, anyone out there?" She winced again.

A moment later, a small round Nepalese woman in soft red scrubs swept into her room. The woman offered Michelle a warm, friendly smile. "Good morning. How you feel?" she said, edging up to Michelle's bedside. She pulled the privacy curtain around them, then took up a tethered device to the bed and pressed down on the button.

"Okay, I think," Michelle said, as the rising mattress under her shoulders took her breath away. "What time is it?" She was pretty sure it was morning, but who knew?

"Seven thirty," the woman said, setting the device down. She wrapped a blood pressure cuff around

Michelle's arm and took her vitals. "You hungry. They be bringing breakfast around soon."

Up until that moment, she hadn't given food a thought, but the mention of it reminded her she was hungry. She spied the woman's nametag. "Actually, I am, Pritti."

"That's a good sign," Pritti said as a knock came to the door outside.

"Hello, Hello! Dr. Thapa here," he said. He pulled the curtain aside and ducked in. "How are you? You looking much better."

"I think the jury's still out," Michelle said, and all at once, a million questions came to her mind. "So, what happened to me? I don't remember a lot, other than we were trapped in a house during the snowstorm and there was an avalanche and then..." She shrugged, and as she did, a sharp twinge in her side took her breath again. "Ouch!"

"Yes, you need to be careful for a bit. You've been through a lot, which I will let your husband tell you about when I'm done here."

Husband?

"What I will say to you is we had to remove your spleen. It was damaged from the accident you had in the mountain house. It is no problem to live without it, but there will be some adjustments you must make, which I will tell you of before you are discharged. Right now, I am going to check your incision, okay?"

He pulled the cover back from her, along with the dressing over the wound and as he did so, she heard Cam's voice outside the door. She was talking with someone, but she couldn't hear the voice coming back. "Hey, Cam, come on in," she said.

"Be right there. I'm on the phone."

My phone! She glanced around, searching for her cell phone as the doctor palpated her abdomen. *Where is it?*

My father, he must be going nuts! "Have you seen my phone?" she said to Dr. Thapa and Pritti.

"No, we haven't. Perhaps one of your friends has it, no?" Dr. Thapa said, replacing the dressing over the wound. He covered her up and pulled back the privacy curtain.

Michelle's mind went into overdrive, imagining her father pacing the floor, waiting to hear from her. "Cam, Cam, you have my phone?" she called out as her heart thumped.

"Coming," Cam said and a moment later stepped into her room, holding her phone up. "Here I spoke to your father, so he knows what's going on. Your brother has an earful for you though." She slid up beside the bed and handed Michelle's phone to her. "Oh, and Don's been blowing up your phone, too. I figured you'd want to talk with him personally." She took a good look at her. "It's good to have you back. You scared the hell out of us, John especially."

"John?"

"Yeah, he's hardly left your side since the accident."

Michelle was surprised, but was warmed by the thought of him caring so much about her. *I guess that explains what the doctor meant by my husband clarifying things to me.* "Really? Huh! Well, that's sweet of him."

Cam shot her a crooked smile, the smile she knew meant there was more to the story. "What?"

"Nothing." Cam paused. "So, how ya feeling?"

"Sore, and my head is pounding, but nothing I can't deal with. I heard they had to remove my spleen. What does that mean?"

"It means your body is going to be more susceptible to infections and viruses from now on, so you'll have to be diligent about taking care of yourself when you start to feel ill. You'll be okay, though."

Michelle took all that in and as she did so, the memory of pushing John out of the way before everything went black flashed before her. "John, is he okay?"

"Grumpy's fine, just a cut on the arm and a bit of wounded pride," Cam said, pulling up a chair beside her.

"Oh, so that's your nickname for him now?"

"Yeah. Rather fits him, I think," Cam said. She was quiet a minute, then said, "He likes you."

"I like him, too. Underneath all that armor he holds up, he's a pretty nice guy."

"He more than likes you, 'Chelle."

"What'd'ya mean?"

Cam studied her. At last, she leaned forward. "I think he's fallen for you."

"For me? You have such a wild imagination," Michelle said and chuckled. The truth was she'd heard the conversation he'd had with Cam, and then had heard him bare a dark secret later on. Here was a man with a tender soul that had been hidden away for such a long time it was almost forgotten. Here was a man she could see herself with, a man she could get close to, a man she could trust with her damaged heart. She looked up and tossed Cam a sassy smile. "By the way, the doctor thinks he's my husband. Care to share why he might think that?"

"Not a clue. Probably just assumed with John being up here almost round the clock."

"You're serious," Michelle said as the power of Cam's assertion about John galvanized in her mind. She sat, thinking about how she felt about that. She couldn't deny if things were different, she could see herself with him. "Well, we live in different worlds."

"Yes, you do," Cam said, as breakfast came through the door.

Michelle smiled at the orderly as he set the food on a rolling tray table and brought it over to her. "Thank you." She lifted the top off the tray and regarded the bowl of steaming porridge, the hard-boiled egg and a glass of what looked like fruit juice. As she unwrapped the cellophane around her plastic-ware, she heard footsteps come to her doorway. She looked up to see John staring in at them. He offered her a tired smile and walked in.

Cam got up. "I'll talk to you later."

"You don't have to leave," Michelle protested.

"Oh, I think I do," Cam said. She smiled, eyed John and patted him on the arm as she passed him by.

Michelle smoothed out the blanket around her as John drifted to her side.

"Hey," he said. "How ya feeling?"

"Okay, I guess. Pretty sore. I feel like I've gone a few rounds in the ring. But how are you? You look tired."

"I'm fine." He shuffled his feet and stabbed a hand into his pants pocket. "Looks like breakfast is here. What's that ya got there. Porridge. Looks yummy."

Michelle smiled. "Haven't tried it yet. Sit. So, Cam tells me you've been hanging close by."

"Just making sure you didn't cause any trouble." He fidgeted a moment, then sat. "The gang's been asking about you."

"That's nice. Tell 'em thank you," Michelle said, drizzling honey on her porridge. She eyed John from the corner of her eye as he sat rigid in his chair. They were quiet for a moment as she ate. Finally, she said, "So, everyone made it back okay?"

"Yeah."

"And Brenda?"

"Not sure. She's here somewhere."

She took a sip of her juice. "And Brian?"

"Haven't seen him. I guess he's on a plane back home."

"I see." Michelle set the cup down as she contemplated the direction she wanted to take the conversation. At length, she took a bite of her porridge, wiped her mouth with the napkin on her tray. "So, what's next for you? I assume with what happened, there won't be any more treks to the mountains for a while."

"Not sure," he said. "Probably go back to my off-season job."

"Which is?"

He shifted in the chair. "Bartending."

Somehow, she could see him doing that, but had a good feeling he didn't like it. "I bet you're good at it."

"It's a job. You must be anxious to get home."

"I am. And you're probably anxious to get back up on the mountain."

He shrugged. "I'm not sure I want to go back. Tell you the truth, I'm thinking about going back home."

"To the States?" Michelle said.

"Yeah. Just not feeling like I have a future here anymore."

"What would you do there?"

"Not sure. My brother-in-law is a mucky-muck in one of those sport shop chains. I suppose I could find something to do in one of those."

"Well, if you come east or west, whichever way it is, maybe you could stop by on your way and say hi."

"Sure, I'd like that," he said, and smiled.

She set her spoon down and peeled her egg, furtively watching him chew his lip. She could tell he was nervous about something. Finally, she said, "Maybe we could exchange email addresses? Write to each other a bit, that is if you want."

"Yeah. Have to warn you...I'm not much on writing."

"That's okay," she said, salting her egg. "I won't hold you to any deadlines."

John smiled, and as he did so, she noticed his knee subtly twitch. He took a breath, turned to her, and in his deep blue eyes she saw uncertainty. "What would you say if I said I was thinking of settling in a little north and east of the States?"

"Where do you mean?" Michelle said, and held her breath.

He shrugged. "Canada?"

"Canada, where 'bouts in Canada?"

"Well, I hear Cornwall's a pretty nice place. That is...if you think I could find work there."

Oh my God!

She set the egg down as her heart thudded and looked back, wondering if she was hearing him right. Suddenly, her headache vanished and everything around her melted away. She studied his bristled face, committing every straggling wave of long blond hair, every wrinkle, every nick, every bump to memory, and said, "I think there would be a lot there to keep you busy."

"Yeah?" he said.

"Yes, really!"

He leaned toward her. "You're sure? I don't want to…"

"Stop, Mr. Patterson," she said, cupping her hand around his face. "There's nothing I'd like more than to have you in my life."

He reached over and lightly ran his long, calloused fingers over her brow. "When you were lying unconscious in that room up on the pass, I was scared for the first time in my life. I thought you were gonna…"

"Well, I didn't, and I'm not going anywhere." She stroked his cheek. "You dear man. Such a marshmallow under all that thick crust. Come here," she said raising her arm, ignoring the sharp stab in her side as she invited him in for a hug.

He got up and leaned over her, and as his powerful arms gently slipped around her shoulder, she inhaled his earthy scent. It'd a been so long since she'd allowed herself to feel the comfort of a man's embrace, and she held him for a long time until at last he pulled back. As he did, she sensed his yearning for more.

She traced her finger over his jaw and smiled. "If you want to kiss me, I wouldn't object."

He studied her a moment, then bent his head down and softly pressed his lips against hers. And in her heart, she knew Adam wouldn't object to this honest, hard-bitten man she'd been on her way to for the last two years.

Chapter 25

John

Pokhara, Nepal – Oct. 22ⁿᵈ

John stepped into Sanjay's Internet café and looked around. He was late getting there but then again, he was never all that punctual, and Mick knew it. The place was busy this morning. People huddled up around their laptops and computers, drinking tea and chatting about the storm.

On the wall, a TV squawked out the morning news. A radio sang out the latest Indian hit song somewhere. In the back corner, one of Sanjay's waiters was waiting on tables. It saddened John to think Nabin was gone. The place just didn't feel right without the over-attentive young Nepali kid who had such a bright smile and future ahead of him. A future stolen away from him by a senseless accident.

He waded through the hodgepodge of scattered tables, catching a waft of seasoned potatoes as he looked for Mick. He found him sitting at the breakfast counter near the back. As usual, Mick was slurping his God-awful butter tea and reading the morning rag. He tapped the burly expedition manager on the shoulder and took a seat next to him.

"Hey, Shanks," Mick said, setting his paper down. He took a good long look at him. "Well, you don't look any worse for wear. How ya doing?"

John considered the man. "I'm still here."

"That was a hell of a storm. Where were you when it hit?"

"On our way to Thorung Pedi."

Mick nodded. "Man, that was where it really hit hard from what I heard. You weren't anywhere near that avalanche, were you?"

"Actually, right in the middle of it," John said as Sanjay came over with pen and pad.

"Namaste, John-ji," Sanjay said. "Good to see you. We worry about you."

"Thanks, Sanjay."

"Get you something to drink?"

"Yeah, ginger tea, and I'll take one of those sweet rolls over there on the counter."

The wiry Nepalese proprietor smiled. "Can do."

When the man left, Mick said, "You're kidding me. Right in the middle of it?"

"Yeah, we'd gotten into a shepherd's house out of the storm, trying to wait things out when it hit."

"Christ!" Mick said. "That must've been one hell of a ride."

"You have no idea," John said as Sanjay set his tea and roll in front of him. He eyed Mick. "So, did any of your boys get caught up in it?"

"Unfortunately, yeah. Binod, you heard me speak of him, and the kid from the States got held up in one of the tea-houses."

"The Madden kid?" John said, and could just about imagine the mother going nuts over that.

"Yeah. They're all right. Unfortunately, I can't say the same for some of those other poor bastards who went with that greedy tea house owner."

"How do you mean?"

"The guy tried to make a quick buck off the situation, talked a bunch of them into giving him money to lead them back down to Manang. It cost them their lives. They're still looking for the bugger, but the general opinion around here is he's lying in a pile of snow somewhere frozen, like a cheap T.V. dinner."

John shook his head and bit into his roll.

"So, tell me...one of your clients ended up in the hospital? Frost bite?"

John shook his head and paused as the memory of the roof crashing down over Michelle's head flashed before him. At last, he said, "No, not frostbite. The avalanche crashed into the house and collapsed the roof over our heads, and a woman took the brunt of it."

"Damn! She all right?"

"Yeah...thankfully."

"That must've been hell. How long were you trapped?"

"Two and a half days. Kembe managed to get out with a couple of my clients and went for help."

Mick slurped his tea and shook his head. "Well, you're back safe, and that's what matters."

John eyed Mick. He was back, but he wasn't staying, and though he'd decided to give up the land he'd called home for the last twenty years, leaving Mick behind would be hardest of all. Mick was a good man, and had been a loyal friend, although up until now, he hadn't thought of him that way. Then again, he'd never thought of anyone as a friend, just people who came in and out of his life, staying for a season or two before moving on. He'd told himself he liked it that way, but now he saw he was fooling himself.

He sucked a sip of tea. "I'm going home, Mick. I've had my fill here."

"Home?"

"Yeah, it's time to get out, I think."

Mick was quiet a moment. Finally, he said, "Well, you do what you need to do. I'll miss your ugly face around here, but I get it. So, when you bugging out?"

"Couple weeks. Have a few things to take care of," John said, looking straight ahead. He couldn't bear to meet eyes with the man. "Know anyone who'd be interested in some gear? Don't think I'll be needing it anymore."

"Sure, I'll ask around."

They both fell quiet then amid the din of banter and the coming and goings of people around them.

Oak Creek, Colorado, USA – Nov. 5th

John pulled his rental car up in front of Bob Murphy's home and sat in the front seat looking out over the street for some time, thinking about what he was going to say to the man when he went up to the front door. Tact had never been one of his strong suits, but he thought he owed it to Bob to hear him out before he said anything he might regret.

He got out of the rental, shut the door, and tugged his collar up around his neck. The neighborhood was quiet; people were off to work. Down the street, a mailman was going about his deliveries. He eyed his mother's house. The For Sale sign was still up. The old oak in front had lost half its leaves. A row of stuffed lawn-and-garden bags sat on the curb waiting for the DPW to come collect them.

At length, he turned away and started up the walk to Bob's front porch. A Jack-O-Lantern sat there on the stoop. Bob was always big on handing out candy to the kids. He stepped past it and rang the doorbell.

A moment later, the door opened. "John, you're home. I was worried about you, what with all that happened over there."

"Yeah, it was…umm…not very good."

"Well, come on in," Bob said, stepping aside. Can I get you a beer or anything?"

"Sure."

"So, you been home for a while?"

"No, got in yesterday."

"Staying with Peg?" Bob said over his shoulder as he went for the kitchen.

"No, I didn't want to barge in on her, so I parked myself in the Blue Moon motel in town," John said as Bob returned with a beer in each hand.

"You're welcome to bunk here if you want. Got plenty of room," Bob said and found a seat in the wingback chair across from the couch. "Have a seat."

"Appreciate the offer, but I'm fine," John said, plunking down on the couch. He glanced around the room, taking in the faded blue walls, dated lamps, end tables, and dark brown, braided throw rug. Pictures of Bob's wife, Miranda, and people he didn't know peppered the mantel over a brick-faced hearth. The room looked like it had grown old right along with the man sitting across from him.

He sucked a sip of beer and filled Bob in about the disaster on the pass, omitting his own experience to buy time before launching into what he came here for. Finally, he dug his wallet out and plucked the photo from it. He looked down at it for a moment then got up and handed it to Bob.

"I found this in my mother's house before I left last time. Care to tell me about it?"

Bob looked at it a long time. "So, your mom kept it." He sighed and handed it back. "It was taken when we were in Vale. Your mom insisted I hold you."

John figured he'd say something like that as he put the photo away. "I see. Just the three us were there?"

Bob crossed his legs and eyed John. "No, your sister was there. She might have been off playing at the time."

"And your wife?"

"She was at her sister's in Denver."

"So it was just the four of us in Vale. Sounds a bit cozy, you being married at the time."

Bob set his beer down and licked his lips.

John let him stew for a moment. "Would it surprise you to know my father was dead at the time? Is there something you want to tell me?"

Bob sat back and looked off into space. "I guess it's time you knew the truth. I don't like to speak ill of the dead, but suffice it to say, your sister's father was a difficult man. He liked his freedom a little too much, was gone long stretches of time. I'd see your mom from time to time, trying to keep things up around the house. At the time, Miranda and I were going through our own stuff. She went to stay with her sister for a while. Anyway, one day I offered to give your mom a hand and eventually, we came to be good friends, supporting each other during hard times. This was all before you were born."

He sucked a gulp of beer and set the can down on the table beside him.

"Then one day, your mom got word David, Peg's father, had gotten killed in a car accident. I'm not going to go into the details of it, only that it was out of town. He'd been away for quite some time, understand, and she was quite sure he'd run out on her. With his death and my marriage in tatters, our friendship grew into something more, and we began to make plans for the future. I have to stop here to tell you, your mom wasn't one to sleep around. She had her job and Peg to think of and you know small towns, how people like to talk.

"But we're all human, and I'm not going to apologize for the few times we were together, one of which led to you. I started divorce proceedings, and the two of us were planning on getting married as quickly as we could, but divorces take time and there was no way we could make everything work before you were born. Your mom was in a pickle. She was pregnant and with her husband being dead there was no way she'd be able to explain things away, until she got to thinking that she'd never mentioned his death to anyone in the church or her job. And why would she have? He had run out on her and she was deeply embarrassed about it when it happened.

"So, since everyone knew he traveled extensively for his job, it wasn't a stretch to omit certain details to you of when and how he died, only saying that he was your father. I wasn't a fan of this plan, but I had to respect your mother's wishes. Besides, she told me we'd all be together, and eventually, you'd look to me as such. Having decided that, we moved forward with our plans to be together. My divorce would move ahead and by the time you'd turn two, we'd be a family, officially.

Bob picked his beer up and took a swig.

"Then, the worst thing happened. I got a call from Miranda's sister. Miranda had suffered a bad stroke. Her sister, having her own health issues, said she couldn't take care of her, and with the two of them having lost their parents back east, the only person Miranda had in the world was me."

Bob shook his head. "What could I do? I couldn't leave her to die alone, and your mother wouldn't let me anyways. So I took her back and cared for her until she died, but by then you were in high school. I suppose I could've said something then, God knows I wanted to, but your mom said, 'What's the point of it after all this time?' So there you have it. I suppose you hate me now."

While John could understand why the secrets were kept, he couldn't help feeling like he'd been cheated out of the one thing that really mattered, a relationship with a father he should've been told about. It didn't matter that Bob had doted on him growing up because he'd always believed Bob was just a nice man across the street who'd ironically been cheated out of having children of his own. The whole thing was a huge mess of lies and secrets to hide dirty laundry from the tight-knit community of busybodies. And so here he was, sitting across from a man who no doubt had longed for years to tell him, to be a father, and he couldn't say he hated him for all that had happened.

At last John sucked a lip and shook his head. "I'm gonna need some time with all this."

"I know."

"I'm sorry."

"Me, too."

"So, you heading back to Nepal, I suppose?"

"No, I'm done with Nepal," John said and smiled as an image of Michelle flashed before him.

"Your sister will be happy to hear that."

John took his beer up and gulped a swig, well aware his sister wouldn't be the only one happy about it. He leaned forward with his hands across his knees, and said, "She will be until I tell her I'm moving to Canada."

Bob blinked. "What's in Canada?"

"My future!"

Notes from the Author

This novel is part of a larger story in the 'Hearts of Nepal' series and is based on the tragedies that occurred in the Himalayas and other parts of Nepal in 2014. The first occurred on Everest (Chomolungma) on April 18th and took the lives of sixteen sherpa men who fix the lines on the route up through the perilous Khumbu Ice Fall on Mount Everest. The second was a flash flood followed by a landslide that hit Mankha and other villages (occurring August 14th). It was brought on by a severe monsoon season. And finally, the Annapurna Circuit disaster in October took the lives of forty-three trekkers and sherpa guides.

These three events rocked the tiny nation and its people. Much of Nepal's economy depends on tourism from adventure seekers and hikers. Permits issued by the government for climbing Everest and other peaks cost tens of thousands of dollars for each individual. On average, between three and five hundred climbers attempt to summit Everest each year, say nothing of the other mountains in the range like Annapurna, Island Peak, (Imja Tse), Ama Dablam, and Makalu. The potential lost revenue for these permits along with all the expedition company permits is enormous. Also lost is revenue from the basic trekking permits to Everest Base Camp, Annapurna Sanctuary, etc., that range from $100 on down along with all the commerce for lodging, food, ancillary activities like hang-gliding and parasailing in Pokhara, safari excursions in Chitwan National Park, and the purchase of souvenirs and treasures to be brought home. For an impoverished nation that depends largely upon revenue from tourism, these tragedies are a recipe for economic disaster. One season with losses of this magnitude takes years to recover from.

Still another side to these events is the impact these disasters and the unpredictable monsoon seasons have on the tiny villages in the mountain passes and the villages on the steppes below. These villages are based on social communal constructs, and the money the sherpa men and women earn doing this hard and dangerous work (sometimes more than a whole year's salary in a single season) goes a long way in supporting a whole mountain community economically. When one of them dies, not only does it affect the family (emotionally and financially), it affects everyone.

The average rainfall in the months of July and August in Nepal is between twenty-five and thirty-five inches monthly. These deluges swell rivers and waterways exponentially, eroding hillsides and creating perilous situations (landslides and flash flooding) for those who live off the land.

The events that occurred in August of 2014 took the lives of over a hundred Nepalese and displaced over 170,000 more nationwide. With a limited economy and under-developed mechanization to address these disasters in an expedient way, these people are often left to their own resources. Yet despite all of these things, they are a resilient and optimistic folk, always offering a smile and hospitality, and that is what I hope to shine a light on in these narratives.

Like all fictional works, I've taken liberties in folding fictional characters into the actual events, sometimes embellishing a bit and other times creating fictional events. The intent is always to be faithful to what happened, while at the same time providing a storyline in keeping with the ongoing series, which began with *The Lion of Khum Jung*. That said, I sincerely apologize to the survivors of these tragedies for any unforeseen slights I may have made during the writing of this work.

Namaste

About the Author

Ron is a practicing architect living in upstate New York. An avid hiker and photographer, he has traveled to Nepal, New Zealand and throughout the United States, Alaska and Hawaii collecting ideas for character-driven stories of romance and adventure. Other novels by Ron are:

Loving Neil – Published by Creativia 2017

The Lion of Khum Jung – Published by Creativia 2017 (Also available on Audio through Amazon)

Beyond the Veil – Published by Creativia 2017.

Starting Over - Published by Creativia 2018.

Connect with Ron via Facebook at R.J. Bagliere or on the World Wide Web at: www.rjbagliere.com

48876447R10373

Made in the USA
Middletown, DE
17 June 2019